Items should be returned on or befor[e] [the last date]
shown below. Items not already requ[est]ed by other
borrowers may be renewed in perso[n,] [in writing or by]
telephone. To renew, please quote the number on the
barcode label. To renew online a PIN is required.
This can be requested at your local library.
Renew online @ **www.dublincitypubliclibraries.ie**
Fines charged for overdue items will include postage
incurred in recovery. Damage to or loss of items will
be charged to the borrower.

"The edgy plot never lets up, touching on the war on drugs, for-profit prisons, and nefarious nonprofits."

—*Publishers Weekly*

"Brackmann has creatted a damaged but likable protagonist."

—*Library Journal*

"Subtle but satisfying."

—*Booklist*

"A pure noir thriller."

—International Noir Fiction

"Brackmann takes the noir formula—things start out badly for a hapless hero and keep getting worse—and gives it a feminist reboot . . . A fun, smart, and fascinating trip."

—Reviewing the Evidence

"A tale of secret identities, for-profit prisons and the all-too-real war on drugs, this modern thriller is a great addition to any suspense lover's bookshelf."

—Brit + Co

"Lisa Brackmann's *Go-Between* pits the supporters of legalized marijuana and sentencing reform against the shadowy forces of the multi-billion dollar private prison industry, and with a deft sleight of hand, she transforms powerful social insight into a nerve-zapping luge run of lies, murder, dirty politics, drug smuggling, love, betrayal and black ops run amok."

—Craig Faustus Buck, author of *Go Down Hard*

"A terrifying political thriller with a powerful message. Brackmann's characters, from cynical Michelle to villainous Gary to damaged Caitlin, are layered and relatable. A compelling read and a thought-provoking story about the dangers of a broken system." —Mette Ivie Harrison, author of *The Bishop's Wife*

GO-BETWEEN

Also by Lisa Brackmann

Rock Paper Tiger
Hour of the Rat
Dragon Day
Getaway

GO-BETWEEN

Lisa
Brackmann

Published by
Soho Press, Inc.
853 Broadway
New York, NY 10003

Library of Congress Cataloging-in-Publication Data

Brackmann, Lisa, author.
Go-between / Lisa Brackmann.

ISBN 978-1-61695-830-5
eISBN 978-1-61695-725-4

1. Marijuana industry—Fiction. 2. Prison industries—Fiction.
3. Prison-industrial complex—Fiction. I. Title
PS3602.R333 G63 2016 (print) PS3602.R333 (ebook)
813'.6—dc23 2015048584

Printed in the United States of America

10 9 8 7 6 5 4 3 2 1

*To my family: Bill, Dana, Dave, Chris, Merrilyn and Gianna,
especially to my mother, Carol. She really liked this book.
I'm glad she had the chance to read it.*

Chapter One

❦

SHE STILL WONDERED IF she'd made the right decision.

She'd spent a lot of time thinking about that, in the two years that had passed since. She'd had a choice.

"I've got some funds stashed," he'd said. "I can set you up with enough to make a fresh start someplace."

"What do *you* want?" she'd asked.

Silence for a long moment. "I'm tired of doing it all on my own."

The other choice she'd made back then, in retrospect, she'd clearly chosen wrong.

At times she could still feel the golf club in her hands, the weight of it, the slightly sticky grip, until it became slippery with blood.

She really should have killed him.

THE PAYROLL WAS SCREWED up, again.

Really, what was the point of hiring a service if they couldn't get it right?

Jesus stood there, still in his work T-shirt and black pants, ball cap in hand. He seemed apologetic, like he was doing something wrong for asking. A middle-aged man, short, wiry, with a shaved head and a fuzzy tattoo on his neck. One of her line cooks.

He probably was here illegally, but she didn't really care. He had the right paperwork, and he worked hard.

She was covered.

She signed the check and handed it to him.

"Thank you, Missus Carmichael."

"Don't thank me. You worked for it. You should get paid."

AFTER HE LEFT, SHE finished entering expenses on her spreadsheet. It looked like it was going to be a decent month. On track for $90K plus in gross receipts. She'd gotten some great deals on wine from Sonoma and Lake County, and she was more than happy with the prices and quality of produce and meat she was getting from the local farmers— well, local and a few hundred miles away. You couldn't be a total purist about these things.

She did some filing. Tidied up the tiny office. It didn't take much to clutter it up. Watered her plants. The lavender wasn't doing well. Probably not enough sun. The office had a window that faced east, and Arcata was foggy much of the time, in any case.

I could buy a sun lamp, she thought. One of those therapy lamps, for seasonal affective disorder.

Maybe she could use it too.

My life's not bad, she told herself. It's not bad at all. And it's way better than it was.

Walking into the seating area of the bistro, she reminded herself of that.

She still felt a little thrill sometimes when she looked at it. The redwood burl tables. The dark walls. The photographs on them, lit by accent lights.

Her work.

It was all her work, really. She'd been very careful about everything. The place settings. The silverware. The glasses.

She'd gone for a simple, elegant look with an unfinished edge. Japanese design. Wabi sabi, the deliberate imperfection, the acceptance that all things were transient.

And good food. Good wine. Microbrews. Single-lot-origin coffee. She kept the prices reasonable, the value high.

"There's some money in this town," he'd said.

College students. Some of them still wanted a nice place to go. Not fussy. Not pretentious. But something for a special occasion. A place to take a serious date, or your parents, when they came to visit. The Cal State faculty made up a good chunk of her regulars too.

Them, and the more professional cannabis entrepreneurs.

Whatever, she thought. They had some things in common, really. The best growers were all about the quality. Perfectly trimmed buds, sticky and sparkling with crystals. No pesticides. Different strains for different highs.

And different medical applications. Indica for insomnia. High CBD for pain management. Sativa for PTSD. You can cure cancer with cannabis oil, some of them said.

She thought they tended to exaggerate.

They liked her wine and cheese selection, her organic, grass-fed beef. Fresh, seasonal vegetables and fruit, artisanal baked breads, estate olive oils.

No GMOs, of course. Arcata outlawed those.

One of her pot regulars, Bobby, sat at a two-top with his girlfriend, Gina, underneath her photo of redwoods and mist. A cliché of sorts, she knew, but technically a nice shot.

She thought that Bobby was more of a broker than a grower. But she wasn't sure, and she didn't really want to know. Bobby kept his business quiet, especially compared to the medical growers, where everything was regulated and registered. They were trying to prove a point, she knew, the medical growers and dispensaries, that marijuana could be a legitimate business, one that paid sales tax, joined the local Chambers of Commerce. Served the community.

The federal authorities busted them anyway.

"Easy pickings, operating out in the open like that," Bobby had said once with a shrug. "No thanks." He wasn't crazy about the latest attempt to legalize cannabis for recreational use in California, either. "Prop. 391's just a tax grab by the state," he'd said. But then, a lot of the growers were split on it. "What's that going to do to price? Who gets the licenses? How can we compete against Big Ag?" being some of the more common complaints. "Artisanal weed," was the usual rejoinder. "Like a fine Napa cabernet versus Two Buck Chuck." But not everyone would be able to make that transition.

What would happen to the economy here, without black market marijuana holding it up? The lumber industry collapsed decades ago. Arcata had the university, at least, but in other parts of Humboldt? There wasn't much else.

Bobby waved. In his fifties, round faced, balding, with the remaining hair shaved short, a wool Kangol cap he nearly always wore, retro Armani tortoiseshell glasses, tweed jacket over a designer T-shirt. Gina, a decade younger, at least, curly hair shot with gray, wearing layers of peasant blouse and yoga T-shirt.

She smiled back and approached the table.

"Emily! How's life been treating you?" he asked her.

"Great. Keeping busy."

"I can see that." Nine P.M., and the restaurant nearly full. "What are we in the mood for, hon?" he asked Gina. "A nice cab?"

"Fine with me."

Know your customer. Appeal to his vanity.

"Try the Rafanelli, if you haven't yet. It's not that easy to get a hold of, and a great value for the price."

Bobby ran a finger down the wine list. "It ain't cheap."

"It is for what it is."

"I'll take your word for it."

She took a half-step toward the bar, thinking she would bring the wine over herself, while Kendra, the waitress, took orders at the four-top by the front window.

"Hey, is Jeff around?" Bobby asked. "I left him a couple messages."

She hesitated. "He's fighting a fire."

"Oh, that's right." Bobby propped his elbow on the bar and leaned back. A studied pose. "The one out near Trinity Forest."

She didn't want to talk to Bobby about this, about whatever it was he wanted, because she was pretty sure that she already knew.

"Right," she said.

"Well, listen, when he gets back, can you ask him to give me a buzz? I have a little gig for him."

Great, she thought. Just great.

"DID YOU KNOW THAT the same bulbs that light our streets are probably used on your indoor garden? Now there's a better solution—Butterfly Bulbs can increase your yield up to thirty percent by maximizing photosynthetic—"

Home.

She switched off the radio.

The tires of her Prius crunched the redwood chips covering the driveway. She decided to just leave the car in the drive. Getting out, opening the garage door and parking in the garage felt like too much trouble.

Outside, fog dripped off the pines.

We really should get a garage door opener, she thought, given how much it rained, but then, it wasn't their house. Not one she'd choose to buy, really. A sixties ranch-style that hadn't changed much since the sixties, with the exception of newer carpeting and paint.

It's a house, she thought. And maybe it wasn't as upscale as the one she used to have in Los Angeles, but it was a place to live, and it wasn't bad. God knows, not too long ago, she'd wondered if she'd ever have a decent place, and this was more than decent, even if it was just a rental.

Not that her old house, when she thought about it, was ever actually hers.

Call it whose it was—her husband's.

But not even Tom's, really. The house had belonged to the bank, or to some obscure hedge fund in Iceland, to whoever it was who'd bought the mortgage.

This rental house was owned by a couple who owned a string of dispensaries in Humboldt and Trinity called "Green Solutions." Three bedrooms, the master, an office and a guest room. A good-sized living room. A kitchen that could use some updating, with those "Colonial" knotty pine cupboards she couldn't stand and a cheap electric stove, but after a ten-to-twelve-hour shift at the restaurant, the last thing she wanted to do was cook.

A hot tub out back, overlooking a stand of redwoods.

The hot tub sounded good. Between the day's work and the session she'd had with her trainer at the gym that morning, she was both pleasantly sore and bone tired.

She used the controller on her keyring to deactivate the alarm. Unlocked the deadbolt and the doorknob key. Stepped inside the entry. Headed to the kitchen.

A glass of wine, she thought. Turn on the hot tub, soak a while, and go to bed.

The kitchen opened out onto the deck where the hot tub was. She flicked on the accent light above the butcher-block island—the one thing about the kitchen that she did like—unlocked the sliding glass door, and turned the dial on the stucco wall to start up the hot tub. The jets came on with a massive burp and a bubbling hum that settled into the wooden planks of the deck like a squad of aquatic mosquitoes.

What wine to have, she thought? Maybe the Sonoma Pinotage she was thinking about adding to the wine list at Evergreen.

She opened the bottle and set it on the butcher-block counter.

It would take about twenty minutes for the hot tub to heat up.

I'll get out of these clothes, she thought. Take a quick shower, put on the thick terry robe, sweats and Ugg boots, and maybe start on the wine. Not too much though. Tempting as it was to just drink until she was ready to crawl into bed, it wasn't a good idea, and she knew it.

Two glasses. That was enough.

She couldn't afford to lose control.

As she stepped into the bedroom, an arm circled around her waist.

SHE ALMOST REACTED THE way she'd been trained. Almost drove the heel of her palm into his groin, slammed the crown of her head into his jaw, stomped her heel on his instep, shoved her elbow into his throat, all the things she'd learned how to do.

"Hey."

"Jesus Christ, don't do that," she said.

His hand paused briefly on her hip before letting go.

"Sorry."

She turned. He wore a T-shirt and sweats, his hair damp from a shower, his face freshly shaved, but he still smelled like wood smoke. She could feel her heart beat in her throat, and she swallowed hard.

"Just don't."

He lifted his hands. "Okay."

She knew him well enough to read the emotions: irritation mixed with hurt, followed by a sort of resignation, the half-smile that he wore like camouflage.

She struggled to smile back. To make her voice warm. "I turned on the hot tub," she said. "And opened some wine."

He stared at her for a moment, then nodded. "Sounds good. I'm beat to shit."

STANDING UNDER THE SHOWERHEAD, letting the strong jets of water pulse against her scalp, she asked herself, yet again, what she was doing with him.

She thought that she knew the answers, but she couldn't seem to stop asking herself the question.

Safety. That had been a big part of it. Security. He'd had all the money. Sure, he'd offered to give her something if she'd decided to go it alone, but how much would that have been? How long would it have lasted?

She'd taken the path of least resistance, again—staying with the man.

Things are different now, she told herself. She had the bistro. She had Evergreen. She owed him for that, but she could support herself. *Was* supporting herself.

She turned off the shower, wrapped herself in her terry robe, and went out to check on the hot tub.

HE'D ALREADY GONE IN.

"Hot enough?" she asked.

"Getting there." He leaned against the side of the tub, eyes half-closed.

"You want anything else with the wine?"

"Water'd be great."

She brought out the bottle of wine, two glasses, and then the pitcher of water with a couple of plastic tumblers. Put them down on the redwood deck. Slipped off her robe and draped it on the Adirondack chair by the tub.

He watched her now as she stepped into the tub and sat on the bench next to him.

"I bet you could kick my ass," he said.

She had to smile. "I doubt it."

"Maybe I'd let you."

He leaned over and kissed her. His lower lip had cracked, probably from the fire's heat, and she could taste the hint of blood. She moved closer to him, and his arm circled around her back. His other hand came to rest on her breast, finger-tips gently stroking her nipple.

Just the way she liked it.

This was one of the other answers.

Stupid, she told herself, and shallow. But true.

She couldn't pretend that it didn't matter. She liked look-ing at him, the long, lean body, the black hair shot with gray, the blue eyes and sharp cheekbones. It shouldn't matter, but it did. He loved sex, and he was good at it. Good with her. And after the long drought that had been her marriage, well, why not?

Don't ask that question, she told herself. But of course, she always did.

"I think I'm ready for some of that wine," he said. The bottle and glasses had ended up almost behind him, and he leaned back and started to reach for the bottle. Drew in a sharp breath. "Shit!" he gasped, falling back against the side of the tub.

"Shoulder?"

"Yeah." He managed a grin. "I think I'm getting too old to be a fireman."

He wasn't that old. He'd just turned forty-two. And he was in good shape. But she could see the scar from the injury even in the near dark: a jagged oblong the size of a large grape, bigger than it needed to be because they'd waited to treat it, white edges around a dark, red-brown hollow.

She poured the wine. They toasted silently. Sipped.

It was smooth. Smoky. Which seemed appropriate.

"So how was the fire?" she asked.

"Fun. You know. Worked our asses off. Lost a house by Junction City, but that was it in terms of structures."

"Are you really thinking about not volunteering any more?"

He gave a one-shouldered shrug. "I dunno. I mean, I need *something* to do."

"The charter business . . ."

"Too slow. Not enough to cover the Caravan. Hangar rental's going up next month."

"Evergreen's doing really well. You own the plane. We can cover the hangar."

"It's not enough."

He poured them both more wine. "Bobby left me a couple of messages. Said he has a gig."

She hesitated. She knew that he probably wouldn't listen. "Is it really a good idea?" she asked anyway.

"Minimum risk, maximum reward."

"It's not minimum risk," she said, feeling a surge of irritation. "You know, the rest of the country isn't Humboldt."

"Compared to what I used to do?" He gulped some wine. "Look, setting up here took most of my bank." Which might have been aimed at her. Opening Evergreen hadn't been cheap. "And there's no way I want to be without some real cash. In case, you know?"

Then he grinned. "Besides, it's patriotic. Supporting the local economy. Taking business away from the Mexicans. Win-win."

She fought the urge to get out of the tub, storm off, slam a few doors. Not her style. Not the person she wanted to be, anyway.

Also, he had a point.

"Okay," she said. "But you have to promise me. If we're . . ."

Her throat closed. She couldn't get the words out. She wasn't sure what the words even were.

It wasn't like they had a commitment. What did they have in common, really? They'd been thrown together, and they'd stuck together because it seemed to make sense.

It wasn't love, or anything like that. She wasn't sure she even remembered what being in love felt like.

It was attraction. Pheromones. It was making the best of the situation. He kept things light, and so did she.

Maybe I can't feel anything deep, she thought.

But she liked him. He was funny, and he was kind. And he'd kept his promises to her.

"If we're going to stay together," she finally said, "there needs to be a point when you're done. With things like gigs for Bobby."

He let out a long, slow sigh. Nodded. "Yeah. I know. You're right."

"I'll clean up," she said. "Why don't you go to bed? You look exhausted."

He smiled, because that was how he was. The good guy. The one who let things slide. Who appreciated what he had. Pretended to, anyway.

"Thanks. I'm wiped."

She shut down the hot tub, put on the cover. Washed the wine glasses and put them in the dish rack to dry. Threw the bottle in the recycling bin. Decent wine, she thought, and she liked that it was local. If she could talk them down a little on the case price, she'd stock it.

By the time she went into the bedroom, he was sound asleep.

She rinsed off in the shower, put on a T-shirt and pajama bottoms—no need for lingerie—and slid under the covers next to him.

Lying there, she thought, he's not perfect, but god knows, neither am I.

Maybe this is close enough, she thought.

Not a life she ever could have imagined living. But it wasn't bad.

☞ ☞ ☞

TWO DAYS, HE'D SAID. "Texas. Flight plan's for Houston, if anyone asks."

One day down, one to go.

Almost 10 P.M. Time to close up shop, she thought, and go home. She shut down her computer, turned off the office light, locked the door.

Tuesday night. A slow one. The kitchen was already closed, except for bar snacks for another hour. She wasn't sure if the hour would be worth it. The bar empty except for two stools. The four-top settling their bill. Only one other customer that she could see, sitting at the two-top tucked into the alcove to the right of the front window. A dark corner, she thought. Maybe she needed to install another accent light. Kendra, the waitress, was there, laughing at something the customer had said, blocking her view of him, except for his shoulder, the side of his torso, some curly gold hair.

As she walked toward the door, a part of her already knew. Before Kendra stepped away and she saw him clearly, her heart had already started racing, raw adrenaline coursing through her body like a flood of melted ice.

The man at the two-top smiled and lifted his hand.

"Well, hello there, Michelle—how nice to see you again."

Fucking Gary.

Chapter Two

A PART OF HER wanted to run. It was the rage that stopped her, coming in hard after the rush of fear.

Gun. She carried a .38 Smith & Wesson in her Be&D hobo. Tucked in a holster sewn into the leather. She'd had it made custom. Her hand snaked toward the flap.

Gary's smile broadened, his eyes trailing the movement.

Fuck, she thought. She couldn't just shoot the son of a bitch down in her restaurant.

Could she?

Kendra paused at her side, whispered in her ear: "He said you were old friends. He's been waiting. Do you want me to—?"

"It's fine." She forced a smile. "I was just surprised."

"Did he call you 'Michelle'?"

"An old nickname. Excuse me a minute."

She waited until Kendra had gone over to the four-top to pick up the check, and then she approached Gary's table.

"Why are you here?"

"I thought you might have time for a glass of wine." He chuckled. "We have some catching up to do. Don't you think?"

The last thing she wanted to do was sit down and have a drink with fucking Gary.

"What do you recommend?" he asked, running a finger down the wine list. "You know a lot more about this stuff than I do. Something nice. And smooth. My treat."

She kept her voice steady. Smiled like she would if he were any other customer. "Kendra? Would you bring over a bottle of the Turley, please? Two glasses."

She turned back to Gary. "Anything else?"

His eyes moved from hers, slowly down her body. Taking everything in. "I've already eaten."

She rolled her eyes. He was so fucking predictable.

Michelle pulled out the chair opposite Gary, and sat.

Kendra brought the wine.

"Well, thank you . . . Kendra, right?" He smiled. "Kendra was telling me about her studies at the college here, while I was waiting for you. Getting your master's in . . . environmental . . . *systems*, is it?"

"That's right," Kendra said. "It's a great program. I think your friend's son would really like it. But there's a lot of options. Environmental engineering, environment and community . . ." She was fresh faced and earnest, her enthusiasm for her subject close to the surface, like her enthusiasm for most things. A sweet girl.

Not someone Michelle wanted to put in front of Gary, not for another minute.

"Kendra, why don't you go ahead and punch out. I'll pay you for the rest of the hour."

"I still have some side work—"

"It's been so slow. Don't worry. Matt can handle it."

The bartender. In his late twenties, tattooed and pierced, hard bodied from mountain biking and rock climbing and whatever else he did.

Not that he'd be any match for Gary.

Michelle's heart started pounding again, and she thought, Matt will be okay. He's over at the bar, where he won't hear anything we say. He won't know anything. He won't be a threat.

She just didn't want to be left alone with Gary, even if Matt was no real protection.

"Thanks, Emily—see you tomorrow!" Kendra said over her shoulder.

Gary raised his glass.

"If you think I'm going to toast with you—" Michelle said.

"Now, now. We're two old friends, having a drink. How's it gonna look to your boy-toy at the bar if you don't?"

She pasted a smile back on. Lifted her glass. Clinked. Watched Gary sip.

She wasn't going to ask how he found her. He wouldn't tell her the truth, she knew.

Most probably, somewhere along the line she and Danny had been compromised, by someone who'd claimed to be on their side.

"Well, this is really nice," Gary said.

If he meant the wine, it was. She'd been tempted to order the cheapest glass on the menu for him, but even those were decent. Might as well make him pay for it.

"The whole place, I'm just so impressed. I bet those are your photos on the walls, right? I always did think you had a real good eye."

"Right."

"You look like you've been working out," he said, sniffing at the wine. "I mean, you always were into that as I recall, but seems like you've taken it to another level."

It was true, but she wasn't going to tell him that. Wasn't going to tell him about the self-defense classes, the kickboxing, how all that activity was one of the few things that helped her relax.

"You know, you kind of inspired me, actually. I've been working out a lot myself." He sat up straighter. Displaying himself. "You notice?"

Oh please, she thought.

But taking the opportunity to really focus on him, she could tell that he looked different. Thinner, for one. Harder. Even his face. His eyelids looked less puffy, the bags below them almost gone.

Good god, had he gotten his eyes done?

The mouth was the same, the cherub lips. And the hair, the gold curls, with their salon highlights.

"You've lost some weight," she said.

"Well, you know, I was in the hospital for almost a month, thanks to you. Yeah, I lost a lot of weight. When I got out, I had to do a bunch of physical therapy, and after all that, I just thought, well hey, why not turn over a new leaf while I'm at it?" He rubbed a patch on his cheekbone. "Still numb. Multiple fractures." Touched the bridge of his nose. "Yeah, and that bump's left from where they reset it. I could've had more work done but I kinda like it, actually. Gives me a distinguished touch, I've been told."

Deep, calming breaths, she told herself.

"So is that why you came here, Gary? You want to compare injuries? Because you know, I have a few. Thanks to *you*."

"Be nice if we could just call it even. Wouldn't it?"

At that, she laughed. "Are you really going to tell me that you came here to kiss and make up? Do you think for one second I'd believe that?"

"No, I don't expect you would." He settled back into his

chair. "But one thing I hope you do believe, Michelle. You know how I used to tell you that I thought you had a lot of potential? A natural aptitude? I meant that. I really did."

A sinking feeling. How many times had she read that description in a book, not really thinking about what it actually described? She felt it now, a hollow plunging in her gut.

She didn't need to know exactly what was coming to have a pretty good idea of its shape.

"No," she said.

"You haven't even heard what I have to say."

"I don't need to."

Now he chuckled. Took a hearty swallow of wine. "You really think you get to say no?"

Red pulsed behind her eyes. She thought about the gun. "I should have fucking killed you," she said.

"Yeah. You probably should've," he said without heat. "Rookie mistake. It's always best to finish the job."

He drank some more wine and finally pushed his glass away. "Tell you what. I know this is a lot to absorb right now. I'm staying at a little bed and breakfast just off the square. The Lady Jane Grey. Cute place. Got a hot tub and everything. Why don't you come see me tomorrow morning, nine-ish, and we'll get caught up?"

Michelle nodded. It was easier to agree than to argue.

Now he stood. Retrieved his wallet from a back pocket. "One glass is my limit these days." He pulled out three one hundred dollar bills and tossed them on the table. "You can take the rest of the bottle home." He smiled. "On me."

AFTER GARY LEFT, SHE stayed where she was. Picked up her wine glass. Thinking she wanted to snap the stem between her fingers, hurl the glass against the wall. At the redwoods photo, maybe. Because it really was a cliché.

Instead she had a sip, and then another.

She finished the glass. Picked Gary's money up off the table, grabbed the bottle of wine, and went over to the bar.

"For the Turley on number five," she said, handing Matt the money.

"Wow. That's a big tip."

She shrugged. "Make sure it gets divided up."

"What about the bottle?"

Michelle glanced at the two customers on bar stools. Students, she thought, a girl and a boy who looked like they'd barely reached drinking age. On a date, probably. Nursing draft beers.

"You like wine?" she asked them. "It's on the house."

OUTSIDE, THE FOG WAS thick, leaving her face damp with its chill. She kept one hand on the butt of her .38 as she clicked on her key to unlock the Prius, parked behind Evergreen.

Stupid, she thought, sliding into the front seat. He's not waiting out here to kill me, or kidnap me. He wouldn't have come into the restaurant that way if that had been his plan.

Whatever it was he wanted her to do would be his version of revenge. Or the start of it. He'd put her in some situation that she couldn't get out of. Where she'd be afraid, all the time. Terrorized.

She remembered the things he'd threatened her with, before. She remembered the things that he'd done.

It's all a game to him. It's fun.

She arrived home, not remembering the drive.

Still keeping her hand on the pistol, she clicked off the alarm and went inside.

No Danny. He wasn't due back yet, but still, she'd wanted desperately to find him here. She wanted to tell him what had happened. To have him hold her.

She went out to the garage and retrieved one of the burner cell phones.

They could have kept the phones in the house safe, but that looked bad, Danny had said. "Just throw them in a box of crap in the garage. Like it's a piece of junk we haven't taken to the electronics recycling. If anyone finds one, you don't know what it is or how it got there." A cheap phone, with no GPS. Prepaid minutes, bought with cash at a big-box store in another state.

She dug out the charger, stashed in a different bin on the workbench. Plugged in the phone. Went to texts, and punched in a number.

A two-character text: 86.

She waited. No response.

Okay, she thought, it might still be okay. He could be on his way back. He could have already tossed the phone.

She went back into the house. Grabbed her iPhone. Her "Emily" phone. The one with the plan through AT&T, the one that she paid for out of her "Emily" bank account every month, like a normal person.

She called Danny's "Jeff" phone. "Hey," his recorded voice said, "Sorry I missed you. Leave a message."

"Hi, it's Emily. Can you call me back, as soon as you pick this up. It's important."

He turns his phone off all the time, she told herself. If he's still doing his run, it would definitely be off. Stashed in a signal-blocking bag, to make sure it couldn't be tracked.

But he was supposed to have his burner cell on, if he was still doing his run.

She went to her bedroom closet. Retrieved another cell phone from her other hobo, a Marc Jacobs she didn't use much any more. Her "Michelle" phone. Also prepaid. A risk, she knew. But she didn't keep any numbers in the phone book. Deleted the calls she made after she made them, as well as any incoming.

The only person who had the number was her sister, and Michelle had already changed it twice.

She couldn't tell Maggie what had happened in Mexico, or after. Where she was now, what she was doing. She'd seen Maggie and Ben once, eight months ago, meeting them in Santa Barbara for a "getaway weekend."

"You can't ask questions," she'd told Maggie. "Only call me if it's an emergency. I mean, a *real* emergency." She'd given Maggie an email address too, that she accessed through a VPN. "Use that first. I'll check it every day."

It wasn't foolproof. Cutting off all contact would have been the safest thing to do. But she'd lost everything else. She wasn't going to lose what was left of her family.

Their parents had been older. They'd gone from retirement community to assisted living to nursing home, the kind of journey where the horizons shrunk to a room and a wheelchair. Mom was gone. Dad had Alzheimer's. It was a weird blessing, in a way, that there wasn't enough left of him to miss her.

She put money into an account for his care, every month. Derek, their lawyer, took care of that. It was supposed to be untraceable.

She didn't necessarily trust Derek.

Michelle dialed Maggie's number. If her sister's phone was tapped, so what? She didn't have to worry about them pinging the cell phone tower, about them locating her. Gary was here. They already knew.

It took five rings for Maggie to pick up.

"It's me," Michelle said quickly. "Is everything okay there? Just answer yes, or no."

"Yes. Michelle?" Maggie sounded sleepy. It was almost 11:00 P.M., and she usually went to bed around now, so she could get up in the morning, make Ben his lunch, drop him off at school and get to the office on time.

"You're sure? There's no one . . . no one's making you say that?"

"*No.* Jesus. What is this, a spy movie or something?"

Michelle nearly laughed.

"Look, do me a favor," she said. "Can you, can you just . . . take a few days off? Go somewhere. You and Ben. I'll cover the cost."

"No, I can't 'go somewhere.' Lucia's on maternity leave, I'm covering her desk, they'd *kill* me. Seriously, Michelle, what the fuck is going on?"

Maggie sounded royally pissed. Michelle supposed she couldn't blame her.

"I can't get into it right now. It's . . . it's complicated."

What could she tell her? If they were listening, what could she say that wouldn't make things worse?

"I'm glad everything's okay," she said. "Just . . . if you have any problems, if anything . . . call me, okay? If the number doesn't work, email me."

"Okay." There was silence on the other end of the line. "Look," Maggie finally said. "Whatever's going on, just tell me. We'll figure out how to deal with it. This, this whole mystery act of yours, it's ridiculous. It can't be that bad." She laughed, a nervous chuckle. "I mean, you didn't kill anyone, did you?"

MICHELLE TOOK AN AMBIEN. She didn't like taking them, but the natural sleep aids, the melatonin spray, the herbs, weren't going to work tonight, and she knew it.

Better a chemically induced sleep than none at all. You can't sleep, you can't think straight, and she needed to be able to think.

Even with the Ambien, her thoughts went in circles.

AT 6:33 A.M., HER Emily phone rang. She might have been awake before it rang.

Danny had programmed her ringtones. She'd never cared about that stuff, but he liked doing it, and his choices made her smile.

"Lawyers, Guns and Money." The ringtone for business.

Derek Girard. Their attorney.

Her heart pounded. If she hadn't been awake before, she was wide-awake now.

"Hello?"

"Emily? Derek Girard. Sorry to call so early. But we have a situation."

Chapter Three

֍

MICHELLE PULLED INTO THE Evergreen parking lot just after 9 A.M. She could have parked by Lady Jane's, but she needed to steady herself, and the walk would help. No matter how scared she was, no matter how angry, she had to play this right.

She cut across the green expanse of the Arcata Plaza, past the statue of President McKinley at its center, then down G Street by the Arcata Hotel, ignoring the panhandlers begging for change, or if not that, a joint. Normally she enjoyed lingering in the Plaza, with its mix of Settlement, Victorian and Craftsman buildings, wondering what previous owners of some of them had been thinking when they'd covered up historic buildings with modern facades, or, more happily, watching the progress of the latest restoration.

She was tempted to linger now. To put this meeting off, just a little while longer. But it was better to get it over with.

Better not to be late.

Her destination was a Victorian a few blocks off the Plaza.

Lady Jane's served breakfast in the garden when the weather was decent, Michelle knew, and it was nice enough today. Mid-sixties. Almost sunny. She missed the LA heat, sometimes. It was hardly ever really warm in Arcata.

At least the climate here is good for my skin, she thought, and then she wanted to laugh.

Gary sat at a table in the back of the garden, under a

wicker archway threaded with ivy, his legs stretched out, feet propped on a chair in front of him. He wore a baseball cap, the first time Michelle had ever seen him in any kind of hat, and sipped from a teacup. He seemed to be staring at the fountain, though she couldn't be sure. The centerpiece of the fountain was an Indian-style Buddha. Not really a good fit with Victorian. She'd always wondered about that.

"Well, good morning, Emily." He bowed his head a fraction and pinched the brim of his ball cap.

Michelle took in the logo. "The Humboldt Crabs?"

"Champions of the Far West League," Gary said, grinning. "You know they beat the Healdsburg Prune Packers last night?"

Michelle pulled out the other chair and sat. "I missed it."

"Right here in Arcata." He shook his head. "I have to say, this town . . . it isn't really *you*, Michelle."

"How would *you* know?" she snapped back.

"I'm actually a pretty good judge of character."

The waitress approached. One of the owners: Jennifer. A few years older than Michelle. Patagonia vests, hemp skirts and handmade soft leather boots.

"Emily, so nice to see you!"

Michelle forced a smile, and nodded. "Great to see you too."

"What can I get you?"

"Just coffee. Thanks."

Gary watched Jennifer pick her way down the gravel path that led to Lady Jane's kitchen. "Interesting woman, don't you think?"

"Do not fuck with anybody else here, Gary."

For a moment, he was silent. "Well, well," he said.

Jennifer returned with coffee. "Is there anything else I can get you? We have fresh baked scones."

"No thanks," Gary said. "I have to watch my gluten."

Michelle sipped her coffee. She made a better cup at Evergreen, but this wasn't bad.

"All right," she said, when Jennifer could no longer hear. "What do you want me to do?"

"That's it? You're just gonna agree?"

He sounded oddly disappointed.

"No. I'm going to hear what your job is first. And then I'm going to think about it."

Gary leaned back in his chair. "You know, I gotta admit, I was pretty surprised to see you and Danny still together. I never would've thought that would last."

"Just tell me what you want."

Now Gary smiled. "So you're willing to go to the mat for him? Who'd a thunk?"

You can't lose it, she told herself.

More to the point, you can't pull out your .38 and shoot him in Lady Jane Grey's garden.

"What's the job, Gary?"

"Babysitting," he said. "I need you to look after somebody. She's rich. And tragic." He shook his head. "Such a sad story."

"Babysitting?"

"Well, she's gone a little overboard with the self-medicating, and she operates in the kind of social milieu that I figure you're familiar with. Fund-raisers and such."

"What would I do?"

"Look after her. Manage her appointments. See if you can get her to take a yoga class or two." He snorted. "Right in your wheelhouse."

No way it could be that easy.

"That's it?"

"Well, there might be a couple other things. Nothing you can't handle."

Great, she thought.

"So who is this woman, exactly?"

"You take the job, I'll tell you. Otherwise, you can pretend it's one of those gossip columns, where you're supposed to guess. '*This* wealthy socialite with a tragic past is known for her charitable efforts and social conscience. But when she's out of the public eye, she likes to drink till she pukes and take pills till she passes out. Friends fear she's gonna drown in her own bathtub.'" He chuckled. "I never can figure out who it is. Can you?"

"I don't try."

Gary pushed his baseball cap back on his forehead and tilted his face up toward the sun, which had just managed to break through the coastal fog.

"Well, you take a day or two to think about it. Examine your situation, and decide what your priorities are. I'll be in touch." He smiled. "You got a number you prefer for me to call?"

"THERE'S NO REASON FOR you to come out," Derek had said, on that first phone call.

"I need to talk to him."

"Look, we'll have the arraignment Friday, we'll hear the complaint, and we'll find out what the bail conditions are. Best-case scenario, he's back in Arcata in a couple days."

"Worst case?"

"Well, there's a whole range of possibilities with bail,

home detention, electronic monitoring, surrender of passport . . ."

He hadn't said anything about the court not granting bail at all.

"ON WHAT GROUNDS?"

"They consider Jeff . . . a flight risk, apparently."

"A flight risk."

Michelle laughed. It wasn't a bad call.

She sat on a stool in her kitchen at home. Derek had scheduled the phone call for 9 P.M., after his flight home to San Francisco, and she'd left Evergreen to take it. No way she wanted to deal with this at work, not even in her office.

"Look, I know this is all pretty scary. And it is serious, but it could be worse."

"How so?"

"They're charging him with trafficking under a thousand kilograms. If it had been a thousand or above, he'd be facing a ten-year mandatory minimum. As it is, it's his first offense, so he's looking at five."

"Five *years*?" She could hear the edge of hysteria in her voice. But why was she so surprised by this? So flattened? She'd known the kinds of risks he was taking.

"At a minimum. On the high end, as much as forty."

"Jesus."

"Now, I don't think that's a likely scenario. My goal is to have Jeff spend as little time in jail as possible and to walk out of there with a clean record. But I'd be remiss if I didn't inform you of all the potential outcomes."

Michelle tilted back the bottle of Napa meritage she'd brought home to sample and poured another glass.

"There's another thing we need to discuss. Odds are they'll get a warrant to search your house. And at some point, they're going to want to talk to you. I strongly advise you to not have any conversations without having an attorney present. A case like this, they're looking to find evidence of a conspiracy. And they love rolling up a girlfriend because she's holding cash or drugs."

"I'm not holding anything," she snapped.

"I know, I know," he said quickly. "I just want you to be prepared."

Was there anything in the house? Anything that could incriminate her, or Danny? She didn't think so. The gun she carried was legal. The cash they had on hand, well, there was about $5,000 in the safe, but that wasn't illegal, was it?

"Because of that, I'm going to ask you for an additional retainer up front," Derek was saying, "in case your asset situation gets . . . complicated."

"How much?"

"Ten thousand if you can. That should be more than enough, assuming this doesn't go to trial."

"Fine," she said. "I'll take care of it.

"Try not to worry. I'll call you as soon as I have news."

"I'm coming out," she said. "I need you to arrange the visit. To the jail."

"Emily, look . . ." There was a considered silence on the other end of the line. "Jeff feels . . . it might be uncomfortable for you to . . . present yourself to the authorities. It's . . . not a nice situation."

Which probably meant, Danny was worried about their fake identities being exposed to too much scrutiny.

Too fucking bad.

"Just tell me what I need to do to see him," she said. "And I'll be there."

SHE FOUND A LATE afternoon flight from San Francisco that would get her into Houston just before 11:30 P.M. on Saturday, with an unavoidable layover in Phoenix. The flight from Arcata to SFO wasn't much cheaper than the flight to Houston.

She had a few hours to kill at SFO. She sat in the Mission Bar and Grill, had a quesadilla, and drank a glass of wine. Watched the jets pull up to the gates, through the smoked Plexiglas windows.

She didn't know what Derek knew. How much he knew about Danny and his background. He knew about some of it, obviously. That Danny was involved in the drug trade, certainly.

Who Danny had really worked for before, who he was working for in Mexico?

Michelle didn't know if Derek knew that much.

When they'd set themselves up in Humboldt, Derek had been there. He'd arranged the payments to her father's nursing home. To Ben's college fund. "Untraceable," he'd assured her. "I know that you have some privacy issues."

Did he know enough to have sold them out to Gary?

THE MOMENT SHE STEPPED off the plane and onto the jetway in Houston, she could feel the heat. Even at 11:30 P.M., it clung to her: thick steam perfumed with burnt jet fuel. Puerto Vallarta wasn't this bad, she thought. There was an ocean there, at least. This, this was some kind of malarial fever dream. Endless freeways looping around a flat plain, strings of Christmas tree lights marking the way. Houston was a drained swamp; she thought she'd read that once. No physical landmarks. No hills. No valleys. No ocean.

Strip malls. Condos. Warehouses and big-box stores. High-rises, clustered here and there like outbreaks, transplants from some other city.

She'd been the last stop on the Super Shuttle. She'd picked an inexpensive hotel that wasn't too far from the jail, but far enough away to get some distance from whoever might be watching Danny's visitors. Far enough away for her to relax, or try to, at least.

The hotel was nice enough. The room had a view of the freeway, and of a water tank on the other side of it. She thought it was a water tank, anyway. Shaped like a mushroom, painted a sea-foam green and surrounded by a spiderweb grid of wire.

Maybe it was a gas tank, she thought. This was Texas, after all.

"You can't bring anything with you," Derek had said. "No purse, no cell phone, no notebook, no pens, nothing. You have to put it all in a locker at the jail. The only thing you can bring in is the locker key. Be careful how you dress. No tank tops. No short skirts. Nothing see-through. And if you wear an underwire bra? Switch it out. You only get a couple tries through the metal detector. Oh, and don't forget your driver's license. They won't let you in without a valid state or federal ID, with photo."

She'd nodded, even though he couldn't see that. Taken notes. Sipped her meritage.

"What happens next?"

"We'll petition for another bail hearing. Line up witnesses and documents showing that Jeff isn't a flight risk."

Good luck with that, she'd thought.

"You'll do that from San Francisco?"

"There's no point in my staying in Houston. You don't want to get billed for all those hours, and I'm limited in what I can do for you right now. I'm not licensed to practice in Texas. But I'm working with a local firm and petitioning the judge for *pro hac vice*—that's representation 'for this occasion.' They usually will grant motions like this, and I should be able to act as Jeff's official counsel going forward. In the meantime, my counterpart in Houston, Marisol Acosta, is on the case and a very sharp gal who specializes in federal drug trafficking. If you have any questions or concerns, call her."

MICHELLE LAY ON THE queen bed in her hotel room and listened to the fan blowing cool air through the room. She'd closed the blinds and the curtains so no light leaked in, but she could still hear the rush of cars from the freeway, like a low ocean wave that never stopped hitting the shore.

Christ, she thought. How are we going to pay for all this? She'd paid Derek the ten thousand, but in a case like this . . . the bills would add up.

Plus, asset seizures. Derek had warned her about that. Things you owned that might be funded by drug money, police departments and federal agencies, they seized those. All the time. People in Arcata complained about that, how the federal authorities would confiscate property if they could reasonably claim it was connected to drug profits.

Vehicles. Houses. Businesses.

Like Evergreen.

You can't worry about that now, she told herself. First things first. See Danny. Tell him what was going on. Find out what he thought she should do.

She'd worked through all the options, and she thought she knew what the best one was, but maybe he had a better idea. An angle she hadn't thought of. Because the best option she'd thought of for this situation wasn't very good at all.

Chapter Four

MICHELLE HOPED SHE WAS in the right line.

The jail reminded her of a bank in a seedy neighborhood crossed with a DMV. It had that institutional smell: stale air, dust and old sweat, mixed with the chemical tang of industrial cleaner, chilled by air conditioning. White brick walls. Plexiglas windows. Long lines. The people who waited were mostly women. Black women. White women. Latinas. Some Asians too. A lot of them looked poor, going by their clothing, by the extra weight they carried.

She'd found a tiny metal table with white paper slips that had to be filled out with Danny's information, "Jeff's," rather: his SPN number—the number for the jail, his cellblock, his bunk. Found the lockers farther back, and stowed her purse in one for a quarter. Stood in the line for the 6th floor, at least, she thought it was. The line stretched the length of the institutional lobby. She'd glimpsed a row of Plexiglas windows, where the deputies waited, the ones who would process her request, and check her for outstanding warrants.

"This your first visit?"

Michelle flinched.

The woman who'd asked the question stood behind her in line. A tall, middle-aged black woman, dressed in a matching turquoise skirt and cardigan, like she'd wear to an office. Processed hair neatly curled.

"Yes," Michelle said. "Yes, it is."

"It gets better after you've done it a few times."

"It does?"

The woman shrugged. "Well, not really. You just learn what to expect, that's all."

Her name was Deondra, and she was visiting her son.

"Off his meds," she said with a sigh. "Not that it's clear they work. At various times they've diagnosed him manic-depressive, mildly schizophrenic, ADD, Asperger's . . . Anyway, he was creating a disturbance and had some marijuana on him, and that was that. A hundred eighty days for the marijuana and a hundred eighty days for disturbing the peace."

"How much marijuana?" Michelle had to ask.

"Oh, it was about half an ounce or so."

Great, Michelle thought. Half a year for half an ounce. And Danny? Coming in between 200 pounds and a ton?

"That seems pretty harsh," she said.

"Well, it was the second time he got caught with it." Deondra's smile was more of a grimace. "At least he might get some treatment, if I can get him transferred to MHU."

"MHU?"

"The mental health unit. They've got more resources inside here than they do out in the community, I'm sorry to say."

They'd reached the front of the line. The Latina woman standing at the window stepped aside. It was Michelle's turn.

She pushed the piece of paper with Danny's information into the battered aluminum trough.

"ID?" the deputy asked.

She gave him her California driver's license. Emily's license.

There was nothing to worry about, she thought. Emily didn't have any outstanding warrants.

She wasn't so sure about Michelle.

The deputy held up the license, studying the photo, then shifted his attention to her face.

Sweat beaded on her forehead, dripped down her back.

Well, it's over 90 degrees outside, she thought, so he won't think that's strange.

Will he?

She shivered in the cold draft from the air conditioning vent.

"California?"

She managed a smile. "Yes."

He turned away to stare at a computer screen, and started typing on a keyboard.

She stood there. Waited.

Finally, he scribbled something on the white slip of paper with Danny's information, and slid that under the window.

"You get the license back after," he said. "Have a nice visit."

THE NEXT LINE WAS for the metal detector.

It should have been quick, but it wasn't. The detector seemed to buzz for every third person passing through it.

"They've got that thing set so sensitive," Deondra said, rolling her eyes. She busied herself taking off her earrings, her necklace, a bracelet, and putting them in a Baggie. "You never know what's going to set it off. Sometimes it's the hooks in your brassiere, I swear."

Michelle was glad that Derek had warned her about underwire.

It took her two tries to get through the metal detector, the second time passing it by removing her shoes. On the other side of the metal detector was an elevator. She stood at the back of the crowd waiting for it to return from the upper floors.

Behind her, Deondra asked. "Did you bring a wet wipe?"

"A wet wipe?"

Deondra reached inside the Baggie she'd used for her jewelry and pulled out a small packet. Stretched her hand out to Michelle.

A sanitary wipe.

"I brought two. Believe me, you'll want to use it."

INSIDE THE ELEVATOR, MICHELLE faced the doors. She was nearly pressed up against them. Close enough to stare at the scratches in the aluminum that spelled out, SUCK PUSSY.

ANOTHER PLEXIGLAS WINDOW WITH a uniformed deputy behind it. Another line, a short one this time. It was colder than downstairs, ridiculously cold. "Yeah, that's why I wear the sweater set," Deondra told her. "Supposedly keeping it cold helps with sanitation. There's a lot of diseases here. Staph infections. Chicken pox."

She hadn't seen a single window on the floor. Nothing but artificial light. The visitation room reeked, the scent of stale sweat and sewage carried on the chilled air. To her right were a series of windows, barely separated by narrow acoustic dividers. Visitors crowded around them, most leaning against the cement pillars that served as stools rather than sitting on them, some even perched on the narrow counters, carrying on conversations in shouts.

"You just hand the deputy your slip." Deondra explained, over the din. "Then you go find a window and wait. They'll bring him in."

It was nearly Michelle's turn. "Thanks," she said. "Thanks for all your help."

Deondra made a little shrug, smiled her grimace of a smile. "It's best we help each other. Believe me, you won't get much help from anyone else."

MICHELLE FOUND AN EMPTY window. At the window to her left was what looked like a family: a young Latina and two small children, the mother holding the smaller of the two up to the glass, so the kid's father could see. At least, she assumed the young man on the other side was the father. To her right, a rare male visitor, white, middle-aged. She watched as the visitors changed positions, putting their mouths and then their ears up against the circular metal speaker. Even so, how could anyone hear the other? Every word seemed to be bellowed.

She studied the speaker grate, the Plexiglas around it. Dried spit. A smear of lipstick.

She opened Deondra's wet wipe and cleaned the area as best she could. Then sat on the pillar and waited.

The visitation room on the inmate side had two banks of windows, the one she faced, and one on the wall opposite. She could see the visitors on the other side of those windows, and she had a sudden flash, a vision, of an endless series of windows, of prisoners and visitors, lined up, yelling through the glass.

She fought off a wave of dizziness, of nausea. Suck it up, she told herself. After almost two hours in various lines, the visit would be over soon enough—you were only allowed twenty minutes.

Finally, a deputy brought him in.

Like the other prisoners, he wore orange scrubs with HARRIS COUNTY stenciled in black, and rubber shower shoes.

Unlike most of the other prisoners, he was handcuffed, hands behind his back. Why was that?

He didn't see her, at first; she watched his head swivel back and forth, trying to spot her. She stood up and waved.

His eyes fixed on her. His face changed. She wasn't sure what to make of the expression. Sad? Worried? Angry? Then he put on the familiar half-smile. The one he used to cover everything up.

The deputy walked him over to the stool. He moved stiffly, like he was guarding an injury. He hadn't shaved today. His eyes were bloodshot, the lids dark with fatigue.

For a moment, Michelle didn't know what to say. "Are you okay?" she managed.

He frowned a little. He hadn't heard her. She pressed her lips against the metal speaker grate and yelled, like everyone else. "Are you okay?"

"Yeah," he said. But his eyes and expression said something else. A fractional headshake. A warning. Don't ask.

He leaned in toward the grate, wincing as he did, arms pressed tight against his sides, his torso held too straight. Had he hurt his ribs? She remembered moving like that, when she had that injury. She put her ear up to the grate. "I'm sorry," he said.

Michelle closed her eyes for a moment. As tempting as it was to say, "I told you so," it didn't seem like the time.

And besides, that might sound incriminating.

"We'll deal with it," she said.

"You didn't need to come. We'll have another bail hearing in the next two weeks, and Derek's sure I'll be getting out this time."

Now it was Michelle's turn to shake her head. She gestured for him to listen and spoke as clearly as she could into the speaker without shouting.

"Gary's in Arcata. He showed up Tuesday night."

She pulled away from the window so she could see his face. For a moment he looked stunned. Then he swallowed, and his face turned still with rage.

"Motherfucker," he mouthed.

"Yeah."

She gestured for him to listen. Waited as he shifted position, grimacing as he did, and pressed his ear against the grate. "He's got some kind of job for me."

"*No.*"

Michelle didn't need to put her ear to the speaker grate to hear that.

"I think I need to take it."

"You can't." His voice was faint, tinny. This wasn't something he was willing to shout to be heard. She pressed her ear against the speaker and let him have his turn.

"You know what his endgame is," he said. "No matter what he promises."

"I don't think there's a better choice."

"There is. Call Sam."

One of Danny's old contacts, who'd helped set them up in Arcata with their shiny new identities. Michelle wasn't sure she trusted Sam either. He'd be in an even better position than Derek to have sold them out. But she nodded anyway.

"I will. But look . . ." She forced a smile. "We're going to need the extra money to pay for Derek, and this other attorney here. And the job sounds like it could be fun."

That, of course, was a lie, one she told on purpose, in case anyone was listening. Danny knew it, too.

"What about Evergreen?" he asked suddenly. "I mean, you put so much work into the place."

The rush of affection she felt for him just then, the intensity of it, took her by surprise. Suddenly it was clear to her how she felt about him, like a switch had been flipped.

Great timing, she thought. Just great.

"I can hire someone. Don't worry about it."

"Em . . ." He drew in a deep breath, and flinched. "Why don't you . . . just . . . get away for a while? You know? Go someplace nice. Until this gets settled."

Run, he meant. Hide.

"No. I want to help."

"But this—"

"It's the best option."

"It's not." He laughed shortly. "Believe me, I can think of a bunch of better ones."

Like you doing time? she wanted to ask. Because if she knew one thing for certain, it was that Gary had set Danny up, and people that Gary set up were pretty thoroughly screwed.

"I'll handle it," she said. "Don't worry. It's temporary."

AFTER SHE LEFT THE jail, all she wanted to do was go back to her hotel and take a shower. A long one. The jail's stink clung to her clothes, to her skin, her hair. Her own stink clung to her as well, the panic sweat from when she'd given the deputy Emily's license.

And have a drink. God, did she want a drink.

But she didn't have time to do either of those things. She'd made an appointment with Marisol Acosta, the Houston attorney Derek had partnered with, and the offices weren't far from the jail. Especially since she hadn't rented a car, just taken a taxi here, it made sense to go see Marisol first.

It was almost 6 P.M. They didn't start visits in the jail until afternoons, 4 P.M. weekdays on the days they allowed visitors, and 3:30 on weekends.

Crazy, she thought.

She stood outside the jail, in its massive shadow: a brick and concrete building that looked like a warehouse, nine stories high, squatting by the bayou. She couldn't stop thinking about how many prisoners were held in that windowless place, piled on top of each other.

What had happened to Danny? Why was he in cuffs?

Who had hurt him?

Get to the lawyer, to Marisol Acosta. Maybe there was something she could do. Some way she could help to keep him safe.

I should call a cab, Michelle thought. But the idea of waiting for one here, of spending any more time in the shadow of the jail, made her shudder.

Hotter than hell outside, but at least it was real air. She thought she caught the scent of river water, a hint of decaying moss.

Taking another deep breath, she tapped Marisol Acosta's contact information on Emily's iPhone, and mapped it. Under a mile. I could walk there, she thought.

She'd be a sweaty mess by the time she arrived, but what the hell? Maybe the sweat would cleanse her, just a little bit.

THE LAW OFFICES OF Carlton, Farris and Pollard weren't far from the theater district, Marisol Acosta had told her. The attorney had agreed to meet her there, even though it was Sunday. There were no prison visits on Monday, and Michelle had told her that she wasn't sure how long she could stay in Houston.

"It's not a problem," Marisol had said. She sounded young. "I have a loft downtown just a few minutes away. So long as you don't mind that I won't be in my office clothes."

Did attorneys charge time and a half for weekends?

She started walking.

As unpleasant as Houston had seemed by freeway, on foot she was seeing some charm to downtown. Not a lot of people, but it was Sunday. Still plenty of late summer light. There were older buildings, nicely restored, a light-rail line that ran down one of the main streets. Then, the theaters. The Houston Grand Opera. They'd done a lot of interesting work, she recalled. Not that opera had ever been her thing, but she'd tried to stay current on cultural stuff, when she'd lived in Los Angeles.

She almost laughed, thinking about it. The concerts she'd go to. The gallery openings, the museums and plays.

Goodbye to all that. Hello, Harris County Jail.

God, it was hot.

MOST OF HER MEMORIES of Mexico were accompanied by heat. The day she'd met Danny on the beach. That night with him in her hotel room. Later, when things had gone from bad to so much worse.

It was supposed to have been a vacation with her husband. A celebration of a business deal he'd been trying to put together. Tom had been lying about the deal, as it turned out. Or engaging in wishful thinking, more charitably. She supposed she could afford a little charity now. Knowing him, she didn't think he'd intended to commit criminal acts. He was going to repay those investors, he really was. The fix was just one contract, one funding source, one deal away.

It always was.

Tom's death had been a shock. He'd crashed his car into a concrete bridge abutment, at a high speed. It might have been a heart attack. Why else would he have lost control that way? That was what she'd thought, until the shocks had continued after his death.

She'd gone ahead and taken the vacation. It was the one thing Tom had actually paid for before he died. He'd left her with nothing, well, unless you counted massive debt and a few lawsuits. She'd go to Puerto Vallarta, spend a few days on the beach, away from her troubles, and figure out what she was going to do next.

What would she have done, she wondered now, if she hadn't met Danny, hadn't gotten sucked into Gary's craziness, had just gone back to Los Angeles and faced the mess she'd left behind? Would she be working in an office somewhere? Still living in her sister's spare bedroom?

She wouldn't be running her own restaurant, most likely.

Wouldn't be living with the man who'd helped make that happen.

Of course, she wouldn't have nearly died, had to change her identity and be stuck in another one of Gary's insane schemes either.

But none of that was Danny's fault, if you looked beyond what it was he used to do for a living anyway. He hadn't asked to get involved with her, either.

That had been Gary's idea. Having her spy on Danny, whom Gary no longer trusted.

It had taken her a while to put the pieces together, what the relationship between Danny and Gary really was. It hadn't helped that telling lies came as easily to Gary as breathing. He loved a good lie, just like he loved fucking with other people's lives. And Danny had kept his own truths to himself.

She'd gotten into trouble in Mexico, and Gary had offered to get her out of it. It hadn't taken her long to figure out he'd set her up in the first place.

What had taken her longer was determining the type of man Danny was.

She thought, suddenly, of her last night in Vallarta, when Danny had knocked on her door. She hadn't expected it, not after everything that had happened between them.

She remembered lying in bed with him, battered and bruised, sweating in the unrelenting heat of the tropical night. "I'll come back for you," he'd said. "I promise."

He'd kept his promise.

"I'll get you out," she said aloud.

She just had no idea how.

Chapter Five

⚓

"You walked from Harris County Jail, in this weather?" Marisol Acosta handed her a bottle of water. "You can get heatstroke if you aren't careful."

"It was only a mile," Michelle said.

Marisol laughed. "This time of year, in Houston? It's better to do miles in an air conditioned gym."

She looked like she put in some time at a gym. A dark-skinned Hispanic woman in her early thirties, round but muscular, with a cute, disarming smile that Michelle suspected she deployed strategically. She wore long jersey shorts and a Texas Longhorns T-shirt. Michelle had noticed a trophy plaque on the wall, third place in a national archery tournament, right next to her University of Texas School of Law diploma.

"You do archery?" Michelle asked.

Marisol grinned. "I love it. Nothing better than hitting the bull's-eye."

"The defense on a crime like this generally centers around search and seizure issues," Marisol explained. "We'll challenge the legality of the search, first thing. See what evidence we can have excluded."

"That's the best defense?"

"The DEA busted Jeff with a plane full of pot." She sounded exasperated. "Other than his claims that he didn't know what the cargo was, illegal search and seizure's what we've got to go on."

Michelle rested her forehead on her fingertips for a moment. "And, and this defense . . . does it work?"

"It certainly *can* work."

Marisol perched on the club chair across from the black leather couch where Michelle sat, sipping from a juice-box sized container of coconut water.

"The other possibility is a plea bargain. Or some other kind of arrangement." She took a final slurp from her straw, and looked up at Michelle.

Some other kind of arrangement. Michelle shuddered a little. She remembered what happened when Gary had offered her an "arrangement," to get her out of trouble in Mexico.

Trouble he'd created.

"What kind of arrangement?"

"The prosecution may consider a reduced sentence for providing information. Or no sentence at all, if your information is valuable enough."

There was no mistaking her significant look, this time.

Did Marisol know what Danny had done in the past? About some of the things he knew?

If she did, and she wanted to use it to make a deal with the prosecution . . . or to expose the things Danny knew to the public . . . or blackmail somebody powerful enough to get him out . . .

Or, maybe Marisol was just trying to gauge what he might be willing to reveal. How dangerous he might be.

Michelle felt herself spiraling. It was the opposite of a rush, more like the ground was being slowly sucked out from under her feet.

You can't trust Marisol, Michelle thought.

"Okay," she said. "So what you want is for Jeff to inform on someone. Maybe agree to some kind of undercover deal?"

Marisol put down her box of coconut water.

"I think that's premature. I'm just trying to give you a sense of what the options might be."

Michelle managed a smile. "Thanks. It's . . . it's good to have an idea."

She hesitated. Then thought, if she's on our side or not, either way, it won't hurt to bring this up.

"I'm worried about what's going on with Jeff right now, actually."

Marisol didn't exactly move. It was more like she became taut. Pulled back the string on the bow. "What do you mean?"

If she's on our side, maybe she can help. If she's not . . . I'm going to let her know that I know. That I'm paying attention.

"Was there something that happened when he got arrested? I mean, did he get hurt?"

"Not that I heard about. And he looked fine when I talked to him."

Michelle thought about how to put it. "Something happened," she said. "He was having a hard time moving, and he didn't want to talk about it. And he was cuffed. Hardly anyone else was cuffed. And I know him. He's not . . . he's not violent. Something happened."

Marisol sighed. "Harris County Jail does not have such a good reputation."

"I want to make sure that someone's checking on him when I'm not here. I'll pay you. Or the firm. However you do this kind of thing."

"We'll make sure he gets regular visits," Marisol said, eyeing her across the coffee table. "Don't worry about that."

BACK AT THE HOTEL, Michelle took a long, hot shower. When she was done, she put on a hotel robe and lay down on the bed. She wasn't sure what she wanted to do. Eat something? Go to the gym? Go to the bar, and have a few glasses of wine? Just take an Ambien and go to bed?

It's only 8 P.M., she thought. Too early to sleep. Wasn't it?

Emily's iPhone rang. The *Get Smart* theme. The ringtone she'd assigned to Gary.

It's what Danny would have picked, she thought.

"So, you have some time to think about things?" Gary asked.

"I have. Maybe we should meet."

"Good! Have you eaten?"

OF COURSE, GARY KNEW where she was. Of course, he was in Houston.

"There's a nice Mexican place that specializes in shrimp not too far from you," he said. "Real Gulf shrimp. None of that farmed Asian shit. I'll have a table ready when you get there."

"Fine."

He could have had her followed from Arcata. With his connections, he probably could've tracked her on her Emily phone, not even needing to physically hack it—he could just get the GPS information from the provider.

Whatever. She'd expected he was watching her. She hadn't been trying to hide.

She'd been so stupid about it before, in Mexico. But she'd never thought of her phone that way until Mexico. Never realized that it could track her, that every app she used to reach out pulled her in, held her close and followed her home.

THE RESTAURANT WAS LOUD, colorful and crowded. Mariachis. Birthday parties. Twentysomethings out for drinks. Gary had secured a table at the back of the big patio, away from some of the noise. A soft mist cooled the area, glass bricks with colored bulbs inside helping to light it.

"So, what d'you think of Houston?" he asked, after she sat.

"It's hot."

"That it is." He signaled the waiter. "I ordered us a couple skinny margaritas." He laughed. "Skinny margaritas. You ever heard of such a thing? But it's about half the calories of a regular one, and you don't get all that sugar. I've taken a liking to them."

Of course he hadn't asked her if she'd wanted one, and as much as she'd wanted a drink before, drinking with Gary was another thing entirely. But it wasn't worth arguing about.

She waited for the drinks and to order—"I'd recommend the small portion of the grilled shrimp—plenty of food for a light eater like you"—before she said, "I have some conditions."

Gary snickered. "Do you, now?"

It was a good thing she'd left her gun in Arcata, she thought. Though if she *did* shoot him, given this was Texas, maybe she'd get off easy.

"You really want me to do this? Because I don't care anymore. I'll just start telling people what I know about you and your friends."

"You've got no evidence," he said. "And no credibility either."

"Maybe not. But maybe Danny does. Maybe we've made some arrangements."

Gary stared at her for a long moment. His predator look. The one that said, you are nothing to me. I will kill you if you get in my way.

Then he grinned. "I knew I had you pegged right, Michelle. You're a born operator." He sipped his margarita. "Not that I'm really all that worried about anything you and Danny might have to say. Danny knows better than to do something like that. Especially where he is right now. Things can happen to a guy in jail, you know."

Hearing that, she shivered, the cooling mist chilling her skin.

She couldn't back down. Even though she knew Gary was right, and that he still had the upper hand.

She shrugged. "Are you okay with being embarrassed? I'm thinking your bosses might not like it very much."

"Well, you might be right about that." He settled back in his chair. "So tell me what you have in mind."

"I want Danny out of jail. I want the charges dropped."

"That's up to a federal judge and a US attorney, not me."

"Bullshit."

Don't lose it, she told herself. She drew in a deep breath. "I know you set him up. I know you used your influence to get his bail denied."

"Say that I did. Say that I can get Danny out. What's to stop the two of you from doing another runner?"

"We won't."

He shook his head. "You can't expect me to take that on faith, now. Can you? I'm going to have to see some effort on your part first. What else?"

"Money."

"How much?"

"How long is the job?"

"Say, two months." He grinned. "Though who knows, you might end up liking it."

"Five hundred thousand."

"*What?* For two months' work?" From the expression on his face, this might have been the funniest thing she'd said yet. "I'll tell you what, sweetie, you've got some balls, asking me for that kind of money."

"I've got obligations, Gary," she said, voice tight. "A federal drug trafficking defense to pay for. A restaurant manager to hire. And probably an airplane to replace."

"Two hundred K, and don't ask for any more. You work past the two months, we can renegotiate."

"What about Danny?"

"You work the first month, I'll see what I can do."

It was his best offer, and she knew it.

Better than she'd expected, actually.

THEIR DINNERS CAME. THE shrimp was pretty good, Michelle had to admit.

"Her name's Caitlin O'Connor," Gary said. "You heard of her?"

"No, I don't think so."

"Think about it, I bet you have. Rich lady. She and her husband and their little boy got carjacked. Kidnapped. A couple of crazy crackheads. They didn't think the whole thing through. Drove them around to a few ATMs to withdraw money. Shot the husband, threw the kid out of the car. Raped her a couple times. Kid died in the hospital."

He tore the tail off a shrimp and sucked out the little bit of flesh from it. "Anyway, she made it through, more or less. Became real active in promoting victims' rights and public safety. Started a foundation, Safer America. Ringing any bells yet?"

It sounded familiar, one of those stories running 24/7 on cable news networks, along with missing blonde women, kidnapped girls forced into sexual slavery, and the mom who drowned her kids and pretended that the black guy did it.

Background noise.

"Right," she said. "I think I know who you mean."

"I'll email you some articles tonight. Read them over, and we can probably set up an interview for tomorrow or the day after."

"Tomorrow? Where is she?"

"Here in Houston." Gary ripped off the shell and legs of his next shrimp and popped the meat into his mouth. "I try and make things convenient."

"CALL ME AFTER YOU'VE looked this over," he'd written. "I imagine you'll have a few questions."

Sitting in her hotel bed, reading the news articles on her iPad, she remembered the story. The rich, perfect couple and their five-year-old son, coming home from a Pixar movie in their Range Rover. The carjackers, two black men, who'd held them up at a gas station, not even caring that their faces were caught on a surveillance camera. The son, tossed out along the side of the road like garbage, though the killers had claimed they'd only wanted him out of the way. The husband, shot in the head while kneeling among the weeds and the scrap and the trash of a vacant lot down by one of the bayous.

The wife, raped. Shot. She should have died, but she didn't. The two men had been out of their heads, drunk and lit up, so high that they couldn't think straight, and they'd left her bleeding in the backseat of the Range Rover while they argued about what to do, and somehow, she'd managed to open the door and stumble away, into the night, while they continued to fight outside the liquor store where they'd stopped to buy more beer.

Michelle studied a photo of the family. One of those corny studio portraits against a backdrop of hand-painted blue-gray muslin. You'd think with their money they could have done something more interesting, she thought, and then she pushed that thought away. I'm a horrible person, she told herself. This was a tragedy, after all.

She made herself look at them. At Paul O'Connor, brown hair, square jaw, broad smile, in his suit and tie, staring up and to the right, per the photographer's direction, no doubt. At then toddler Alex, blond, burbling on his father's knee.

At Caitlin.

Blonde, like her son. Big hair, but not ridiculously so. Small frame, cheerleader pretty. Smiling, like her husband, at some beautiful and amusing vision to the upper right.

"THE ONLY THING YOU can do when you have something like this happen to you is to try and keep moving."

Her voice was soft, well modulated. Quiet enough that you found yourself leaning forward to listen. Or in Michelle's case, holding the iPad closer to her face.

"So, you founded Safer America," the interviewer

prompted. Some cable news channel flack. Along with the articles, Gary had sent a collection of video links in the body of his email.

On screen, Caitlin nodded. It had been four years since the attack. Seven since the family studio portrait. Her blonde hair was now cropped closer to her head. She'd lost that cheerleader prettiness. It had turned into something else, something more fragile, almost ethereal.

That can work for you, Michelle thought. Lots of people found vulnerable-looking women attractive. They weren't threatening. They needed protection.

"Yes. I felt that not enough attention was given to the victims of violent crimes. So we try to act as advocates for them."

"But you push for stronger public safety measures as well."

"Well, that goes hand in hand with supporting victims." Caitlin sat on a couch in what might have been her own home. An expensive cream-colored sofa in a large living room. Michelle couldn't make out many details the way the shot was framed, but she thought that the sofa might be a Barbara Barry.

"When people have been victimized, they are desperate to have their sense of safety restored. And by knowing that violent offenders will be locked up where they can't hurt anybody else, they get just a little bit of their own security back."

She smiled. A sad, tentative smile.

It wasn't just that she looked vulnerable, Michelle realized. If anything Caitlin was beautiful now, instead of merely pretty.

"DRUGS HAVE TAKEN OVER our cities." A deep, bourbon-voiced narrator, who Michelle was pretty sure also did trailers for Hollywood movies.

Grainy black and white shots of addicts drawing on crack pipes, white smoke swirling around their pockmarked, skeletal faces. Graffiti-bombed street corners, with furtive dealers exchanging brown paper bags of contraband.

"Yet Felix Gallardo insists that drugs aren't a problem."

A shot of a politician at an impromptu gathering—outside a courthouse? City Hall? Surrounded by news mikes. "Drugs aren't the problem," he said in quick staccato rhythms. Michelle wondered if the bite had been edited. "We're spending too much money on law enforcement solutions—"

A freeze-frame on his face, his expression caught so that he appeared to be half-drunk. A crawl of text with statistics, with the narrator reading highlights: the percentages of violent felons with illegal drugs in their systems, drug-related traffic accidents, the crimes committed by addicts, the number of kids who'd smoked pot last year, rolling by so quickly they were hard to read.

Then, a smash cut to a young black man wearing prison scrubs, sitting at an institutional aluminum table, clasped hands resting in front of him. "I was so high I was crazy," he said, staring at his awkward, knobby hands. "So, yeah, I shot them. I killed them."

Back to the freeze-frame of the politician and the voice-over artist.

"Drugs aren't a problem. Really, Felix?" The shot fading to a black screen. "Paid for by Safer America."

Michelle picked up her Emily iPhone and called Gary.

"I do have a few questions. Are you free tomorrow, for breakfast?"

Chapter Six

✵

"So, if it doesn't say 'organic,' and it uses canola oil, doesn't that mean it's genetically modified?"

"Probably."

"And same thing with soy?"

Michelle gritted her teeth and nodded.

"What's the world coming to, when you can't even trust tofu?" Gary said with a sigh.

"Just coffee," Michelle told the hotel waitress.

"Yeah, me too." Gary settled back in his bucket chair. "I've been doing intermittent fasting anyway."

They sat in a corner of her hotel's coffee shop, underneath a painting of an offshore oil rig done in Day-Glo colors, which looked to be part of a series also decorating the adjoining bar and lobby.

"So, I want to make sure that I understand the situation," Michelle said. "Caitlin's actively involved with fundraising for this foundation of hers. Right?"

"Right."

"And the foundation contributes to political campaigns."

Gary nodded.

"And there's a national election coming up in November."

The waitress arrived with their coffee and a white ceramic pitcher and a matching container of sugar and sweetener. Gary took a sip of his coffee and made a face. "Is that half-and-half?" he asked. He winked at Michelle. "I'll risk the bovine growth hormone."

"So Caitlin's going to be in the public eye a lot," she continued, after the waitress left.

"Yeah. That's one of the reasons we need you for this job. She can go a little overboard on the cocktails, and we can't afford to have that happen on the national stage."

"And I'm her babysitter." Michelle had a sip of her coffee. He was right; it was pretty bad. She poured a little half-and-half from the pitcher into the cup. "How does that make sense?"

"What do you mean?"

"I have a boyfriend in jail on pot charges," she said in a low voice. "Odds are I'm going to get questioned by, by the FBI, or whoever's investigating this at some point. Even if I'm just standing in the background, things like that get found out. So if you really want this to work—"

He snorted. "Oh, I see where you're going on this—I should get Danny's case dismissed. Actually, I have a better idea. *Emily* might have a pot-smuggling boyfriend. *Michelle* doesn't."

It took her a moment to get what he meant.

"Wait . . . you want me . . . you want *Michelle*—?"

"Sure! We can work that tragic widow angle. Maybe you and Caitlin can do some bonding over it."

Sucker punched again.

Stupid, she told herself. You're so stupid. He's already thought two steps ahead of you.

She sipped her coffee, which tasted even worse as it cooled off. Thought about Gary's move. And realized, it still didn't quite make sense, not on the surface, anyway.

"I guess I don't get why that's better," she said. "So Danny's a pot smuggler. My husband *cheated* investors. If he hadn't died, *he'd* be in jail."

"Well, we've been doing a little cleanup on your late husband's business. He still doesn't come off great, but more like, incompetent and in over his head, rather than an outright crook." He pointed at her, grinning. "*You*, on the other hand, were safely out of the loop. Which is the truth." He leaned closer. "Right?"

She felt her cheeks flush. She knew what he was implying. He'd accused her of being Tom's accomplice before.

She hadn't known. But she'd suspected. And she hadn't done a thing about it.

"Right," she said, keeping her voice steady.

"And your motivation is, you're trying to move beyond the pain of the loss by helping others. Plus, you need the money."

"Where have I supposedly been for the last two years?"

"Mexico, and then you traveled. You know, looking for meaning, or romance, or what have you. Like in all those books you women love. Not staying in any one spot for too long. India, China, Vietnam, Bali . . . all places you've been, don't worry about that."

"Places I've been a long time ago. Gary, this, this is . . ."
Crazy.

She stopped herself from saying it. "Crazy" was how Gary operated.

"Yeah, maybe skip China," he muttered. "Too many changes."

"Problematic," she said.

"It'll work. Everything will check out."

"I left some loose ends. The lawsuits—"

"Fixed. Turns out a little hedge-fund group came in and bought up the remaining assets of your husband's business. As a part of the deal, they settled with the original investors."

She hadn't thought there *were* any remaining assets. Just the shell of Tom's company and ownership on paper of a project he hadn't been able to develop, the one that had taken their house, taken their savings, that had bankrupted his business. As far as she'd known, anything left had been hopelessly encumbered when she'd gone to Mexico over two years ago, for her five-day vacation.

Given the people Gary knew, given whom he worked for . . .

"And I guess I signed off on this deal?" she asked. The question tasted bitter.

"I guess you did. And you were real happy to, apparently. Cause you know, you hated the idea of leaving people out all that money because of your husband's poor business decisions."

The truth was, she hadn't even thought about those people, not since she'd become someone else and they were no longer her problem.

"And now you're ready to start over fresh. With a clean slate."

Which in a way, she'd already done. Only it hadn't lasted.

She could call her old attorney to confirm some of this. He had to have helped draw up the hedge-fund deal. He must have thought she'd agreed to it.

"So, how did you do it? Faked some emails from me? Forged my signature?"

"Something like that." Gary studied her face, without his usual leer or threat. "Don't you *want* to be Michelle again?"

he asked. For once, he seemed genuinely curious. "Have your old life back?"

She hesitated. Actually thought about it. How she'd lived, back in Los Angeles. How she'd lived the last two years.

"Not really."

"THE INTERVIEW'S JUST A formality. You'll be meeting with Porter Ackermann, the executive director of Safer America. He's already heard all about you."

"*All* about me?"

"Well, what he needs to know. That you're the right person for the job. That you know how to handle the kinds of situations you'll find yourself in."

She hoped he meant fundraisers and cocktail parties.

"After that, you'll see Caitlin. That won't be a problem. She'll go along with whatever Porter tells her to do."

She knew there was a big piece of the puzzle missing, and that Gary wouldn't tell her what it was if she asked him. But she decided that she might as well ask. Maybe something in his reaction would give her a clue.

"There's another thing I don't get, Gary. Why do you care about this?"

"What do you mean?"

"I mean, Caitlin and her foundation. Why is it so important to you and your friends?"

"What, you think we don't care about a safer America?"

No clues. Just his typical shit-eating grin.

He raised his hand to call the waitress. "Anyway, that's nothing you need to worry about."

Which in her experience meant she should worry about it, a lot.

"When do I get paid?" she asked.

"Your official salary's seventy-five K annually, so expect your first check in a week or two." He reached into the pocket of his sports coat and pulled out a sealed 5" x 8" manila envelope. "Here's some walking-around money to get you started. Five thousand." A little smirk.

Five thousand was what he'd given her the first time, in Mexico.

She tried not to shudder as she took it from him.

"And the rest?"

"Four payments. What the hell, I'll make them fifty K each. That's a little more than we agreed on, but let's just call it a bonus. A third of your salary's going to taxes anyway. We'll get the first one to you in a couple of days." He started to rise, and then added: "You might want to put some thought into how you're gonna manage all that cash in the meantime."

It was true. She hadn't considered that at all.

"Oh, better not forget this." He retrieved another envelope from his sports coat. Thicker than the first. Something solid inside. Gary slid the envelope across the table. "Go ahead. Open it."

Inside was a wallet. Her wallet. A black leather Gucci that had been a gift from Tom.

The one she'd lost in Mexico, the night she almost died.

"New credit cards," Gary said, "since you cancelled the old ones. Address for those is your sister's place in LA. But the rest of your old stuff's there."

She took a quick look. Driver's license. Auto Club. A new AMEX and Chase Visa. Pilates and yoga studio memberships. A photo of her nephew and her sister. Another of her parents.

✧ ✧ ✧

SAFER AMERICA'S OFFICE WAS in a section of Houston called River Oaks. "Close to where Caitlin lives," Gary had said. "She doesn't like having to go far when she comes into the office."

The office was across the street from a mall topped by condos. The anchor store there was a place called Tootsie's. "Oh, yeah, that's where all the rich ladies shop," the cab driver told her. Michelle had never heard of the store. She made a note on her iPhone to check it out. She needed to figure out how things worked here, in Houston, what the landscape was like, what the different neighborhoods meant. She'd known all that stuff in Los Angeles, but this wasn't Los Angeles.

She paid the driver and got out. Stood on the sidewalk and immediately started to sweat in the dead heat of the afternoon. Stared up at the innocuous office building in front of her, where Safer America was.

She'd worn her black Armani suit, which she'd brought in case she'd needed to go to court. She didn't have many nice things like this any more. A little black dress for parties, a couple of decent sweaters and blouses, a few good skirts and pairs of slacks. She mostly wore jeans and cardigans. Long-sleeved T-shirts. Sweats. Even thermals.

Sweat trickled down her back. If I get the job, I'm going to need to buy some new clothes, she thought briefly. Hardly any of her Arcata wardrobe would work for Houston, especially not this time of year.

Stupid, she told herself. Stupid to even be thinking this

way. Danny was right. She shouldn't have agreed to this. She should have called Sam, seen what he could do.

But she didn't know if she could trust Sam.

I will call him, she thought. But this way, going along with Gary for now, maybe she'd bought a little more time, for her safety, and for Danny's.

"You come highly recommended."

Porter Ackermann sat behind a large walnut desk. He was middle-aged, in his late fifties, Michelle guessed, heavy, squat and immobile, like a piece of expensive furniture.

Overall the headquarters of Safer America were as modest and unassuming as the building in which they were housed. A receptionist in a vestibule decorated with bland corporate art. A small suite of offices grouped around a short corridor. Still, there were signs of money. Porter Ackermann's desk. Porter Ackermann's suit.

"That's good to hear," Michelle said.

"Yes, very good, because from your résumé, well, we've had other candidates who on paper would seem to be better qualified." Porter glanced at the résumé sitting on his desk, the résumé Gary had provided, and then looked up at Michelle, managing a flick of a smile. He had a pear-shaped face, with a wide jaw and heavy jowls, and kept the remains of his gray hair short.

"I know my résumé looks a little thin," she said. "But I've had a lot of experience managing the kinds of social situations that Ms. O'Connor has to deal with."

"So I've heard." He made a show of studying her résumé. "Well, I for one weigh your references very heavily. But it really is all about the kind of personal connection you have with Caitlin." He smiled again, an action that seemed like a mechanical arrangement of facial muscles. "Why don't we head on over to her place and see if the two of you hit it off?"

PORTER STEERED HIS ESCALADE down a broad, quiet street. "River Oaks is mostly old money, in Houston terms. Oil and real estate." He chuckled. "Of course, Houston is a relatively new city."

Michelle could certainly see the "money" part of the equation. The houses they passed were on the order of estates. Some of the older houses had charm, sturdy-looking American Colonials and Tudors, modest when you compared them to the newer mansions going up. Others were faux plantations. Colonials on steroids. Even a castle or two.

She'd had a nice house in Brentwood, but nothing like these places. River Oaks rivaled Beverly Hills, and to her eye the lots and homes were bigger here. Cheaper land, probably.

They followed the sweeping curve of the street around to the left. Out the window she saw a dog walker, a wiry Latino wearing all white, with two Dobermans pulling on a sturdy leash. She assumed he was a dog walker, anyway, and not the owner. His clothes, a short-sleeved white shirt and shorts, looked almost like a uniform. The dogs looked like guard dogs, their sleek coats showing the bunched muscle beneath.

Other than a lone female jogger, this was the first person Michelle had seen on these streets. The whole place felt like a ghost town. An expensive, well-manicured one.

"It seems very quiet here," Michelle said.

"Well, a lot of the River Oaks set like to summer in Colorado."

"But not Ms. O'Connor."

"Not Ms. O'Connor," he agreed. "She's a dedicated woman."

He turned the car into a drive blocked by a black wrought iron gate, flanked by brick columns, the entire property surrounded by a high stone wall.

"Excuse me," Porter said with a sigh, putting the car in neutral. He opened the door, swung his heavy body around and heaved himself out of the car.

Michelle watched as he walked to the gate, punched a number into a code box there. There was a surveillance camera atop the column, she noted. A sign for a security company that promised an armed response beneath it.

Well, it wasn't too surprising that Caitlin O'Connor would be concerned with security, Michelle thought.

By the time Porter returned to the car, he was beet red and sweating. "I'll tell you, this weather's almost enough to make a person believe in global warming," he said.

Caitlin O'Connor's house wasn't one of the biggest ones Michelle had seen on the drive through River Oaks. The grounds weren't as extensive as the larger estates either. The house looked to be older, a comparatively modest two-story Colonial set back from the street by a neatly trimmed emerald lawn. Greek Revival—wasn't that what the style was called?—with four columns flanking the entrance. A portico? It had been a long time since her architectural survey class at UCLA.

Three old oak trees shaded the house and yard. There were flower beds, a few in bloom even in the late July heat, and big shrubs that rose almost half the height of the front door, surrounded by low hedges.

"Azaleas," Porter explained. "They don't look like much now, but you should see them in the spring."

"It's beautiful," Michelle said. Not to her taste, but it really was.

Porter parked the car in the driveway, in the shade of one of the oak trees.

A middle-aged Latina woman wearing a white shirt and white shorts answered the door. "Oh, Mr. Ackermann—how are you today?"

She immediately stepped aside so that Porter and Michelle could enter.

"Very well, thank you, Esperanza. Except it's too damn hot."

"I think so too! Crazy, huh?"

They stood in the foyer for a moment. Michelle had the impression of white and beige: the tiles and walls, the staircase leading up to the second floor.

"This here's Michelle Mason." Porter tilted his head in Michelle's direction. "I think Caitlin's expecting us."

"She's waiting in the Great Room," Esperanza said.

They followed her through the foyer and into the living room beyond.

A beautiful room, big, twice the size of her living room in Arcata and two stories high, with plush carpet, French doors, and a wall of windows, done in different shades of white, cream and beige, with dark brown accents. That and the cool air made Michelle think suddenly of an ice cream sandwich.

Caitlin O'Connor sat on the couch, the eggshell-colored sofa from the video that Michelle had seen.

She rose to greet them. She wore a cream-colored,

cowl-necked jersey top and slightly darker linen slacks, both pieces expensive to Michelle's eye.

"Hi, I'm Caitlin," she said, extending her hand. Her blue eyes and blonde hair were the brightest colors around, but she still blended into the room.

Michelle took her hand and clasped it briefly. "Michelle Mason."

Caitlin's hand was cool. Nearly the temperature of the conditioned air. Her eyes seemed a little unfocused, Michelle thought. Or maybe she was imagining it, based on the seeds that Gary had planted.

"So nice to meet you." Caitlin smiled and gestured toward the couch.

"Well, I'll let the two of you get acquainted," Porter said as Michelle sat. He glanced at his watch, an expensive one, though she hadn't been able to catch the brand—Phillip Stein? "How 'bout I pick you up in, say, a half hour or so? Around four-fifteen." He looked over at Caitlin. "That give you enough time?"

"I think so," she said, smile still in place. She turned to Michelle. "I've already heard so many good things about you."

"Well, I'll leave you to it then." Porter lifted his hand to his forehead in a mock salute. Michelle watched him walk away, almost seeming to tiptoe, a big man remaining light on his feet.

"I'm an admirer of your work," Michelle said, after he'd left.

Caitlin sighed out a chuckle, lifted her shoulders a fraction. "Would you like a glass of white wine? It's awfully damn hot out."

Michelle hesitated. If this was a job interview, saying yes

to a glass of wine might be the wrong answer. But if Caitlin was a drinker looking for someone to drink with her, then "yes" might be what she wanted to hear.

"Only if you're having one," Michelle said, smiling back. "Otherwise, water is fine."

"Oh, let's open the wine. Esperanza," Caitlin called out. "Hon, can you bring us that bottle of chardonnay in the fridge?"

Esperanza must have been hovering within earshot. A minute or two later, she arrived with a bottle of Calera chardonnay and two glasses. As she started to open the wine, Caitlin said, "How about bringing out an ice bucket?"

So she wanted to drink the entire bottle, Michelle thought.

"I can open that," she said to Esperanza.

Esperanza handed her the corkscrew. "I'll go get the ice."

A nice waiter's corkscrew, thankfully. So many households used butterflies or Rabbits, and those just weren't as good as a decent waiter's corkscrew.

She cut the foil and popped the cork. Poured Caitlin the proper-sized pour—not too much, you didn't want it to get warm, but enough so that you could catch the nose.

"You look like you've had some practice," Caitlin said.

"I've hosted a lot of parties. When they weren't big enough to hire a bartender, I was the stand-in." Michelle smiled. As artificial an expression as what Porter had given her earlier. Could Caitlin tell? "I make a great margarita."

She poured her own glass. A little less than what she'd poured Caitlin. Lifted it. "Cheers," she said.

Caitlin smiled, and raised her glass. "Cheers."

Michelle sipped her wine. Over oaked and heavy on the butter, but not bad.

Esperanza returned with an ice bucket. "I'll bring out some snacks," she said.

She came back a moment later with a couple of cheeses, some crackers and a small bowl of nuts.

Caitlin cut off a corner of Brie and spread it on a cracker. Michelle took a piece of the Gouda and ate it alone.

"I understand you lost your husband," Caitlin said.

Michelle wanted to laugh. She had the sudden image of having misplaced Tom, like you would your set of keys. "Yes. It's been about two and a half years."

"Not so long, then." Caitlin took a healthy swig of wine.

With everything that had happened, it seemed like forever, but Michelle couldn't really get into that. "It was unexpected," she said, because that was what she'd gotten into the habit of saying.

Caitlin made a tiny snort. "I wonder if it's easier when you know it's coming. Something like cancer. When you have some time to settle things. To say goodbye. What do you think?"

How the hell was she supposed to respond to this?

"I think it would be," she said. "I wish I'd . . ." She took another sip of wine, trying to figure out what to say. She didn't exactly want to confess all to this woman she didn't know, whose own tragedy made hers look small by comparison.

But Caitlin had opened the door. She obviously wanted to talk about it. Wanted to hear Michelle's story.

Maybe she was tired of telling her own.

"My husband left a lot of loose ends," Michelle finally said. "It was . . . it was a real mess. His business . . . well, things were really bad. He made a lot of mistakes. And all I can think of was . . . that he was too embarrassed to tell me about it." Her turn for a minimal shrug. "I wish I'd known. I wish we'd had a chance to talk about it. Not because I could have fixed it for him, just so that . . ."

She didn't have to fake the wave of emotion that closed her throat. "After he died, I finally just took off," she said. "Left the mess behind and traveled for a while. It wasn't the most mature thing to do, I guess." She looked up. Met Caitlin's eyes. Her somewhat distant gaze. "But now it's time for me to be a grownup. To get to work." She smiled.

"So here you are."

"If you think it's a good fit. This is about what *you* need."

Caitlin poured herself more wine. "Well, I need someone to keep me on track, basically. Manage my appointments. Book my travel. Make sure I get places on time. Tell me who it is I'm seeing and why they're important. There'll be some event planning involved, most likely."

All work that Michelle had done before, during her ten-year marriage to Tom (all those parties and fundraisers), her stint as "associate director" of the photo gallery before that (when a wealthy collector or artist came in the door, you'd better know who it was), the clerical and admin jobs she'd had during and just after college.

She nodded. "Those are things I have experience doing."

"Also . . ." Caitlin hesitated. "I don't know how you'd feel about this." She chuckled in a way that sounded almost embarrassed. "Porter tells me you . . . well, that you like going to the gym and doing yoga and that sort of thing." She waited for Michelle's nod. "I guess I could use more of that. Everyone tells me I should. I just haven't . . . I'm not very motivated, I guess. And it's tough with my schedule, sometimes."

"Well, I'm not a trainer, or anything. But if you want a workout partner, I'd be happy to do that. It would help keep me on track too."

Nothing you can't handle.

"Good." Caitlin smiled. Her eyes seemed to brighten. "There's times when you know you should make some changes. You just need a little push."

"YOU AND CAITLIN SEEMED to be having a nice sit-down," Porter said, as they walked down the drive to his Escalade.

"I hope so. I really enjoyed meeting her."

According to Gary, she already had this job. Porter had acted as though she'd needed to at least pass the test with Caitlin. Michelle thought that she'd passed, but she couldn't be sure.

"Where can I drop you?" Porter asked.

Michelle hesitated.

She assumed that Porter knew Gary. That it had been Gary's "recommendation" that had gotten her this far. But there could be a layer between Gary and Porter for all she knew.

Better to not make the assumption, at least not yet.

"I guess that depends," she said. "If you think I'm a good match for the position, then how about the Galleria?"

"The Galleria?"

"I'll need some new clothes for this weather." She smiled at him. "If not, my hotel's fine."

Porter grinned back. It might have been sincere. "Well, I'll have to run it by Caitlin first. But why don't I go ahead and take you to the Galleria? You can try on a few things. See what you think about the fit."

Chapter Seven

⚘

SHE BOUGHT A COUPLE of pieces at Neiman Marcus: a fitted shirtdress and a jacket by Burberry Brit, two simple silk tees from Eileen Fisher and two pairs of Stella McCartney slacks. A black leather Cole Haan tote with a padded laptop pocket. Things that were stylish but not flashy. She'd need another suit, but she wasn't going to spend that kind of money until she knew she'd gotten the job.

After that she stopped at the Best Buy and bought a new burner phone, just in case. Then treated herself to dinner at a "Contemporary American" restaurant close to the Galleria that had gotten a lot of good reviews: "pan-seared wild king salmon in red cherry barbeque sauce, with heirloom baby potatoes and broccolini drizzled with truffled lemon butter," paired with a Washington pinot noir.

By the time she got back to the hotel, it was close to 9 P.M. She smiled at the friendly desk clerks, took the elevator to her floor, unlocked the door to her room with the card key, hung the "Do Not Disturb" sign on the door. Tossed the bags of clothes on a chair. Kicked off her shoes, shed her Armani suit, hung it in the closet.

She put on a baggy T-shirt and fell back onto the bed.

This is insane, she thought. Danny is in jail, someone hurt him, and I'm eating truffled broccolini.

Her iPhone rang. The *Get Smart* theme. Fucking Gary.

"Hey, there. You do some shopping?"

"Yeah, Gary." She felt exhausted. "I did some shopping."

"Good. Looks like you'll need the wardrobe. I gather you made a good impression."

"You talked to Porter?"

He chuckled. "Now, did I say that?"

"So, you talked to someone else? Why don't you give me a hint?" The rush of adrenaline lifted her up on her elbows. "You don't tell me things I need to know. Do you *want* me to fuck up? Is that it? Because I've thought a lot about what happened in Mexico. And the way it seems to me is, you don't really care one way or the other."

For a moment, there was silence.

"Of course I care," he finally said. "Mexico was different."

"Different, how?"

"Well . . . in that situation, there were a couple of scenarios I would've considered a success." A snort. "Not the one that ended up happening, as it turned out."

"Such as?"

"If you'd gotten good intel on Danny and what he was up to? That would've been great. If you'd . . . served as a reminder to him? You know, of what his situation was? That would've been useful too."

Don't scream, she told herself. Don't lose it.

"Oh, you mean that someone who was fucking him might be spying on him? *That* situation? Is that what you're getting at?"

"That, and what happens to people who don't do what they're told."

He sounded very calm.

There it was, the threat. And the admission. That he'd tried to have her killed.

Of course, she'd already known that.

Gary's sigh rattled the speaker of her iPhone. "Look, try to see it from my point of view. I didn't know you back then. But I've moved beyond that, Michelle. I really have. Now I know you're too valuable an asset to burn that way this time out."

She laughed. This was all such bullshit. "You're blackmailing me into this. Just like you did before."

"Well, that's where you're wrong." He sounded so calm she could almost believe that he wasn't a crazy man who'd once tried to kill her. "See, you could've walked away from this if you'd wanted to. This is about saving Danny's hide. Not your own. Still surprises me, to be honest."

"And you wouldn't have tried something else if Danny hadn't worked? Threatened my family? Implicated me in my husband's scam, maybe?"

"Heh. Well, yeah. You're probably right about that."

She took a moment to think. She knew a part of it was revenge—she and Danny had gotten away from Gary before, and that wouldn't sit well with him. But the trouble he'd gone to, the money he was willing to spend . . . there had to be more to this particular op than just that.

"You seem really anxious to have me look after this woman," she said. "What's so important about Caitlin O'Connor, Gary? And why me?"

A chuckle.

"Well, you know how it is, Michelle. It's really hard to find a reliable babysitter these days."

I give up, she thought.

She flopped back down on the bed.

"So, Porter. What does he know? What can I tell him that's safe?"

A pause. "You've been recommended by several major donors. Porter's inclined to look positively on you."

"And are you considered one of the donors? If I drop your name, is he going to recognize it?"

A longer pause.

"He'll recognize my name," Gary said. "But not as a donor. I'm just . . . an intermediary. You know, a go-between."

"Right."

"Expect a call from Porter tomorrow."

After he disconnected, Michelle lay on the bed for a while without moving.

"Major donors" who used Gary as "a go-between."

This could not be good.

THERE WERE A LOT of things that she didn't know about Gary. But there were a few things that she did know. He was one of the Boys.

"Not everyone in the Company's dirty," Danny had said. "Most of them aren't. It's mainly that group, and they've been fucking the rest of us over since World War Two."

Them, along with several generations of very rich men. The Boys were their provocateurs, their shock troops. The ones who helped pave the way, who cleared the road of inconvenient obstacles.

The Boys did what they wanted, regardless of who was officially "in charge."

"It's the Deep State," he'd explained. "Finance and dirty energy. Oil, mostly. Defense stuff, like ordinance and high-tech weapons systems, private contractors. The drug money keeps things running, especially the black ops that are off the books."

Michelle hadn't wanted to believe any of this. Why not just bring on the UN black helicopters and the tinfoil hats? That was how crazy it had all seemed.

But you get smacked in the head with the crazy hard enough, and what else were you supposed to believe?

The Boys liked to keep some separation from the guys who did a lot of their dirty work. Danny had been a contractor, an "asset." Gary, a few steps up the food chain from Danny—"Not exactly an asset. Not exactly official," Danny had said. The "major donors" Gary worked for . . .

What did they want with Safer America?

"WELCOME ABOARD."

Porter extended his hand across his expensive walnut desk. Michelle took it. He squeezed a little too hard. She'd never understood that, why some men felt the necessity to show their dominance through grip strength.

"I'm really happy to be here," she said.

"We'd like you to start as soon as possible. Today, if you'd like. But if you need a little time to wind down your other obligations . . ."

What had Gary told him?

"I do have a few things I need to deal with." She kept her voice cheerful. Reminded herself to smile. "If I could have a week, that would be great."

"That's fine." Porter seemed distracted, maybe by something on his computer screen. "Make sure you talk to Carla in personnel so you can fill out the W-4."

"Will do." Great, she thought. Didn't you need an address for a W-4? What was she supposed to put down? She couldn't exactly use Emily's address in Arcata.

Her sister's condo, maybe. Where the credit cards Gary had given her called home.

"Do you have ideas about a place to live, here in Houston?" Porter asked suddenly. As if he'd read her mind.

"Not really."

"Well, I've got a line on some corporate housing, if you're interested. Semi-furnished. Not too far from here. Convenient, especially with all the travel you'll be doing."

Michelle smiled at him. "Thank you. I'm very interested."

SHE NEEDED TO SEE Danny one more time, before it got any more complicated. Better to go as Emily—that's how she'd gone before. Explaining Michelle's presence there would be more than problematic. And if she was accompanying Caitlin on her media events and availabilities, to her high-profile charity events, her parties . . .

How easy was it to get known here?

ON TUESDAYS, YOU COULD visit between 4 and 9 P.M.

She waited in various lines. Put on a thin knit silk cardigan she'd brought for the refrigerated air. Avoided the horror that was the bathroom for the sixth floor visitors near Danny's pod. Gave the guard the white slip of paper with his information. Sat on a cement stool with no padding, and rubbed down the speaker grate with a wet wipe, the shouting and laughing and crying of everyone around her blending into something like a human version of an orchestral warm-up.

They brought him out. He wasn't cuffed this time, which was a relief. He looked okay, she thought. Tired, mostly. Managed his half-smile when he saw her.

"Hey," he said. "Thanks for coming."

"How are you doing?"

He shrugged. Stood up and spoke into the grate: "The food sucks, the place stinks and there's a large contingent of assholes."

"Other than that?"

He grinned. At least she could still make him smile.

"Are you still . . . are you having any problems?"

That look again, the fractional headshake. Don't ask.

This time, she gave him a look back. The hint of a glare. Tell me.

"One-time thing," he said. "Just to let me know . . . what the situation was."

That he was vulnerable here. That they could get to him, any time they wanted.

She'd suspected that. She'd known it, really. But still, it felt like a gut punch.

"Shit." She sat back and closed her eyes. It was all too much, this whole thing. How was she supposed to handle it?

"Hey."

She opened her eyes. She had to look at him. To face this. He gestured toward the speaker grate. She put her ear back up to it.

"Don't . . . don't worry. Just take care of yourself. I know you can do that." His voice sounded warm, and urgent. She nodded.

"Did you call Sam?" he asked.

Her heart beat a little harder. She didn't want to have this conversation. *Couldn't* have it, more accurately. Not here.

"Not yet."

He pulled away from the speaker, his expression once again weary. Studied her.

"Look," he finally said. "I get it if you're done. I don't blame you. But I need you to make that call for me."

"That's not it," she said, "That's not it at all. It's just that . . . Derek can't?"

He shook his head. "These aren't people he talks to. It's better if you do it. You can probably explain things better."

Things like Gary? she wondered.

She leaned forward. Spoke into the grate. "I'm just a little worried. Because of the job. I'm not sure if . . ." How to put it? That she didn't know if Sam was trustworthy? That she didn't know what might happen if she exposed one of Gary's operations to someone else? If Sam was working with Gary, then telling him was a problem. Gary hated it when people talked, and he'd punish her, or someone around her, if he found out. If Sam was on their side, could he get Danny out, or would he just make things worse? If he compromised her with Gary and didn't have the juice to get her away from him . . .

"Gary's job?"

She nodded.

"I'm telling you, don't do it."

She felt suddenly, irrationally angry.

"You know, coming from a guy who . . ."

She couldn't finish. Because the rest of the sentence was, "Got busted for flying hundreds of pounds of pot to Texas and never paid much attention to my opinions on taking those kinds of gigs."

"Because it's a bad idea?" she asked instead. "Or because you're telling me not to?"

"Because it's a bad idea. You know it is."

It was, and she did.

"Jesus, Em. I wish you'd listen to me."

"I'm listening," she said. "I'll make the call."

He seemed to relax, the line of his shoulders softening. "Okay. Keep me posted."

"I'll try. It might get a little complicated."

"It doesn't have to be. Do what Sam says. He'll take care of you."

Right, she thought.

"I'm going home tomorrow," she said. "To take care of a few things. I should be back in a few days."

She hesitated. She wanted to make some gesture, something to show him that she cared. She'd seen women actually press their lips against the window, but she wasn't going to do that.

Instead, she flattened her palm on the Plexiglas, just for a moment.

It still felt fake. Like a scene from a bad prison movie.

He watched her do it. Stared down at his own hands held flat on the counter. "Be careful," he said.

She wasn't sure, but she thought he seemed ashamed.

"I will. I'll see you as soon as I can."

Once she got out in the hall, she tore open her second wet wipe and cleaned her hand with it.

STUPID. YOU'RE SO STUPID.

The words repeated in her head like the world's worst mantra. While she stood in the shower, washing the stink of the jail away, while she lay on her hotel bed, not able to sleep, until she finally gave up and took an Ambien.

Seeing him in jail that first time, the rush of affection and fierce protectiveness she'd felt, now she thought it had been like she was acting out a part in a romance novel—save the handcuffed, wounded hero.

This time, seeing him, the thrill was definitely gone.

The jail was a horrible place, full of petty indignities. It was about waiting in lines, filling out forms, screaming into a spittle-flecked speaker, having to pee in an overflowing, shit-smeared toilet that no one seemed to care enough to clean. Watched every step of the way by guards, some of whom wore leather gloves padded with buckshot. It was horrible and stupid and mundane, like some kind of nightmare version of a prom at a poor public high school, men and women lined up on opposite sides of the glass.

If I really care about him, I'm going to have to see this through, she thought. There's no quick fix. What were the odds that Gary or Sam could just snap their fingers and make it all better? Or if they could, that either of them were willing to do so?

She lay there, the Ambien slowly dissolving the knots in her head, and thought about it. How she really felt. Did she love Danny, really, without the fantasy? Considering who he was, and all the things he'd done?

He'd done good things as well, she told herself. She'd believed him when he'd talked about the missions he'd flown. They hadn't all been criminal.

But what was the point of rationalizing it? That was what *he'd* done, what had helped him keep doing his job, until the bad things had piled up too high and tipped the balance.

Did she owe him? On the one hand, he'd saved her ass. On the other, her ass wouldn't have needed saving if she'd never met him.

Though she'd probably be bankrupt and living in her sister's spare room.

She was finally dozing off. Once, twice, a fragmented thought broke through her drift towards sleep, jerking her awake, and she was irritated with herself for not being able to control her thoughts, for depriving herself of the relief that sleep would bring.

Jesus Christ, I'm in love with a criminal.

And not for the first time.

That hadn't ended well, either, she thought, before she finally fell asleep.

Chapter Eight

✧

SHE GOT INTO ARCATA at 4 P.M. She'd left her car at the airport, with a fleece jacket in the trunk, which was a good thing, because it had to be thirty degrees cooler here than it had been in Houston.

She made it home before 5 P.M. The house smelled stale and cold. She resisted the temptation to take a nap. It had been a long day of travel, and her shoulders ached with fatigue, but there were things she had to do.

Call Sam.

She didn't want to. But she'd promised.

Funny. Danny had told her to memorize Sam's number, and she thought that she had, but she was still afraid of forgetting it. So she'd written the number down on page 122 of her Alice Waters *Art of Simple Food* cookbook, on the margins of a recipe for pan-fried pork chops.

She flipped through the cookbook to page 122.

There it was.

What phone to call him from? Emily's? Michelle's? A burner?

She had a sudden flash from the night she'd met Sam. They'd flown over the border, landed on a dirt airstrip somewhere in New Mexico. Danny by that time was shocky, pale and drenched in sweat, wavering on the edge of consciousness at times, the blood on his shirt dried to rust. He'd called Sam. "Hey, Sam," he'd said. "Hey. Can you pick us up?"

She shuddered, thinking about it. It had been a bad night. A burner.

She retrieved the new burner phone from her luggage that she'd bought in Houston at a Best Buy and plugged it in to charge. Went out to the garage and got the other phone, the one she hadn't used to call Danny the night he was arrested. She'd tossed that one before going through security at SFO.

The area code for Sam's number was 703, Virginia, but that didn't mean anything much. She had no idea where Sam's base of operations actually was.

"Hi, Sam? This is . . . this is Michelle. Danny's friend." She hesitated. "Is this a good time?"

"Let me call you back."

Sam had the hint of an accent. She wasn't sure from where. His last name was Kolar, but who knew if that was his real name? At times she thought she'd imagined the accent, or that maybe it was just an inflection he'd picked up from foreign-born parents. Or that it was some kind of disguise.

Five minutes later, her burner rang. He was using a different number now. A burner of his own, maybe.

"Is there a problem?" he asked.

"Yeah. You know Gary, right?"

A brief silence on the other end of the line.

"Just tell me what happened."

She kept it short. Didn't talk about her visit to Houston, or Gary's job. Just that Gary had been responsible for Danny's bust.

Sam knew who Gary was. He had to. She hadn't heard everything Daniel had told him that night in New Mexico, but he had to have told Sam about Gary.

"So, Gary," Sam said when she'd finished. Then silence. She waited.

When it was clear that he wouldn't speak first, she asked: "Is there anything you can do?"

Another pause. "What does Gary want?"

She felt the acid churn in her gut. This was what she'd wanted to avoid. "I don't know, revenge?"

Sam chuckled softly. "Is there something he wants you to do?"

She was afraid to tell him the truth, but she couldn't come up with a good enough lie.

"So you know Gary," she said.

She listened to the silence on the other end of the line. He wasn't going to answer. "I'm afraid if I tell you that he'll find out," she finally said. "And that you won't be able to protect me."

"A legitimate concern. But Danny told you to call me, didn't he?"

She couldn't say what she wanted to. Which would have been something like, "Yeah, and he also thought that smuggling pot into Texas was a great idea."

"Gary wants me to take a personal assistant job," she said. "For a woman named Caitlin O'Connor. She has a non-profit called Safer America."

She thought she heard the clicking of a keyboard, but she couldn't be sure.

"Interesting. And what did you tell him?"

"That I'd do it."

"All right." Another pause. "We'll work with that, then."

"What does that . . . what do you mean?"

"Just that you're cooperating, that's all. It gives us a few different options. Negotiation. Compromise."

She didn't believe him. She'd been around these people enough now that she knew there was almost always a hidden agenda. Another option. "Or something else?"

"Perhaps." If she could have seen his face, he would have been smiling. She was sure of it. "For now, just go along with him. Let's keep this conversation between the two of us. I'll do some fieldwork, and we'll see what makes the most sense, how we should play this."

"What about Danny?"

"I'll work that angle too. Find out who else aside from Gary might be backing the charges, if I can. See what can be done."

After that, Michelle drove to Evergreen.

She still had a restaurant to run.

Joseph, the executive chef, the guy who'd designed the menu and the recipes, was working tonight. She didn't expect that he'd be working there much longer. The line cooks had learned his recipes, and one of them, Guillermo, was a natural talent who was coming up with ideas of his own. Joseph was getting bored, she could tell, and was ready to move on to the next project, maybe a bigger place in another town, maybe his own restaurant, though she doubted he wanted to take that step. He was a hired gun, and she'd known that from the beginning.

Which made him the perfect person to talk to now.

Six o'clock. The early dinner crowd had drifted in, the ones who came for happy hour, half-priced wine by the glass tonight. All the bar seats were taken, and between that and the tables, two-thirds full, Matt was having a busy night.

"Emily, hi!"

Helen, her head waitress—not an official title, but that was how Michelle thought of her—waved from the back of the restaurant. She worked more hours than anyone else on the serving staff. Helen was in her late twenties and had dropped out of Humboldt State a year ago. Michelle hadn't asked why. It wasn't any of her business, and anyway, someone shares something with you, sometimes they want an exchange of confidences in return.

What she knew was that Helen worked hard, that she was smart and reliable.

Michelle headed in her direction.

"Everything going okay?"

"Yeah, you know," Helen said with a shrug. "We missed you."

"That's nice of you to say."

Helen stood her ground. Clasped her hands together. She was stocky, brown skinned and freckled, her caramel-colored hair done up in two braids that swirled around her ears like elaborate cinnamon rolls.

"Seriously. We're running low on some produce, and it's like, we can still get it if we switch up our suppliers, but I don't know, I'm thinking it might be time to adjust the menu." She suddenly seemed embarrassed. Twisted her clasped hands. "Somebody just needs to decide."

"Okay," Michelle said. "Thanks."

She went into the kitchen.

JOSEPH WAS THERE, WORKING on the finishing touches of a salmon dish; Copper River, she thought. She caught a whiff of the fish through the general smoke and chaos of the kitchen and suddenly realized how hungry she was. Had she even eaten today?

"Hey, Emily," Joseph said, glancing at her for a moment, then returning his attention to the garnish.

"When you can, would you take five and meet me in the office?"

He paused for a moment and actually looked at her, his expression some combination of concerned and annoyed. Maybe he thought she was about to fire him.

"Nothing bad," she said with a quick smile. "Just some business."

SOMEONE HAD BEEN WATERING her plants, at least.

She sat down at her desk, booted up her computer and logged onto the restaurant's receipts and inventory system.

Receipts were connected to the registers out front, so it was fairly easy to see how business had been in her absence. Not bad. Not bad at all.

Inventory and expenses were a different matter. As much as she wanted to standardize it all, different vendors had different ways that they liked to do things. You could have one artichoke grower at the farmer's market who used an iPad and then a winemaker who only took cash or checks and wrote out all his receipts by hand.

And of course, the restaurant did a lot of cash business as well. Pot dealers like Bobby tended to have an excess of it.

"Shit," she said aloud. Bobby. He had to know by now that something had gone very wrong on Danny's run. What should she do about it? What made the most sense?

A perfunctory knock on the door. Joseph entered without waiting for her response.

He really is kind of a prick, she thought. But a lot of chefs were like that.

"Hey." He came over to her desk, pulled the guest chair beneath him, the legs scraping the battered linoleum floor, and sat. He was a big guy, in his thirties, curly red hair, big belly, big, thick hands that were scarred from knives and grills and hot oil.

"How's it been?" she asked.

"Good." A shrug.

"Glad to hear that." She hesitated. How to put it? "So I imagine that you're getting ready to move on," she said.

Joseph's head canted back and he frowned, like he was surprised that she was that perceptive. She supposed that was understandable, given Emily's cover story: a hobbyist with money to burn (thanks to her boyfriend in the pot trade; "Jeff's" sideline was pretty much an open secret in town, or at least a well-trafficked rumor) who'd decided to buckle down and get serious about her dream of owning a restaurant. Which wasn't that far off from the truth, really, except for the "dream of running a restaurant" part. It was more that she'd had to do *something*, and a photography business or gallery hadn't seemed like much of a moneymaker. And she did know about food. About wine. About how to create an atmosphere. She'd hired a consultant to help set the place up, to teach her the basics, but he'd left a couple of months after the opening. "You don't need me from here out," he'd told her. "You've got a knack for this business."

Who knew?

"Yeah, well, things run pretty well," he said. "It's a good group."

"That's good to hear." Again, she hesitated. Then plunged

ahead. "Because the thing is, I'm having a family situation. An emergency. That's why I had to go out of town. And unfortunately . . . it looks like it's going to be dragging on for a while."

"Sorry to hear that." He actually did seem sorry. He looked down at his lap, at the grease stains on his apron, maybe. "Parent?"

"What?"

"You know." He shrugged. "Aging parent."

It was as good an excuse as any. "Yes. My dad."

He shook his head. "Fucking drag."

"Yeah."

Joseph shifted in his chair. She didn't know much about his personal story, next to nothing, really, but this seemed to be an issue that had some resonance for him. Might as well play it, she thought.

"We're not a big family," she said. "And there really isn't anyone else in the position to help. So, it's pretty much landed on me."

"I know how that goes," he muttered.

She nodded. "So I'm going to have to be out of town a lot for the next few months. And what I was wondering was, if you'd be willing to . . . take on a little more of a managerial role while I'm gone. I'll pay you for it."

Now Joseph looked alarmed. "The paperwork and stuff, it's not really my thing."

"I know that," she said quickly. "I mean as an executive chef. For the administrative end, I was thinking about promoting Helen. She seems really organized to me, and like she has a sense of the big picture."

The truth was, Helen already was a de facto manager

during the times that Michelle wasn't there. She did everything but the accounting, and there was no reason that she
couldn't do that as well, at least do enough of it to keep
things running for the next few months.

"Yeah," Joseph said slowly. "Yeah, she's good."

"We'll need to find another server. Do you know anyone?"

"I can find someone," he said.

SHE'D CALLED SAM. HAD Evergreen squared away,
to the extent that it could be.

One thing left on her to do list.

Bobby.

As it turned out, she didn't have to go looking for him.
He leaned against the end of the bar, having a glass of wine,
holding up the goblet and checking out the red's legs.

"Hey, Emily," he said.

"Bobby."

He could have someone at the airport. Someone in the
restaurant. A customer. A busboy. The bartender. And it
didn't have to be sinister. Just, "give me a call when Emily
gets in, okay?"

"You have a few?" he asked.

"Sure. Let's take a walk."

No way she wanted to have this discussion inside
Evergreen.

FOG DRIPPED ONTO THE flagstones of the plaza, and
someone had hung a large red bra from the outstretched arm
of the McKinley statue. Double D?

Bobby adjusted his Kangol hat low on his forehead.
Michelle zipped her fleece up to her chin.

"So, I guess Jeff ran into some trouble," Bobby said.
Michelle nodded.

"How's he doing?"

"He's doing okay."

"Does he . . . I mean, do you need anything, or, is there something I can do . . . ?"

Can you get him out of jail? she wanted to ask. "Not really."

Bobby paused at the foot of the statue. It was a quiet night on the plaza. The fall term hadn't started yet. A group of homeless men, passing around a paper bag. A couple of tweakers, a guy with a neck tattoo and a woman with sunken cheeks and skeletal limbs. A few knots of college kids who lived in town kicked a hacky sack around, and a violinist dressed in a 49ers hoodie played a concerto—a famous one, but she couldn't remember what it was called. No one seemed to be listening.

"Look . . . Jeff does me a solid, I'll do him one. You know?"

"No, I *don't* know," she said, irritated. A "solid"? Who talked like that, other than a frat boy? And Bobby was somewhere in his fifties. "What are you saying, exactly?"

"Just that he stands up for me, I'll stand up for him."

"And what, what does that even mean, you'll stand up for him?" she snapped. "What can you actually *do*?"

Bobby glanced around. Made sure no one was in earshot. "I'm not tied to any of it, okay? I mean, whatever he says, there's nothing to back it up."

"He hasn't *said* anything. Jesus."

"I know, I know," Bobby said quickly. "Jeff's a stand-up guy, no worries about that."

"If you're not worried, then what's this conversation about?"

He readjusted his cap once more. Michelle fought the urge to knock it off his head.

"Just checking in. Making sure we're on the same page. Because there's some guys who're pretty pissed off they didn't get their delivery. They're gonna want to take it out on somebody. So we need to stick together on this. Right?"

He stared at her a moment, his eyes unusually steady behind his round tortoiseshell glasses.

"Right," she said.

Chapter Nine

✧

SHE BOOKED AN EXTRA day in San Francisco. She needed a break between the obligations that she had in Arcata and the craziness she'd committed to in Houston.

Also, she needed to do something about her hair.

She'd always worn her hair shoulder length or longer. "Don't cut it," Tom had murmured, twining her hair in his fingers. "Don't ever cut it."

"You have such great hair," everyone had always said.

The problem was, the last thing she needed was her face turning up on CNN or whatever, her standing at the shoulder of Caitlin O'Connor looking exactly like the Emily that people knew back in Arcata.

Changing her hair wasn't foolproof, but at least it might discourage people from looking twice.

"I'm thinking short," she told the stylist who stood behind her chair, the two of them staring into the three-sided mirror. "And maybe we should have some fun with the color."

"You want to just go for blonde? I mean, obviously fake blonde." He framed her face with his hands. "I think you could pull it off."

"Sure. Why not?"

"OH, I LOVE THE hair!"

Michelle smiled and twitched a shrug. "I figured it was time for a change."

"Change can be good, or so everybody tells me." Caitlin laughed. "I don't know, I'm pretty sure they're full of shit. Change is overrated, in my book."

As before, Michelle had met Caitlin in the Great Room. It was just after 4 P.M., and Caitlin had a bottle of chardonnay on ice. She looked to be on her second glass.

"I guess it depends," Michelle said. She'd been ready to leave Tom, at the end, or so she told herself, but who knew if she actually would have gone through with it? When the change had finally happened, she hadn't had a choice.

She thought about Danny. "I've had both good and bad," she said.

Danny being both.

Caitlin poured a fresh glass of chardonnay and held it out to Michelle.

"Thanks, but I should probably get settled in first."

"Oh, don't worry about that." Caitlin waved like she was shooing off a fly. "We can start tomorrow. I don't have anything going on till that fundraiser in . . . I think it's Los Angeles. But it's not till next Tuesday." Her brow wrinkled. "Or maybe Wednesday?"

"I'll make sure to check."

She'd gotten into Houston yesterday. Rented a car at the airport. Gone to the corporate housing Porter had recommended, on the outskirts of River Oaks but still only a ten-minute drive to Caitlin's house. The rental office was sleek, soothing, a large room that resembled a community center at a condo complex, with tall ceilings, fabric-draped walls highlighted by sconces, a coffee urn and water with lemon slices, and a large salt water aquarium.

She'd picked the smallest, cheapest unit available. One

bedroom. Second floor. Two easy points of entry, the front door and a window close to it. She'd have those wired with a cheap alarm system. Nothing that would stop a pro, but it might surprise someone who didn't expect it.

The apartment was furnished with industrial uphol-stered chairs and a love seat done in rust and hunter green. The back window overlooked a main street, which in the direction of Caitlin's house was lined largely with oaks and the backs of estates. Then, at the intersection where her complex was, it shifted to a mix of businesses: restaurants, realtors, a florist. From her window she could glimpse the sign for a "gentlemen's club" called The Zone Erotique.

Was there any zoning in Houston, she wondered?

Think of it as a hotel room, she told herself. That's all it really is.

AFTER THAT, SHE'D GONE to the AT&T store to get a new phone, and a new number. Michelle could have a real phone now, though she'd have to be careful with it. Anything other than a burner, anything attached to a regular account, with GPS, with useful apps, Gary could easily track.

I need to buy more burners, she thought.

"ARE YOU SURE THERE isn't anything I can help you with today?" Michelle asked Caitlin now.

"No, I don't think so, hon. Come on by tomorrow morn-ing, and I'll make sure someone's here from the office to help you get set up on the computer here, and bring you over a laptop for the road. Make sure we get our calendars in sync."

"All right." Probably for the best. She needed to do some

shopping, buy bedding and a coffeemaker and a few other things for the apartment.

Michelle took a last sip of her chardonnay. Too bad she shouldn't finish it. Much better than what Caitlin poured the last time.

"Then tomorrow afternoon, there's the board meeting. You don't have to come to that if you need some more time to settle in."

Board meeting. Michelle felt a prickling down her spine.

"Would . . . am I allowed to attend?"

"Well, if you want. We have them every other week or so. I don't attend every time, to be honest." Caitlin laughed briefly. "They'd rather do them without me, I'm pretty sure."

"It feels like a good way for me to get a better sense of what you're doing, how things work," Michelle said. "But if you have things you'd rather have me do—"

"No, of course not—if you want to go, well then, I think you should." Caitlin sipped her chardonnay. "Just be warned—there's lot of talk that generally doesn't lead to much."

"Consider me warned. But I'm actually really excited to have the opportunity."

Gary wanted her babysitting Caitlin for a reason. Safer America was important to him. The people on that board might give her a clue as to why.

"You back in Houston?"

"What do you think, Gary? Like you don't know."

She heard Gary chuckle through her earbuds.

"I guess I can't put one over on you anymore, can I?"

Michelle lay back on the bed in her new apartment,

covered by her brand-new sheets. "You know, it's late, and I've got to get to work tomorrow."

"You enjoying it? The work?"

"It's a little soon to say."

"Well, you'll like why I'm calling you. That first installment we agreed on—you can pick it up tomorrow."

"Great," Michelle said. She felt a little rush of enthusiasm. She needed the fucking money, after all, to pay for this place, to pay for her new sheets, to figure out what she was going to do about a car in this sprawling city.

"You'll get some instructions tomorrow night. You're not going to have a big window, time-wise—you'll have to hustle to the drop."

"Okay. You going to tell me what time?"

"It'll be after seven P.M. Just be ready." A snicker. "Don't let Caitlin talk you into cocktails."

PORTER ACKERMANN LOOKED AT his tablet. "So, back to 391. Everybody's had a week to think it over. Are we in agreement?"

They sat around a walnut table in a dark-paneled meeting room with a view of the mall across the street. The meeting had started at 3:30 P.M. By now it was 4:45. It seemed to Michelle that not very much had actually happened.

"I agree it should be a priority. But do we really want to focus that large a percentage of our resources on one campaign?"

The speaker was a middle-aged white man—all seven of the board members save Caitlin and the Secretary of the Board were middle-aged to older white men.

This one had a square head and gunmetal gray hair

brushed back close to his scalp—the Donald Rumsfeld look. His name was Randall Gates, and he was involved with a company named Prostatis.

"I don't think we have a choice." An older man—white hair, big gut, genial expression, the perfect shopping mall Santa Claus: Michael Campbell, who represented something called ALEAAG. "We do public advocacy for law enforcement issues," he'd explained when he'd introduced himself, giving Michelle a pillowy handshake.

They'd all introduced themselves at the beginning of the meeting, after Caitlin presented Michelle as her new "right-hand woman"—"any time you need to set something up for me, just talk to Michelle here."

"She's a real go-getter," Porter had added.

Michelle, for her part, smiled, accepted handshakes and a few lingering looks—a couple of the men doing their "how fuckable is she?" inventories—and took notes. There was nothing strange about Caitlin's new assistant wanting to know the names of the board members, was there?

"As California goes," another one of them said, a compact, balding man with crow's feet around his eyes reminding her a little of Danny—that look a person gets who's spent a lot of time outdoors, or staring into the sky. She thought his name was Steve. He hadn't named the organization he represented.

"If this proposition passes, we are looking at marijuana legalization sweeping across the country," Steve said.

Of course. Proposition 391: Legalize cannabis for recreational use in California. She felt an electric sensation in the palms of her hands, a little adrenaline rush.

Danny in jail for pot. Maybe there was no meaningful connection.

Maybe there was.

"So what if it does?"

It was Caitlin who spoke. The first words she'd said since her introduction of Michelle. You could feel a little wave of shock go around the room: everyone suddenly more attentive, expressions ranging from surprised to skeptical to carefully neutral.

Caitlin waved a hand. "I don't know, it's getting to the point where all the fuss over pot just seems silly to me. I mean, how many people in this room have ever smoked pot?"

Michelle wasn't about to answer that question.

"Well, I never have." Debbie Landry, the secretary of the board, sat up straight. Probably in her fifties, but she looked younger—long, carefully dyed blonde hair, cheeks a little too taut, maybe some Botox on the forehead—but she was in great shape, too, her bare arms toned and cut.

"It's one thing for kids from stable backgrounds to engage in some youthful experimentation," she said. "And even then you never know who might be susceptible to mental and emotional problems from taking that drug. For kids from disadvantaged backgrounds? We might as well just consign them to failure."

Another one of the men, Matthew Moss, nodded. Barrel-shaped, a helmet of brown hair, big head, full cheeks, like a Lego mini-figure. Moss had been the more obnoxious of the "is she fuckable?" crew (Campbell was too jovial for her to take seriously), holding her hand a little too long, doing the overt checking out of her cleavage. He'd introduced himself with the attitude that she should already know who he was and what he did. She didn't.

"It comes down to, what kind of America do we want?"

he pronounced. "One that's populated by a bunch of stoned slackers? It goes against our values as a country."

Had she seen him on TV, maybe? On one of those stupid political talk shows with shouting heads?

"It's not that I disagree with you," Randall Gates said. "I'm just wondering if it makes sense to put all our eggs in one basket, resource-wise. We've also got 275 in California, and I don't need to tell you what the implications of changing those sentencing guidelines are. And if we can't hold the line in California, and I'm not convinced we can, we'd better start focusing on shoring up our defenses elsewhere. There's a couple of Congressional races where, as you know, we definitely have dogs in those hunts."

Porter nodded. "That we do. I think the obvious answer here is, we'll just have to raise more money."

A round of chuckles.

"We're on track to raise thirty-seven million this year," Debbie said.

Porter smiled. "I think we can do better than that."

"The polling on 391 shows a six percent majority in favor," Steve said. "Those are numbers we can move. If we're willing to devote the resources."

Matthew Moss nodded. "I think we have to make a stand on this."

"We'd better," Steve said. "Things are going to get trickier in California if this new disclosure bill gets traction."

"Disclosure bill?" Moss asked.

"We'll have to report donors over one K to the secretary of state for any California races."

They didn't have to already? Michelle thought. That didn't seem right. Maybe she misunderstood.

"Surely there will be work-arounds," Porter said.

Steve nodded. "There will be. But this is an easier campaign to run now. In the future?" He shrugged. "The momentum and optics may not be on our side."

"You find me a single user of meth or heroin who didn't start with marijuana," Campbell said, wagging a finger. "And then there's the correlation with criminal behavior—"

"Do we want our children exposed to the temptation of legal marijuana?" Debbie Landry asked. "Knowing they can buy it just as easily as they can buy a beer?"

Caitlin laughed, a light, silvery chuckle. "Well, hon, I'd have liked my child to have lived long enough to've been tempted."

Silence.

"Oh, hon, I'm so sorry," Debbie said.

Caitlin waved her hand again, this time with a shake of her head, her eyes closed. "No, *I* am. That was . . . I'm just a little tired today."

"We can finish up without you," Porter said. "There's not much left on today's agenda."

"Why don't you do that?" Caitlin said. She rose slowly. She looked frail.

Michelle rose as well. "Wonderful meeting all of you," she said, gathering up her iPad and notebook.

She followed Caitlin out of the meeting room.

CAITLIN WALKED DOWN THE hall and through the reception area without stopping. Michelle wasn't sure what to do. Caitlin seemed like a woman who didn't want to be interrupted, who just wanted to get somewhere private and hole up, sink into her deep, warm well of unending grief. It could be a comfortable place, Michelle knew.

It's my job to look after her, she thought.

"Caitlin?"

Caitlin stopped. Her hand gripped the corner of a file cabinet. She turned to Michelle, her eyes a little red, her smile back in place. "Oh, I'm sorry, Michelle. Didn't mean to run off and leave you."

"That's okay. I just wanted to know if there was anything I could do for you, anything you wanted to work on this afternoon, or . . ."

Caitlin snorted. "Hell, let's just go get a drink."

Don't let Caitlin talk you into cocktails.

THERE WAS A TAPAS place close by that Caitlin liked.

"Just for a glass of wine," she'd said. "And they have small plates, if you're hungry."

It was just after 5 P.M., and though Michelle wasn't hungry, she figured she'd better have something to sop up her glass of rioja.

She wasn't going to have any at all, but Caitlin ordered a bottle, and Michelle had a feeling Caitlin wouldn't be leaving any of it on the table. And she barely seemed to eat. Just a few olives. One bite of the tortilla. Small as Caitlin was, Michelle wondered how she'd manage even the short drive home.

Not that Michelle was eating a lot either. Her stomach, her chest, everything felt tight. She'd be getting a call from Gary at some point, and he'd tell her where to pick up her money. Only with Gary, you could never trust that it would be anything simple. He'd find some way to twist it, to fuck with her, just because he could, and because he enjoyed it.

The restaurant was dark, a lot of stained wood, wrought

iron and dark red booths. "It feels a little private, don't you think?" Caitlin said, taking a tiny nibble of octopus.

Michelle nodded. Of course, nothing was really private. Gary could have someone spying on her, right now. He could have already hacked her new iPhone for all she knew. If he knew the number, he could ping it, find out what cell tower it was in contact with, approximately where she was. She didn't know if he could get into the GPS without having physical contact with her phone, without infecting it with spyware, but she'd never assume that he couldn't.

That he wouldn't have some way to turn on the microphone without her knowing.

"It's very nice," she said.

"I don't get out enough," Caitlin said. "I mean, it's funny to say—I do all this travel, these fundraisers, parties . . . but I don't just go *out* very much. It's always business." She chuckled. "I suppose this is, too."

What do I say to her? Michelle thought.

What does she want to hear?

"I know what you mean," Michelle said. "You get wrapped up in your business, it gets to be your social circle too. I've made some great friends that way. But it's good to have a life outside of work."

Another weary chuckle. "I don't know if I have a life *inside* of work."

Michelle hesitated. It was tempting to push. To dig. But they barely knew each other. If she started asking too many questions about Safer America . . .

"You've done some great things," she said.

"Here's hoping," Caitlin said, raising her wine glass.

ॐ ॐ ॐ

THE WINE BOTTLE HOVERED over Michelle's half-empty glass. "No, thank you," she said to the waiter. Maybe James Bond could belt back a couple of martinis and go do spy stuff, but she wasn't going to risk it.

Caitlin, meanwhile, kept drinking, as Michelle had guessed she would.

"I don't know," she was saying. "I'm really not sure about this whole pot thing."

"Oh?"

"Just if it's worth pouring all kinds of money into opposing something that's eventually going to pass." She tilted her glass to her lips. The swallows were getting bigger now, sips turning into mouthfuls. "It's like trying to hold back the tide."

Michelle nodded.

Caitlin suddenly leaned forward. "I mean, what do *you* think? You've lived in California. Y'all have had medical marijuana for how long now?"

"Close to twenty years," Michelle said. Her heart was beating a little faster. This was getting too close, too close to her real life. Or Emily's real life.

"And you haven't fallen into the ocean yet, in spite of what some of my friends here think." She laughed. "Of course I can't use California in any kind of an argument with them. They'd look at y'all to prove their point it's the devil's weed."

Michelle glanced down at her iPhone. 5:52 P.M. She still had plenty of time.

"I guess there's plusses and minuses," she said. "I'm sure there's some abuse of the medical-marijuana system. It's easy to get a card if you want one. But pot really seems to help some people."

"Well, then, maybe we ought to be treating it more like real medicine. Make it a little harder for any ole' kid with a hangnail to walk into a clinic and get a Baggie full of weed."

With the quality and cost of the stuff you could get in the clinics, your kid with a hangnail probably wouldn't be coming out with a Baggie-full, Michelle wanted to say. More like a tiny plastic bag with a couple of nice buds.

Instead she nodded and said, "I'm sure there are ways things could be improved."

"Hell, I don't know." Caitlin tilted back her glass and swallowed. "Sometimes I think we ought to go in a different direction altogether."

"With medical marijuana?"

"With Safer America. I don't know, like promote after-school programs. Job training. Maybe community gardens." She laughed, as if the whole idea was absurd.

"Why don't you?"

"Well, it isn't up to me. We have a charter. We have the board."

"But you're the founder."

"I'm the figurehead." Caitlin shrugged and tossed back the rest of her wine. "Sometimes you start something, and it takes on a life of its own."

"Why don't I drive you home?"

"Oh, don't be silly. It's just a few blocks."

Michelle hesitated. Another situation where she wasn't sure how hard to push. But she could just see it: her first day on the job, and Caitlin gets pulled over for a DUI, crashes her car into a fire hydrant, or worse.

"Well, it's part of my job," Michelle said lightly. "So you can relax and not have to worry about driving."

It wasn't just that Caitlin had drunk almost the entire bottle of wine. Michelle wondered if she'd had anything else, meds, maybe, whatever it was she took to manage anxiety, to sleep. She had to be taking something, Michelle was willing to bet. She wasn't weaving, exactly, but it took her an extra effort to plant her foot each time she stepped, and her eyes seemed unfocused.

"Maybe I should take you up on that." Caitlin stretched a little. "I'm pretty tired. I can send Rodrigo for the car tomorrow."

LEAVING THE CAR WAS fine with the restaurant manager. They knew Caitlin here. "I left them an extra-nice tip," Caitlin said, sliding into the passenger seat of Michelle's rented Prius.

"This your car?" she asked.

"A rental. But . . ."

It's like the one I have at home, Michelle almost said.

"I've always liked them."

"Well, no need for you to be renting a car. There's an extra one in the garage you can use."

"That's very generous, but—"

"Now, no arguing." Caitlin wagged a finger. "It's supposed to be used for Safer America business, and it's just sitting there rusting away as it is."

They'd just turned down the broad avenue that led to Caitlin's house when Michelle's iPhone rang. Emily's, rather. The ringtone, "Get Smart."

Fucking Gary. And it was only 6:29 P.M.

"Sorry," Michelle said. "I have to take this." She pulled over. No hands-free setup on the rental, and even if she had one, she wasn't about to put Gary on speakerphone.

She fumbled around in her new tote for her phone. Her Emily phone.

"Well, hey there."

Just the sound of his voice, that phony flirtatiousness, made her shudder.

"Hi, listen, I'm going to have to call you back—I'm . . . driving someone home."

A chuckle. "Now, what did I tell you about cocktails with Caitlin?"

God, Michelle hoped Caitlin hadn't heard that. She pressed the phone closer to her ear.

"Five minutes," she said. "I'm just about there."

She disconnected.

"What was that, *Get Smart*? How funny!" Caitlin gave Michelle a friendly pat on the arm, giggling a little. "And here I thought you seemed so serious."

Michelle supposed that she *was* serious. It was Emily who'd learned to lighten up a bit, to laugh at Danny's jokes.

What was he doing right now? How was he?

She pushed the thought aside. She couldn't take the time to worry about him. Not now.

"You're early," she said.

"Change in plans."

Of course.

"Gonna need you to make a stop first, pick something up. Got a pen?"

"What am I picking up?"

"Never mind that. You're just the delivery gal. You'll hand it off, and then you'll get your money."

Not good. But so predictable.

It was close to sunset.

At first the neighborhood she'd driven through seemed okay. Nice, even. Well-kept older houses, big oak trees, trimmed lawns. Restaurants and clubs that looked funky and hip. Then the main business street turned into peeling beige stucco fast-food chains and auto-part shops: radiators, mufflers, tires. A strip club called Purple Passion that looked like one of the auto-part stores, with faded tin siding. No sidewalks in places, just dirt.

It hadn't cooled off much, and Michelle was glad she'd kept the air on, the windows rolled up. She was drenched in sweat as it was, her heart racing like she'd been running. But of course she hadn't been.

Danny was right. She should have turned Gary down. Should've run. Should've done . . . something. *Anything* other than taking this job and driving down a sketchy-looking street in god knows where, Houston, so she could "pick something up" for that fucker Gary.

She'd packed a change of clothes this morning: jeans, Nikes, black T-shirt, a light-weight women's cut hoodie she wore on nicer days in Arcata. But she hadn't had time to change, so here she was in her black silk Eileen Fisher T and her black Stella McCartney slacks.

She did take the time to put on the Nikes. In case she had to run.

The address Gary gave her was for a trailer park called "Shady Acres."

Shady Acres. She had to roll her eyes at that. Fucking Gary. She'd bet good money this was his idea of a joke.

Probably you'd call this a mobile-home park as opposed to a trailer park, she thought. The homes here were single-wides, long rectangles that looked like flimsy shipping containers made out of plastic siding, plywood and corrugated tin, the skirts around the bottoms warped and buckling, satellite dishes clamped or bolted onto the structures like the remnants of some advanced alien technology.

There were trees, at least, patchy attempts at landscaping here and there, kids' bikes sprawled on the dirt. Not that many people outside. Maybe it was still too hot.

At the end of the road was her destination: #52.

It looked like most of the others. Single-wide, two-toned, in this case cream with ochre trim, rusting here and there around the edges. A Harley and some kind of late-model Ford sedan were parked on a tiny patch of asphalt next to the entrance. A flag fluttered from a skinny pole stuck into a stanchion mounted on a wood beam holding up the canopy that shaded the door. It was one of those flags with a black coiled rattler on a yellow background with the legend DON'T TREAD ON ME.

Please don't let there be a pit bull, Michelle thought.

She parked. Took a deep breath, then another. Thought, I'm not going to get killed here, that wouldn't make any sense, this whole setup with Caitlin and Safer America is too elaborate, there's more at stake, this is just Gary fucking with me, because he can.

She got out of the car, stood by the door for a moment. *Breathe. Just breathe.*

Get it over with, she thought.

She walked past the Harley, up four mold-stained cement steps, paused on the landing. Listened for a moment. Voices. A burst of laughter and music. Something on TV.

She knocked on the door.

Chapter Ten

⚯

AN EXPLOSION OF BARKING greeted her knock: high-pitched yapping.

That doesn't sound like a pit bull, she thought.

Though had she ever actually heard one bark?

She could hear movement behind the door: a scrabbling of blunted claws on linoleum, more barking, then a heavier, human tread.

She smoothed the wrinkles in her black silk T-shirt and ran her fingers through her hair. Because I want to look my best for whatever maniac Gary sent me to meet, she thought briefly.

The door cracked open.

"Yeah?"

In his late fifties or early sixties, thinning gray hair combed back from his forehead, falling over the collar of a short-sleeved button-down checked shirt. A small-ish man with a round gut that made him look almost pregnant.

Behind him, she heard more high-pitched yapping and nails scrabbling on linoleum. "Get back, Roscoe," the man snapped.

For a moment, her mind went completely blank. A fresh wave of sweat broke out on her forehead and back. Gary hadn't told her what to say. Gary hadn't told her anything.

"I'm here for the pickup," she said.

The man's head tilted back. He looked her up and down. "Come in."

A SMALL DOG WITH long cream-colored hair scampered around her feet, rearing up on its hind legs and barring its overbite of tiny fangs with a high-pitched growl.

"Shih tzu," the man said. "They're very loyal. Chinese."

She nodded.

Past the small rectangle of linoleum of the entrance was a stretch of rust-colored pile carpet. The living room. The TV she'd heard, a large flat screen, took up most of the narrow end of the rectangle. It was playing a reality show. *The Bachelor*. An overwrought woman in a Little Bo Peep costume and lots of lip gloss wrung her hands at another woman dressed up like a cowgirl—that is, if cowgirls wore short shorts and crop tops with their cowboy boots.

The man aimed a remote at the TV and muted it. He indicated a loveseat-sized brown and gold upholstered couch across from a leatherette recliner with a TV tray table parked at its side.

Michelle sat.

"Something to drink? Water? Sweet tea?"

"I'm fine, thanks."

He shrugged. "Be right back."

As he headed down a truncated hall, the dog skittered over, sniffing at her ankles with bared teeth and quivering with barely suppressed canine rage.

"Roscoe! Go sit!" the man yelled over his shoulder.

The dog retreated with one last outraged trill, and hopped up onto the recliner.

She heard metal catch on metal: a key, sliding into a

lock. A door opening. Her mouth was dry. I should've taken that water, she thought. She stared at the Remington print framed in battered walnut, a cowboy on a bucking bronco, hung on the opposite wall.

All this place needs is a wagon-wheel lamp, she thought.

The man hobbled back into the living room, a canvas duffle bag on each shoulder, laboring under the weight. He lowered them down onto the shag carpet, the longer bag on his right shoulder landing with a solid thud. Muffled metal.

"Everything's there," he said. He leaned over, stiffly, and unzipped the larger bag. "Check it if you want."

She didn't want. Not at all. But maybe she was expected to. She stood. Looked into the bag.

Bubble-wrapped objects. About three feet long. Rifles.

"Four Colt AR-15s, two Bushmasters, six Sig Sauer 226s. Good condition." He shrugged. Or maybe he was just working out a kink in his shoulder. "I threw in a couple of Colt full auto kits."

"Oh," she said. "Great."

"You need a hand out to the car?"

"I . . ."

She thought about it. There was something she needed, all right.

"Do you have any revolvers?" she asked. "Any .38 specials?" She smiled. "For me. I'm new in town."

HIS NAME WAS TERRY. He tried to talk her out of a .38. "Wouldn't you rather have a nice semi-auto? I have a sweet nine-millimeter Beretta you might like. Fits great in a purse."

"Thanks," she said, "but I'd rather have a .38."

Something small, reliable and that she already knew how to shoot. She'd spent a lot of hours on a gun range with her .38, back in Arcata.

"Well, I do have a Smith and Wesson Chief's Special. Really nice piece. And clean. I can let you have it for four hundred. That's a discount."

SHE PAID HIM CASH for the pistol. He threw in a cheap nylon concealment holster ("So you aren't carrying it naked"). He never said anything about payment for the rest of the guns. Already taken care of, she had to assume.

TERRY INSISTED ON HELPING her out to the car, wobbling under the weight of the duffle bags, the little dog dancing around his heels.

He slammed the hatchback shut. Took a moment to smooth out his plaid short-sleeved shirt. Like she'd done when she'd stood at his door.

"Pleasure doing business with you," he said. "You're a nice change from the usual suspects."

FUCKING GARY.

Her hands gripped the wheel, so tightly that her wrists were aching. His directions had led her somewhere northeast. She had no idea where, what kind of place it was. Just street names that didn't mean anything. Anonymous broad avenues with beat-up convenience stores, an occasional gas station, a stucco hospital complex. Skinny condos where the faded paint was peeling off the wood siding. A lot of chain-link fencing, graffiti sprayed on beige-coated brick.

It had to be a bad neighborhood, she thought. Because, fucking Gary. She'd bet anything he was sitting back with a scotch—well, maybe not, given his health kick—but she'd bet he was laughing his ass off right now, thinking about the situation he'd put her in. He got off on it.

Why do dogs lick themselves, right? she heard Danny say.

Given that she was using the GPS on her iPhone, Gary probably knew exactly where she was.

"Fuck you, Gary," she muttered, in case he was listening.

"In four hundred feet, turn left," her phone said.

She'd turned into a housing tract. Late 1950s, she guessed—smaller ranch-style homes, single story. Rundown, most of them, from what she could see in the dark and the few sputtering streetlights. Dead lawns. FOR SALE signs here and there, BANK OWNED slapped on some of them.

Boarded-up windows. Junked cars.

Abandoned.

"Your destination is on the right."

A brown stucco house with a darker brown paint trim, a withered oak tree in the front yard and a bug zapper by the door doubling as a porch light.

She pulled over to the curb. Sat there for a moment with the engine running, breathing hard.

Deep, calming breaths, she told herself. Think about what you're going to say.

Like what, she thought? What could she possibly say? "Hi, I'm here with your guns"?

If she'd been sweaty before, she was drenched now, shivering in the chill of the air conditioner, stomach clenched and roiling.

She turned off the engine, killed the power. In the silence

that followed, she could hear faint strains of *ranchera* music coming from the house, the scrape and chirp of crickets.

It's a long game, she told herself, Gary's playing a long game. He doesn't want to see me dead, not yet. Not so soon.

That wouldn't be fun for him at all.

She took one last deep breath. Got out of the car. Locked it, put the keys in her purse. Put her hand on the butt of her new revolver, tucked in the concealed holster in her purse, next to her wallet, comb and lipstick. Stupid, she told herself. What good would that gun really do her if she was walking into a house full of the type of people who would buy illegal weapons?

Still, she kept her fingers wrapped around the rubber Pachmayr grip. It felt like muscle and bone, hard beneath a slight yield. You know how to shoot this if you have to, she told herself.

You're not going to die.

THE DOORBELL DIDN'T WORK. She knocked. Rapped three times, the first one tentative. The second two, harder.

The music quieted. She waited.

She didn't hear footsteps, just the sudden scrape of the dead-bolt as it retracted into the door, then the rattle of the chain lock, pulling taut.

"Yes?"

She could see a slice of his face: smooth brown skin, short black hair, a dark eye.

"I have your delivery," she said.

It was the best she could come up with.

"Delivery?" he asked, in accented English.

"You're expecting something, right?"

A pause. "Excuse me. One moment."

The door closed.

She stood there, heart pounding, hand clutching the .38 in her purse, mouth so dry the sides of her throat stuck together as she swallowed.

The chain lock rattled again. This time, the door opened wide.

"Sorry," he said. "We did not expect *you*."

He wasn't that young. In his thirties, at least. Short, barrel chest, close-cropped hair, round, full cheeks. Not quite baby faced, but close. He wore a green-striped polo shirt and jeans. She could see the blurred blue ink of a tattoo on his neck, disappearing into his shirt collar. The letter L, and a number that she couldn't make out.

"It's in the car," she said.

The man in the green-striped polo shirt and another younger Latino wearing a white undershirt and baggy shorts followed her to the curb.

She popped the hatch. Gestured at the duffle bags. "There," she said.

The man in the green striped polo shirt stepped up to the bumper while the younger man in the white undershirt waited behind her. Watching her. She could feel it. She relaxed her hand that rested on the edge of her purse, poised above the pistol. Don't make him nervous, she thought.

The man in the green striped shirt leaned over and unzipped the larger duffle. Took a quick glance. Zipped it up and nodded.

The younger man trotted forward and hoisted the two

duffels onto his shoulders, then turned and jogged slowly across the dead lawn to the front door.

She and the man in the green striped shirt stood across from each other. Close enough now that she thought she could make out the number tattooed on his neck, in an elaborate font that reminded her of medieval manuscripts.

73.

His face, with its smooth, round cheeks, showed no expression. He stood there, seeming to stare at a point just past her.

I just want to get in the car, she thought. Get in the car and drive away.

But she was supposed to get her money. Wasn't she?

Fucking Gary, she thought. Of course he wouldn't make it clear.

Should she ask?

Something in 73's expression suddenly changed, a sort of wince. He shifted back and forth on his feet. Then his face turned hard again.

What did it mean?

She let her fingertips slip down and graze the grip of her revolver.

"Sorry," he suddenly said. "For making you wait."

SHE FELT A SUDDEN flush of sweat, of something close to relief. "Oh. That's all right. No need to apologize."

A moment later, the younger man in the white undershirt came trotting back, pulling a navy-blue wheeled suitcase behind him. Too big for a carry-on.

He pushed the handle into the suitcase, hoisted it up and laid it in the trunk of her Prius.

The man in the green striped shirt gestured at the suitcase. Was she supposed to inspect it? Like she did the guns?

She leaned over and unzipped suitcase. Lifted up the flimsy canvas.

Money. Banded bundles of it. Hundreds and fifties and twenties. She had no idea how much it was. But it looked like a lot more than fifty thousand dollars.

She zipped the suitcase shut. What was she supposed to do? He had to know how much money was in there. She couldn't exactly tell him he'd made a mistake.

Something of her confusion must have shown on her face when she looked up to meet his eyes.

He nodded slightly. "Our . . . donation."

Chapter Eleven

SHE SAT CROSS-LEGGED ON the floor of her bedroom, trying to count the money.

The suitcase weighed at least fifty pounds. Most of the bundled bills were hundreds, but there were bundles of twenties and fifties as well.

One hundred bills in each bundle. So each bundle of hundred dollar bills was $10,000. There were sixty of those.

$600,000 in hundred dollar bills.

She counted out the stacks of fifties and twenties. Sixty bundles of fifties. Another $300,000.

Fifty bundles of twenties. Another $100,000.

A million dollars.

Michelle rolled onto her back and stared at the popcorn ceiling.

What was she supposed to do with all this money?

"Why don't you . . . just . . . get away for a while?" she heard Danny say. *"Until this gets settled."*

Just take the money and run.

She took in a deep breath. Exhaled slowly. Thought about places she might go.

Where? What made sense? Was there anyplace far enough away?

Maybe that was what Gary wanted her to do, to try to make a run for it.

How far could she really expect to get?

Besides, that would leave Danny right where he was.

She felt like she was adrift in a dark sea, all the things that made up her life shipwrecked, bobbing up and down in the black water just out of her reach. Nothing was solid. Nothing was hers.

She'd made a promise to herself that she was going to help him. Not because they were going to be together for the long haul. Maybe they wouldn't be. Maybe it would be just this one time, maybe not ever again.

Just this once, and call it even. But she had to keep that promise.

She had to hold onto something.

She rolled up to her feet, retrieved her phone and called Gary.

"WELL, HELLO THERE." HE sounded typically cheery. "Everything go okay tonight?"

"Sure. It went fine."

She'd thought about what to say. She couldn't be sure who might be listening, that Gary wouldn't use her words against her, somehow.

"It was a little more than I was expecting," she said.

"Oh, yeah." A chuckle. "The stars just kind of lined up for that."

"What am I supposed to do with it?"

"Just hang onto it for a spell. Somebody'll be by to pick it up."

"When? I can't exactly just . . ."

Stash a suitcase with a million dollars in it under my bed.

"I'm not comfortable having it here. This apartment . . . it's not that secure."

A long, drawn-out sigh. "I suppose you have a point," he finally said. "I'll send somebody over in an hour or so. Just sit tight."

THE FIRST THING SHE did was separate out her share of the money and repack the suitcase.

She took three bundles of hundred dollar bills and four bundles of fifties. Her $50K.

It's not that bulky, she told herself. She could hide it, somewhere.

Not in the freezer. People were always hiding things in freezers in the novels she used to read, and they always seemed to get caught.

Not under her mattress. This too was a cliché that never ended well.

Finally she put half of it in one of her suitcases that she stored in the bedroom closet. She'd make that a go-bag, in case she needed to leave in a hurry. She tucked another couple of bundles between folded towels in the hall closet. The rest she divided between her purse and under a couch cushion, which really needed to be vacuumed.

I'd better get a small safe, she thought. Not for all of the money, but for some of it. So if someone broke in, that's where he'd look first. A decoy.

Gary was right about one thing. She needed to figure out what to do with all this cash.

She wasn't unfamiliar with the problem. Danny had done some cash business back in Arcata, like those gigs for Bobby. Some of the money they'd funneled into Evergreen. She knew this was technically money laundering, but she preferred thinking of it as an investment. The rest, he stashed wherever it was he stashed such things. "Don't worry," he told her once, when they were lying in bed together, her back pressed against his chest, feeling his half-erect cock on the curve of her ass, "I'll make sure you can get to it, if something happens."

What might "happen," they never talked about.

Well, something had happened, all right, but she still didn't know how to get to Danny's money, if there even was any.

SHE CHANGED INTO CLEAN clothes. Yoga pants and an old Air Force T-shirt that Danny had given her. She desperately wanted a shower. But "an hour or so" in the Gary-verse could mean anything from 3 A.M. to five minutes from now.

It was just after 10 P.M. She put on the local news. Watched a segment about a rodeo fashion show that was some kind of fundraiser for kids in foster care. Turned off the TV. She couldn't focus on it.

She got out her iPad and surfed for a while. Looked at the *New York Times*, then Zagat and Yelp for Houston restaurants. There were supposed to be some good ones here. Might as well do a little research.

None of it engaged her. She kept on clicking. Anything to keep her mind off of where she was, and what she'd been doing.

Who would he send? A cartel thug? Some white supremacist militia crazy?

One of the Boys?

Whose money was this?

Our donation.

She pulled her purse next to her on the couch, holster side next to her, so her hand could easily grasp the .38.

10:35 P.M.

At 11:05, the doorbell rang.

Michelle flinched. Snatched the gun and jumped up. Then thought, fuck, I'm wearing yoga pants. There are no pockets in yoga pants. I can't walk to the door with a gun in my hand. If they see it . . .

That might make things much worse.

She grabbed her purse, slung it over her shoulder and went to the door.

On the other side of the fish-eye peephole was a woman, with long brown hair and glasses.

Michelle kept the chain lock on and cracked open the door. "Yes?"

"I'm supposed to pick something up?"

She sounded younger than she looked. In her early thirties, Michelle thought. A little heavy, her flat brown hair parted in the middle and falling past her shoulders. Wearing sky-blue shorts and a white, scoop-necked top, sturdy pewter-colored wire-framed glasses. A gold necklace with a Tinkerbell charm.

This was who Gary sent?

"Right," Michelle said. "Come in."

HER NAME WAS CARLENE. "Cute place," she said.

"Thank you." Michelle supposed she was being polite. There was nothing about her industrial-upholstered hotel furniture decorated apartment that was remotely cute.

"Can I get you something to drink?" she asked. "Some water? Some . . ."

What did she even have here?

"Wine?"

Carlene hesitated. "A Coke or sweet tea, if you have it."

"Sorry, I don't."

"I'm fine, then."

Shit, Michelle thought. She needed to stall her, somehow. To get a hold of Gary. To make sure that she was actually supposed to hand over nearly a million dollars in cash to a sort of dumpy woman wearing a Tinkerbell necklace.

But why else would Carlene be here?

Her phone was in her purse, which was still slung over her shoulder.

"You know, let me check the fridge," she said. "There might be a Coke left in there."

"Oh, thanks," Carlene said. She smiled at Michelle. Something about her eyes looked blank.

Michelle shuddered, in spite of the heat.

Out in the kitchen, she retrieved her phone and dropped her purse on the counter. Opened the refrigerator and shuffled around the bottles of Pellegrino and cartons of coconut water with one hand and texted Gary with the other. One word:

CARLENE?

She moved a few more bottles around, hoping for an answer. Got out a Pellegrino and poured it in a glass. Nothing.

Shit, she thought again. She wanted her phone, and she wanted her gun, because the woman sitting on her hunter green industrial upholstered couch might look harmless, but if Gary sent her?

She tucked her revolver into the waistband of her yoga

pants, at the small of her back, not sure about the holster Terry had given her. Felt the steel cylinder press against her skin. The T-shirt she was wearing was pretty baggy. She hoped it hid the gun well enough. She hoped the waistband was tight enough to hold the gun in place.

She especially hoped she didn't accidentally shoot herself in the ass.

She left her phone on the counter.

I will never wear pants or shorts without pockets again, Michelle thought.

As she took a step toward the living room, glass of Pellegrino in hand, her phone skittered on the counter. A text.

:D

That was it.

Fuck you, Gary, she thought.

Back in the living room, Carlene still sat on the couch, texting on her big phone . . . no, not texting. Playing a game, it sounded like. As Michelle drew closer, she saw that it was something that involved cartoon birds.

"Sorry," she said, putting the glass down on the wood veneer coffee table. "I thought there might be a can of Coke in the back of the fridge, but there wasn't. I brought you some sparkling water. Just in case you're thirsty."

"Thanks."

Carlene picked up the glass and took a sip. Her lips puckered, like she'd sucked on a lemon. Maybe because there was no sugar in it. "I should probably get going," she said. "It's past my bedtime."

"Oh. Sure. I'll be right back."

Michelle pulled the blue canvas suitcase out of the bedroom closet and slid the mirrored door shut.

Gary had to have sent Carlene, as unlikely as it seemed. If he was going to LOL in response to her questions, what else was she supposed to do but hand over the money?

Besides, this wasn't her money. As tempting as it was to think about keeping it, about running away with it, it wasn't hers, and nothing good could come from keeping it.

"Here you go," she said as she wheeled the suitcase out to the living room. "You need help with this out to your car?"

"Maybe getting it into the trunk," Carlene said. "I have a bad back."

MICHELLE HEAVED THE SUITCASE into the trunk of Carlene's car, a late-model silver Hyundai with a bumper sticker that said OWNED BY A PUG. After that, she stood by the door for a moment as Carlene slammed the trunk shut.

"Thanks for coming out on such short notice," Michelle said.

"Not a problem. Just doing my job." Carlene gave her one last, unblinking look. "That's a not a very good way to carry," she said.

My back's fine, Michelle thought, and I lifted with my legs.

And then she got it. The gun tucked into the waist of her yoga pants, pressing against her back.

"Yeah," she said. "You're right. Thanks."

Chapter Twelve

✣

"I don't know, hon, where do you think we should stay?"

"Well, it depends on what you like," Michelle said.

She and Caitlin sat in the Great Room at Caitlin's house, Michelle with her Safer America-issued laptop, a tiny Sony VAIO. It was just after 3 p.m., which meant that Caitlin had opened a bottle of wine. Another chardonnay, which seemed to be her go-to.

Maybe I can get her into sauvignon blanc, Michelle thought, or a good rosé or even vinho verde. Something light and crisp for a horribly hot day like today.

But that wasn't why Caitlin was drinking, was it?

She'd arrived at ten this morning per Caitlin's instructions to find that Caitlin was still in bed.

"Is she okay?" Michelle had asked Esperanza.

"Sometimes she just sleeps late," Esperanza had replied, with an eloquent shrug. "You know . . . she doesn't always feel so good."

When Caitlin finally did show up, just after 11:30, her face looked puffy, her eyelids swollen. "Sorry to keep you waiting. I had a little bit of a migraine."

Maybe she'd kept drinking after Michelle had dropped her off last night. Or maybe she'd just been too depressed to get out of bed. You couldn't be too hard on her for that, Michelle thought. She'd had a few days like that herself, after Tom had died.

"I guess we might as well stay at the Century Plaza," Caitlin said now, leaning back against her beige-wheat couch. "That's where the fundraiser is."

"There's nice hotels in Santa Monica," Michelle found herself saying. "Right by the ocean. It's a really great area with a lot of good restaurants. Maybe you could . . . take a little extra time. Enjoy yourself."

It's not that I really care, she told herself. Caitlin's problems were Caitlin's problems, and Michelle had plenty of her own.

But the way Caitlin looked, the dark circles around her eyes, the slight tremor in her hand . . .

I'm supposed to be taking care of her, Michelle thought, and she doesn't look good at all.

"I know some good yoga classes in that part of town," Michelle said. "Plus there's great hikes, there's the beach . . ."

Caitlin's smile remained in place, but her eyes looked puzzled. Lost.

"You wanted to start working out, right?"

"I suppose I did," Caitlin finally said. "All right." Something in her shifted. Focused. "Why don't you pick the hotel? Arrange an extra day on either end. We'll get started on that."

STUPID, MICHELLE THOUGHT, AS she checked hotel prices and availability on the desktop in Caitlin's office. Really stupid.

She'd lived in Brentwood for seven years. She had friends who lived in Santa Monica. She'd *taken yoga* in Santa Monica.

What were the odds she'd run into someone who knew her?

Maybe she should book a hotel in Beverly Hills.

She shook herself. And thought: So what if someone recognizes me? So what? I'm Michelle again, not Emily. It might be a little awkward, she'd have to trot out Gary's stupid story about traveling around the world to find herself or rekindle her passion for life, or whatever it was she was supposed to have been doing for the last couple of years. But she didn't have to worry about getting arrested.

And her late husband was magically no longer a crook.

The Shore was booked. Too bad, she'd heard great things. It hadn't opened yet when she'd left for her vacation in Mexico.

Emily's phone buzzed. She'd set it to silent, but she could see it light up at the bottom of her purse, see the tiny tremor in the objects around it.

Carrying Emily's phone felt dangerous. Stupid, even. But so did leaving it behind. And this was a phone call she couldn't afford to miss.

Their lawyer, Derek.

She swiped the screen to answer. "Can you hang on a minute?"

Outside, the late afternoon heat felt like plunging into a bowl of hot soup. She made her way to the shade of one of the old oaks.

"So we have a date for the new bail hearing," Derek said. "It's next week, Wednesday."

"Shit, I . . ." she began, then stopped herself.

Won't be in town, she'd almost said. Michelle would be in Los Angeles, babysitting Caitlin for the big fundraiser.

Emily wasn't supposed to be in Houston at all.

Her phone was already slippery with sweat.

"I don't know if I can make it. I . . . my father . . . he's in the hospital, and . . ."

"Understood. Look, don't worry about it. We've got your statement. We've got letters from the fire chief and from a few other businesses about Jeff's ties to the community, what an asset he is. I even got that couple he helped find when he volunteered to fly search and rescue."

Jeff's a standup guy, she heard Bobby say.

"Do you think . . . is that going to be enough? Should I . . . should I try to come? Would that help?"

There was a moment of silence on the other end. "I don't think it'll make a difference one way or another."

"So it doesn't look good." It wasn't a question. She didn't really need to ask.

"I'll be honest with you, Emily. They're a taking a pretty hard line with Jeff. I'm not sure why, given his lack of priors. It may be they want to push us into taking some kind of deal."

"A deal? Like what?"

"Immunity or a reduced sentence in exchange for information. Maybe. They're not showing their cards yet."

She couldn't say what she wanted to say, that she doubted this was why "they" were taking a hard line, that assuming Gary had arranged the bust, the last thing "they" wanted was for Danny to talk.

"And you know, I could be reading the situation incorrectly. I just want to prepare you for the possibility of an outcome we're not going to like."

"Right," she said.

"Emily . . . has anyone contacted you? I mean, any law enforcement agencies, for questioning?"

"Not yet."

"Well, that's good news," he muttered.

"Who should I expect?"

"Most likely, Arcata Police or the DEA. It's not clear to me how they're handling this investigation so far."

"What do you mean?"

"I think they're still scrambling to put the pieces together. Jeff's arrest . . . it didn't happen because of a long investigation, as far as I know. There was a confidential informant involved, and we won't have access to his or her identity until a week before the trial."

Not Gary. He wouldn't put himself directly on the line like that. Most likely someone he or another intermediary had paid off.

"Okay," she finally said. "Keep me posted. And . . . tell Jeff to call me. Okay? Can you do that?"

She couldn't call him. The jail didn't allow it. He had to call her, collect.

"Marisol's seeing him tomorrow. I'll make sure she tells him."

THE NEXT DAY, THURSDAY, she left work a few hours early, bought a car, and opened two bank accounts.

She didn't want to keep the rental—she'd bet they had some kind of black box tracking device in it. Using the Safer America car for anything other than Safer America business was out of the question.

She took a cab to a used car lot on Southwest Freeway, not too far from the hotel where she'd stayed her first night here, when she'd come to visit Danny in jail.

She picked out an eight-year-old silver Toyota Corolla that had about 60,000 miles on it. $9,500, plus tax and registration. Something you wouldn't notice.

"So, let's talk financing." They sat in a tiny beige office. The salesman, a young guy with a thatch of blond hair, leaned over his veneer desk. High-school athlete, Michelle thought, whose shoulders strained against a wrinkled blue button-down shirt that was damp with sweat.

"That won't be necessary."

She got out an envelope she'd earlier stuffed with cash and counted out the bills.

The salesman took in the stack of money. Sat back with raised eyebrows and gave her a lopsided grin. "That's a lot of cash."

She smiled back. "Babysitting money."

AT THE FIRST BANK, one in River Oaks not far from Tootsie's, she opened a checking and a savings account, depositing $3,000 in checking and $3,000 in savings. She could have her paychecks direct-deposited here. Her official bank.

For the second, she drove out to a bank near George Bush Intercontinental Airport. Opened a checking account under Emily's name with $2,000 and rented a safe-deposit box, where she stashed another $9,000.

"How about a savings account?" the teller asked.

"Maybe later," Michelle said. "After I've saved a little up."

THAT LEFT CLOSE TO $25,000 in her apartment.

It wasn't ideal. But none of this was ideal, was it? Gary could easily find out where she'd opened bank accounts. Could have that money taken away as quickly as she'd deposited it.

Probably quicker.

Sitting in evening traffic in her silver Toyota, she asked

herself what the point of all this was. Opening different bank accounts, packing a go-bag, would any of that really help?

She had the money for now, was promised more, but could she hold onto it?

Would Gary really let her walk away from this situation?

Would he let Danny go?

The freeway was a sea of red lights. Barely crawling.

DANNY DIDN'T CALL. NOT that night. Not the next day.

Caitlin had a Friday morning appointment at the hairdresser, she'd told Michelle on Thursday, as she topped off her first glass of chardonnay, "So there's no need for you to rush on in."

Michelle went to the gym in her complex first thing Friday morning after a cup of coffee. It wasn't a very good gym. Most of the space was taken up by a couple of machines, a cable setup, two treadmills, an elliptical trainer and a recumbent Lifecycle, but there was a rack of dumbbells, two bars and some plates, a good enough bench, a set of bands and a couple of fitness balls. Enough for her to come up with a decent workout and clear her head with sweat.

After that, she stood outside the gym on the lumpy common lawn that smelled vaguely of dog shit and called Marisol Acosta.

"I saw him, and he's fine," Marisol said. "He's in good spirits. And he told me to tell you not to worry."

"Did you tell him to call me?"

A pause. "Yes, I did."

"He hasn't yet."

"Well . . . I really think it's just because he doesn't want you to worry."

Her heart started to race in her chest, and she wasn't sure if what she felt was anger, or panic.

"Tell him that not talking to me is what's worrying me. Okay? Tell him that."

"I will," Marisol said. "I promise." Another pause. "Do you have a landline?"

"A landline? No. I mean . . ."

Michelle didn't have a landline. Emily did, back in Arcata. Which did her no good at all here in Houston. "I'm running around so much, I'm not close to a landline most of the time."

"That might be why you haven't heard from him."

"He can't call my cell?"

"He can, but you'll need to go to Securus and set up an Advance Pay account. It's pretty easy. They have a website."

"Securus?"

"The company that runs the prison phone system. They've got contracts all over the country." A dry chuckle. "I'm guessing they make good money, from the amount they charge for those calls."

HE FINALLY CALLED ON Sunday afternoon, while Michelle was packing her bags for Los Angeles.

An automated phone tree called, rather, that same flat, cheerful woman's voice that was always sorry when you spoke and it "didn't get that," and asked if she was willing to accept a collect call from an inmate at Harris County Jail.

"Hey."

"Hey."

She sat down on the edge of the bed, her Armani jacket spread on her lap. She could hear noise in the background, men's voices, shouting, laughing, what sounded like metal doors slamming, now and again.

Now that he'd called, she didn't know what to say.

"How are you doing?" she finally asked.

"Okay. You? Things are good?"

She couldn't actually tell him anything. Couldn't tell him where she was, what she'd been doing, where she was going. These phone calls were monitored, and not just if you had a Gary in your life.

"You know, it's complicated. But I'm okay. Keeping busy."

He snorted. "Yeah, I figured."

He got it. God knows, if she told him the story of how she got her first $50,000 payoff, he'd probably nod, roll his eyes and say, "Fucking Gary."

That Gary, such a crack-up.

"Did you get a hold of . . . ?"

Sam. He had to mean Sam. "Yeah. He's looking into it."

"Good. Thanks."

What could she tell him might actually help?

"I'm sorry I can't come to the hearing," she said.

"Don't be. Look." A long, drawn-out exhale. "You don't need to be anywhere near this. I don't want you to. Just . . ."

He couldn't say what he wanted to either.

"I really think you should take a break from all this, Em. You've got other stuff on your plate. Me and the lawyers can handle my situation. You need to take care of yourself."

Was this code? Was it truth? She didn't know.

Maybe it was a particularly awkward breakup.

"Okay, I don't know how you're feeling right now, but the reality is, we're *both* in this situation. I can't just . . . run away and take a vacation from it."

Her words came out on a rush of irritation. The two of them were stuck together, whether he wanted to be or not, and even if he'd said it because he cared about her, practically, it made no sense.

She wasn't going to outrun Gary on her own.

Silence.

"Yeah," he finally said. "I hear that. Just . . . take care. Okay?"

"Okay."

Was there something else she should say?

"You too."

Chapter Thirteen

✦

Los Angeles.

Stepping outside from baggage claim, she saw and felt it: the unmistakable quality of the light, that stretched-out, faded blue, the air that wasn't desert dry but still slightly astringent.

She scanned the curb for the town car that was supposed to pick them up.

"Does it feel good to be home?"

Michelle turned. Caitlin stood slightly behind her, hand resting protectively on her suitcase, which sat on the luggage cart.

They could have done without the cart, really; the things cost $4.00, and Caitlin's wheeled suitcase wasn't even that big. But Caitlin had insisted. "Oh, hon, I don't feel like dragging that thing around. Let's just get a cart." She'd drunk a few glasses of wine on the plane, and Michelle suspected she'd also taken whatever it was she took for anxiety; she had that blurred quality to her, like a charcoal drawing that the artist had slightly smeared.

Michelle smiled. "It's nice to be back."

She wasn't really sure that it was.

LA wasn't her home anymore; she was sure of that.

MICHELLE HAD BOOKED THEM at Shutters, because Caitlin had wanted something special, and because it was on the beach. She'd been reluctant to book herself in a place that expensive, but Caitlin insisted. "It wouldn't make much sense for you to be at a different hotel. Besides, this is a special occasion." She'd smiled. "I'm going to get started on those changes I need to make."

Now they stood in the lobby, wood, and leather and brocaded couches with striped pillows, all very Cape Cod. The whole hotel looked like that, wood with light gray siding, white balconies and dark gray slate roofs, like they'd shipped it from the Hamptons.

"Oh, this is lovely," Caitlin said.

"It has a spa and a nice gym, and a restaurant with a really great wine list. Plus there's all kinds of places we can walk to from here."

"Now, I thought nobody walks in LA," Caitlin said, with an obligatory laugh.

Michelle forced a smile. Nearly every out of towner she ever encountered seemed compelled to make that joke. "Well, this area's a little different."

"Why don't we change and go get a glass of that wine?" Caitlin said. "Maybe take a little walk on the beach." She laughed, this time with an edge of embarrassment, or at least it seemed that way to Michelle. "I don't think I'm ready for yoga today."

"Sure," Michelle said. It was almost 4:30. She was tired, aching, and though yoga would do her a world of good, a glass of wine sounded better. Easier, anyway.

THE GLASS ENDED UP being two.

"Oh, this is so nice," Caitlin said. It wasn't the first time she'd said it. But though repeating herself could be a sign of too much wine and whatever else Caitlin had taken, Michelle had to admit, it was very nice.

She'd forgotten what it was like, being in places like this.

They sat out on a terrace with a view of the beach and the ocean stretching to the horizon, the sky streaked with clouds glowing from the late afternoon sun. She'd ordered a glass of sauvignon blanc; Caitlin stuck to her chardonnay. They'd also ordered a few small plates: roasted baby vegetables, charcuterie and cheese. Watching Caitlin eat, Michelle could see how she stayed so thin in her late thirties without getting much exercise: she hardly ate anything. Most of her calories were in wine.

"So, for the event tomorrow," Michelle began. They had barely discussed it.

Caitlin did her dismissive wave. "There'll be drinks and hors d'oeuvres, people will mingle, we'll have dinner. Then speeches and presentations. Lord, I hope it doesn't go on too long."

"And you're speaking."

"Yeah." She sighed. "The usual heart-rending appeal." She drained her glass, and lifted her hand to call the waiter.

"It sounds like you're a little tired of it," Michelle said cautiously.

Caitlin shrugged. "Well, what else am I going to do with myself?"

"Ladies, can I get you another round?" The waiter had appeared, a young man with sandy hair who Michelle would bet had a headshot.

"Absolutely." Caitlin beamed at him. "How about you, Michelle?"

"Well, if we want to take a walk . . ."

"Look how high the sun is. We have time for another glass."

BY THE TIME THEY reached the boardwalk, the streaky clouds were turning a watercolor wash of pink, orange and yellow. Beach cruisers, rollerbladers and skateboarders wheeled by. The air was soft, moist, with a snap of salt and kelp.

Caitlin took in a deep breath. Smiled. "If this doesn't look like a TV commercial."

"They do film a lot of them here," Michelle said. "Is this your first visit?"

Caitlin laughed. "Oh, no. I've been out to LA more times than I can count. We've actually got a condo in San Diego." She paused for a moment and gazed out toward the water. "*I* do, I mean."

"I'm sorry," Michelle said without thinking. Without stopping herself from saying it.

"Yeah, I know. Everyone is." Caitlin stared at the horizon. "It's a funny thing. I keep waiting to feel better. Four years out. I don't, really." She turned to Michelle. "Do you?"

"I . . ."

What could she say? That her loss didn't come close to Caitlin's?

That she hadn't loved Tom?

I did once, she told herself. I really did.

But it was the betrayal that had hurt, that she couldn't confront him with because he was already gone, the anger that she hadn't been able to let go of.

Until she'd met Danny.

"I do," she said. "But I don't think it's the same. What you had . . ." She shuddered.

That everything you had could be taken away in an instant, she understood that.

"Losing a child . . . I can't imagine that."

"I wish you could've met him," Caitlin said. "Alex. He was . . . he was such a fun kid. Happy. He was obsessed with trucks. He knew all the models. He'd shout them out when we were driving. 'Peterbuilt!' That was his favorite." She laughed. "I think he mostly just liked yelling 'Peterbuilt.' I'd buy him Hot Wheels, Legos, Tonka Trucks . . . his room looked like a toy truck stop. Except without the lot lizards." She laughed again.

Why did Gary think I'd be good at this, Michelle thought? What was she supposed to do? Give Caitlin a hug? Offer words about how God must have wanted an angel? It was horrible, and tragic, and senseless, and there were no good words, no comfort she knew how to give.

"I took all the family pictures down. At the house." Caitlin was no longer smiling. "I just couldn't look at them anymore. Sometimes I feel like I'd be better off if I couldn't remember them at all."

Michelle thought about it and realized that she'd never seen a photo of Caitlin's husband or son at the house in River Oaks. The place was so carefully decorated it felt like a set, as opposed to a home. But she hadn't found that particularly unusual. A lot of people she'd known in LA kept their houses that way. The personal stuff was elsewhere, in a bedroom or family room, maybe. Offstage.

"You know what's funny?" Caitlin said suddenly. "All the times I've been here, I've never put my feet in the water."

Michelle felt a wave of relief. This was something she could handle. "Well, why don't we take care of that?"

⚘ ⚘ ⚘

THE BEACHES IN VENICE and Santa Monica were very wide. Michelle thought she recalled reading that this breadth was artificial, created by dredging and massive amounts of sand brought in from elsewhere. But she wasn't sure.

The two of them shuffled through the deep sand to the water's edge, where the sand was packed and wet. The sun was low now, breaking through the bank of clouds hanging offshore. A runner jogged by. A half-dozen people did yoga on the flat sand, a class, it looked like. She could hear the congas and the bongos of the Venice drum circle in the distance, celebrating the sunset.

She thought about the day she'd met Danny, on the beach in Puerto Vallarta. She'd had a couple of margaritas. The two of them had a few more. It was the kind of thing you did on a vacation, wasn't it? Meet a good-looking stranger. Have some drinks. Go back to your hotel room together.

She shivered now, thinking about it. She'd been lonely. Drunk. Just wanting someone to make her feel good.

So incredibly foolish.

On the other hand, it wasn't all that much to ask for. Was it?

And to be fair, Danny hadn't wanted trouble either, had no idea he'd tangled her up in Gary's game. He was just looking for a good time. Maybe he'd even been lonely too, like she had been. She'd never asked.

Danny, you asshole, she thought. Sure, Gary would've figured out another angle, but Danny had made it so easy.

Why did he have to take stupid risks? Like he needed the buzz?

How was he doing right now?

Caitlin exhaled with an audible sigh. Kicked off her Tory Burch thong sandals. Scrunched her toes into the sand.

"Tell me why I stay in Houston again?"

"I . . . the weather?"

Caitlin threw back her head and laughed. A studied gesture, maybe. But this was still the liveliest Michelle had ever seen her.

"I don't know, maybe I'll just pack up the house and retire to my condo out here. Just . . . start over."

Seeing Caitlin, her face lit up by the orange glow of the sunset like some illuminated renaissance painting, Michelle wished she had her camera. It was a beautiful shot.

She felt a sudden rush of protectiveness. It surprised her. She hadn't gotten into this expecting to care. Not about Caitlin. But whatever Gary had in mind for Safer America, she couldn't assume that Caitlin was safe.

More realistic to assume the opposite.

But what could she do about it?

"Is there something stopping you?" she asked.

"Just laziness, I guess. Starting over in a new place . . . what would I do with myself?"

"I don't know. Just . . . be there for a while? You can take some time to figure that out."

"Maybe I will."

Caitlin walked toward the lapping waves, and kept walking until the water was up to her calves. Stood there facing the ocean while the waves surged and ebbed.

She turned back to Michelle. "This is perfect!"

"Watch out," Michelle said.

The sneaker wave rose and crashed into Caitlin's back,

almost knocking her over. Caitlin shrieked, laughing like a five-year-old. She stumbled out of the water, still laughing. "Well, so much for this dress," she said. "And, oh hell, there goes my sandal."

The receding wave had pulled one of her designer flip-flops into the surf, where it bobbed like a toy boat. Hiking up the skirt of her dress, Caitlin waded back into the water and snatched up the sandal. "Well, I wanted to get my feet wet," she said.

By THE TIME THEY got back to the boardwalk, the last light was fading to deep indigo. The hotel was a short distance away, lit up by small white bulbs that looked like oversized Christmas lights.

"So, for tomorrow—"

Caitlin waved her hand. "Really, you don't have to worry about it. Just shadow me and be ready to take down notes if I promise somebody something."

"I mean, do you want to, I don't know, maybe do a little hiking in the morning? Or some yoga? I'm sure the concierge can arrange for a private instructor if you'd like."

"Oh." Caitlin sounded vaguely surprised. "Well, I guess the yoga sounds nice. So long as I don't get so sore I can't get out of my chair at the event."

"Spare some change?"

He was standing under a streetlight. Homeless guy, Michelle thought automatically. Skinny, wearing a filthy T-shirt and torn pants, face caked with black grime and crusted sores. She shook her head and turned to go.

"A few dollars so I can get something to eat?"

"Sorry," Caitlin said. "I don't have anything."

He stared at her. "You don't have anything? *You don't have anything?*" He started laughing.

Michelle put her hand on Caitlin's arm. "Come on," she said. "Let's go."

"Fuck you, you stupid bitch. Fuck you!" He took a few steps toward them, face bright with rage, his hands balled into fists, driving his fists into his thighs. "I've got something. I've got something for you. You want it in your pussy? You want it up your ass? You fucking filthy cunt, I'll fuck you till you bleed!"

Michelle raised her arms, palms out, legs braced, the defensive posture she'd been taught that said she wasn't going to start anything, but she was ready if she had to.

He was probably harmless. Most of them were.

"You don't want to get into trouble, do you?" she said to him. "We're going now." She took a sideways step toward the hotel.

Caitlin didn't move.

"Caitlin. Let's go."

Caitlin nodded rapidly. "I'm sorry," she said, to Michelle or to the man, Michelle wasn't sure which.

Michelle steered Caitlin behind her. "Don't worry. Just walk away. I've got your back."

She could hear Caitlin's rapid breathing behind her. She took a few steps backward, shielding Caitlin, watching the man clench and unclench his fists.

Then his arms went limp, flopping down like that part of him had died.

"I'm sorry," Caitlin said in her ear.

As Michelle guided Caitlin up the path, she glanced back over her shoulder at the homeless man. He stood there, shuffling back and forth from one foot to the other, muttering to himself, his arms flapping feebly against his thighs.

"I FEEL SO STUPID." There was a tremor in Caitlin's hand as she picked up her wine glass.

"Don't. That was pretty disturbing."

They sat in the hotel lobby now, on one of the overstuffed couches. Anything Michelle had wanted to say about how as a part of a new beginning maybe Caitlin shouldn't drink so much, she set aside for another time.

Hell, *she* wanted a glass of wine at this point.

For all that she'd read about what had happened to Caitlin, that she'd been raped, that her husband had been murdered, that her child had died . . .

Rape. What woman didn't think about that? Fear it? Calculate the odds of it? Sometimes say "yes" because it felt less risky to say than to say no?

The violent death of someone you loved . . . of your child . . .

Of course, she understood those things. She knew what they meant. But she'd kept those thoughts abstract. At a distance.

Seeing Caitlin's reaction just now . . .

She hadn't really gotten it before.

"No, you were right," Caitlin said with a sigh. "He was a crazy guy. He wasn't going to do anything. I just . . . I just get nervous sometimes."

"I think we should do some yoga tomorrow morning, it's a great way to get more centered."

Michelle could hear the frantic edge in her own voice. She hoped that Caitlin couldn't.

She had to stay calm. Had to keep it together. She couldn't afford to think about what had happened to Caitlin.

Couldn't afford to think about the things that had happened in Mexico.

She couldn't let herself feel those feelings, not now. There was too much at stake for her to lose it, too much at stake for her and for Danny.

For Caitlin.

If I tell her what's going on, Michelle thought, would that help? Could Caitlin handle it? Would she believe it?

How could I even begin to explain? she thought.

And if Gary found out . . .

Michelle smiled. Sipped her wine. "Maybe we should schedule a massage after yoga. It might help you relax a little."

Chapter Fourteen

⚑

YOU COULDN'T CALL CENTURY City a neighborhood. It was a business district, built on the former 20th Century Fox Studio's backlot, which the company had to sell when *Cleopatra* bombed at the box office. There were very few reasons to go to Century City if you didn't work there. Lunch at the Fox Lot, a screening at CAA, dinner at Craft, maybe, but there were nicer parts of town to eat expensive meals. There was the Century City Mall, but it was just a mall like any other mall, and Michelle had generally gone to Santa Monica when she needed to pick up a couple of T-shirts from J. Crew or a mascara from Sephora.

The Century Plaza was a hotel that Michelle associated with presidential visits, foreign affairs lectures, conventions and fundraisers. Not a place where anyone she knew from out of town actually stayed.

If you had a meeting on the Fox Lot or CAA, maybe.

Or if you were a part of Safer America's fundraiser, like board member Matthew Moss.

She'd been right about him being a talking head, a cultural commentator. He hadn't been that well-known, back when she used to pay more attention to such things. And he wasn't anyone you could call "famous" now. He didn't have his own cable show, or anything like that. But she'd done a little Googling and found that he was a regular guest on those cable shows and a columnist who'd gotten his start on a popular blog.

"Hello," he said now. "Michelle, isn't it?"

She nodded. "Nice to see you again." Which was a lie. He stood too close, a bulky man who radiated heat in an expensive suit. Sweat glistened at his forehead. Up this close, his hair looked even more like a plastic fiber helmet.

"You look very sharp tonight," he said, slowly sweeping his gaze up and down.

She told herself to smile. It wasn't like she'd dressed to attract any attention. She was wearing her black Armani suit, because it was LA, and when in doubt, wear black, and she was barely showing any cleavage.

"Why, thanks! So do you."

He snorted. "My wife dresses me. I'm pretty sure I'd be helpless without her."

She took a step back. The banquet room was crowded, but not so crowded that he needed to stand this close.

"Oh," Michelle said. "Well, she does a great job. Is she here tonight?"

"No. She's more the stay-at-home type." He continued to stare at her, with a fixed smile. As plastic as his hair. "Speaking of, how's our little leader?"

"You mean Caitlin? She's great. We've had a really nice day."

This was not entirely a lie. She'd arranged a private yoga session for Caitlin in the morning, not too early, then a "healing organic red-flower therapeutic massage followed by a smoothing sea-salt exfoliation and hydrating sea-algae masque."

Caitlin seemed to like it.

"I'm so relaxed," she'd said to Michelle over a sushi lunch on Ocean Boulevard. She'd actually eaten something for a change, and only had one glass of chardonnay.

And she'd reached out across the sushi bar, and grasped Michelle's hand. "Thank you," she'd said. "Thanks for, I don't know . . . giving me a little push."

Thinking about it now, Michelle felt a sick, acid churn in her stomach.

Caitlin had latched onto her hand, and Michelle feared she was leading her someplace very, very bad.

"Good to hear," Moss said. "She's one brave little lady."

MICHELLE FOUND THE BRAVE little lady over at the bar.

"Oh, hi," Caitlin said. "What do you want to drink?"

Michelle very much wanted something to drink. But that wasn't a good idea. Not right now. "Just a Pellegrino," she said.

Caitlin did her little wave, with more emphasis than usual. "Come on, I'm not gonna judge. There's not that much for you to do, anyway. Just shadow me when we're mingling and take down any names of people I talk to. Not that I really wanna talk to any of them." She laughed. "I just wanna do my talking-dog act and get the hell out of here." She took a slug of her wine and laughed again, more loudly this time. "You know that joke about the talking dog? It doesn't have to talk well. It's just that it talks at all."

Had she already had more than one drink? A pill? Something? She'd seemed okay when they'd ridden over to Century City from Santa Monica, if somewhat quiet and distant, wearing one of her beautiful white and beige outfits that threatened to blend her into the furniture. Pre-event jitters, Michelle had assumed.

They'd arrived at the Century Plaza some fifteen minutes after the event had officially begun, in the Constellation Room on the Plaza level. "I need to go check in with the event coordinator," Michelle had told Caitlin. "Are you going to be okay, is there anything I can get you?"

The little wave, weak this time. "No, I'm fine. Go do what you need to do."

She'd gone, found the coordinator, a stringy, slightly frantic woman named Cyndee, who Michelle was pretty sure had been in one of her Pilates classes a few years ago, but she wasn't about to bring that up.

"Okay," Cyndee had said, "So, here's the schedule, we do cocktails and mingling till seven, then salad, we'll have the introduction from Perry Aisles, Matthew Moss for the main course, and Caitlin O'Connor for dessert. Then Perry comes up and closes the deal."

"Sounds good."

Cyndee's oversized eyes darted around the room. "Everything looks great, don't you think? Fantastic turnout."

Doing a quick count of the tables, Michelle had estimated the crowd at around or over three hundred people, close to capacity for this room. Good enough. Men in suits, women in cocktail dresses. An older crowd, mostly, and very white.

They'd hung huge plastic banners around the room, photos of smiling multi-ethnic children's faces, mostly, with the occasional suburban home and green lawn and more little kids running through sprinklers and riding little bikes with big training wheels, the words A SAFER AMERICA written across every other panel. Floral centerpieces, white chrysanthemums in blue and red bunting, decorated the tables.

"It looks great. Excuse me—I'd better get back to Caitlin."

She hadn't been gone that long, maybe fifteen, twenty minutes between the conversations with Cyndee and Moss. But here was Caitlin, apparently already on her second glass of wine, and not scheduled to speak for another hour at least.

"Come on, let me get you something," Caitlin said. "Believe me, you don't want to try and get through one of these things sober."

"I'm going to need to keep my hands free to take notes," Michelle said. "While you're mingling. We still have half an hour before dinner starts."

Caitlin sighed. "You know, the last thing I want to do is talk to any of these people. And I'm not in any kind of mood to hear Matthew go on and on the way he does. Let's go downstairs and get a drink."

"You *have* a drink, Caitlin," Michelle snapped.

For a moment, Caitlin stood there, wine glass in hand, staring at Michelle like she'd been slapped.

She put the glass down on the bar.

"Not any more." Caitlin made a face and smiled, like a kid who knew she'd been bad but figured she could get away with it. "It wasn't very good, anyway." She put her hand on Michelle's arm. "Tell you what. I just want to get out of here for a few minutes. Get some air. I promise I'll be back in time for dinner, even if that means I have to listen to Matthew. You don't have to come with me."

Oh yes I do, Michelle thought.

"I'll come," she said. "I wouldn't mind some air."

❧   ❧   ❧

ON THE WAY OUT, they passed Cyndee, who stood by the sign-up table at the entrance to the banquet hall. An older man wearing an expensive suit was there, signing a check with a flourish. "In case I have to leave early," he said, presenting it a volunteer who sat behind the table. Michelle couldn't read his name or the amount, but she was pretty sure she saw a lot of zeros.

"Oh, hi, this is Caitlin?" Cyndee asked. "I'm such an admirer of yours!"

"That's so sweet of you, hon," Caitlin said, meeting her eyes and clasping her hand for a moment, before heading out the door.

Michelle could see now that Caitlin had that particular gift, the ability to connect with someone in an instant, and then break apart without a backwards glance.

"Where is she going . . . is everything okay?" The tendons in Cyndee's neck looked ready to snap.

"Fine," Michelle said. "Just fine. She needs some air, that's all. We'll be back in a few minutes."

"But the donors—"

"There'll be plenty of time for them to talk to her, I promise."

She hoped there would be, anyway.

THE CENTURY PLAZA HAD an outdoor bar off the lobby, with round tables and dark wicker furniture and overstuffed earth-tone pillows, illuminated by warm-hued lanterns. "Just one drink, I promise," Caitlin said. "As long as you join me."

"Okay." Better to have one drink with Caitlin if that kept her from having two, Michelle figured. She hoped that wasn't just a rationalization. The drink was tempting.

They sat at a small table next to a low wall made from stacked wooden cubes that separated the bar from the gardens and reflecting pool. Faux votive candles sat in the wall's open-air alcoves. Flattering light all around, Michelle noted.

"Just a glass of red wine," she told the waiter.

"Pinot, merlot, cabernet, zin?"

"How's the pinot?"

"I'd do the cab."

"I'll have that too," Caitlin said.

After the waiter left, they sat in silence. Michelle wasn't sure what there was to say. Did she owe Caitlin an apology? She didn't think so, but she hadn't exactly been the deferential employee back there in the ballroom.

And what she said . . . it had all kinds of implications. Inferences.

"Look, there's something that you're gonna have to trust me about," Caitlin finally said. "I realize I'm not . . . I don't take care of myself as well as I should, and I know I have to change that. But this?" She gestured toward the hotel lobby. "I know how to do this."

"I'm sorry," Michelle began. "I was—"

"Don't apologize. I know why you're here."

For a moment, Michelle froze in her chair. She couldn't know. Could she?

"You're here to make sure I don't get into any trouble. Maybe help me clean up my act. Look, part of that was my idea anyway. I understand, you're just doing your job."

The waiter appeared with their wine.

"Enjoy, ladies!" he said, depositing their glasses in front of them.

Caitlin lifted up her glass. "Just realize that I know how to do mine."

Michelle raised hers. What else could she do? They clinked.

"You know what I don't know?" Caitlin said with a sigh. "Whether I want to keep doing it."

They'd worked together how long, a little over a week? And how many times had Caitlin already said that she was feeling ambivalent about Safer America?

Were those doubts important? Was that why Gary wanted her here?

Why would it matter if Caitlin stepped away from Safer America?

For some reason, Michelle thought of the check she'd seen upstairs, the one with multiple zeros. Safer America was on track to earn $37 million dollars this year, hadn't Debbie said that, back at the board meeting?

It was always about money.

Caitlin was the draw. The rainmaker. If she quit, would Safer America raise as much money?

Maybe Gary and the Boys got a cut somehow. Maybe it was some kind of money-laundering scheme, where Safer America was taking in money that wasn't exactly clean, freshening it up, and funneling it to some CIA shell company that was "off the books."

Did that make sense, or was it something simpler?

Our donation.

Those tattooed Mexican mobsters buying some guns and throwing in over $900K extra . . .

Some of that money had been her payment. Where had Carlene taken the rest of it?

Maybe it really was a donation.

A drug cartel wouldn't favor marijuana legalization, would it?

And the Boys were all about buying elections, from what Danny had told her.

"Michelle, are you all right?"

"I'm fine. Sorry. I was just, just thinking about what we have to do tonight."

"Oh, trust me, it's easy. We talk, we drink, we eat, we talk some more. And then we take their money." Caitlin grinned, and tilted her wine glass to her lips.

"Excuse me."

A deep, male voice. Michelle turned.

A big black man in a rust-colored suit and black shirt. Shaved head.

"I'm sorry to interrupt. Are you Caitlin O'Connor?"

Caitlin hesitated. Michelle could see her shrink back into her seat. Then she straightened up and nodded. "I am."

The man stuck out his hand. A big hand, like a basketball player's.

God, stop thinking in clichés, Michelle told herself.

Besides, he really looked more like a football player: muscular, solid, a little thick through the middle.

Caitlin took his hand, with that same hesitation she'd shown before. Her hand was dwarfed in his. He handled her hand gently, Michelle thought. Not a squeeze, just letting it rest there a moment.

"I'm Troy Stone. I was really hoping to meet you tonight."

"Oh," Caitlin said, with a sort of brightness that sounded more studied than sincere. "Are you coming to the event?"

He let out a chuckle. "Not exactly. I'm with PCA. Positive Community Action."

"I think I've heard of you," Caitlin said distantly.

"I'm not surprised. Though we've been playing opposite ends of the field, it seems like."

He crouched down next to Caitlin. Michelle could see him better now. His face was all planes joined at sharp angles. She hadn't thought he was handsome at first glance, but his eyes were nice, she thought: big, dark and expressive. Now they were focused on Caitlin.

"I'd really like to talk to you about your efforts here in California. I've heard a lot of what you have to say, and I think we want the same things. We just have different ideas of how to go about it."

"Very different ideas, from what I understand."

Caitlin's body language—sitting back in her chair, arms crossed—was clear. She wanted nothing to do with him.

He shifted on his haunches, like something was hurting him, and then he held very still.

"Mrs. O'Connor . . . I've lost people too."

They stared at each other. Michelle had the oddest feeling just then, that she'd somehow intruded on a private moment.

"All right," Caitlin said abruptly, uncrossing her arms. Still watchful. "There's no reason we can't talk. Michelle, would you make sure to get Mr. Stone's contact information? We'll set up a time."

"Now, in the months coming up, you're gonna hear a lot of talk."

Matthew Moss stood at the podium. He'd been talking for a while. In her seat at Table #1, Michelle was close enough to see him sweat.

"You're gonna hear talk about how pot is harmless. You're

gonna hear talk about how we're sending too many people to prison. You know what they aren't gonna talk about?"

He paused. Put both his hands on the podium. Leaned forward.

"How since we got tougher on crime, crime rates in the US have gone down. Way down."

Michelle watched a bead of sweat roll down his forehead, getting caught on his eyebrow.

"What we've done is made America safer. And anyone who tells you otherwise? Is either deluded, a criminal . . . Or a *poverty pimp*."

If that was one of his catchphrases, he really ought to practice saying it in front of a microphone without popping his Ps, Michelle thought.

"There are people out there who profit from keeping poor people down. From keeping them dependent on big government. On handouts from Uncle Sugar. *Poverty pimps*." He laughed. "You know what they *don't* want? They don't want people helping themselves. Working their way up. Taking responsibility for their own actions. Because if that happened? They'd all be out of a job!"

Polite laughter.

Did the people in this crowd really buy any of this? Michelle wondered. They seemed to be willing to write big, fat checks for it.

"All this talk about how we need to put fewer people in jail, well, I do agree with that. But I disagree with how we make that happen. We don't let criminals go free." He slapped the podium. The low, hollow thud echoed through the ballroom. "We demand people take responsibility for their own actions. We examine cultural dysfunctions, honestly, without letting special interests and politically correct garbage get in the way." He slapped the podium again. "Why aren't we talking about black-on-black violence? Why isn't anyone willing to look honestly at that?"

Next to her, Caitlin sighed. She leaned over to Michelle. "Honey, can you pass me some of that wine?"

Michelle really didn't want to. If she'd counted correctly, Caitlin had polished off four glasses already. And as usual, she hadn't eaten much, though the dinner was several cuts above the usual banquet fare—the poached Skuna Bay salmon with red quinoa and ratatouille from local vegetables wasn't half-bad, Michelle had thought.

"You don't agree?" Michelle asked. "With what he's saying?"

"Well, there's some of truth to it, of course," Caitlin said quickly. "It's just that . . . I've heard it so many times before." A slight hesitation. "Let's just say I think he oversimplifies. And frankly?" She leaned in closer. "He's such an asshole."

Michelle couldn't entirely repress a snort.

"Now how about that wine? Just a half a glass. I promise." Caitlin grinned. "And you can drag me to another yoga class in the morning."

"You don't want to go to jail?" Another podium slap. "Don't break the law. It's that simple."

"Well, let's get this over with." Caitlin pushed her Swiss Black Forest cake aside, braced her hands on the edge of the table and stood. She hadn't been announced yet, but it was time for her to take her position by the podium for her introduction. Perry Aisles, the bundler who was the official "host" of the event, had already risen from his seat, and he was the one introducing Caitlin.

Was she okay? Michelle wasn't sure. She had that frail, faded look that Michelle had seen before.

Michelle stood too. "I'll walk you up."

"Oh, you don't need to come," Caitlin said, with her usual wave. "Sit down and enjoy your dessert."

"I don't really eat dessert."

Caitlin laughed. "Of course you don't."

"It's better if I come with you. I might need to, to take notes."

Her stomach was in knots, and she wasn't sure why.

Nothing was going to happen here, was it?

Caitlin laid a hand on Michelle's arm. "You're sweet. Come if you'd like, but I'll be fine."

"I CAN'T EVEN BEGIN to express how much I admire this woman . . ."

Aisles was a TV producer who had made his bones on police procedurals dealing with serial killers. Sixty-ish, close-cropped hair, thin and as tanned as leather, looking like an aging surfer in a designer suit.

". . . whose bravery, courage and commitment is why we're all here tonight."

Wasn't that redundant? Michelle thought.

"Ladies and gentlemen, Caitlin O'Connor."

CAITLIN LOOKED SO SMALL up on the podium.

People applauded. She glanced at them briefly and smiled. Took a moment to adjust the microphone. Then picked up a couple pages of notes and appeared to study them.

She put the notes on the lectern and looked up.

"I'm going to keep this short. I know y'all support what

we're doing. You're here, aren't you? And I so deeply appreciate that."

She wasn't looking at the audience. She seemed to look past them, somewhere just behind them and above their heads.

"Lately I've spent a lot of time thinking about what a Safer America really means. What it might look like. And I can't really see it quite clearly yet."

Now her head tilted down. Focused. First on a table in the front. Then on one next to it, and one behind.

"But what I want y'all to know is, I'm going to keep looking. *We're* going to keep looking."

It was a neat trick, Michelle thought. Caitlin really *was* good at this. You could feel the connection she was making, the way she drew people in.

"We're committed to finding real solutions to America's problems. We're not going to be hemmed in by any partisan straightjackets. We're going to look for answers everywhere, regardless of party, regardless of ideology."

Funny, Michelle thought. You couldn't stop watching her. She was mostly so still, awash in all that cream and beige, and it was as if every small gesture she made had some special significance.

"Y'all have seen what we've managed to accomplish so far. So I'm asking you to have a little faith. I promise you that every dollar you contribute is going to be spent carefully and thoughtfully."

Now Caitlin smiled. Tilted her head and her eyes up. There was something private about the smile. Something that made you want to weep.

"There's no such thing as absolute safety. If there's one thing I've learned, it's that."

She looked at the audience again. "But we can do better. We *must* do better. For our communities. For our kids. For the America they will inherit. If you feel the same way I do, help us get there. Help us build the America of our dreams. It can be done. And it *will* be done. If all of us, together, are willing to work for it."

She bowed her head.

"Thank you."

"See?" Caitlin said, grinning, as Michelle walked her back to their table. "I told you I know how to do this shit."

Chapter Fifteen

✧

DANNY'S HEARING WAS TODAY.

She forgot about that for a while, during yoga. That was one of the reasons she liked yoga, because she could get out of her own head. "Breathe. Breathe." And sweat. Take her body to the edge and then pull back. And this was yoga on the beach, just Michelle, Caitlin and their instructor, feet in the sand, waves pounding in front of them, seagulls and pelicans wheeling in the late morning sky.

She was fine as long as she was moving.

But as soon as they lay down on the packed sand for Corpse Pose at the end of the session, the point where you were supposed to completely relax, sink into the earth and feel nothing, the thought snaked back.

Danny's hearing was in an hour.

Why am I even worrying about it? she thought. Derek could produce letters from half of Humboldt County saying what a great guy Danny was, how much he'd contributed to the community, it wasn't going to make any difference.

They weren't going to let him out.

"That was really fun," Caitlin said, as they scuffed up the beach to the bike path.

"I'm glad you liked it," Michelle said.

"I did. I mean, you know, I used to work out. Do Zumba." She snorted, like the whole notion was too absurd to contemplate. "I need to get back in the habit of doing this kind of thing."

The reasons she'd stopped, the great fracture in her life, seemed to yawn in the air between them.

"Is there anything in particular you'd like to do today? Anything . . . anything I can do?"

"I don't know. Find us a place for lunch, I guess."

They paused at the bike path, waiting for a pair of roller-bladers and a family on rented beach cruisers to pass by.

"Oh, and why don't you see if you can get a hold of that man from, what was it, PCA? The one we met last night."

"Troy Stone?"

"Yeah. Might as well see if he's available. Since he wanted to meet with me."

Caitlin said this casually, but Michelle had a feeling she'd been giving the matter some thought.

Why would Caitlin want to meet with Troy Stone? Was she really interested in what he had to say, when they'd "been playing opposite ends of the field"? By that Michelle figured he was a supporter of the two propositions on the ballot here, to legalize pot and reduce prison sentences for non-violent crimes. The propositions Safer America was raising money to defeat.

We're going to look for answers everywhere, Caitlin had said last night.

Michelle hadn't thought she'd *meant* it.

After seeing the way Caitlin had performed, seeing Caitlin's acknowledgment after her speech that it had in fact been a performance . . .

What did Caitlin really want? Who was she, underneath the performance, underneath the role of tragic victim?

You can't trust her, Michelle told herself. For all you know, she might be part of Gary's game.

"WELL, IT'S NOT GOOD news."

"I didn't expect any."

Why lie?

"Emily, this is far from over," Derek said.

"Just tell me what happened."

She'd slipped outside the hotel and powered up her Emily phone while Caitlin was finishing up a spa treatment before their lunch. Walked to where the sand was deep and powdered and checked for a signal—cell service had always been spotty around here.

Hardly anyone hung out on this middle part of the beach. Most people went down closer to the water, where the sand was packed, or stayed on the boardwalk.

"They denied bail."

"You were expecting something different?"

"To be honest? No. For whatever reason they've really got a hard-on for Jeff. The judge might as well be taking dictation from the prosecution."

She could feel the rage and panic rising up from her gut, taste the acid bile in her throat. She wanted to scream.

Instead she said, "So. Tell me. How is this 'far from over'?"

"Well, there's no trial date yet. They say they need more time to prepare their case."

"And that's good?"

"For us, yes. If they hadn't delayed, I'd be doing it myself."

"Why?"

A moment of silence. Michelle stared at the shoreline.

Was that a dolphin, surfing in the waves? She'd have to get closer to be sure.

"I don't think they want this to go to trial," Derek finally said. "I think they want to make a deal. They're making things rough on Jeff, threatening a long sentence, denying bail, to increase the pressure so he'll take it."

A deal? Was that even possible, with Gary pulling the strings?

"What kind of deal?"

"Well, there's no way to be sure. No one's put anything on the table, yet. But typically, they'll want any information Jeff could provide on the other players involved here. If they can roll up a couple of bigger fish, that might be enough for Jeff to walk. Or at least get a lesser sentence."

How does this make sense? Michelle wanted to ask. There was no way Gary was going to let Danny go if he informed on Bobby and whoever it was who'd bought his cargo. Those people weren't worth anything. Not to Gary.

And the last thing that Gary would want was for Danny to really start talking. About what he knew. About the things he'd done.

She tried to think it through.

Maybe Gary could set Danny up. But maybe he couldn't control what happened after that. Maybe the prosecutors were honest actors, in their own way. Maybe they'd be willing to cut some kind of deal.

She wanted to believe that. But she really didn't.

"You know Jeff," she said. "Not that I think he did anything wrong, but . . . he really values loyalty. So . . . this whole idea that he'd, well, betray other people, if he had any knowledge like that . . ."

"I do know," Derek said. "But I'm telling you, it may be our best option. And I might need you to convince Jeff of that."

Like she had that power. When had Danny ever listened to her?

"Because look, Emily, realistically . . . you're one of the points where they can apply pressure. It's only a matter of time before they do."

"I'll talk to him," she said.

TROY STONE WAS AVAILABLE to meet later that afternoon.

"I'm in Venice," he'd said. "So easy for you to get to. How about Hal's on Abbot Kinney? They have valet parking."

"Do you think . . . is it safe for us to walk down?" Caitlin asked.

The question took Michelle by surprise. "Sure," she said. "It's a nice walk. People come here from all over the world."

"I hate arriving places all in a sweat. But it's not too hot. And the breeze is nice. I just thought . . ." Caitlin hesitated. Her cheeks reddened. "I need to start getting out more. And it's a pretty day."

So they walked. It *was* a pretty day. Most of them were, here. One thing Michelle supposed she missed. The sky was that slightly desiccated blue, with high, wispy clouds; you could follow the quiet roar of the low waves as they rolled across the long, flat beach, heading up the coast, like some kind of stereo demonstration. Her parents had an old vinyl LP like that, with airplane and train sounds. She and Maggie played it incessantly when they were little kids.

The Venice boardwalk hadn't changed much. The same

T-shirt and sunglasses stores, a poster shop, a lot of food stands and restaurants—a couple of which did seem more upmarket than what had been here a few years ago—interspersed with newer condos that looked like concrete bunkers had mated with aquariums. On the beach side, vendors sold crafts, incense, political bumper stickers and buttons and 9/11 Truther literature. There were tarot readers, a freak show, performers, some playing music, others juggling chainsaws, and that guy who wore a turban and roller blades and played an electric guitar, singing about a man from Mars. He'd been in so many TV shows and commercials that he had to be living pretty well off his residuals by now, Michelle thought. The crowd was the usual mix of tourists and locals, people riding beach cruisers and skateboards, street kids begging for change, would-be gangsters walking their pit bulls. A homeless man worked on a cartoonish sand sculpture of a mermaid with huge breasts, the magic marker scrawl on a piece of cardboard requesting no photos without a donation. Another man with a boa constrictor wrapped around his neck pedaled past on a unicycle.

"Oh, would you look at that!" Caitlin said, with an exasperated chuckle.

Michelle looked to where she pointed.

MEDICAL MARIJUANA EVALUATION, the sign said. Also, BOTOX BY THE BEACH.

"Nice to know you can get everything you need in one place," Caitlin said, rolling her eyes.

They passed another cannabis clinic, this one a smaller fluorescent-green storefront, tucked between a tattoo parlor and a shop that sold "tobacco water pipes and smoking accessories." Two women barely out of their teens wearing bikini tops, cut-off shorts and leis made of fake marijuana leaves stood out in front. "Get legal!" they called out. "Free evaluation!" The customers waiting inside looked mostly young, scruffy and stoned, some holding skateboards and grimy backpacks.

"I'm sure there's all kinds of legitimate medical needs going on there," Caitlin muttered.

"I think we go this way," Michelle said. This was not a subject she wanted to talk about.

ABBOT KINNEY HAD GENTRIFIED a lot in her last few years in Los Angeles, but walking down the street now, Michelle could see it had gone even more upscale during her time away. Expensive boutiques, designer-furniture stores and foodie restaurants filled the mostly low, vintage brick and California Spanish stucco buildings, with the occasional modernist cube thrown in. New faux lofts had sprung up behind the main street in places.

When Michelle was younger, Venice had been bohemian, cheap and somewhat dangerous. It looked like none of those things now.

Michelle watched Caitlin as she paused to look at a purse in a display window. "Now that is cute," she was saying. Like they were two girlfriends out for an afternoon of shopping and cocktails.

There was danger here, all right, but not from gang-bangers or meth heads. The danger came from very high places, likely from Caitlin's own inner circle, and it was following them both, Michelle knew.

And Caitlin had no idea.

At least, Michelle didn't think she did.

✿ ✿ ✿

"THANK YOU FOR AGREEING to see me." Troy Stone rose, and offered his hand. He'd secured a booth on the bar side of Hal's restaurant.

Hal's was a neighborhood fixture and Industry hangout, even back in the days when Abbot Kinney had been on the border of a gang war. Michelle had always liked the place. Dark granite floors, white walls with rotating art, a high ceiling, and acoustics that during the day actually allowed for conversation. A good choice for a meeting.

"My pleasure, Mr. Stone," Caitlin said, taking his hand briefly. Her guarded look was back, the politeness held at a distance.

"Troy, please."

Today he wore a Lacoste mustard polo shirt and khaki chinos. The polo showed his broad chest, the sleeves cutting across his biceps. If he hadn't been an athlete, he looked like one, a recently retired jock who still hit the gym to keep his gut in check.

Caitlin and Michelle sat down across from him.

"What can I get you ladies to drink?"

Caitlin wanted chardonnay, of course. Troy opted for beer. Michelle stuck with Pellegrino. "She's trying to be a good influence on me," Caitlin said with a grin, that flirtatiousness typical of her returning for a moment. "I'm not sure it's taking, though."

Troy chuckled. "In wine there is wisdom. In beer, there is strength. In water? There's bacteria. I don't know if that's true, but I saw it on a T-shirt once."

They both have their charming masks on, Michelle thought.

"Have you lived in Venice long?" she asked.

He leaned back and sipped his beer. A Red Stripe. "You might say that. I'm in my grandparent's old house, a few blocks from here. We were able to keep it in the family, when they passed."

"Oakwood? Michelle asked.

He held himself still for a moment.

Was he insulted? Maybe it was another assumption she shouldn't have made.

"Yes," he said. "You're familiar with the history here, I take it."

"I lived in LA for a long time."

Troy smiled easily. Turned to Caitlin. "Oakwood has been a black neighborhood from the time they built Venice, over a hundred years ago. Mostly due to employees of Abbot Kinney, the founder. He wanted to make sure there was a place where his chauffeur could live, seeing how black folk couldn't own property in much of Los Angeles. Of course there's fewer of us here now, with all the gentrification going on."

"I heard Google moved in," Michelle said.

"Yep, and a Whole Foods. Now, don't get me wrong, I'm enjoying that Whole Foods. But there are still plenty of people around here who can't afford it. They're living just a few blocks away, but it's a different world."

He was working his way into his pitch. So many people in LA had a pitch, and Michelle had heard so many of them.

Their screenplays. Their bands. Their high-concept restaurants.

Their charities.

Now it was Caitlin's turn to smile. "Tell me more, Mr. Stone—Troy."

Caitlin, apparently, had heard her share as well.

A small grimace crossed his face, and then a short burst of a sigh. "Look, we can sit here and talk about economic opportunity and social justice and all of those big issues, but that's not why I wanted to talk to you, and I think you know it."

Caitlin seemed surprised. Maybe she'd expected a little more small talk before getting down to business. "I'm not sure that I do. Though I assume it has to do with our election efforts here."

"It does. Look, I believe your intentions are good, but those propositions have the potential to make a positive impact in a lot of communities here."

"Really? Legalizing pot is good for communities?" She smiled deliberately. "Like liquor stores are?"

He leaned forward. Not quite in her space, but closing the gap. "What you need to understand is that people of color who are not wealthy tend to have very different interactions with law enforcement and the justice system than white, affluent folks do."

"I do understand that, actually." Her voice had turned hard. Defensive. "I realize there are some problems with how the law is applied. But that doesn't change the need for appropriate laws. And it doesn't remove the danger of being too lenient in how we deal with criminals."

This had gotten offtrack very quickly, Michelle thought. Troy and Caitlin were bristling at each other when they'd barely started talking.

"It goes beyond 'some problems,'" he said. "If you need statistics, I can quote them all day. But here's one that's relevant to your efforts. Whites and blacks smoke marijuana at about the same rates. On average, a black kid is four times more likely to get arrested for possession. In some places? Up to thirty times more likely. In poor neighborhoods where there's a heavy police presence, a lot of black kids end up with a so-called extensive criminal history that's nothing but minor possession busts. And that record follows them around for the rest of their lives. You know that blacks are ten times more likely to go to prison for a drug offense than whites?"

Michelle could see Caitlin's grip tighten on her wine glass. She had to know these statistics already. And hadn't she expressed doubts about the whole marijuana focus at the last board meeting? But her tone, her body language—she didn't want to hear it now. Not from Troy.

"I'm not saying there aren't problems," she said. "But addressing them by wholesale legalization? You really think that's a way to help poor kids of color do better in life? Making it easier for them to smoke pot all day?"

"I'd rather have them smoking pot than sitting in prison, learning nothing except how to be better criminals. But you know what, I can understand why people have doubts about legalization. I can understand why your group is against that, even if I'm not so clear on why an organization from Texas is dumping a ton of money on an election in California. Shouldn't we be left to make our own decisions about this?"

Caitlin snorted. "What happens in California doesn't stay in California. I think you know that."

Now Troy sat back in the booth. He chuckled. "Well, all right, you have a point there. And look, I know I'm coming on strong. I get impatient sometimes. I've just seen too many kids get screwed up by the system. You see them when they're little, running around and playing without a care, and you watch them turn hard and hopeless. It's got to stop. Even if we disagree on legalization, can we at least agree on that?"

Caitlin nodded slowly. "I guess we just disagree on how to go about it."

"Can we talk about sentencing reform, then? Because I'm having a hard time understanding why Safer America is so dead set against it."

"Because longer sentences work. Why else have we seen crime rates drop the way they have?"

"Now, there's absolutely no proof that longer sentences have anything to do with that. Rates started dropping before longer sentences kicked in."

"What *does* it have to do with it, then?"

"Demographics. Not as many young people since the Boomers aged up. Smarter policing in some cases. Less opportunity to commit crime in others—increased surveillance, cell phones—"

She lifted an eyebrow. "Cell phones?"

Something had shifted between them. Michelle couldn't exactly call Caitlin's attitude playful now, but she was interested. Engaged. Troy had relaxed, too, leaning back against the bench, arm stretched along the back.

"Yeah. Cell phone videos. Crime's just harder to get away with than it used to be."

"But you can't just pretend punishment doesn't play a role in that. A criminal in prison doesn't have an opportunity to commit crimes, now, does he?"

"All right, I'll grant you that. But how does a drop in violent crime correlate to locking up non-violent offenders for longer and longer periods? There isn't a country in the world that incarcerates a greater percentage of its people than the United States. And about a half a million of those people are behind bars for drug offenses. That's over a thousand percent increase since the War on Drugs started in 1980. You can't tell me that's what winning a war looks like."

"Maybe not. But legalization? Isn't that just giving up? We passed a few of your pot 'clinics' on the way over here. Aren't those bad enough? Waiting rooms full of kids working the system to get high legally? You want even more of that?"

"Oh, you were down on the boardwalk." He rolled his eyes. "Yeah. Look, I agree there's abuse. I just disagree that this abuse is worse for our communities than criminalizing behavior kids are going to engage in anyway."

Caitlin nodded slightly. Not because she agreed with him, Michelle thought, but just to show that she'd heard what he had to say.

She sipped her wine. He drank his beer.

"Besides, some of those clinics are doing good work," he said. "I can take you to one, if you're interested."

Caitlin laughed a little, uncomfortably. Maybe she was picturing all those stoned kids on skateboards and not particularly wanting to mingle with them. "I don't know that we have time for that."

"It's just up the block. I mean, literally. On this street."

ABBOT KINNEY'S MARIJUANA DISPENSARY was hiding in plain sight, between an old bungalow turned shoe boutique and an art gallery. It had a cheerful neon green sign that said ORGANIC MEDICINE, a display window with hoodies and Chinese herbs and medicinal teas. Outside, there was a rack of T-shirts and a table and chairs, with a big aluminum water bowl for dogs. But the most unusual thing about it to Michelle's eye was the large, open door. That wasn't how these places generally did business. Usually if they even had windows, they were shuttered, protected by iron bars.

This one looked like an ordinary retail store.

"We're an open clinic," the young woman at the counter explained. "You don't have to have a prescription to come in and look. We sell all kinds of other medicinal products. And our herbalists can recommend things other than cannabis, if you'd like."

She didn't look like the sort of person you'd expect to find working at a pot dispensary. She wore a tailored white blouse and black slacks, tortoiseshell-framed glasses. The store didn't look like the dispensaries in Humboldt Michelle had seen either, with its neat racks of T-shirts and sweat-shirts, shelves of teas and herbs, aromatherapy burners and neti pots.

But then there was the main counter, filled with pipes and vaporizers and edibles, and the large glass jars of buds that lined the shelves behind it, the pungent scent somewhere between pine sap and skunk that they couldn't completely seal up.

There were a couple of customers at the counter, being serviced by two twentysomethings, a man and a woman wearing logo T-shirts.

"I'll take two grams of the Fire OG Kush and what do you have in a top-shelf Sativa dominant today?"

He looked like a studio exec, thirtysomething, swept-back hair, expensive, slouchy suit.

"I've got a dank Jack Herer," the clerk said.

"Organic?"

"It's indoor. This time of year, that's what you're going to get."

The other customer was a woman in her sixties, frail, with the sort of gray pallor that came with a serious illness. "Why don't you try the 420 Bar?" the clerk was saying. "And another thing you might like are these tinctures. They're great for making tea."

"Well, this is pretty interesting," Caitlin said. She turned to the woman behind the register. "So if I told you I had a particular condition, you'd recommend something for me?"

"I wouldn't," the woman said. "I'm not an expert. I mean, I know the basics. But it's really best if you consult with one of our herbalists and decide on a course of treatment."

"I'm just curious," Caitlin said. "You medical-marijuana people make all kinds of claims on what it's good for. If I came in here with a doctor's note, saying I wanted something to treat, I don't know, insomnia or PTSD or something, you'd tell me there's some kind of pot that's good for that?"

"A lot of our patients use cannabis for insomnia. And there are a few small studies where veterans are finding cannabis helps them with their PTSD. You really should talk to one of our herbalists about it, if you're interested."

Caitlin hesitated. "That's all right," she said. "I'm from out of state, anyway."

"Yeah, that's a problem with edibles," the clerk was saying to the older woman, nodding. "They can take a long time to kick in. If you don't want to smoke, have you considered vaporizing? There's a couple vaporizers I can recommend that don't cost too much."

"I think I do want to try that," the woman said. "I'd like something that works right away."

❦ ❦ ❦

AFTER THAT, THEY WALKED up to the Oakwood Recreation Center. All the years she'd lived in Los Angeles, and Michelle had rarely been to this neighborhood. It had been the 'hood, after all, one of the few places on the Westside where the '92 riots had flared, where rival gangs murdered each other. That's how she'd always thought of the place, anyway. The truth had probably always been more complicated (if she'd learned anything the past few years, it was that).

And Oakwood had been changing for a while. Expensive houses were being built. Tom had looked into projects here, though he'd never managed to put anything together, as far as she knew.

Oakwood didn't feel dangerous now. Tree-shaded streets with low bungalows and Craftsman cottages, a few dense stucco housing project apartment buildings, new concrete condos here and there, and designer bunkers that looked as though they'd been dropped onto a lot that was too small to contain them. People pedaling slowly by on beach cruisers, kids on scooters and skateboards, a Mexican vendor selling ice cream from a pushcart.

"Yeah, it was pretty heavy for a while," Troy said. "Things have calmed down a lot. I don't know if it's because most kids now don't want anything to do with the crack cocaine, seeing what it did to their elders, or if enough bangers got priced out of the neighborhood, or what. I think maybe people just got tired of it all."

"Or cell phones," Caitlin said, with a sideways smile.

He laughed. "Yeah. Maybe."

"How're you doing today?" a man called out from his porch.

"Oh, just fine," Troy said. "You?"

"Can't complain. It's a beautiful day."

"You know, it really is," Caitlin said.

At the rec center, Latino kids played soccer. On the other half of the field, there was a kickball game going on, two teams of mostly white hipsters. A few middle-aged black men and women sat at the picnic tables around the fringes.

"There's all kinds of great programs here for the kids," Troy said. "Not just sports. Music, art, cooking, tutoring for school. What we really need are more things like that. Support for kids who have problems at home. A better education. And jobs at the other end. Not a pipeline to prison for smoking weed."

Caitlin stared at the soccer field, watching the children play. Michelle thought they looked to be about seven or eight years old. They played with a combination of intensity, laughter and tears.

Had her little boy, Alex, played soccer?

He probably had, Michelle thought. Most kids his age did these days.

THEY STOOD OUTSIDE SHUTTERS by Troy's Path-finder, where valets parked a succession of BMWs, Porsches and Benzes.

"I appreciate you taking the time to meet with me today," he said.

Troy had driven them back to their hotel. "Come on, it'll take forever for a cab to come. And it's really no problem. I need to get back to the office, anyway."

"Well, thank *you* for the discussion and tour." Caitlin shook herself, like a cat who'd gotten sprinkled with water. "And I mean that."

"I don't imagine I talked you into anything though."

Caitlin stood just at the edge of his open car door. "It's a little soon for that."

Troy paused by the door frame. "Can we keep talking?"

"I can't see any reason why not."

"Good."

They smiled at each other. He got into the car, swung his legs inside like his back was hurting, reached to close the door.

"Lead," Caitlin said.

"Lead?"

She seemed almost embarrassed. "I read somewhere that there's a strong correlation between lead in the environment and violent crime. And the decline of lead tracks with the decline of crime."

"Really? I'd love to read that."

"I'll see if I can dig up the link."

Watching the two, Michelle could still sense tension between them, but a different kind than there had been before.

She'd bet money what she was seeing now was attraction.

The back of her neck prickled.

She was pretty sure that this could not be good.

Chapter Sixteen

✦

WELL, SO WHAT?

Michelle leaned back in her business class seat and sipped her wine. Caitlin dozed in the seat next to her. It was about 8:30 P.M. Los Angeles time.

So what if Caitlin liked Troy? So what if the feeling was mutual? Caitlin was flying back to Houston. He was in Los Angeles.

Of course, with Caitlin's money, she could fly back to LA any time she wanted. And with this election going on, she'd have plenty of reasons to be in LA.

Just because they were attracted to each other didn't mean they'd get together, Michelle told herself.

What if they did?

You're not thinking this through, she told herself. It wasn't the attraction that was the problem. The problem was Caitlin coming out of her shell. Opening herself up to new ideas. Maybe wanting to quit Safer America.

Or worse. What if Caitlin decided to steer Safer America in a different direction?

Follow the money. She was assuming a lot of things, but if it all came down to money, the people funding Safer America expected results from their contributions.

Who exactly was funding Safer America?

Was there any way she could find out?

Don't go there, she told herself. She needed to focus, on

doing her job and not pissing off Gary. On getting Danny out of jail.

But if her "job" was taking care of Caitlin . . . what did she owe Caitlin? Anything?

And Gary would almost certainly fuck her over in the end.

It wouldn't hurt to know more about what she was up against. There were things she could find out without taking stupid risks—more about the backgrounds of the board members, for one. She could do that on her iPad. *That* shouldn't be dangerous.

Assuming Gary hadn't somehow hacked it.

MICHELLE HAD ARRANGED FOR a car service to pick them up at the airport. Caitlin was mostly silent on the ride. Tired, Michelle supposed, and feeling the effects of the wine she'd had on the plane. As they approached River Oaks, Caitlin stirred. A smile crossed her face, as though she'd recalled a pleasant memory.

"You know, that was a really great trip," she said.

"It was," Michelle said, mustering whatever fake enthusiasm she had left.

Caitlin suddenly turned to her.

"I know I make a lot of jokes, but you really have been a great help to me. And, okay, I'll admit it, a good influence." She reached out and briefly rested her hand on top of Michelle's. "Thank you."

You need to tell her, Michelle thought. You have to.

"You're welcome," she said.

HER APARTMENT FELT LIKE a stale sauna, smelling faintly of old moldy carpet. She switched on the air conditioner. Dumped her suitcase by the bed. Checked to see if her cash was still in the other suitcase in the closet. She was a little surprised and vaguely pleased to see that it was.

She took a quick shower, changed into a pair of jersey shorts and Danny's old Air Force T-shirt. Powered up her Emily phone.

One message.

"This is a collect call from an inmate in . . ." A pause. "Harris County Jail . . . If you are willing to accept, press one."

Click. A hangup.

Danny.

HE CALLED AGAIN THE next day, while she was dropping off Caitlin's clothes at the dry cleaner. She'd risked keeping her Emily phone on, in case he called back.

She waited for the prompt from the recorded voice, pressed the button to accept the call.

"I'm sorry," she said to the clerk at the cleaner's. "I, I have to take this." Scooping up the clothes she'd laid on the counter, she slung the laundry bag over her shoulder and left the air-conditioning to stand outside on the sidewalk, in the steaming heat of a Houston late morning.

"Hey," he said. "Hope this is an okay time."

"It's fine."

For a moment, there was silence on the line.

"I . . . I'm sorry, " she said.

She wasn't even sure why she was apologizing. For not being there at the hearing. For the way the hearing had worked out. For everything.

She was crying now, and she didn't know why she was doing that, either.

"Listen," he said. "Calls get dropped a lot, so I need you to listen." He sounded exhausted. But not just that. There was something else, something underneath. Something urgent.

"I miss you," he said. "I . . . I just want to see you. I know it's a lot to ask, with everything you've got going on."

He couldn't be asking to see her just because he missed her. There had to be something else. Something he didn't want to communicate through the lawyers.

Something important.

The thought steadied her somewhat.

"I miss you too. I'll be there as soon as I can."

Whatever it was, good or bad, she needed to keep herself together.

WHEN SHE GOT BACK to the house, she found Caitlin sitting on the oatmeal couch in the Great Room, tapping away on her laptop.

"The dry cleaning will be ready tomorrow afternoon," Michelle said.

"Oh, hi." Caitlin continued to stare at the screen. "Thanks for taking care of that."

"No problem. Is there anything I can help you with right now?"

"Mmm, not really. I'm just finding that article for Troy. The one about lead and criminal behavior."

Now what, Michelle thought? There was nothing on the schedule for today. No plans for upcoming events that she knew of. No work she could do. And if she took the afternoon off, she still couldn't see Danny. There were no visiting hours today.

What was it he needed to tell her?

"Is there anything in particular you'd like for lunch?"

"Lunch?" The little wave. "Whatever you feel like."

"Well, okay, I'll figure out something."

Caitlin nodded, attention fixed on her screen.

"I'll be in the office if you need me," Michelle said.

WHEN SHE CHECKED THE Outlook calendar on the office desktop, she saw an event had been added for Friday.

She went back into the living room. Caitlin was still working on her laptop.

"There's a staff meeting tomorrow?" Michelle asked.

"Yeah. A sort of debrief on the LA event and a pre-planning meeting for the next swing through California."

"Okay. I'll try to get up to speed on that."

"I already heard back from Troy on that lead article. He really liked it." Caitlin's lips curved in a small smile.

Michelle managed a smile of her own.

"That's great!"

Maybe Caitlin's connecting with Troy was nothing to worry about, she thought. Maybe she was overreacting.

And maybe Safer America was a perfectly legitimate nonprofit doing perfectly legal election work.

Figure the odds.

SHE COULDN'T SEE DANNY until Saturday. There were no visiting hours until then. That left the rest of today and tomorrow to occupy herself, somehow.

The staff meeting tomorrow, that could be interesting.

How much could she investigate Safer America without arousing suspicion?

Whatever was on the office computer was fair game, she figured. If there was some kind of scam, some kind of money laundering or illegal donations going on, the evidence probably wasn't going to be sitting on the computer here in plain sight.

And the board members, who they were, what interests they represented, surely there was nothing too suspicious about her looking into their backgrounds, was there? As Caitlin's assistant, she should have an idea who the players in the organization were, shouldn't she?

In the nearly two weeks she'd been working for Caitlin, Michelle hadn't spent a lot of time on the computer in Caitlin's office. Mostly she'd used the laptop, and the times she'd been on the desktop, she'd been doing scheduling and researching hotels. Hell, most of what she'd been doing had been exactly what Gary had said it would be: Babysitting Caitlin. Chaperoning her on the trip to Los Angeles. Monitoring her drinking, which so far had been excessive but not drowning-in-a-bathtub drunk. Michelle wondered about that. Maybe she'd been lucky so far. Or maybe Gary's version of Caitlin was an exaggeration, if not an outright lie, to suit his own purpose, whatever it was.

Or maybe Caitlin had changed. Was changing. The doubts she'd expressed about Safer America, meeting with Troy Stone . . .

And asking if Michelle wanted to work out with her tomorrow morning at a local River Oaks gym.

"If you don't mind," Caitlin had said, with some hesitation. Might as well, Michelle had thought. The River Oaks gym had to be better than the shitty "fitness center" at her apartment complex.

Now, she was here in the office with nothing to do, except possibly arrange lunch.

She booted up the computer.

There weren't that many folders on the desktop. "Speeches." "Research." "Receipts." "Contacts." "Disclosures."

She checked the applications menu. One of the icons was a stylized globe held up in cupped hands. "DonorSoft."

As good a place to start as any. Michelle clicked on the application.

It opened onto a welcome page. She could see a menu bar across the top: "Home." "Search." "Accounting." "Reports." "Donors." "Campaigns." "Events." "Volunteers." "Prefer-ences." "Help."

She felt a tingling in her hands. She clicked on "Donors."

A pop-up box appeared. User Name. Password.

"Shit," she muttered.

She entered the user name and password she'd been given to log on to the computer here.

User name or password not recognized.

Hardly a surprise.

She tried a couple of the other tabs, less sensitive areas, like "Volunteers" and "Help" and got the same result.

Could she go to Caitlin, ask for access?

What would her excuse be?

I'll think about it, she told herself. Come up with something.

What else could she explore?

"Disclosures" sounded promising.

She clicked on the folder.

Eight PDFs with the file names "Public" followed by years. Half were labeled "SAF," the others, "SAA," one from each year. The most recent were from last year. She clicked on the one labeled "SAA."

It looked like a tax return. "Form 990. **Public Disclosure Copy** Return of Organization Exempt From Income Tax."

The name of the organization was "Safer America Action."

She started paging down.

The first page looked a lot like a 1040. Caitlin was identified as the "principal officer" of a "501(c)4." There was a brief description of the organization's mission: "To advocate for the victims of crime in the United States and for effective strategies to reduce crime and build safer communities." Then, a checklist for "Activities and Governance," followed by "Revenue," "Expenses" and "Net Assets."

They'd raised over $32 million last year.

She kept scrolling. The document looked to be around fifty pages.

Statement of Program Service Accomplishments. Checklist of Required Schedules. Statements Regarding Other IRS Filings and Tax Compliance. Governance, Management and Disclosure.

Compensation of Officers, Directors, Trustees, Key Employees, Highest Compensated Employees, and Independent Contractors.

There was a long list of directors, forty-one of them in alphabetical order, split in two for some reason, with some names that Michelle recognized: several retired politicians, a few famous businessmen, Perry Aisles, the television producer who had introduced Caitlin in Los Angeles. That was where she found Michael Campbell, the Santa Claus representing ALEAAG, the law enforcement officers lobby; Randall Gates, the man from Prostasis, whatever that was; and Debbie Landry, the board secretary.

All of the directors were listed as working for two hours a week, one hour at Safer America Action, the other at a "related organization," for zero compensation.

The directors' list was interrupted by a section for "Independent Contractors." A couple of them were easy enough to figure out: The travel service they used for hotels and airfare. Professional fundraisers. A company that printed annual reports and mailers. A hotel in town that seemed to be where Safer America booked its guests.

But two of the contractors were simply listed as "Consulting Services": Edgemore Media Consulting and Red Seas Research Ltd.

Edgemore Media received $539,372 in compensation. Red Seas Research got $348,191.

Michelle paged ahead.

In the next section of directors, she found Matthew Moss. Also listed for two hours a week at zero compensation.

The final board member, Steve . . . she still didn't know what his last name was.

She continued to scroll.

Next came the highest compensated employees.

The first was Caitlin O'Connor, President.

Caitlin worked thirty-three hours a week, according to the disclosure form: twenty hours at Safer America Action, thirteen at "related organizations." Her annual salary was divided between three columns, D, E and F. The first was "Reportable compensation from the organization," which had to mean Safer America Action. The second column was for "Reportable compensation from related organizations." Maybe from SAF, the other group of PDFs, whatever that was? The third column was "Estimated amount of other compensation from the organization and related organizations."

From Column D, from Safer America Action, Caitlin received $159,286. From Column E, "related organizations," she got $127,776. From Column F, "other compensation," $45,113.

Michelle added up the numbers in her head.

She was getting paid $75K, so she guessed it wasn't that surprising that Caitlin was making close to $300K, even without adding in "other compensation."

Not real wealth, not like the hedge fund managers and the Fortune 500 CEOs and the new tech millionaires, maybe not even that much for a person living in River Oaks.

But wasn't this supposed to be a nonprofit?

The Vice President of Finance/Administration, Porter Ackermann, was next. His salary and compensation were about $50K less than Caitlin's. He too was working thirty-three hours a week, with a similar split in who paid him.

She had a sudden flash of Porter in his expensive suit, sitting behind his expensive walnut desk. He had other income, she was willing to bet on it.

"Hon?" she heard Caitlin call from the Great Room. "Did you make any reservations yet?"

"Not yet. Anything in particular you feel like?"

"Oh, I don't know." Caitlin hugged the doorframe. "How about . . . something healthy?" She grinned. "Sushi, maybe?"

"Sure," Michelle said.

She scrolled past the other highest compensated employees. She didn't have much time before lunch.

Statement of Revenue. Statement of Functional Expenses. Balance Sheet. Reconciliation of Net Assets.

A lot of big numbers. Tens of millions in places. There was no way for her to make sense of it skimming like this.

Public Charity Status and Public Support. Reason for Public Charity Status. Support Schedules. Public Support Percentage and Investment Income Percentage. A page for Supplemental Information, left blank.

Then, finally, there it was:

Schedule B. **Public Disclosure Copy**.

Schedule of Contributors.

Her heart beat a little a faster, and she could feel the sweat break out on her scalp and back, in spite of the air conditioning.

She paged past the Organization Type and General Rules versus Special Rules to Part 1: Contributors.

The first contributor's contributions totaled $8,500,000. The type of contribution checked was "Person."

The other information, the name of the contributor, the contributor's address, was blank.

"What?" she muttered. That couldn't be right.

She scrolled down the page.

The next contributor kicked in $7,000,000. A "Person." No identifying information.

$5,500,000. $3,300,000. $1,500,000. Two more pages with decreasing amounts. The lowest was $5,000.

No information about the donors at all.

"You about ready for lunch?" Caitlin called from the other room.

"Lunch sounds great," Michelle said. She closed the program and rose. "Oh, would you mind if I ran a quick errand after? I just need to pick something up at the drugstore."

"Sure, go ahead. There's not a lot going on today anyway. Take the rest of the afternoon off, if you'd like."

"Well, I won't say no to leaving early," Michelle said quickly. "There's just a few things I want to do here first."

"Do you want to stop at the CVS now?" Caitlin asked after lunch, some $175 of sushi and premium sake. Caitlin had drunk most of the sake, so Michelle was driving. "It's on our way back."

Michelle hesitated. She couldn't think of a logical reason to say no, but she didn't like the idea of Caitlin knowing she'd gone to buy a flash drive.

"I don't want to put you out," she said.

Caitlin made her weary wave. "Oh, you're not putting me out. I'll just wait in the car with the air on."

"Okay, thanks. I'll be quick."

She left Caitlin in the passenger seat fiddling with the radio, the car parked in the middle of the small CVS parking lot.

She bought a box of Kleenex, a bottle of Mrs. Meyers counter cleaner and a bar of hand soap along with the flash drive.

When she exited the CVS, she felt like she'd walked into a sauna, especially after the store's overly chilly air conditioning. Why do places do that? she wondered. It just made going outside worse.

There was a car parked two spaces over from Caitlin's White Pearl Lexus SUV. A late model silver compact, one of those anonymous economy imports that you saw everywhere and couldn't necessarily identify. Something about it nagged at her. What was it? A Kia?

No. A Hyundai.

She drew closer.

A Hyundai with a bumper sticker that said OWNED BY A PUG.

Carlene's car. Gary's errand girl who'd picked up the suitcase of cash from her apartment.

From behind, the car looked empty, but Carlene wasn't very big. Maybe she was crouched down, blocked by the front seat.

Maybe she can't see me, Michelle thought. She circled around to the passenger side.

She's Gary's person. You have to assume she's dangerous.

Michelle had her .38 tucked in her hobo with the custom holster. She wrapped her hand around the grip now. Approached the car and peered through the window.

Empty.

Michelle straightened up and scanned the parking lot, swiveled her head around to check the exit of the CVS.

Where was she?

Just get out of here, Michelle thought. She turned and half-jogged around the Hyundai toward the Lexus.

And saw Caitlin slumped in the passenger seat, head lolling to one side.

Michelle froze, heart hammering in her throat. She took a step toward the passenger door, then another. She couldn't see Caitlin's face. Was she breathing?

Michelle rapped her knuckles on the window. Caitlin stirred. Turned her head and opened her eyes.

Relief flooded through Michelle like cool water.

Caitlin stretched and sat up.

"I can't believe I feel asleep," she said when Michelle opened the driver's door. "It hasn't been that long, has it?"

"Not really." Michelle managed a smile. "This heat takes a lot out of you."

It was Carlene's car, she was sure of it, parked in a place where Michelle was likely to see it. Obviously Carlene wasn't trying to hide her presence, wherever she might be now. She wanted Michelle to know she was here.

As Michelle pulled the Lexus into the parking lot exit, she saw a woman standing by the bus stop on the sidewalk to her left, wearing a sun visor and accompanied by a leashed brindle pug.

Carlene.

She stared at Michelle, the fingers of her free hand finally wiggling in a fractional wave as Michelle steered the car onto the street, turning right, away from her.

Gary's way of saying that he was always watching.

Chapter Seventeen

⚓

IT TURNED OUT IT was perfectly legal to shield the identity of donors in a 501(c) organization from the public.

She'd copied the "Disclosures" file onto her new flash drive. Thought about trying to copy the DonorSoft files but decided against it, for now. Without the password, she was only guessing what files might be useful, and she had no way to open or make sense of them.

And Michelle had plenty of material to keep her busy tonight.

She leaned back into the pillows she'd propped against the headboard of her bed and put down her iPad for a moment. Took a sip of her wine.

She'd thought over the last few years that she'd gone beyond being surprised by much of anything. She'd known that politics was a manipulation by the powerful to get what they wanted. But she'd figured in this case she was looking for something more, well, *illegal*. Money laundering, bribery, things like that. Not something so obviously corrupt that was hiding in plain sight.

Of course, donors' identities did have to be reported to the IRS. And she had little doubt that *something* illegal, in that it was against the letter of the law, was happening with Safer America. But this system just made it so easy to get away with.

No wonder they called it "Dark Money."

Safer America Action was a 501(c)(4). A "social welfare"

organization that was allowed to do political work. It could lobby, it could support or oppose candidates, thought it could not legally coordinate with candidates' campaigns. A 501(c)(4) could work for or against legislation, as Safer America was doing in California. It could also contribute funds to a 527, an organization whose only purpose was politics and that could actually field candidates. But 527s were required to disclose their donors. So a 501(c)(4) donating to a 527 was a way to get around that requirement.

There were all kinds of ways to manipulate this, she thought, to shield who was advocating or attacking. One 501(c)(4) could donate to another, which could then donate to another, and eventually to a 527 to directly support a candidate. A tide of Dark Money could be transferred from organization to organization, and no one would know where or who it came from.

Companies and corporations could donate as much as they wanted, too. That check box for "Person" was what they marked as well. It seemed ludicrous, but she double-checked, and that was how it was done.

And how hard would it be to disguise that money? If, say, the Boys wanted to contribute something? They had all kinds of shell companies to funnel money through. Donations to a 501(c)(4) weren't tax deductible, but why would they care about that?

They cared about buying influence. About purchasing elections.

Would an IRS auditor reviewing a 501(c)(4) look at a contribution from, say, a Blue Sky Enterprises and bother to check where that money came from, how Blue Sky had gotten it, as long as the paperwork looked okay?

"SAF" stood for "Safer America Foundation." It was a 501(c)(3), so not involved in political work. She'd hardly started to dig into those forms yet, so she wasn't entirely sure what Safer America Foundation did. The mission statement was almost the same as Safer America Action: "To advocate for the victims of crime in the United States and to research and implement effective strategies to reduce crime and build safer communities."

Caitlin was president of both organizations.

Even with more time and a greater understanding of what these organizations were and how they were supposed to function, she still couldn't tell if Safer America was doing anything illegal from these forms. Things like "office expenses" and "other salaries and wages" and "total lobbying expenditures" and "other exempt purposes expenditures," "temporarily restricted net assets," "endowment funds" and "leasehold improvements"—none of these entries was broken out in any way. It was impossible to look at this paperwork and know how Safer America received and spent its money.

There were a couple of entries that she had to wonder about. "Land" and "buildings" listed under assets. Safer America Foundation owned some property, she could tell that much. One million dollars in land and some $650K in "buildings."

Caitlin was receiving a housing allowance. It was listed on the Schedule J for Safer America Foundation, $50,000. And if she was reading the instructions correctly, this should have been listed in Column F, "other compensation," for the Safer America Foundation.

But it wasn't. The numbers didn't add up.

Maybe it was included as part of the over $500K of "other

employee benefits" that weren't broken out in any way that she could tell.

And why was a woman already making a nearly $300K salary receiving a housing allowance in the first place? For a house that she owned?

Safer America owned $1,650,000 in land and buildings.

How much was a house in River Oaks worth?

She did a quick Google search. That amount wasn't out of line.

Was it possible that Safer America Foundation owned Caitlin's home?

But there was no way to tell from this public disclosure what the property was. Just that Safer America Foundation owned it.

The one thing she could be sure of was that Caitlin made decent money from this charity. And so did Porter Ackermann.

"I DON'T KNOW, MAYBE there's some way we can work together," Caitlin said suddenly.

"I'm sorry?"

Caitlin and Michelle were finishing up their workout on the treadmill at the fancy River Oaks gym where Caitlin had a membership. "Except I never use it," she'd said with a laugh. "Don't worry, I'll have Porter sign you up. You shouldn't have to pay for it on my account."

It was a nice, clean gym, not crowded, obviously expensive, with its brand new equipment and track lights and wooden lockers. A big black dog greeted them in the foyer, "the gym mascot," Caitlin explained.

A neighborhood gym in a very wealthy neighborhood.

"Troy Stone and me. Well, Safer America." Caitlin blushed. Or maybe it was just the cardio.

"Oh? What would you want to do?"

"I'm not sure. It's just that . . ." Caitlin's steps slowed down a fraction. "You know, he has a point. If we really want to build safer communities, maybe we should be looking more to what we can do to strengthen them. Instead of just locking people up for longer and longer times."

"But on Prop. 391, on legalizing marijuana . . ."

"I'm not sure we're going to agree on that. But on the sentencing guidelines? I think he's right. It costs too damn much to keep so many people in prison for such a long time."

"Oh."

It wasn't that Michelle disagreed. If she was being honest with herself, she'd barely thought about the whole issue. It was only now, with Danny in jail, with her doing so many things that were so far from legal, that any of this had seemed relevant to her own life.

It's not my fault, she told herself. It wasn't like she deserved to be in jail.

She was just taking payoffs from drug cartels, that's all. Thanks to a black ops agent embedded with a cabal of powerful men trying to run the country from deep in the shadows.

But god forbid she should get caught with a joint in Texas.

"Something on your mind?" Caitlin asked.

"Not really, just . . ." She hesitated. "Are you sure it's safe?"

"Safe? What do you mean?"

"Well, I mean . . . Troy. What do you know about him?"

"Oh, honey, I've already started checking into him. His

organization looks legit. He's gotten some nice press cover-
age the past couple of years, too, for the work they're doing."

"That's . . . great. I'm just wondering . . . what will the
board think?"

There was no way for Michelle to say what she really
wanted to say. That going against the board might be
dangerous.

Caitlin shrugged. "They can think what they want." Her
steps picked up speed. "I'm still the president and founder. If
they don't like it, they can find somebody else." She grinned.
"Now, *that* would be a mess."

MICHELLE HAD FOUND OUT a few things about several of the board members just by using Google.

Michael Campbell had been a police chief in several
midsized California and Midwestern cities before he retired
and took on his position at ALEAAG, the American Law
Enforcement Agencies Advocacy Group. He was the Vice
President of Communications there. As far as she could tell
from their website and a few other hits, ALEAAG advo-
cated for "vigorous support of law enforcement officers
and agencies in their mission to protect and serve American
communities," which meant, among other things, increasing
police department budgets and police officer salaries, supporting programs that supplied local law enforcement agents
with surplus US military equipment (apparently local police
departments really needed armored personnel carriers), lobbying for laws that empowered local police departments to
seize assets from lawbreakers, particularly drug-related lawbreakers, and then use said assets to fund police programs.

Then there was Randall Gates, of Prostatis.

Prostatis owned and operated prisons, along with "other correctional facilities."

The private prison industry was a big business. Prostatis was not the largest private prison company—it came in third—but the company's revenue last year was still close to a billion dollars. They housed around 30,000 offenders in some twenty-plus facilities, on contract with federal, state and local governments. Their annual report talked about Prostatis's business model, how they required a steady stream of income, a certain number of beds filled, reliable profits for their shareholders. It came down to occupancy rate, as much as anything else. Like they were running some kind of hotel.

A hotel with a government contract guaranteeing 90% occupancy and a certain charge per bed.

"Our fully modernized facilities and state-of-the-art technology enable us to promote staffing efficiencies," the annual report said.

Meaning fewer guards.

Prostatis was guaranteed a price per inmate, and the lower the operating cost, the more of that money they got to keep. What other corners were getting cut Michelle wondered.

Prostatis advertised its prison labor force on the company's website.

"Correctional work opportunities promote individual responsibility by offering offenders a chance to pay back their debts to society and learn valuable new skills. We are privileged to play a part in inmate rehabilitation through labor and also to offer cost-effective, high-quality workers for some of America's best companies. Our inmate workers provide staffing for industries ranging from computer, garment and aviation manufacturing to telemarketing to farming and harvesting. We are especially honored to produce helmets, bulletproof vests and more for our armed forces."

At nineteen cents an hour, with no benefits. She'd found that number with a little extra Googling.

The annual report also dealt with potential risk factors for investors.

"Demand for our services is greatly influenced by local, state and federal law enforcement and judicial practices. Increased leniency in enforcement, sentencing and parole policies, as well as the decriminalization or legalization of activities previously classified as criminal, could result in a decreased demand and therefore smaller than forecast profits."

The CEO of Prostatis made $2.5 million a year. Randall Gates, the CFO, made $1.7 million.

It wasn't hard to see what stakes Michael Campbell and Randall Gates had in steering Safer America's priorities in certain directions.

What about Debbie Landry? She came across like a typical society lady—one invested in her charities and fundraisers, because that was what you did in her position.

Like I used to do, Michelle thought.

But she couldn't assume this was all there was to Debbie. She couldn't assume anything about any of these people.

Like Matthew Moss. He had to be getting something out of this beyond travel expenses to make speeches. No way he was doing all this for free.

And Steve? She didn't even know his last name.

❧ ❧ ❧

THE STAFF MEETING WASN'T all that interest-
ing. Porter was there, but there was no one else from the
board meeting except for Caitlin. Instead it was the VP
of Development, the Managing Director, the Director of
Communications, the Events Manager, some assistants,
people Michelle had met in passing or hadn't met at all,
cloistered as she generally was with Caitlin in her River
Oaks home.

The campaign to defeat Prop. 275 and Prop. 391 had a
name now: "The Coalition to Protect Our Communities."
The event in Los Angeles was "a great success." They hoped
for great things in San Francisco, though this event would be
"smaller scale, in a more intimate setting."

"We'll have two more email blasts going out. But I think
we need to work on the buy-in for donors who can't be there
in person."

"San Francisco's not the most fertile territory for us."

"We'll do all right." Porter sat to Caitlin's right, his bulk
settled into the conference room chair, watchful and still.
"The prison guards union will send some folks our way, for
one. And there's plenty of concerns about public safety there,
for another, even if all those terribly enlightened folks like to
pretend otherwise." He snorted a little. Amused at his own
joke.

"CCPOA has its own PACs," the Director of Development said.

"Sure. But I think they also appreciate what we can bring
to the table. And they've got a lot of money to spend. You
find me a bigger heavyweight in California politics than the
prison guards union. And it so happens that our interests
align."

At that, Porter shifted in his chair. "I'm going to have to run. I have an appointment across town."

Caitlin leaned over to Michelle. "I'm with him," she whispered. "Let's get out of here."

MICHELLE PULLED CAITLIN'S LEXUS SUV into the garage. It wasn't just the possibility of Caitlin's drinking that had Michelle playing chauffeur. Caitlin really didn't like to drive very much. "I don't know, the traffic's so bad here these days, it's just not fun," she'd said with an offhand wave.

"I'm happy to drive," Michelle had said, suspecting that Caitlin's nerves had more to do with her attack than Houston traffic.

"I was wondering," Michelle said now, as the garage door closed behind them. "Would it make sense for me to . . . familiarize myself a little with the donor database?"

Caitlin frowned. "Well, I don't know. Is there some reason you want to? I don't know that it enters in much to the work you're doing for me."

Shit, Michelle thought.

She ran over the arguments she'd worked out in advance. Opened the driver's door and stepped out, slammed the door shut. Drew a deep breath, taking in the scent of stale gasoline and hot concrete. She waited for Caitlin to exit the SUV, punching in the access code to unlock the door that led into the house, through the kitchen.

The blast of air conditioning prickled the sweat on her skin.

"There's a couple of things. I noticed there's an Events section, and I thought it might make sense for me to be able to enter miscellaneous travel expenses directly into that. I mean, I'm assuming it tracks expenses for the events?"

"I think so." Caitlin paused in front of the refrigerator and opened the door.

Was she buying this? Michelle couldn't tell. She couldn't see Caitlin's face. She could only see Caitlin's back as she grabbed an open bottle of chardonnay from the refrigerator.

"You want a glass, hon?" Caitlin asked.

"No thanks."

For all she knew, Caitlin was complicit in this whole thing, whatever it was. Some of that money, from the unnamed donors, from the "other compensation and benefits," could easily be ending up in her pockets, and there was just no way to tell.

Caitlin hesitated by the refrigerator door. "Maybe I'll skip it too." She replaced the bottle and closed the refrigerator, almost gently, as though she might have regretted her choice.

Michelle took a moment to hang the Lexus keys on the hooks by the garage door, then followed Caitlin through the kitchen.

"Also I thought it might be a good idea, when we go to an event, for me to have a little background on the donors. Like for this San Francisco trip. Who's going to be there, what they've contributed. And other donors in the area who you might want to reach out to." Michelle smiled, gave a little chuckle. Don't overplay this, she told herself. "Just so I can back you up a little better."

They'd entered the Great Room. Michelle could hear the distant whine of a vacuum cleaner, somewhere in the house.

"Well, I guess that makes sense," Caitlin finally said, tossing her beige Prada tote onto the sofa. "Tell you what, let's dig into it first thing Monday morning. Cause you know what I'd really like to do right now? A yoga class."

"Okay," Michelle said. "Sounds good."

Deep, cleansing breaths.

IT WAS A RISK going to see him, now that she was Michelle again. She had to go as Emily, but what if someone recognized her as Michelle?

Not likely, she told herself. Who among Caitlin's friends and the Safer America crew would be visiting an inmate at Harris County Jail?

SATURDAY, 5:30 PM. THERE were so many visitors here tonight. Michelle supposed that made sense. No visiting hours at all on Thursday and Friday, no visiting hours until 3:30 on Saturday. The weekend, so people had time off. Maybe. Looking at the crowd around here, as usual, mostly women, she wondered how many of them had the kind of jobs where they worked Saturdays and Sundays. Fast food. Retail. Jobs that didn't pay well. Some of them likely didn't have jobs at all. Deondra, the woman she'd met on her first visit here, she'd looked like she worked in an office, put-together outfits, styled hair, but so many of these women, dressed in T-shirts and leggings and cheap, bright cotton chinos, she could picture them running registers in a McDonalds somewhere, stocking shelves at Walmart.

She wasn't sure, of course. She couldn't know. Her brain was just spinning scenarios as she waited in line after line in the refrigerated, chemical, stale-piss chill of Harris County Jail.

She noticed it more, this time, how many of the people waiting were black, and brown. Oh there were white people too, about a third, she estimated, but surely the population visiting this jail didn't reflect the overall demographics of Houston. More than a third of the population of Houston couldn't be African American, but more than a third of the people waiting here—the women waiting here—were black.

Well, they just must commit more crimes.

Was that a friend's voice she heard, some embarrassing relative's, Matthew Fucking Moss's or her own?

If they do, there are reasons.

Whose voice was that?

You know that blacks are ten times more likely to go to prison for a drug offense than whites? Even though they use drugs at about the same rates?

That was Troy Stone.

She looked around, at the lines of people, of women, shuffling along on scuffed-up linoleum, at the guards in their uniforms, at the metal detectors, thought about the pods and floors of prisoners in this massive building, and felt for a moment that the weight of it all might crush her.

Who was making money off this?

"Hey. I like the hair."

"You do?"

"Yeah." He grinned. "You look like a rock star."

She had to smile. "I don't think so."

His own grin wavered. He looked so pale, from what she could see through the glass. Maybe the light in here did that to everyone, but she didn't think it was just the light. Had he been outside at all since he'd been arrested?

He leaned closer to the glass. His cheek was bruised, she noticed now. Not badly. But she could see it.

"What happened?" she asked.

He closed his eyes and shook his head. "It's not . . . there's no point. There's nothing . . ."

"Tell me."

There's nothing you can do.

"I fell, that's all," he said.

"Love you, baby," the woman to her left said loudly.

He gestured to the speaker grate. Michelle put her ear close, grateful that she'd remembered the wet wipe.

"Have you heard back from Sam?"

"Not yet."

"*Fuck*," he muttered. "What did he . . . when you talked, did he have any recommendations for you?"

"He thought I should just keep . . . doing what I'm doing. Working."

"For *Gary*? That . . . that's it? He didn't offer to . . . to help you, or . . . ?"

"He's checking into things," she said, hoping it would calm him. "It's just going to take a little time."

She could hear his ragged breaths through the speaker grate, and then she couldn't any more. She looked through the glass. He'd pulled away from the grate, braced his hands against the edge of the counter, eyes closed, breathing hard. Trying to get a grip.

"Dan—" she started. "Jeff. What's going on?"

"*Nothing*. The same. I just . . ." He shook his head like he was trying to shake something off of it and let out a long sigh. "Sorry. Just a lousy couple of days."

Christ, she thought. She'd seen him in a lot of moods, in some very bad situations. But she'd never seen him like this.

Panic rose in her throat. She tasted bile.

He was watching her. Something in his face changed. He seemed calmer now. She guessed that was for her benefit.

"Are *you* okay?" he asked.

"I'm fine."

She *needed* to be fine right now. Needed to be calm. Panic wasn't going to help.

"How's . . . how's work?" he asked.

"I told you we don't have the money. Now what am I supposed to do?" the woman to her right said.

"Oh, you know. Complicated." She wished she could tell him about it. He'd be the one who could help her make sense of it all. If they could actually talk to each other, maybe between the two of them they could figure out a way out of this. A way to win Gary's game.

"Don't you give me that shit," the woman next to her half-shouted into her speaker. "This is the last thing I need to hear from you right now."

"I don't want your life to get any more fucked up because of me," Danny said.

"It's not," she said, suddenly exhausted, even though it was. But she'd chosen this life with him. She'd had her chances to leave, several times. She'd stuck with him. And now she was well and truly stuck.

She got as close to the speaker as she could, and though she didn't want to touch it, her lip brushed against the cold metal. "My life was pretty fucked up before," she said. "And . . . I like the life we have. I miss you, and . . ."

Her throat closed up, and she could feel the tears gathering. Stop, she told herself. This wasn't a time for tears. He was already on edge, and she wasn't going to make it worse. "We're going to fix this," she said.

He leaned close to the grate. "I wish I could protect you. Make sure you have what you need. It's just . . . I don't have a lot of options." He laughed shortly, like he was making a joke, but something in his voice had shifted, to an urgency that sounded like business. He pulled back from the speaker grate and stared at her.

"I'm doing all right," she said. "Really. You don't need to worry about me right now."

He gestured at the grate. His turn to say something he didn't want to half-shout.

"There's a book at the house. It's called *Taking Flight*. You remember it?"

"I . . . think so." She didn't, specifically, but he had a collection of books about aviation, along with big coffee table books of exotic landscapes and wildlife. "It's not the same on a screen," he liked to say.

"It kind of explains how I'm feeling right now, about being locked up like this. You know me, I don't like being inside all the time."

He drew back from the speaker but stayed close to the Plexiglas. Met her eyes. Held the gaze.

That was the message he'd wanted to give her.

She nodded. Message received.

"I wish I could send it to you," she said.

"I do too. Because the reading materials here pretty much suck." He smiled a little. "I guess I can request to buy books from an approved vendor. If I'm stuck here much longer, I probably will."

"You won't be," she said. "We'll figure out something."

We *have* to, she thought. And soon. Whatever Gary's game was, she had a feeling that the clock was winding down.

Chapter Eighteen

TRAVEL TIME FROM HOUSTON to Eureka was around eight hours if she wanted to leave tomorrow morning. If she flew at 7:20 A.M., she could be in Arcata by around 1:30 P.M. or so.

She could, conceivably, get back to Houston before work on Monday morning. There was a flight leaving Eureka at 8 P.M. But did that make sense?

Maybe it would be as simple as picking up the book. Maybe not. She had no way of knowing.

On the one hand, she hated having to ask for a day off. To make up some story why she needed it. She'd only worked for Caitlin for two weeks, after all.

On the other . . . what were the odds that she'd be tracked? That Gary would find out where she'd gone? She'd have to assume he would. If he did . . . how could she possibly explain a one-day jaunt to Arcata that would cost well over a thousand dollars?

She had to try to set this up.

She got out her Emily phone and called Evergreen.

She'd called Helen, her interim manager, several times since she'd been in Houston, in the mid-afternoon, when the restaurant wouldn't be too crowded. She'd sounded harried, but insisted things were going well. Michelle had preferred to believe her—what could she do if they weren't?

This time, she'd push. Anything that would give her a plausible excuse for going to Arcata, in case Gary was listening.

"Oh, hi, Emily. Yeah, it's busy. You know, Saturday night."

Helen sounded like she was in the middle of something, which she undoubtedly was.

"How are things with Joseph?" The chef.

"Oh. Fine. He's . . . experimenting a little."

She could just see Joseph trying to steamroll Helen.

"Oh?"

"Yeah. I mean . . . you know. Some of it's interesting."

"Would it help if I came in?" Michelle asked. "Just to get everyone on the same page?"

"You don't have to," Helen said quickly. "Things are fine."

"It's okay if they're not, Helen. Really. I dumped a lot on your plate."

A hesitation. "Well, if we could have a meeting . . . I mean, we'll be okay, you don't have to rush, but . . . when you can . . . I think it would help."

"I'll see how soon I can get freed up, and I'll let you know right away. Hang in there. You guys are doing great."

One thing you could almost always count on: things going wrong in a restaurant.

A pretty thin excuse to go to Arcata, but it was some cover, at least.

9 P.M. on a Saturday. Later than she felt comfortable calling Caitlin, especially on a weekend.

She opened up a new message on her email and thought about what to say.

Don't overexplain. Come up with a believable story if Caitlin asks.

Dear Caitlin, I'm so sorry, but I have a family emergency and need to handle it ASAP. Would it be a huge problem if I missed Monday? I can be back early evening, so I could deal with any emergencies then. Best, Michelle.

"Home" would be . . . Los Angeles.

Her father. Her sister. Her nephew. Something.

She thought about hitting "send." Hesitated.

She had to assume anything going to and from Safer America was monitored.

On Wednesday, she and Caitlin were supposed to fly to San Francisco for another fundraiser on Thursday.

Maybe I should just wait and go to Arcata after that, she thought. Surely Caitlin could handle a flight on her own back to Houston. If she had too many glasses of wine on the flight, well, so what? As long as Caitlin kept it together for the fundraiser, what difference did it make?

But if Danny wanted her to see this book . . . maybe it couldn't wait that long.

Michelle padded out into the kitchen and poured herself a glass of sauvignon blanc. Flopped on the couch, Safer America laptop and her own iPad by her side, and sipped her wine. Fuck it, she thought, taking a gulp. She got up and grabbed the bottle from the fridge.

This was all too fucking much.

Forget about the big problems: Danny in jail, Gary up to god knows what, having to deal with bags of dirty money, a shady charity helmed by a likeable, unstable woman and a board of sketchy directors. She couldn't even decide on a travel itinerary.

She settled back down on the couch and topped off her glass.

Here's how you play it, she told herself. You had a sudden family emergency. You just found out about it. You emailed as soon as you knew, and you're so sorry for the inconvenience.

She'd wait a few hours. Book her flight. Send the email.

In the meantime, she'd do a little more digging into Safer America.

"Edgemore Media Consulting" and "Red Seas Research Ltd." Those two companies had stood out on the list of independent contractors. It wasn't obvious what they did, and they'd gotten a lot of money for doing whatever it was.

Edgemore first.

The website was easy enough to find. Edgemore Media "is a full-service political consulting firm specializing in media management and production coordinated across multiple platforms: television, radio, direct mail, email and web, including social media and SEO. We are constantly pushing the boundaries of technology to develop new communication tools that will engage and mobilize your target audiences."

So they produced Safer America's commercials. Michelle found a few examples under "Our Work," a mix of upbeat pieces promoting particular candidates and initiatives and attack ads condemning others, including the one Gary had sent her . . . it seemed like ages ago. Had it been only three weeks?

She clicked on the ad. Something about it nagged at her.

"Drugs have taken over our cities."

The voice was Matthew Moss. She was sure of it.

She listened to some of the other ads. He'd done the voice-over on several.

It was not a huge surprise to find Matthew Moss listed as an Edgemore "messaging strategist and media consultant."

So Moss served on Safer America's board for free. But a company he was a part of got paid over half a million dollars to handle media for Safer America. Of course some portion of that money was going into Matthew Moss's pockets. For a gig that required him to show up at a few board meetings and make speeches at fancy fundraisers.

Nice work if you can get it.

Red Seas Research also had a website. But it was more notable for what it didn't say than for what it said.

"Strategic research and intelligence for forward-thinking clients. We provide the information you need to recognize opportunities, optimize outcomes and manage risk."

Good graphics, Michelle thought. There were customer testimonials, tabs for their advisory services and research products, all couched in the same vague corporate-speak. A page with headshots and brief bios of the company's chief executives. None of whom were named Steve, unfortunately.

But that didn't mean he wasn't working for them.

What did they do for Safer America?

"Strategic intelligence." Were they advising Safer America what to focus on?

If ever there were a candidate for a cutout company run by the Boys, this would be it.

SHE SET AN ALARM for 2 A.M. Woke up enough to book the flight on her iPad and send the email to Caitlin on her Safer America laptop.

She booked the flight out of Houston to San Francisco as Michelle, the flight to and from Arcata as Emily, using American for the Houston leg and then switching to United, the only carrier that flew in and out of Arcata. That way

she'd be going through two different security lines at SFO—
less chance that someone would notice the identity switch
that way. And she used two different IP addresses on her
VPN to book the two different flights.

It wasn't foolproof, not even close. But it was the best she
could do.

She couldn't show up in Arcata as Michelle. The Arcata-
Eureka Airport was small, and the odds of her running into
someone who knew her as Emily, too great. She'd been to
the one bar/restaurant at the airport enough times where the
bartender acted like he recognized her, anyway.

And if federal investigators were in Arcata looking into
"Jeff's" life—she couldn't risk traveling as Michelle.

She had to keep that identity safe.

Before she fell back asleep, she heard the chime signaling
an incoming email on her Safer America laptop.

Caitlin. Did she always stay up this late, Michelle
wondered?

*Absolutely no problem. Take all the time you need. Anything I
can do to help?*

Thank you so much, Michelle wrote back. *I'll let you know.
But I should be back Monday evening. If you need me for anything,
don't hesitate to call/email.*

THE FIRST THING SHE did when she got to the Arcata
house was throw open the windows and sliding glass doors to
let the fresh air in. It was in the mid-sixties, a nice day, and
after the soupy heat of Houston, just feeling the cool air on
her skin seemed to dissolve the knots that had accumulated
in her shoulders from the lack of sleep, the flight, her life in
general.

The house was fine, at least. No break-ins. The property crime here wasn't as bad as in Eureka, but it was worse than you'd think, for a relatively small city in the redwoods. People blamed it on the tweakers, and on transients who drifted through Humboldt in search of cheap weed. Another good reason to have a home security system.

After that, she made a pot of coffee. Sat on a stool at the wooden chopping block island and contemplated the knotty pine cupboards. They really didn't look that bad, she thought.

She took in a couple deep breaths. Drink your coffee, she told herself. She had a couple hours before the meeting at Evergreen, which she'd set up when she'd landed in Arcata-Eureka.

Drink your coffee, and then go look for the book. Like it's not a big deal.

She didn't know if anyone was watching.

AFTER SHE'D DRUNK ABOUT half her cup, she wandered out into the living room.

Some of Danny's larger books were out on the coffee table, appropriately. One on the Antarctic. Another on tigers.

So, the bookcase.

You're just looking for something to read, she told herself. Even if no one was watching, pretend like someone was. Live the part. Something to read before she went to sleep tonight, and for the long trip home tomorrow.

More coffee table books, many of them gifts they'd given each other. Nature and animals, countries he'd been to or wanted to visit. One on Paris that he'd given her, because she'd never been: "Don't all women love Paris?"

he'd said, half-joking. "We'll go there someday. Promise."
Books on fighter jets with names like *Viper* and *Eagle*, and
several on his beloved Cessna Caravan. Her photography
books were out here as well, and the big cookbooks and
wine books that were as much about pretty photos as they
were recipes and varietals. "Food porn," Danny liked to
call them.

Amazing how many things they'd managed to accumulate
together in two years.

There was another bookcase in the bedroom. That one
had novels, mostly hers, plus the history and biographies he
sometimes liked to read.

She found it on the second shelf, between a history of
Timbuktu and a book about how societies collapse under
environmental pressure. Funny, she hadn't known he was
interested in that kind of thing.

But she didn't have time to think about that. Here was
Taking Flight.

A thick trade paperback. The cover had what looked like a
red electronic bull's-eye over a surreal cloudscape. Michelle
looked at the back cover copy. A novel. That alone was
unusual—Danny didn't read a lot of novels.

> *Air Force Captain Lex Telluride flies his missions*
> *and doesn't think much about their purpose, until he sees*
> *something in the skies above Iraq that he can't explain.*
> *He wants to forget what he saw, but the image comes*
> *to him in dreams: A golden disc, a fluttering of wings.*
> *Slowly but surely, his life falls apart . . . or is it coming*
> *together?*
>
> *A modern-day Catch-22 that combines surrealist*

travelogue and Pynchonesque conspiracies into a howl of
rage against the absurdities and outrages of war, while
somehow remaining a celebration of flight as a metaphor
for the elevation of the human spirit.

"Lex Telluride"?

Though given that Danny's Air Force nickname was Jink, and he had buddies called Bagger and Punch, maybe the name wasn't completely far-fetched.

Or maybe it was just Pynchonesque.

She sat down on the living room couch with the book and her coffee.

Flipping through, she didn't find any notes, anything obvious to explain why Danny had wanted her to see this.

She started reading.

> *In fact, the worst day flying was* not *better than the*
> *best day working. Sometimes flying was just work. Some-*
> *times, when the Lawn Dart you're flying is a bag of balls*
> *and Bitching Betty chimes in to let you know things are*
> *well and truly FUBAR, flying's not much fun at all.*
> *"What a goat fuck," Telluride said.*

Michelle hoped she wouldn't have to read this entire book.

When she got to page 4, she saw it—a faint pencil underline of the number 4. Okay, she thought. Maybe this wasn't anything, but she grabbed a pad of paper sitting by the landline and wrote it down.

The next underline was on page 10. Just the zero. Then, two lines down, an underlined period that ended a sentence.

40.

She kept going. On page 48, the 8 was underlined. On page 57, the 7. Then 1, 8, 0, 5.

40.871805.

The next markings she found were of letters. The "min" in "minute." Then the word "us."

Minus?

More numbers. 124.0610.

Letters and words followed.

At the end, what she had was this:

40.871805 minus 124.0610 between north side bridge and big tree by tree. Dig 1 ft.

She was pretty sure she knew what the numbers were, from the times Danny had taken her flying in the Caravan: latitude and longitude.

Directions to something he wanted her to find.

How could she figure out where these coordinates were?

She thought about her iPhones, both of which were switched off and stored in signal-blocking bags. She didn't have any illusions that Gary couldn't find her some other way—he was probably tracking her credit card spending, for one—but she hoped this would at least slow him down.

There had to be apps for finding someplace with the latitude and longitude—could Google Maps do that? But she had to assume her phones were hacked. Entering these coordinates into either of them, even using a VPN, was too risky. She didn't know enough about how that technology worked to know if a VPN was enough protection.

There were handheld GPS units out in the garage.

"You're out hiking, you can't count on your phone." She remembered Danny telling her that. "They're not as accurate as one of these, and the battery life sucks." He had them for his volunteer firefighting and for backup on the Caravan. That one was probably gone, seized along with the plane. But the unit he took when he was out fighting fires, and the one he'd given to her, the extra stashed in the earthquake kit, those were still out in the garage.

Maybe they hadn't been hacked.

Danny, bless him, had included the manual with the unit in the earthquake kit, with plenty of extra batteries. She grabbed a pack and went into the house to the kitchen. Poured herself another cup of coffee and sat down at the butcher-block island.

She skimmed through the manual and found the section she needed.

Press MARK *for your current location. Your current position will appear in the latitude/longitude window. Press* ENTER *and then enter your desired coordinates. Name your waypoint and hit* ENTER *again to save.*

She didn't recognize the map that came up at first. A topographical map with a lot of green that she assumed meant forest. Then she saw the street name near the bottom of the screen: Fickle Hill Road.

The coordinates lead to a location in the Arcata Community Forest, not more than two miles from here.

All she had to do was press GO TO to lead herself there.

It was 2:45 P.M. The meeting at Evergreen was at 4 P.M. Did that leave enough time to get to the location, dig a foot-deep hole, retrieve whatever was there?

What if someone saw her? Would it be better to wait until later, after dark?

But if Gary was tracking her, maybe the only advantage she had was moving quickly.

Maybe not even that.

Shit, and her car. It had just been sitting here in the garage for the past few weeks. If he wanted to plant some kind of tracker in it, god knows he'd had plenty of time and opportunity.

How to get there?

Not the rental car, all those had GPS trackers in them, and she couldn't risk it.

Her mountain bike.

SHE RODE DOWN ONE of the trails in the Arcata Community Forest, following the directions on her GPS unit, her Emily phone in the signal-blocking bag so she could call Evergreen in case she was running late, the handle of a short shovel sticking out of a GORUCK backpack that was one of Danny's favorites.

She also wore a fanny pack with a hidden holster, her .38 tucked inside.

Sunday afternoon, and there were people here, walking or jogging on the trails, riding horses and mountain bikes. Not huge crowds, but she couldn't count on privacy, either. It was a nice day, mid-sixties, light slanting through the tall, straight redwoods, which absurdly reminded her of telephone poles with Christmas trees stuck on top, the scent of pine and the hint of fog to come infusing the air.

By now she'd turned off a multi-use paved road and onto a trail, roughly in the middle of the over 2,000-acre forest. She passed two hikers and a couple pushing a baby carriage with oversized wheels that looked like a tiny dune buggy. She was getting close.

Up ahead was a small bridge that spanned a creek.

That had to be it.

About two feet from the north side of the bridge was an older redwood.

She got off her bike and wheeled it over, leaning it against the tree.

The leafy green ground cover around the tree—ferns and sorrel, she thought—looked thin compared to the others. There was a patch of nearly bare soil covered over with pine needles beneath the tree, between the tree and the bridge.

She got out the shovel, swept the pine needles aside and started digging.

Chapter Nineteen

"YOU GEOCACHING?"

"What?"

Michelle had seen the hiker coming: a college-aged kid with a rainbow bandana tied pirate-style over his head, leading a mid-sized mutt on a leash. She'd also smelled the weed he was smoking. She'd put the shovel aside, leaning it against the tree, and rested her hand on the fanny pack with the .38.

"Geocaching. Is that a cache?" He was a skinny white kid, not that tall, wearing a worn long-sleeved T-shirt and Patagonia vest.

"I . . . haven't quite gotten there yet."

He peered into the hole. "I didn't think they usually buried them like that."

"It's . . . actually a scavenger hunt."

"Oh. Cool."

His dog, which looked like a cross between a beagle and an Australian shepherd, nosed at the pile of dirt and needles she'd dug up.

He held out the joint he'd been smoking. "You want a hit?"

"Thanks, but no. I have to work later."

He took another draw, nodding, stubbed the joint out on the sole of his shoe and tucked it in his shirt pocket. Crouched down and gave his dog a two-handed scratch behind the ears.

Now what? Michelle thought. He seemed harmless, but he didn't seem to be going anywhere, either.

"Well, I have a deadline," she said. "So I better keep digging."

"Cool."

She picked up the shovel. He stood there, watching her.

Christ. If someone like Carlene could be one of Gary's people, who's to say this kid wasn't?

Just dig, she told herself. If he tries anything, hit him with the shovel. But she didn't think he was going to try anything. He was just hanging out, watching her dig, and he seemed extremely stoned.

Her shovel hit something solid. A tree root?

No. Something metal.

A steel box in military gray-green, about ten inches long and seven inches high. She grabbed the handle on the top and tugged.

"Need a hand?"

She forced a smile. "That's okay. I've got it."

He crouched down on his haunches, his dog sniffing at the dirt.

"Oh wow. It's an ammo box."

Michelle brushed it off. Whatever was in there shifted with a soft thud—a solid weight, but not too heavy. She unzipped her pack and put it inside.

"You aren't going to open it?"

"No, it's part of the game," she said. "We have to bring what we find to the party, and we'll open it there."

"Oh." He seemed disappointed, a kid who wanted to know what the present was. "Well, have fun with that."

"I will. Nice meeting you!" she added. She used the shovel

blade to push dirt back into the hole, quickly as she could, glancing over her shoulder at the hiker as he ambled down the trail, his dog pausing to sniff at a fallen branch.

"I'M NOT TRYING TO 'stifle your creativity'!" Helen made finger quotes, the rising red on her cheeks making the freckles stand out. "I'm just saying that all that fancy shit doesn't *sell* here!"

"Bullshit. You're not even *trying* to sell it!" Joseph's face was even redder, but then, he was a redhead.

It was feeling very cramped in her little office.

Guillermo, the line cook, leaned back in his chair and sighed. She'd included Guillermo because if Joseph walked, he was the one who'd be taking over.

Michelle lifted her hands. "Guys . . . None of us has time for this."

She hadn't even had a chance to open Danny's box yet.

"Okay," she said. "Joseph, this isn't El Bulli or Moto. You can't go crazy with experiments. Our customers want high quality, locally sourced food with seasonal ingredients at a reasonable price point—"

"You're not giving people here enough credit. They just need some education—"

She raised her hand with more force. "I'm not finished. You want to do one special a night that's as complicated and wild as you want to make it, go for it." She turned to Helen. "And I want you to sell it hard. We'll offer half-price on an appropriate wine pairing. Nice bottles. Call it 'Chef's Adventure.' We'll see how it goes."

Helen gave a little shrug. "Okay. Sounds good."

"Are we all on the same page?"

"Yeah," Joseph said, clenching and flexing his big, scarred hands. "Sure."

"Works for me, Emily," Guillermo said, stretching in his chair. "Okay if I get back to the kitchen? I still have some prep to do."

"Sure," she said. "I just want to let you know . . ."

She hesitated. Not because she didn't know what she wanted to say, but because the words were getting caught in her throat. "All of you are amazing. I know I've been asking a lot from you, and . . . I just really appreciate it." She squeezed her eyes shut, hoping that would stop the tears, because crying at this point was just too embarrassing.

When she opened her eyes, all three were staring at her.

"Sorry," she said. "I've had a long day."

Helen took a step forward, like she was thinking about giving her a hug, but she didn't quite get there. "Is there . . . do you need anything, or . . . ?"

"No. No, I'm fine. Just tired." She managed a smile. "I'm going to take a little time to go over the accounts and let you guys do what you need to do. Helen, why don't you and I meet for a few minutes after I'm done? And Joseph . . . put me down for one of those chef's specials tonight. I haven't had a decent thing to eat all day."

After they all left, she closed the office door and collapsed in her chair.

She knew that she came across as cold much of the time. Oh, she did the right things. Holiday bonuses and bottles of wine. She thought that she treated people fairly. But she'd been so closed off for so long, keeping a part of herself behind walls. She couldn't admit who she really was. And she wasn't sure she even knew anymore.

But who had time to worry about that?

She unzipped the GORUCK and pulled out Danny's ammo box.

THREE VACUUM-SEALED PLASTIC BAGS.

The first one was money. Five bundles of hundreds, so probably fifty grand. She sighed. She had enough trouble with excess cash as it was. What should she do with it?

Deposit some to her Emily personal account, maybe. Under $10K to avoid the reporting requirements. She could use some extra cash to cover the rent, since she wasn't paying herself what she usually did from Evergreen. And of course, there were the lawyers. It was Sunday, but she could deposit up to fifty bills at her bank's ATM.

Except large cash deposits . . . as the girlfriend of a man jailed on federal drug charges . . . didn't that just scream "Drug money! Freeze my bank account!"

"Shit," she muttered.

Next, a smaller package, the size of a sandwich bag. Passports.

She opened the package. There were two. The first had Danny's photo, with the name "Justin Terrence Carver."

The second was for her. "Meredith Evelyn Jackson."

If she needed to run, now she could. He'd made sure of that.

She took in a deep breath. Let the tears flow, this time, until one dripped onto the passport.

No time for that.

The last package was a notebook. Longer than it was tall, about 8" x 6", with a sturdy, slightly battered dark-blue pebbled cover. A pair of wings, like the Air Force logo, and PILOT LOGBOOK stamped in silver, faded in places.

She opened it. Light-green pages, like a ledger book. Columns for date, route, aircraft category and class, conditions of flight, type of piloting time. Some columns had no headings or ones that were handwritten; one of those was labeled "Account." The last column on the right-hand page was a longish space for "Remarks and Endorsements."

She looked at the first entry. It was dated about ten years ago.

The most recent entry was just over two years old.

When she'd met Danny in Mexico.

She was pretty sure she was looking at the logbook of the missions that Danny had flown for the Boys.

At first the entries were minimal. Abbreviations and numbers that she didn't understand. Locations marked by airport codes and coordinates. But further in, the notes became more detailed. Names. Dollar amounts. "Kilos" instead of "Load." Strings of numbers that looked like bank accounts. Remarks like: "Exfiltration." "Face Shot." "Dead drop." "Ghost transpo." "Wet job."

"They burned Rami. FUBAR."

"Target was bullshit."

"Fuck this."

There were about twenty unformatted pages in the back, just ruled lines, like a regular notebook. The first few pages were fragmented notes, a few doodles. Then, several pages in, a page of writing dated shortly after they'd arrived in Arcata.

For approx. 10 years I worked as an asset for an off-the-books CIA black ops unit. This log contains a record of those missions, including relevant names, dates, operational details and account numbers when applicable.

When I started I was proud of what I did. I truly believe we accomplished some good things. We took out some real bad guys and helped some good people. But on the balance, what I did wasn't good. I supported missions that eliminated people we had no business targeting. I helped take gold and other valuables out of Iraq and Af-Pak. I ran illegal narcotics into the US and money and guns to Mexico, Central America and South America, all this as a means to continue to fund our missions and other ops, some within US borders. I've recorded what I know about those.

Some of the times when I was moving money around, I don't know for certain what it was for. But from my years of working with these people and observing the behaviors, I believe some of these missions were just about making money. Everybody made good money, including me. But what we made is nothing compared to the people we were really working for.

Like Smedley Butler said, "War is a racket, conducted for the benefit of the very few, at the expense of the very many."

I wasn't serving my country, I was feeding the war machine. If you're reading this, it's because it's time I did something to make up for it.

Captain Daniel Finn (USAF, Ret.)

She slowly closed the notebook. Rested her palms on its pebbled surface.

What was she supposed to do with this?

There was a scanner/printer in the office. Would that be smart, having another hard copy? Was there someplace she could hide it? Someone she could mail it to?

How would that help? Could she really say, "Let Danny go and leave us alone, or all this comes out"? Did things like that actually work?

Gary killed people who found out things they weren't supposed to know.

She needed time to think about what to do.

Scan it and put it on a flash drive, she decided. Easier to carry that way, and she could make as many copies as she wanted.

The printer had a USB port that you could print from or scan to directly. She wasn't sure if clearing the data from the printer really got rid of it, but it had to be better than having it on the computer and hoping "secure empty trash" did the trick.

First things first: she disconnected the printer cable from the desktop.

After she'd finished, some two and a half hours and over two hundred pages later, she cleared the data, plugged the printer cable back in and printed out a slew of reports on expenses and earnings, hoping that would overwrite anything still in the printer memory, having no idea if it actually would.

By the time she was ready to leave Evergreen, dinner was in full swing.

She stood by the end of the bar, sipping a half glass of wine from a bottle of Russian River pinot she'd been wanting to try. A nice crowd for a Sunday night. Everything looked good. The food, the warm lighting, the wood-burl tables, her photos on the wall. She wondered if this was the last time she'd ever see the place.

If nothing else, I proved I could do it, she thought.

"Hey, Emily. Nice to see you." Matt, the young tattooed bartender, took a moment to wipe the counter in front of her. "Can I get you anything?"

"I'm good," she said. "Thanks."

He scrubbed at a sticky spot on the bar. "So, how's Jeff doing?" he said in a low voice.

Had he heard something? Did he know?

"Jeff's . . . he's okay. Why do you ask?"

"Just some things people said." He grabbed a couple of dirty glasses off the bar and scooped up the tip someone had left. "Anyway, hope it works out. Jeff's a good guy."

"Thanks for your concern," she said.

If Matt knew, it wouldn't be long before everyone at Evergreen knew. Maybe they already did.

MAYBE SHE SHOULD JUST take the money, the passport and the logbook, and run. She was pretty sure that was what Danny wanted her to do. How many times had he said it, since he'd been arrested?

Why don't you just get away for a while?

You don't need to be anywhere near this.

You need to take care of yourself.

Her car was parked behind the restaurant. She'd gone out the front door because she hadn't wanted to say goodbye to everyone again. Didn't want to risk the emotion.

The goodbye wouldn't mean much to them. She was the boss, and they expected to see her in a week or two. If they knew about Danny's bust, maybe they were worried about the business, about their jobs. If she disappeared completely . . .

How long would it be before the feds showed up?

They'll be fine, she thought. They weren't involved. They might be pissed as hell that their jobs ended without warning, but they'll survive. They won't know how much they meant to me, most likely.

Their lives would go on.

She rounded the corner to the back parking lot. There were only a few cars there, including hers.

Standing by it were two burly, tatted-up white guys with shaved heads and flat-brimmed ball caps. Out of towners, she guessed, the kind who came here looking to buy weed cheap and move it back east.

But she couldn't be sure. She transferred her keys to her left hand.

She reached into her fanny pack, wrapped her fingers around the checkered hardwood grip of her .38.

"Excuse me," she said.

"Oh. Sorry, ma'am," one of them said. He took a few steps back.

The other didn't move. He was taking a hit off a glass pipe.

What was the logo on his hat? An H over a star.

Houston?

Were these some of Bobby's clients? The ones expecting Danny's shipment?

"Excuse me," she said again. Louder this time. Her heart was pounding hard enough to choke off the words, but she wasn't going to let that happen.

He straightened up with a grin. "Sorry about that. We don't mean to be getting in your way."

She could feel their eyes on her as she approached the driver's side door of her car. She had her finger on the trigger of the .38 now, the grip cool and solid in her hand.

She pressed the key to unlock the door. Opened it. Now her back was to them.

Keep it together. Don't act scared. Get ready to shoot.

She slid into the car seat and slammed the door shut. Jammed the key in the ignition and started the car.

She saw the two of them in her rearview mirror, watching her as she pulled away.

GREAT. JUST GREAT.

The last thing she needed were some Texas thugs looking to recoup the weed money they'd lost. Or the weed. How did deals like that work, anyway? Half the money up front, half on delivery? Were they the ones who'd paid Danny, or was that part of Bobby's deal? She had no idea. She'd never wanted to know very much about Bobby's gigs. That way she could go on pretending that Danny was a charter pilot and volunteer firefighter, she was a restaurateur, and they were living a nice, normal life among the redwoods.

You don't know they were part of Bobby's deal, she told herself. There were a lot of guys like that, drifting in and out of Humboldt.

And if they were, maybe they just wanted to make sure that Danny wasn't talking.

She snorted. Of all the things Danny had to say, their little pissant deal didn't even register.

But if they were hanging around Evergreen . . .

Christ. What if they tried something with Evergreen? With someone on her staff?

What could she even do about it?

She pulled the rental car into the driveway of her rental house.

NOW WHAT?

She'd checked all the doors and windows, twice, to make sure they were locked. Set the alarm.

What made sense to do?

Just get in the car and drive. Drive someplace she could catch a bus or a train to San Francisco. Use the new passport and the cash and buy a plane ticket to somewhere far away.

What about Danny? What did he want her to do with the pilot log? Could she use that, somehow, to get him out of jail?

She was pacing around her living room, mind racing. If she tried to run . . .

She'd left a trail, coming here. There was no way for her not to have. Gary used all kinds of electronic tracking, but he paid people, too. He could have paid anyone here to keep an eye out for her.

This new passport was clean, as far as she knew. She had to use it carefully. Compromise it, and she was completely fucked.

Okay. So stick with the cover story she'd already established. A crisis at the restaurant. Back in Houston tomorrow.

Figure out what Danny wanted her to do with the logbook.

Then run. As fast and as far away as she could.

❧ ❧ ❧

SHE DECIDED TO TAKE Danny's rucksack with her. It was a better choice for a go-bag than the one she had back in Houston.

"This thing is bomb-proof," he'd said, more than once. Danny had a thing about good bags.

Was there anything at the house she wanted to take with her? In case she couldn't come back?

Not really. A couple practical pieces of clothing, too warm for Houston, but who knew how much longer she'd be there? The books were too heavy. The nice dishes, the framed photos . . . what was the point?

She hardly had anything personal here anyway. She'd lost all that two years ago.

She wasn't sure what to do about the money. She'd done a little Googling, and although there were no restrictions on how much money you could carry on planes domestically in theory, in practice, she was the partner of a man in jail on federal drug charges, and she'd booked the outbound flight from Arcata as Emily.

She'd tried to be smart, but she would have been better off traveling as Michelle with this kind of cash. Michelle didn't have a drug-smuggling boyfriend.

Just a dead financial-swindler husband.

Okay, she thought. Stop at an auto-teller before her flight and deposit just under $10,000 in her official Michelle account.

Except she had to assume that account was monitored. As was the second bank account she'd opened in Houston, under Emily's name. The one with the safe-deposit box and $9,000 in cash.

You needed that account to pay the lawyers, she told herself. That's your story.

And Gary knew about that money anyway. He was the reason she had all that cash she needed to account for.

But if thousands of dollars suddenly showed up in either of those accounts, and it wasn't money from Gary . . .

She couldn't risk it.

Okay, she thought. Just deposit a few thousand dollars into your Emily account. She could make up an excuse for that amount that would fit with her trip out here. Cash from Evergreen, to cover her Emily expenses. She could carry five thousand or so in her wallet. The restaurant was largely a cash business; she could claim she didn't have time to make the deposit if she got stopped. The rest . . .

She hated to leave it, but maybe it wasn't worth the risk.

SHE SPENT THE NEXT couple of hours going through clothes, through the things they'd accumulated, deciding what made sense to take. A jacket, and a few other pieces of rugged, practical clothing. She found Danny's Air Force Academy ring. It must have meant something to him; he'd kept it all this time, so she packed it. She found a jade pendant he'd bought her, a cutout woven design that almost looked like a Celtic knot. "You keep it next to your skin," he'd said. "It's supposed to be good for you." Instead of packing it, she put it on.

A few of his favorite T-shirts and a pair of jeans, in case he got out. Her good camera. The memory cards and backup drives. All those images she'd made.

At the last minute, she stashed another $3,000 in the Hadley Pro camera bag, under the padded insert. It's still not a crazy amount of money to carry, she told herself. She could explain it if she had to.

Besides, if she got searched, it was the passports that would really fuck things up. There was no way she'd be able to explain those.

Might as well throw in another $10K, she thought.

By the time she'd finished, it was 11 P.M. With a 6 A.M. flight, she'd need to get up at 4 A.M. at the latest. Hardly worth sleeping. She was still pretty wired, anyway, even though she hadn't really slept more than an hour or two the night before.

Finally, she decided to open a bottle of wine. She had some good bottles here. What were the odds she'd be back to drink them? She chose the 2001 Chateau Montelena Cabernet Sauvignon Estate. In a perfect world, she'd cellar it a few more years.

"Obviously, this is not a perfect world," she said aloud, as she popped the cork.

She poured the bottle into a decanter and got out a proper crystal cabernet glass. She wouldn't be able to drink it all, and it would be a shame to waste it. But might as well do it right.

The wine poured out deep ruby red. The nose was an explosion of dark fruit, chocolate and earth. She sipped, and it was every bit as good as its bouquet had promised.

She stood in the kitchen for a while, savoring the glass. Turned off the alarm sensors on the sliding glass doors and the back of the house and went out onto the deck and stared at the redwoods. All this time, it had been a good life here with Danny, and she'd hardly appreciated it.

After a second glass, she thought she might be able to sleep for a few hours. You'd better, she told herself. You could only go so far on adrenaline before you started making stupid mistakes.

She rearmed the sliding glass doors and deck, double-checked the windows and doors. Made sure everything was locked down tight.

She put the rest of the cash in the office safe, where she'd stored her .38 while she was in Houston. Not tonight, though. She put the .38 under the pillow next to her so she could easily reach it.

Where Danny would normally sleep.

She put the ruck and the Cole Haan tote she'd traveled with next to the bed. She was wearing a nice pair of sweats and a J. Crew T-shirt, so if she didn't have time to change, she could travel as is, her Toms espadrilles parked next to the ruck, ready to go.

She'd packed *Taking Flight*, because, who knew, she might need something to read. And even though she'd erased some of the pencil marks, it felt like something she shouldn't leave behind.

She turned on a little lamp on the dresser. Normally she slept better in dark rooms, but tonight, she didn't want to sleep too deeply. She just wanted to get enough rest to function tomorrow, until she could safely sleep on the flight from San Francisco to Houston.

Hell, maybe I'll upgrade, she thought. She had the cash, after all.

She lay down on the bed, on top of the sheets, and covered herself with a down comforter.

After a minute or two, she got up and retrieved Danny's logbook from the ruck. Even having it next to the bed was too far away. She tucked it under her pillow.

She lay there a long time before she drifted off to sleep.

❧   ❧   ❧

FUNNY HOW SHE COULD see the room still, with her eyes closed. There was the dresser. There was the door. The door was open. The dark shape by her bed—

Someone was in the bedroom.

She flinched, choked back a scream. Get the gun, she thought. Get the gun.

"You're not fooling me, Michelle."

Fucking Gary.

She rolled over and sat up, her back against the headboard. He was lounging in a chair he'd pulled over close to the bed. How long had he been there, watching her?

"What are you doing here?" She couldn't keep her voice from shaking. Of course, he'd love that. He got off on her fear.

"I was gonna ask *you* that. Missing work tomorrow, so soon in your employment—doesn't make you look very reliable."

"I cleared it with Caitlin," she said. Thinking, *gun*. Her fingertips grazed the wood grip.

"You didn't clear it with me."

"I was afraid you'd say no. Besides . . . I knew you'd find out anyway."

He chuckled. "Well, you were right about that."

He stood up, looming over her, his body blocking much of the light from the lamp on the dresser.

"So what was so important you had to run out here on a weekend?"

Her mouth was so dry it was hard to speak. "We were having a problem at the restaurant."

"And you couldn't handle it over the phone?"

"Not if I wanted to make sure it was handled." She sat up

straighter. Body language. Try not to act scared. It's what he wants. Don't give it to him.

"I know you don't give a shit, Gary. But the restaurant's important to me."

Get the gun. She was touching the grip. If she could pull it closer, just enough to get her finger on the trigger.

"You said I could go back to it when I'm done with Caitlin. I need to know I have something to go back to."

Her index finger touched metal.

"You're not going for a gun, are you, Michelle?" His voice was soft.

"No," she said.

"Because if something happens to me, Danny's never getting out. You can trust me on that." He took a step closer. "You wouldn't do too well with that, now, would you?"

She could feel a tremor in the mattress as his knees touched the side of the bed.

"I know what kind of woman you are," he said. "You can't stand being without a man."

Her hand was wrapped around the grip now.

He smiled. "The things I could do to you. I bet you'd like it."

Her finger tightened on the trigger.

"Don't try it," he said. "You won't make it."

If he moves, I'm trying.

He didn't move. It was hard to see his face in the near dark, but she thought his eyes were fixed on hers.

"I'm not gonna hurt you," he said.

"Back up, then." She said it slowly, forcing out each word, her voice hard and harsh to her own ears.

He hesitated. Then lifted his hands. "All right." He took two steps back. "I just came here to make sure we're on the same page, that's all."

Watch his hands, she thought. If he goes for a gun . . .

He sat back down in the chair. Put his hands behind his head and leaned back.

"I'm telling you, you really have an aptitude for this kind of thing, Michelle. A lot of women, a lot of men, for that matter, me showing up like this, they'd just fall apart. But you . . . you really hang tough."

He suddenly straightened up. She flinched.

"Now, now," he said. "Calm yourself down. You want a glass of that wine you poured out? I tasted some—I thought it was really good."

She shook her head. He shrugged. "Your choice. So, tell me about Caitlin."

Breathe, she told herself, her mind a blank.

"What about her?" she managed.

"How's she doing? Where's her head at?"

Was it over, then? Had he had enough fun for now?

Just answer the question.

"I think she's doing better. We've been going to the gym. To yoga. She's not drinking as much. That's what you wanted, right?"

"I want you to keep her on a leash. Make sure she's sober enough to do the events and to stay on message."

Did he know about Caitlin's doubts? About her meeting with Troy Stone?

"Okay," she said. "I'll do my best."

"Anything she's said or done that makes you think she wants to change directions?"

Her heart sped up again. If she told him, what would that mean for Caitlin? If she didn't . . .

Wouldn't Gary already have an idea? She couldn't be his only source of information.

If she lied, he'd know.

"Mostly . . . I think she wants to make a change in her life. Doing Safer America, it's almost like she's constantly reliving what happened to her. I think maybe she's ready to try and be someone other than the tragic victim."

Gary frowned. "We're going to have to keep an eye on that."

She felt that sickening plunge in her gut, the one that came with a betrayal. But there was nothing she could have said that wasn't a risk.

"What do you want me to do?" she asked.

"Keep me posted. If Caitlin starts to go off the reservation, let me know."

"Okay."

"And speaking of . . ." He stood up. Slowly. "Next time you get the urge to make a little jaunt like this, you run it by me first. Because if this happens again? I'm really going to start to wonder if you're being straight with me."

She nodded. "It won't happen again."

"Good. Because you know what? I really like working with you. It's been kind of a challenge, breaking you in, but I'm having some fun with it."

He backed toward the door. Paused in the doorway. "Maybe *you* ought to think about making a change. Leave that old victim behind."

"That's what I was trying to do before you fucked with my life," she blurted out.

"You think too small." He reached for the doorknob and started to close the door behind him. "Let me know how it goes in San Francisco."

The door shut.

She stayed where she was. Brought the gun out from under the pillow, her hands shaking. She strained to listen, for doors closing, for car engines starting and tires crunching redwood bark, for signs that he was really gone.

Chapter Twenty

⚓

JUST AFTER 2 A.M. Whatever Gary had done to the alarm system she doubted she'd be able to fix, but she couldn't see much point in worrying about it now.

She got up, put on a zippered hoodie and went out to the kitchen. A second wine glass sat on the counter, about a quarter full. That son of a bitch. He'd come into her house, taken his time. Drunk some of her wine and watched her while she slept.

She picked up his glass and hurled it across the room. It smashed against the sliding door and shattered. She stood there, breathing hard, staring at the ruby-red drips running down the glass door and onto the floor.

After a minute or two, she got out a broom and dustpan to clean up the mess.

What she said to Gary about Caitlin, that would have consequences. But then, every moment she worked for Caitlin was a betrayal of a sort.

You're not loyal to Caitlin, she told herself. You can't afford to be.

She had to keep her priorities straight.

She needed to figure out what to do with Danny's logbook.

She'd left it under her pillow, for now. She couldn't be sure what kind of bugs Gary had planted in the house, if he'd left a spy cam or two behind. But he didn't seem to know about her trip to retrieve what Danny had stashed in the woods. He didn't know about the logbook. If he'd known, he wouldn't have left the house as easily as he did.

He would have made her pay.

That was the only advantage she had right now.

So, act normally. Whatever "normally" was for a person in her situation.

She poured out one last glass of the Chateau Montelena. While she drank that, she dumped the rest in the sink and washed the decanter, rinsed out the bottle and put it in the recycling.

After that, she took a quick shower and changed into a fresh T-shirt and the light pair of slacks she'd worn on the trip from Houston, and layered on the hoodie. Went back into the kitchen and put on some coffee. She drank a half a cup and poured the rest into a travel Thermos for the drive to the airport.

It was 3:15 A.M.

Now for the logbook.

The ruck and the tote were still sitting by the bed, the tote between the bed and the ruck.

Make the bed, she thought. You wouldn't want to leave the house with the bed unmade, would you?

Since she'd slept on top of the covers, she wouldn't need to do much, just tidy the sheets and blankets and put the comforter on top. She tossed the pillows onto the floor, the two on Danny's side, and then the two on hers, first the extra and then one she'd slept on, and with that, the logbook.

She tugged and straightened the covers, spread out and smoothed the comforter over them. Retrieved Danny's pillows and propped them up against the headboard. Then went to her side of the bed to do the same. She stood close to the wall and prayed that if anything was watching, her body hid what she was doing.

She grabbed the top pillow and put it on the bed, against the headboard. There was the logbook, sitting on top of the other pillow. As she grabbed the pillow with one hand, she picked up the logbook with the other and slipped it into the laptop compartment of her leather tote. Took in a deep breath and placed the second pillow on the bed.

3:22 A.M. Still too early to leave, unless you had a reason to flee.

She forced herself to drink some more coffee. Brushed her teeth. Walked into the living room. Every creak in the house seemed magnified. She could hear the wind in the redwoods, the seeds and needles falling from the canopy to the ground, sounding almost like rain.

Enough. It was time to go.

SHE WAS EARLY, EVEN after stopping at an ATM to deposit $3,000 to her Emily account and dropping off the rental car. Arcata/Eureka was a small airport, looking something like a Holiday Inn lobby version of a rustic lodge, and there wasn't much of anything on the post-security side to do. The one restaurant here was on the second floor pre-screening. But she wanted to get this over with, now, while there wasn't much a line.

She carried Danny's logbook in her tote, $4,376 cash in her wallet.

Her Michelle phone in its signal-blocking bag, her Michelle driver's license and two credit cards, the two fresh passports, one of the $10,000 bundles of cash, all those were stashed in the interior pockets of the Patagonia jacket she'd packed at the bottom of the ruck.

If they searched her bags . . .

You got through Gary, she told herself as she approached the TSA officer. You can get through this.

She smiled at the TSA officer, a young man who looked very bored. "Good morning," she said, and handed him her Emily license.

He looked at it, looked at her, scribbled something on her boarding pass and waved her through.

The x-ray line.

She put the ruck down first, then her shoes and hoodie, her iPad, and finally, her tote. She didn't want to be separated from that tote any longer than she absolutely had to.

Don't stare at the woman stationed at the x-ray monitor, she told herself. Just walk into the scanner when they tell you to. Stand on the yellow footprints. Raise your hands above your head, like a criminal, as the curved plastic door slides shut.

Wait.

The door opened, and she walked out the other side.

"Ma'am?"

It was the TSA officer stationed on the other side of the x-ray machine.

"I'm going to need you to open this bag."

The ruck.

Oh Christ, she thought. Her heart pounded. She was sure that if he looked, he could see the pulse in her throat.

"Sure," she said.

She unzipped the main compartment. He gestured at the camera bag, packed on top of the jacket. "Open that, please."

She did. Oh, Christ, the money in the camera bag. Why had she packed it? Why couldn't she have just let it go?

"Turn on the camera."

She switched it on, and it booted up.

"Okay," he said.

Relief flooded through her like cool water. She turned off the camera, replaced it in the Hadley bag and zipped up the ruck. Grabbed her hoodie and started slipping on her espadrilles as she waited for the iPad and tote to emerge on the conveyor belt.

iPad. She picked it up. Tote.

"Ma'am?"

Oh, fuck. "Yes? Do you need me to . . . to . . . ?"

"You don't have to put your tablet through separately. Just laptops. That's a tablet, right?"

"Right," she said. She managed a smile. "Thanks for letting me know."

SHE SAT IN THE small waiting room on the other side of security and wondered: What should she do with Danny's logbook?

What had he said that last time in jail?

I wish I could protect you. I don't have a lot of options.

Maybe this book was one of them. A weapon she could use.

There was no place she could think of that felt safe to hide it. If she kept it with her at all times, that carried risks as well.

She had the one flash-drive copy, on the same drive to which she'd copied the Safer America tax-disclosure documents.

Maybe I should make another copy, she thought. Mail it

to someone before I get to Houston. Gary might be watching her, might be watching mail going out of her apartment or Safer America, but dropping something in a mailbox while in transit between two terminals in an entirely different city seemed like a pretty good bet.

There were all kinds of electronics stores at San Francisco International. Surely she could buy another flash drive and maybe a cheap tablet to use to copy it. Maybe the iPad she carried was safe, if she turned off the WiFi. But maybe it wasn't. She couldn't be sure.

Who to mail it to? Who did she trust?

The problem was, anyone she trusted—her sister, for example—there was no way she wanted to put them at risk by sending them this thing. She had to assume that Maggie was monitored anyway.

Sam?

Danny might trust Sam, but she didn't. Since she'd gone to him for help, he'd done exactly nothing for Danny or for her, at least so far as she knew.

And thinking of that last jail visit, it wasn't until she'd said she hadn't heard back from Sam that Danny told her to get the book.

Maybe Danny didn't trust Sam either.

There was no way she was going to pull that trigger until she talked to Danny.

Who, then?

Derek?

He'd always done a good job for them. He seemed to be representing Danny to the best of his ability. But he was so close to it all. She didn't know who else he worked for, where his ultimate loyalties lay. The information in that book might be more than enough to make a deal to get Danny out. Or it might be something he wouldn't want anyone ever to see.

There were plenty of people who wouldn't want anyone to see it.

Maybe Danny wanted to come clean, let the world know all about what he'd done. But the logbook was also a bargaining chip. One that might get them both out of this mess.

What if she tried to make a deal with Gary?

The thought made her shudder. If he knew she had the logbook, he'd kill her. He'd kill Danny, too.

If he thought he could get away with it.

When she'd met Gary in Houston, she'd tried that bluff, that Danny had valuable information, that they'd made "arrangements" to get it out there if something happened to either of them. Gary hadn't bought it then, but it seemed that he was still worried enough about what they knew to make a better deal with her.

Now, she really did have the goods. If she could actually make those arrangements . . .

She shivered again. Pulling that off with Gary would be like swimming up to a hungry shark with a bucket of bloody chum and hoping she could get out of the water fast enough.

First things first. Make another copy. Figure out who to send it to.

THERE WAS A BEST Buy vending machine not far from her gate at SFO's Terminal 3. It actually dispensed iPads, iPods, cameras, chargers, smart phones, noise-cancelling headphones, gadgets costing hundreds of dollars.

And flash drives.

She used her Emily ATM card and bought an iPad, two

flash drives, and a portable charger. There was a United Club in this terminal, and she had a pass from a credit card. Gathering her purchases and luggage, she made her way there.

The club didn't have great food, but it had bananas and bagels and coffee, views of the airplanes and runways, and plenty of electrical outlets. "Do you have any stationery, anything I could write a quick letter on?" she asked one of the agents at the club counter.

Airline logo stationery in hand, she took a seat in a club chair by the window.

As the iPad charged, she sipped her coffee and thought about who she should write.

Maybe her Michelle lawyer in Los Angeles, Alan Bach. She'd found him to be honest and straightforward, and he'd done what he could for her. And he wasn't involved in Tom's business, so she had to hope that when Gary had cleaned up her late husband's mess, Alan hadn't been on his radar.

She liked him enough that she almost didn't want to send trouble his way.

Too bad she didn't know anyone she hated whom she could also trust.

Finally, she started writing.

> *Dear Alan,*
> *It has been a while since we spoke. You handled my situation after the death of my husband, Tom Mason, 2 ½ years ago. I'm*

She stopped writing. She really couldn't say she was "doing well." She crossed out "I'm" and wrote:

I've had a number of changes in my life. The enclosed is something that I'd like you to hold onto for two weeks. Please don't open it before then. Sorry to sound mysterious, but I'm in transit and it's complicated to explain. I'll be contacting you shortly and will send you a retainer for your trouble within the next few days.

Many thanks—I've always appreciated how helpful you were to me during a very difficult time.

If that first note came across as melodramatic, she could only imagine what he'd think of what she had to write next.

Dear Alan,

If you are reading this and you haven't heard from me otherwise, the flash drive contains very sensitive information. I know for a fact that it's all true, and that it's dangerous information to have. I'm sorry to have put you in this position but I couldn't think of anyone else to give it to. For your own safety please send this information to as many news outlets as you can. Use a VPN if you email it. Send it to some hackers if you know any, to those sites that publish classified information. The best way for you to be safe is for as many people as possible to have this information too. I know how crazy this sounds but please believe me and do what I've said as quickly as you can.

All it needs is a tinfoil hat, she thought.

THE AIRPORT POST OFFICE was about a mile from the airport; a bus ran every half hour from the BART station, she was told, or she could walk from the BART in 15 minutes.

Normally, she would have liked to walk, to get some air and stretch her legs, but she was afraid of being seen, afraid of being followed. Maybe it would be safer to try and hide in a crowd than on a frontage road where hardly anyone was likely to be walking.

She hadn't noticed anyone following her. The Embraer turboprop from Arcata only held about twenty-five passengers, and she'd scanned them as carefully as she could during the flight. If any of them had tailed her through the airport, followed her into the United lounge, she hadn't spotted them.

That didn't mean no one was watching.

Maybe she should wait and mail it in Houston.

Standing by the entrance to BART, watching the people drag their suitcases up and down the long escalators, she thought, this is pointless.

All of it. Switching identities, putting phones in signal-blocking bags, trying to calculate risks, not knowing if anyone was watching . . . it was impossible. Hopeless.

There was no way she could fight back and win against these people.

Might as well mail it here, she thought. Maybe the flash drive would make it to Alan. Maybe they wouldn't find out. And if they killed her, maybe he'd do what she said, release the information to the entire world and cause these homicidal assholes some embarrassment, at least.

It wasn't much consolation.

BY THE TIME SHE'D finished at the post office and got back to the airport, she had an hour and a half before her flight on American to Houston. Time to check in. Time to become Michelle again.

In a restroom stall before security, she sat on the toilet, opened up the ruck, fished around until she found the jacket pocket where she'd stashed her Michelle driver's license and credit cards. Switched those out with Emily's. Took her Emily phone in its signal-blocking bag and stuffed it in the bottom of the ruck. Got out her Michelle phone and put it in her tote, taking it out of its signal-blocking bag to go through Security, because she thought that might look strange, going through the x-ray machine—a normal person wouldn't have their smartphone in a bag in her purse. The phone was turned off, and it wouldn't be out of the bag for long. She hoped it was enough.

The one in the ruck she could say was a spare, was a friend's, was . . . something.

Hopeless.

One more time through Security. A long line this time. More time to get nervous. Just don't think about it, she told herself. You're Michelle. You're going back to Houston to your apartment and your job. You haven't done anything wrong.

One more time standing in a glass booth with her arms above her head.

She stepped out.

"Ma'am?"

She closed her eyes. Took in a deep breath and let it out. Turned toward the TSA officer standing by the x-ray conveyor belt.

He pointed at the ruck.

"You got a laptop in that bag?"

"No. It's an iPad."

Chapter Twenty-One

⚘

"WE'RE BOOKED AT LOTUS. It's just off Union Square."

"Oh, that sounds lovely," Caitlin said. She sounded distracted.

Tuesday morning. Michelle glanced up from her laptop. Caitlin stared at her phone, thumbs flying on its virtual keyboard.

Texting someone, it looked like.

"You're scheduled for the CIAC convention in Anaheim," Michelle continued. "That gives you an extra day to relax in San Francisco."

"Wonderful."

The chime of an incoming text. Caitlin smiled. She seemed to study it for a moment, then set the phone down on the coffee table.

"Sorry," she said. "Just trying to set up a few things for San Francisco."

"Oh? Anything I can help you with?"

"I don't think so. Besides . . ." Now she focused on Michelle. "You seem to have enough on your plate right now. Is there anything I can help you with?"

Michelle flushed. "No, it's . . . fine, really." The last thing she needed was Caitlin asking questions about her problems. She wasn't ready to make up some bullshit story right now. She could barely keep track of the lies she'd already told.

"If you want to talk about it, hon . . ." Caitlin looked at her with what seemed to be real warmth. "I know it's been all about me and my problems since you started working here, but it doesn't have to be."

Michelle shook her head, not trusting herself to speak. The kindness made it worse. "Thanks," she finally managed. "It's just . . . it'll work itself out."

From the office, she could hear a muffled ringtone. "Lawyers, Guns and Money."

Derek, on her Emily phone.

She started to rise. "Do you mind if I—?"

"Go," Caitlin said, with her off-hand wave. A new text had come in, and she stared at her phone again, smiling.

"EMILY, IT'S DEREK. LISTEN, has anyone been in touch with you from the DEA?"

Great, she thought. Just what she needed. "No, not yet."

"Well, expect that they will be. They called me, trying to find you. I guess they went by your house and the restaurant yesterday."

"I've been in transit," she said.

"Good. I don't want you talking to them without me."

"Is there a warrant?"

"We're not even close to that yet. Jeff's been very protective of you, and as long as your finances are as separate as he says they are, odds are you're going to be okay."

"So there's no warrant."

"No. As I said—"

"Okay. Great."

"Emily, listen, I'm convinced this is more about putting pressure on Jeff than it is about rolling you up in the indictment, but we shouldn't delay this too long—we don't want to give the appearance that we have something to hide."

She exhaled a chuckle. She couldn't help it.

"No. We wouldn't want that."

HELEN CALLED FROM EVERGREEN not long after.

"Hi. So. These two men came by? Earlier today?"

"I know," Michelle said.

"Oh. They left cards. Should I . . . ? Should I give them your number, or . . . ?"

"That's okay. I'm already making arrangements."

A pause. "Um . . . I don't really know how to say this . . . but . . . is the restaurant . . . ?"

Would they close Evergreen? Would Helen and Joseph and Guillermo and everyone else still have jobs?

"It should be fine." Of course, she had no idea if it really would be. And if Emily disappeared . . . what then?

"Tell you what," Michelle said. "When you're doing the payroll this week . . . pay everyone an extra week's salary. Um, a week and a half if the receipts look good. Pay yourself two. Call it a bonus. In case something happens . . . well, in case something happens. Not that I think it will," she added quickly. "It's just a misunderstanding. Things should be back to normal soon."

She doubted Helen believed that. Helen had lived in Humboldt long enough to know the kinds of things that happened when the DEA got involved.

"Okay, will do. I hope . . . I hope everything goes okay."

"Thanks. It'll be fine."

After she disconnected, she wondered if this was the last time she'd ever talk to Helen. Wondered if she never went back to Arcata how long the restaurant would go on running without her, like a ship on autopilot before it ran out of fuel, or ran onto the rocks.

"DO YOU STILL WANT to take a look at the San Francisco donors?" Caitlin asked after lunch.

"Oh, right. Yes. That would be great."

With everything that had happened, she'd completely forgotten about her plan to access the donor database, and as Caitlin logged them in on the desktop computer in the home office, explaining how it worked—"Click on this tab to get location. Here's how to search by donation level. This field is type of donor, meaning person or company or organization"—Michelle quickly realized that it wasn't as revealing as she'd hoped it would be.

Sure, there were some names she recognized, some names that she could make a pretty good guess at what they did, what their interests were. A few famous billionaires. Companies, ones that ran detention centers like Prostasis, others with the word "Corrections" in their title, companies that provided "security technology," others that manufactured guns.

Law enforcement organizations. Prison guard and police unions. Rehab clinics and drugtesting companies.

If she took the time to go through the entire database, maybe she'd find out something useful, some shell company of the Boys, of Mexican cartels. But what good would that really do her? She already knew the Boys were involved because Gary had gotten her into this. And with the Boys came drugs. She didn't need any more proof of that. She'd lived it.

And all these names? They also just confirmed what she already knew. Most of the people supporting Safer America were invested in the policies it promoted.

Follow the money.

THERE'S NO WARRANT.

She told herself that as she waited in line at Harris County jail.

She had to risk it. Had to see Danny one more time before there *was* a warrant—and regardless of what Derek said, her best guess was that there would be one. She didn't know if Gary was pulling those strings or not, but it would be just like him, to reduce her options down to the one path he wanted her to follow.

Soon there would be no going back to Emily.

She'd taken the logbook and passports with her. There was no place she felt secure leaving them. Not in a safe-deposit box under a name Gary knew. Not in her apartment, with its cheap alarm system and personal safe she'd installed in the closet that would be far too easy to crack or steal.

Instead, they sat in a locker here in the lobby of Harris County Jail.

It won't be for long, she told herself. Just long enough to get through the lines. The line for the deputy. The line for the metal detector. The line for the visitation room.

Just long enough to find out what Danny wanted her to do with the logbook.

This would be her last chance before leaving town tomorrow with Caitlin. Maybe her last chance to visit Danny in Harris County period, if Emily had to disappear. Suddenly turning up here as Michelle—too big a risk.

Her turn at the first Plexiglas window and the deputy behind it. She put the slip of paper with Danny's information and her Emily driver's license in the aluminum trough, and waited.

There's no warrant.

The deputy looked at her license first. He was heavyset, with a shaved head and thick neck. He glanced at the license, gave her a long look up and down.

"Oh, you cut your hair," he said, with a smile she didn't like. "Makes you look real different."

She nodded and forced a smile back. Maybe he was just trying to be friendly, and anyway, she needed this to go smoothly.

He faced his computer. Entered in her license number. Waited for the results. She stood there, willing herself to stay calm.

He put her license aside. She tried to keep her face arranged in the same neutral expression. To not show her relief.

The deputy picked up the piece of paper with Danny's information and typed in the SPN number.

"Not available," he said after a moment.

"What?"

"Not available," he repeated, impatience edging his voice.

"I'm sorry," she said, "but I don't understand." Stay calm, she told herself. Swallow the panic that rose in her throat. "Not available . . . can you tell me why?"

He shrugged. "No information. Takes the system a day or two to update sometimes. Check back then."

"But . . ."

He pushed her license plate into the trough. She'd been dismissed.

Smile, she told herself. You need his help. "It's just that this is all pretty new to me. Can you tell me what that generally means?"

"Could be sick and in the clinic. Most likely pulling chain."

"Pulling chain?"

"Transferred." The look he gave her now, the curled-lip smirk, there was no mistaking the contempt. "Like I said, check back in thirty-six to forty-eight hours."

She nodded and picked up her license, her hand trembling. "Thank you," she said, gripping the license, feeling its plastic edges cutting into her fingers, into the meat of her thumb. She turned to go.

"You look better with the hair long," he said.

Chapter Twenty-Two

※

"You're in Houston?"

"Of course I'm in Houston, isn't that obvious?"

"Okay, Emily, try to calm down."

"Calm down? Did you hear anything I just said? They transferred him someplace, or he's sick or hurt and in the clinic, and they wouldn't tell me a fucking thing!"

Michelle had waited until she got back to her apartment before calling Derek. Now she paced around the tiny living room, which felt far too small to contain her rage.

"Okay. Look, I understand you're upset. It's probably some kind of . . . administrative error, or computer glitch. It happens. Have you talked to Marisol?"

"No, because as we've determined, I'm in Houston, and it's almost 9 P.M. here."

"I'll call her. We'll deal with this first thing in the morning, I promise."

"Okay." She felt suddenly exhausted, like someone had pulled a plug and all her energy had drained away, leaving a wash of toxic chemicals behind. Her shoulders ached. She flopped down on the couch, the stiff fabric that reminded her of indoor/outdoor carpeting making her bare calves itch.

"Emily, so." Derek sounded a little tentative. He was probably worried about setting her off again. She'd never lost it with Derek before. Not like this. "Since you're in Houston . . . we should think about setting up that meeting with the DEA. The sooner the better. Marisol can act as your counsel."

"I'm not staying in Houston."

"How long will you be there?"

"I'm leaving tomorrow."

"Where are you going?"

"I'm . . . I'm going to be in transit for a few days. I'll call you from the road."

"Emily, you need to listen to me. Seriously. We need to have this meeting. If you keep stalling, you're just giving them an incentive to look at you more closely. You don't want that. I don't want that. Because it starts making Jeff's case look bigger than it is, and there's nothing the feds love more than turning a simple case into a multi-defendant conspiracy. One where they can add charges and years onto a potential sentence. Do you understand what I'm saying?"

She wanted to cry. Or laugh. *A conspiracy*? she wanted to say. You have no fucking idea what kind of conspiracy this is. Or maybe you do, and you're just playing your part, in case someone is listening.

"I do understand," she said. "I'll call you tomorrow."

Tomorrow she'd be in San Francisco, where Derek's office was. They had the Safer America event on Thursday and a free day scheduled on Friday. If she had to, maybe she could slip away from Caitlin for a while, and meet with the DEA there.

"WE THINK IT'S A transfer," Marisol said.

"You *think*?"

"We were able to determine that it's nothing medical, he's not in the clinic, he's not in Ad-Seg, and they moved over a hundred prisoners yesterday because of overcrowding, so don't worry, he's fine. We just don't know exactly where he is yet."

It was just after 10 A.M., and Michelle was getting ready to leave her apartment and drive to Caitlin's house to meet the town car that would take them to the airport.

"I don't understand," Michelle said. "How can you not know? How is it they don't keep better track of these things? It's crazy!"

"I know. You'd think it would all be computerized, like they'd have barcodes or something, but there's still an awful lot of stuff that gets entered by hand, and they don't make it a priority for *us* to know. Believe me, you'd be surprised at some of the stuff that happens."

"Not really," Michelle said.

After she hung up, she did one last final bit of packing. She opened the safe in the closet and got out the cash she'd stashed in it, and then she retrieved the rest of the cash that she'd kept in the suitcase there.

She decided to put most of it in her checked luggage. If she got ripped off, she got ripped off, but her checked luggage was less likely to get searched.

The logbook and the passports she'd keep close.

Too bad about the .38 she'd bought from the guy in the trailer park with the shih tzu. Declaring she had that in her checked luggage as required seemed like a sure way to get flagged for a secondary search, and she needed to keep the money safe.

She'd need the money if she had to run.

"WHAT A BEAUTIFUL HOTEL!"

"Glad you like it," Michelle said.

Lotus was a new boutique hotel with a vague Asian theme: black and red lacquer accents, mandala paintings and a giant Buddha at the back of a fountain with black stones and stylized lotus blossoms carved from marble in the lobby. Michelle had picked it because of the location and reviews, which noted that the on-site sushi restaurant, spa and fitness center were all excellent. Seeing it now in person, Michelle worried that it wasn't really Caitlin's kind of place—the crowd in the lobby looked to be predominately T-shirted techies and soul-patched hipsters—but Caitlin's smile seemed genuine.

She looked good, Michelle thought. A little blush to her cheeks, and she looked steadier, somehow, not so fragile. She hadn't had too much to drink on the plane, and she seemed more focused than when they'd traveled together to Los Angeles. Maybe she hadn't taken the tranquilizers or anti-anxiety meds or whatever was she was on.

"Ma'am? Take your bag?"

Michelle flinched and shook her head. The bellhop already had Caitlin's massive suitcase and her own smaller wheeled bag on the luggage cart. She'd carried on Danny's ruck and had it slung over one shoulder now. Inside were the logbook and passports and several bundles of cash.

No one was carrying this bag but her.

"You look like you're about to go camping, or invade a small foreign country," Caitlin had said as they'd boarded the plane.

"Hah, well, I thought if you felt like it, maybe we could go hiking in the Muir Woods. And . . . it's a good bag for that."

It was a good bag if she decided to run.

Face it, she thought now. At some point you'll have to.

What were the odds that she'd be able to resume her life as Emily, or continue on as Michelle?

The odds of successfully running weren't great either. She'd have to time it just right.

But with Danny missing . . . the logbook . . .

What made sense?

Caitlin perused a welcome brochure that came with their keycards, as they followed the bellhop to the elevator.

"Did you know this place showcases premium sake and soju, as well as locally produced spirits, premium tequila and small-batch mescals, and that their artisan cocktails are handcrafted to reflect seasonality and creativity?"

"I . . . did not."

"What the hell *is* soju, anyway?" Caitlin asked.

"It's like Korean vodka, except it doesn't taste that strong," the bellhop said. "Stuff'll really kick your butt if you're not careful."

"Well, we'll have to try some," Caitlin said.

"We also have shochu."

"Shochu?"

"That's the Japanese kind."

Caitlin laughed. "You know, I think I'm really going to enjoy it here."

"We hope so, ma'am."

MICHELLE HAD BOOKED THE two of them in adjoining rooms. After she'd tipped the bellhop, had put her suitcase on the luggage rack and her ruck in the closet—should she risk the hotel safe for the logbook and passports?—she knocked on Caitlin's door.

"I just wanted to check and see what you wanted to do for

the rest of the day and tomorrow before the event. Do you want me to book the spa, or make any dinner reservations, or . . . ?"

"Oh." Caitlin looked a little flustered. She'd already kicked her shoes off, and the contents of her big suitcase were spread across one of the queen-sized beds in her suite. Bad idea, Michelle thought. Never put your suitcase on the bed, in case of bedbugs. But Caitlin probably had never had to worry about bedbugs.

"Well, actually, Troy's coming up from Los Angeles tonight." Caitlin's cheeks flushed. "We're going to talk about potential collaborative projects."

Shit, Michelle thought. Caitlin and Troy collaborating— would Gary consider that "going off the reservation"?

"Oh. Well, that's . . . great. Will you want me to take notes?"

"Oh, I don't think so. This is just spitballing."

Caitlin stared out the balcony window, at a view of San Francisco rooftops and hills bathed in late afternoon light. "But I'm hoping we come up with something . . . I don't know. Something different. Something that's gonna change this conversation we've been having." She seemed to shake herself. "Now I gotta figure out what to wear." She gestured at the pile of clothes on the bed, the muted creams and beiges and tans. "I'm just so tired of all this stuff."

"Maybe we could do some shopping tomorrow or Friday."

"Let's do that."

"Do you want me to find you someplace for dinner?"

"That would be wonderful, hon. Though I guess we could eat here." Caitlin grinned. "Maybe try some of that soju."

"Okay." Michelle hesitated by the door. "Just let me know."

"You know what, don't worry about it," Caitlin said suddenly. "Why don't you just go relax this evening? Treat yourself to something nice. You look like you could use it."

"Thanks. I'll do that."

CAITLIN AND TROY COLLABORATING. Did she have to tell Gary?

If she didn't tell him now . . . how long would it take him to find out?

Best-case scenario, she'd be gone by the time he did.

Worst case . . .

Well, it depends on what they come up with, she told herself. If their projects fit within Safer America's mandate, then that wouldn't be a problem, would it?

Figure the odds of that, though. She already knew what Troy's views were on the propositions Safer America had come to California to lobby against.

But telling Gary? She didn't know what he'd do if he decided that Caitlin was taking Safer America in a direction he didn't like. But she did know that he had people killed.

Not telling Gary carried its own set of risks. To her. To Danny.

Fucking Gary. No matter what she did, someone was likely to lose.

Right now, it's just a dinner, she told herself. I'll wait and see what happens. Then I'll decide.

Like the rest of the hotel, her room was decorated with Asian accents. It had a comfortable bed, a view of the city, a great minibar, a big TV and a shower/tub with massage jets. Under other circumstances, she'd really enjoy spending a few nights here.

She powered up her Emily phone and called Marisol Acosta. It was after 6 P.M. in Houston, but Marisol had promised her she'd be there for her call.

"We found him. He's in a facility just outside of San Angelo."

"Okay," Michelle said. "Isn't that . . . isn't that pretty far from Houston?" Her Texas geography wasn't all that good, but she was pretty sure San Angelo was in west Texas somewhere.

"Yeah. It is. A six and a half hour drive."

The way Marisol said that, she sounded almost angry.

"I don't understand," Michelle said. "Jeff . . . he hasn't even had a trial. Why would he get transferred to a jail that's hours away from the court that's handling his case?"

"That's a very good question. It's one we're asking right now. We're going under the assumption that it's a mistake."

"A mistake."

"It's not unheard of, when a lot of prisoners get transferred at once. Hopefully we can get it fixed quickly. Because they're making our access to Jeff more difficult during a time that we need to be working on his case. And I'd hate to think they were doing that on purpose."

"That would be shocking," Michelle said. "What's the name of the jail?"

"Weaver Detention Facility, but look, there's no need for you to go rushing out there. By the time he's allowed to have visitors, hopefully he'll be on his way back to Harris County."

"I was just curious," Michelle said. "Hopefully you're right."

As soon as she disconnected, she got out her iPad, logged

onto the hotel's internet, sat down in the club chair by the window balcony, booted up her VPN and Googled Weaver Detention Facility.

A couple of official-looking sites connected to various government agencies. A Wikipedia entry. A prisoner advocacy group promising information and support. Some news articles.

She clicked on the first hit, which seemed to be the main site for the facility.

A photo of an anonymous low-slung gray building with two flagpoles out front, taken at a distance; next to it a portrait of a broad-faced, buzz-cut white man sitting at a desk. Buttons for "Visitation and Contact Instructions" and "Jobs Available at this Facility." Below that, in polite gray text, a couple of sentences:

Carl Weaver Detention Facility: A medium-security facility with a capacity of 1,027 inmates.

Customer Base: The Texas Department of Criminal Justice, US Marshal's Service.

"Customer Base"?

In the upper left, there was another button that said: "Back to Locations."

She clicked on it. A banner photo of warehouse and factory-like buildings spread over a flat, anonymous landscape, surrounded by warm lights perched atop skinny poles, like cheap Ikea floor lamps that had somehow grown as tall as redwoods.

Find a Facility, it said. And below that, *Prostatis: A Nationwide Network Dedicated to Community Safety.*

It took a moment to sink in.

The Weaver Detention Facility was owned by Prostasis.

Chapter Twenty-Three

☙

FOR A MINUTE OR two she just sat there, staring out the window at the San Francisco skyline, her mind empty except for that one thought.

Prostasis owned Weaver Detention Facility.

Operated, rather.

Same thing.

This was bad.

A sudden wave of panic drove her to her feet. This was very bad.

Why? What were the implications?

Deep, calming breaths, she told herself. Get a grip. Think it through.

Randall Gates was a vice president of Prostatis, and he was on Safer America's board.

Gary, or somebody, had pulled strings to get Danny transferred to Weaver Correctional Facility.

Did Gates know about her connection to Danny? About her other life? If he did . . .

Christ, she thought, did Gary *want* it to come out? That she had a boyfriend who'd been caught smuggling pot? And here she was at the arm of Caitlin O'Connor, the spokeswoman for an organization that preached getting tough on crime.

Why?

Maybe I'm being set up, she thought. Maybe . . . maybe

something's going to happen to Caitlin, and I'm going to get blamed for it.

That sounded like a scenario Gary would enjoy. Something that would end with both her and Danny in a cell. Or worse.

Was Danny safe?

"Fuck!"

"I'M SORRY, I'M *NOT* going to calm down. You need to get him out of there."

"Emily, we're doing what we can."

"Which is *what*, exactly?"

She dropped the phone to her side, dragged her fingers across her forehead.

"Shit," she muttered.

Get a grip. You have to.

She raised the phone back up to her ear.

"Derek," she began. "I've done some research into Weaver. It's a substandard, dangerous facility."

Which was the truth. She'd spent the last half hour Googling on her iPad. Among other things, Weaver had been written up in a few local papers for an inmate-hazing ritual that the guards had not only turned a blind eye toward but encouraged. They called it "Balls on the Wall." Michelle could barely stand to read about it.

"They understaff the prison so they can make more money," she said, because money was easier to talk about. "They've found *maggots* in the food."

"Marisol is going out there first thing tomorrow with the paperwork for Jeff to file a request for a transfer back to Harris County. Assuming this was an administrative error of some kind, that should be all it takes to fix this."

"And if it wasn't?"

"We file the request for a transfer anyway. If the over-crowding in Harris County really is that severe, they can still move Jeff to a facility closer to Houston."

"What if they don't? What are we going to do?"

She drew in a deep breath. It was time for, if not honesty, some kind of acknowledgment of what was actually happening here.

"Look, Derek, you know this whole thing is . . . that it's screwed up. That there's some kind of . . . pressure or vendetta going on."

There was a moment of silence on the other end.

What *did* Derek actually know?

"Jeff is a pre-trial detainee," he finally said. "As such, he's entitled to a higher level of constitutional protection than a convicted prisoner. They're not allowed to punish him when he hasn't been found guilty of anything. If they keep up this bullshit, we claim that it's punitive and they're violating the Due Process clauses of the Constitution."

If Derek knew something, he wasn't saying.

"Do you think that will work?"

"I think we can make a good case."

Which didn't answer the question at all.

"In the meantime . . ." A pause. "It might help if we made that appointment with the DEA."

Shit.

"Okay," Michelle said. "Let me . . . let me figure a few things out."

DID IT REALLY MAKE sense for her to meet with the DEA? How much time would that actually buy her, before someone decided there was enough evidence to arrest her as well?

She'd only been Emily for two years. If they were checking her background . . . if they asked a lot of questions . . .

How much of a life story could she fake?

She started to unpack.

After she'd hung her Armani jacket, slacks and blouses in the closet, her light overcoat she'd brought for unpredictable San Francisco nights, folded up her other clothes and placed them in the drawers under the flat-panel TV, she considered what was in the ruck: The logbook. The passports. The money.

She wasn't sure what to do with the logbook and the passports, but she decided the hotel safe was good enough to store the $10,000 bundle, plus the $3,000 from the camera bag, the $25K from Houston and half of the cash in her wallet. People carried cash. That alone wasn't incriminating. Not for Michelle, anyway.

Christ, she thought. All that money in the safe at the Arcata house. Had they gotten a warrant? Could they search the house? She'd put nearly $25,000 in the safe, and there was already cash in it. What would they make of some thirty thousand in cash in a safe that she and Danny both used?

They'd hang her on that alone.

I should've just carried it on, she thought. It would have been less of a risk.

Stupid, she thought. You're so stupid.

But she couldn't spend too much time beating herself up about that right now. She needed to figure out what to do.

Was there any way to get out ahead of this game that Gary was playing?

She sat cross-legged on the floor in front of the closet safe and started pulling out the things she'd packed from the ruck.

Her camera bag. The money in it. The practical jacket and the $10,000 bundle. The money from Houston. The passports.

She opened one of the passports, the one belonging to "Meredith Evelyn Jackson."

Her hair was dark in the photo. Shoulder length.

Well, there was nothing she could do about the length. But I should dye my hair again, she thought. Back to what it was before.

She was going to have to use this passport. She knew it now. There was no going back to Emily. And she couldn't count on Michelle being safe for much longer.

Danny's logbook. She ran her fingers on its pebbled surface.

What to do with the logbook?

What to do about Danny, locked up in a prison run by Prostatis?

No way that filling out an administrative request for a transfer was going to get him out of there. And how long would building a case based on constitutional law actually take?

I've got to get him out, she thought. I have to at least try.

She pulled *Taking Flight* out of the bag. The Further Adventures of Lex Telluride, she thought.

Have you heard back from Sam?

When she'd told him she'd heard nothing from Sam, that was when Danny had told her about the book.

Maybe Sam wasn't holding up his end of the bargain. Whatever the bargain was.

She considered her choices. There weren't very many.

If she wanted to get Danny out, she'd have to make a bargain with someone, and that someone was either Sam or Gary.

She took her last remaining burner phone out of her suitcase and headed downstairs. She'd make the call outside.

"WHAT CAN I DO for you?"

Where to start?

"We have a situation," she said to Sam.

AFTER SHE'D FINISHED, THERE was silence on the other end of the line. Typical, Michelle now realized. He did this kind of thing and answered questions with questions, making her force the conversation—a way of keeping her off-balance.

Why did Danny have so much faith in him?

"Did you get all that?" she finally said.

"I did."

"And . . . do you have any recommendations?"

Silence.

"You know, this is a burner phone with limited minutes," she said.

A chuckle. "Let the process run its course," he said.

Now it was her turn for silence. "Are you shitting me?" she finally said. "I'm actually curious."

"Of course not. It's always best to see if the easiest path opens up. You waste much less energy and the calling in of favors that way."

"You know, Sam," she said, "it's funny, because Danny really trusted you. He was counting on you to help. And so far, all you've done is make vague promises and tell me to let it all play out."

"You think I haven't helped him already?" he said sharply. "That I haven't helped you? Do you think all of the arrangements I make happen by magic?"

"No. I think they happen because you or somebody else owed him some favors. And now you're adding up who owes who."

Funny. It wasn't until she'd said it that she knew she'd spoken the truth.

She thought she heard his intake of breath. But that might have been wishful thinking. This man was cold. It wasn't about loyalty for him, not primarily, anyway. It was all about the balance, about the calculation, how the numbers added up.

"Our best option is to wait and see if this administrative appeal gets him out of the facility. If it doesn't, then we can escalate the pressure."

"Okay. Then I'll call you tomorrow or the day after. We should know where we stand by then."

After they disconnected, she stared at the burner phone in her hand. She wondered if the low heel on her boot was hard enough to crush it.

What an asshole.

She hadn't told Sam everything. She wasn't going to lay down all her cards at once. She hadn't told him about Danny's logbook or the passports, and she was pretty sure that Sam didn't know about them. Danny wasn't naïve. He was always hedging his bets.

But it was clear that Sam didn't care all that much about Danny being in prison, in a place where it was reasonable to assume people were willing to do him harm. Sam didn't care at all that she was being squeezed by Gary and the DEA, or that she was likely being set up in some kind of scheme to help keep Safer America the convenient little money machine that it was, one pumping out ads to support the interests feeding it all the cash that kept it running.

She was willing to wait a few days. After that, Sam was going to get something in his mailbox that he might not much like.

AFTER THAT, SHE DECIDED to take a walk. She needed to buy another burner or two, for one thing. It was close to 5:30, still plenty of sun left, and the day was pleasant, cloudy and in the mid-sixties.

She wandered around Union Square in search of a Walgreens. Those were everywhere, so she figured it wouldn't take long. She was always struck by what a beautiful city San Francisco was, but she especially noticed it now, after spending so much time in Houston. All these older, elegant buildings, framed against a pink and purple sunset. Now filled mostly with luxury chain stores. Tiffany. Gucci. Marc Jacobs. Kate Spade. Burberry, Brooks Brothers and Bloomingdale's.

So much money here.

By the time she got back to the hotel, it was nearly 7:00.

I should eat something, she thought. Maybe just in the hotel restaurant. It was on Safer America's dime, after all, and sushi sounded as good as anything. After that, she had no idea. Go to the gym, maybe. Watch a stupid movie. Work on her story for the DEA, that is, if she decided to make that appointment. She really wasn't sure if it made sense, if it would actually do any good.

And if they were planning to arrest her, if she met with them and they knew where she was, even if she was traveling as Michelle . . .

Panic fluttered in her chest. I've got to get Danny out of jail, she thought, and then we have to get the fuck out of here.

THE RESTAURANT WAS CALLED Kendo and was decorated in black with red and gold accents, with swords hung on the walls here and there and a sculpture tangle of branches sitting in the center of the space lit by gauzy blue and red spotlights.

There was a place at the sushi bar. Michelle eased her way in.

"Something to drink?" The waitress, dressed in what looked like a fashion version of a black martial arts outfit, was young, cute. Everyone here would be young and cute, Michelle was willing to bet.

"I'd like cold sake," she said.

"Our house cold sake is Ozeki. But we have a big list if you want to try something more unusual."

"What do you recommend?"

"We have so many good ones. But I like Akita Seishu Dewatsuru Hihaku. It's Junmai Daiginjo sake, so very high quality."

"Sure," Michelle said. Why not? She wasn't paying for it.

The sushi chef closest to her seat finished searing the albacore he was preparing, and as he shaped the rice for the *nigiri*, said: "What would you like?"

"*Omakase*," Michelle said, managing a smile. "You choose."

Just let someone else make the decisions.

The waitress brought her the sake, a full crystal glass in a wood box nearly overflowing with sake. Michelle sipped. It really was delicious: crisp, floral, with a hint of some fruit she couldn't place.

I should have some water, she thought. Her mouth was dry—she was probably dehydrated from the flight. She turned to catch her waitress's attention.

There at a table on the other side of the tangled branches were Caitlin and Troy. She couldn't see Troy's face from this angle, but she could see Caitlin, and she was laughing, as though Troy had just told her a joke.

Chapter Twenty-Four

"UNFORTUNATELY, IT DOESN'T SEEM to have been an administrative error."

Michelle nodded, though of course Marisol couldn't see that. The lawyer had called her late in the afternoon, after Michelle and Caitlin had gotten back from clothes shopping, with the news that Michelle had expected.

"We filed the request for the transfer, and if we don't get a favorable response or if they drag their heels about it, we'll take the next step."

Marisol sounded tired. Maybe even discouraged. Michelle didn't know her well enough to be certain.

"How long before they make a decision?"

There was a pause on the other end of the line.

"Two to four weeks. Though I've seen it happen in as soon as five days."

She was pretty sure it wouldn't happen in five days.

Two to four weeks. Could she afford to wait that long? With Danny in that place and with whatever Gary was planning?

"Okay," she said. "And . . . Jeff. How is he doing?"

"Well, you know Jeff," Marisol said. Like she actually knew him. "He's hanging in there, making the best of it."

"Can he . . . is he able to call me?"

"You may have to set up a new account. I'm pretty sure a different company runs the phones there."

"Great," Michelle said. "I'll do that."

Just great.

SHE WROTE DEREK AN email.

> *Hi Derek,*
> *I can't set up that meeting you wanted for another few days. I'm going to send you some additional funds to cover your expenses in the meantime.*
> *Thanks for all your efforts.*
> *Best,*
> *Miche*

She stopped. Erased that portion of her name. Typed in "Emily," and sent the email.

"So . . . how was your dinner with Troy?"

"You know . . . it was really good. We talked so long I think we just about closed that bar down."

Michelle and Caitlin rode in the back of a town car on the way to the event in Sea Cliff. The event was cocktails and hors d'oeuvres beginning at 6:30 P.M. and running until 9:30, but Caitlin wasn't expected to appear until 7. They had some time and the traffic was bad, so the driver took them on a circuitous route along the outer edge of Golden Gate Park, with views of the ocean and the Golden Gate Bridge: a series of postcards of the long, slow summer sunset, the encroaching fog.

"I can't explain why Troy and I've hit it off the way we have. It sure wasn't anything I was expecting. But I'm really thankful for it. You know, he lost a parent to addiction and a brother to violence, along with a lot of friends. There's plenty of pain in the world to go around. Maybe I just needed a reminder of that."

Caitlin looked thoughtful. Not like she'd looked before when mentioning Troy, not embarrassed, not flirtatious, not like a woman who was doing something a little rebellious and enjoying it.

"I've been feeling for a while now that the way we've been approaching things in Safer America is just . . . that we're doing it wrong. That a lot of what we've been supporting isn't productive, and maybe it's even the opposite of that." Now she turned to Michelle, briefly rested her hand on Michelle's arm. "I can tell you these things, right? I mean, you're not committed to what Safer America's been doing the way . . . well, the way the board and most of the employees are. Are you?"

Michelle swallowed hard. "No. No, I'm not."

Caitlin smiled. "Good. I didn't think you were."

I'm not here to help you, Michelle wanted to say. I'm not your friend. And if I'm being at all smart, I need to get on the phone to fucking Gary and tell him that you've slipped your leash. Unless of course that would trigger whatever endgame he has to blow things up and blame me for it.

"So . . . it's not like I met Troy and I suddenly had a come-to-Jesus moment," Caitlin said. "I was thinking a lot of this stuff already. I just . . . I didn't want to think it all the way. Does that make sense?"

"Sure," Michelle said. "Yes. It does."

"He's really helped me take that last step, and . . ." Now Caitlin did blush. "I don't feel so afraid."

But you should feel afraid, Michelle thought. You really should.

"That's great to hear," she said.

"And you know . . . you've been a part of it too. You showed up at just the right time. I really have wanted to make some changes. To . . . to just get moving again. You gave me the push I needed. And I can't tell you how much I appreciate that."

Michelle felt tears gathering in her eyes. Stop it, she told herself. You don't have time.

"That's nice of you to say. But . . . you did it on your own. Without me, and without Troy. You're a really strong person. Just . . . remember that. Okay?"

What the fuck was she going to do?

Caitlin gave her a look that Michelle couldn't quite interpret. Some combination of measuring and amused. "You are one fierce lady," she said. "One of these days you're gonna have to tell me how you got that way."

They rode for a while in silence, the car turning away from the sea road with its cliffs and pines.

"I don't want to embarrass the people who're hosting the event," Caitlin said with a sigh. "Though, I don't know, I also don't want to take peoples' money under false pretenses. Because when we get back to Houston, I'm planning on switching up our priorities. I don't want to put our money into this election. I might not agree with legalizing marijuana, but it's a waste of our resources fighting it. And I definitely don't want to support going after this sentencing proposition. It makes no sense to me at all. But a lot of the folks who're coming tonight, well, they're only showing up because of our positions in this election."

She hesitated.

"What do you think I should do? How should I handle it?"

Oh, Christ, Michelle thought.

"Shake their hands and take their money?" She said it with a smile, lightly, like she was making a joke, but she knew that of all the things that could happen tonight, this would be the safest option for Caitlin, and for her.

"Yeah, except I don't want to deal with the mess when they start screaming for their money back."

Michelle scrambled around for the next best option.

"Maybe . . . say something along the lines of what you did in Los Angeles. That your goal is a safer America, and you're open to new approaches on how to achieve that."

Caitlin grinned. "You know, I invited Troy to come along tonight. He didn't think that was a good idea. Said he could just see people's heads explode. But I'm still gonna put him on the guest list. Maybe he'll show up. Wouldn't that be a hoot?"

"Hahah, yeah."

Please don't show up, Troy, Michelle thought.

This was already going to be bad enough.

FROM WHAT MICHELLE KNEW, Sea Cliff was one of the wealthiest areas in San Francisco, with large homes on actual reasonably sized yards instead of the postage-stamp lots found in most of the city. Still, they were dwarfed by the compounds of River Oaks, by the estates in Beverly Hills for that matter. Land in San Francisco was simply too scarce.

There was a valet station set up at the drive of one of the larger houses in the neighborhood: a yellowish cream Mediterranean-style three-story villa with a Spanish tile roof perched on a corner lot. Michelle suspected it would have an ocean view from the other side, or would it be considered the bay? She didn't know San Francisco all that well, not the way she knew Los Angeles.

"Thanks, hon," Caitlin said to the driver. "We'll see you in an hour and a half or thereabouts."

As they started up the red terra-cotta stairs that led to the front door, Caitlin drew in a deep breath.

"Here's hoping we can get through tonight without completely pissing everyone off," she said. "Wish me luck."

"You'll be fine," Michelle said.

She wished she actually believed that.

THE PARTY WAS HOSTED by one of San Francisco's richest men, a venture capitalist and hedge fund manager named Garth Johannsen. He'd been a big donor to Safer America in the past, one of the more useful bits of information Michelle had gotten from reviewing the DonorSoft database with Caitlin the other day. And it was pretty easy to see what his stake was: he'd invested heavily in the private prison industry and the various companies that provided food and other services to the prisons. Some of his other investments included companies that used a lot of prison labor. It hadn't been that hard for Michelle to track all this down. Just a couple of hours of work during some downtime here in San Francisco, and if anyone asked, she was just getting up to speed on an important donor, one they needed to coddle with informed flattery.

Inside, the house was contemporary, a mismatch with its original style: spare, straight lines and sharp angles, recessed lights, carefully chosen art.

Garth Johannsen and his wife greeted them in the entry.

"Ms. O'Connor, it's wonderful to finally meet you."

He was in his sixties, trim, with a handmade suit and expensive haircut.

"Please, call me Caitlin."

"Caitlin, I'm Mary. Welcome to our home." This was his wife, several decades younger, round cheeked with a pixie cut and eyes set in a permanent twinkle. She was originally from China and they'd met when she'd worked at Johannsen's firm as a new hire out of Harvard Business School. Her family had ties to the Chinese leadership, Michelle recalled.

Wonder how *that* affects his investments, Michelle thought.

"This is Michelle," Caitlin was saying. "If you need anything from me or the group later, just get in touch with her, and she'll make sure it happens."

"What can we get you ladies to drink?" Mary asked. A server in white and black had appeared next to them—Chinese? Michelle wondered.

It looked to be another gathering where most of the guests were white.

"Just water, thank you," she said.

The next half hour passed in a blur of introductions and handshakes as she trailed Caitlin, collecting business cards and making notes. The guests were bankers, business owners, wealthy retirees, a police chief from a nearby city, a representative from the state prison guards union, one of the few non-white faces here, aside from Mary Johannsen and the serving staff.

Caitlin was good. She'd stuck to the one glass of wine,

but it was more than that: she was focused, charming, on her game.

Well, she'd need to be, tonight.

The guests had started to settle in the living room, where Caitlin was to speak. You could see the remodeling here, too, Michelle thought: floor-to-ceiling windows had been installed for the ocean view she'd figured the house would have on this side. She couldn't see the ocean because of the fog, but she could hear the boom of the waves through the double-paned glass.

"Well, look who's here," Caitlin said.

Michelle turned to Caitlin, who was smiling like she meant it.

Coming across the living room was Troy Stone, excusing himself a few times as he worked through the crowd on his way to her side.

Chapter Twenty-Five

"I CAN'T BELIEVE I let you talk me into this," Troy said in a low voice.

Caitlin actually cackled. "You know you love it."

He snuck a grin. "Yeah, maybe I *like* seeing heads explode."

"Well, here comes your first chance. Our host is on his way over."

Garth Johannsen was heading in their direction. Michelle checked her phone: 7:40. Time for Caitlin to give her remarks. Her pulse quickened.

It'll be okay, she told herself. Caitlin's a pro. She'll handle this, and it won't be a disaster.

"Michelle, nice to see you again," Troy said.

She smiled back. "Likewise."

He didn't actually seem happy to see her. But then, she sure wasn't glad to see him.

"Hello," Johannsen said, extending his hand in Troy's direction. "Garth Johannsen."

Troy took it.

"Troy Stone."

It was always interesting to watch the male handshake ritual, Michelle thought. Garth would want to show his dominance, but there was no way he'd be able to crush Troy's broad hand.

A vigorous, quick shake.

"Troy's a friend of mine from Los Angeles," Caitlin said.

"He heads up an organization called PCA, Positive Community Action. Maybe you've heard of it?"

She was enjoying this, Michelle could tell.

Johannsen's brow crinkled. "Sounds familiar." He knew, or had an idea, Michelle thought. He just couldn't make the knowledge make sense.

"Your group's working on Prop. 275?" he asked.

The sentencing reduction proposal.

Troy stretched out a smile. "Yes, yes we are."

"Oh. Well." Garth looked to Caitlin, the question showing as clearly on his face as if he'd asked it.

"We've been having some discussions about approaches to crime reduction and community safety," Caitlin said.

"Have you, now?"

"Do you think I should do a little talk now? Have folks had enough chance to settle in?"

"I think so." He didn't sound all that certain.

A waitress had appeared at Michelle's elbow. "Something to drink?"

"Yes. Please. A glass of red."

"WELL, I'M JUST DELIGHTED to be here."

Caitlin stood with her back to the wall of windows, illuminated by a soft pool of light cast by the overhead spots.

"I'm a little worried, though, about some of the things I want to talk about tonight, because I don't think they're what y'all are expecting to hear. I apologize for that."

She did that trick of hers, the one where she looked around the room, making brief eye contact with people in the audience, making you believe she'd connected with you, if just for that instant.

"But lately I've been doing a lot of thinking about our mutual goals—about creating a safer America—and asking myself, what does that actually mean? Does it mean making sure that more and more people go to jail? Is that really making us safer?"

She paused. Surveyed the room again.

"Now, we all know there's dangerous folks who belong in prison, who do violent things and hurt other people. But I'm gonna admit to y'all here, I'm not so sure putting people in a cell for selling weed or shoplifting a couple pieces of pizza is getting us where we want to go. Which is to safer, stronger communities that are better for us and better for our kids."

She spread out our hands. "So . . . I'm open to suggestions. I'm talking to a lot of different people"—she gestured in Troy's direction—"like Troy Stone here, from Positive Community Action, about the kinds of things we can do together to truly build a safer America. And what I'd like to do now is get some of *your* ideas on that."

For a long moment, no one spoke. Finally, a man at the back of the room raised his hand.

"So . . . are you *not* supporting No on 275 and 391?"

"To be honest with you? I'm not sure any more."

An audible buzz started up in the audience.

Oh shit, Michelle thought. This was bad.

"OUR PRISONS HAD NEARLY twice the number of inmates they were designed to hold. The overcrowding was so bad we're operating under federal court orders to fix it. We're sending prisoners out of state, we're releasing inmates to local jails, we're double-celling in administrative segregation, and you want to starve the system even more?"

This was the representative from the prison guard's union, standing toe-to-toe with Troy.

"You've just stated the case for changing sentencing guidelines better than I could," Troy said.

"What about community safety? How's releasing offenders into communities with no supervision going to help with that? What we need are more facilities, more resources—then we can get to more of the rehabilitation functions people like you are always going on about."

Troy raised an eyebrow. "People like me?"

"Activists," the union rep spat out.

"Now, isn't it true y'all are already spending more on prisons than you are on colleges here in California?" Caitlin said, neatly stepping into the conversation.

"Mostly because we're spending more money per prisoner to improve healthcare and rehabilitation opportunities."

"And salaries," Troy said. "Let's be honest, your members make fifty to ninety percent more than correctional officers in the rest of the country."

"Yeah, and so do California highway patrol officers. We got prisons in some of the most expensive areas of the country here. My officers are professionals who deserve to be compensated decently. Unless you'd rather see a bunch of poorly trained rent-a-cops like what the private prisons are hiring for shit wages."

Michelle took a few steps back, toward the wall of glass that overlooked the water. She'd drunk most of her glass of wine as the question and answer session broke into a general discussion, with Caitlin working the room and chatting with guests.

Would a refill be a bad idea? She felt sick to her stomach.

Not everyone here was hostile, from what she could tell. Many seemed interested in talking to Caitlin and hearing what she had to say. But much of this crowd had come to raise money to defeat the two propositions that Caitlin said she was now on the fence about. In the case of Prop. 275, she'd already decided, Michelle knew.

"Looks like Ms. O'Connor's had kind of a turnaround, doesn't it?"

Standing next to her was a man about her age. Sandy brown hair, rimless glasses with titanium frames, wearing an open-collar blue button-down Oxford cloth shirt and a blazer.

"Her views are evolving, I think," Michelle said.

He chuckled deep in his chest. "I've been telling Garth he's going to get caught out on the wrong side of this issue. If Caitlin O'Connor's coming around, I'd say the tide has officially turned."

"Are you working on one of the propositions, Mr. . . . ?"

He stuck out a hand. "Shane. You're Caitlin's person?"

"I'm her assistant, yes. Michelle."

"I have a fund," he said. "We've taken some positions on cannabis-related industries. I'm in with both feet, and I'm advising others to do the same." He leaned over. "Heard of Budly? Or Skunkish? Green Goddess LTC?"

She'd vaguely heard of Budly. "Budly . . . isn't that . . . Facebook for weed?"

"Potentially—more like Amazon. But you have the right idea." He was watching Caitlin across the room as she listened intently to a red-faced man who was chopping at the air with his hands: Angry. Frustrated.

"People are going to get very rich off this business," Shane said.

"People already have," Michelle said.

He laughed again. "I mean, legally. It's already happening, with the medical industry. Once states start legalizing cannabis for recreational use . . ."

"You'll still have to deal with the federal government."

"This too shall pass. I'm not going to pretend it isn't a little tricky right now, especially the banking end. But it'll all get worked out. I can afford to be patient."

Michelle glanced past him, out the window. By now it was completely dark, the night muffled in fog. She could make out a haloed string of lights somewhere out in the water. A bridge? A ship?

"There's a lot of money being made right now with the way things are," she said. "A lot of the people in this room don't want things to change."

Shane gave an easy shrug. "In any scenario like this, you have winners and losers. And you have people who know how to adapt to changing circumstances and stay winners regardless. If I'm wrong about this, I'll lose money, but it's not going to break me. If I'm right, I win big. And I'm pretty sure I'm right."

He continued to stare at Caitlin. She'd calmed the man she'd been talking to by the look of things, clasping his hand and resting her left hand on his forearm for a moment.

Shane turned to Michelle. "How about introducing me to your boss?"

"Sure," she said. "I'd be happy to."

Dread sat in her gut. She thought she might actually be sick. She knew she'd never been in control of this situation, far from it. But now she had a palpable sense that things were spinning far, far out of her grasp.

☙ ☙ ☙

SHANE SUGGESTED THEY ADJOURN to a "speak-easy" in the Tenderloin after the cocktail party.

"There's a private bar down there that's good for conversation," he'd said. "Just follow me. I'll get us in."

Michelle had Googled him on her iPhone. He looked like he was who he claimed to be: a very successful venture capitalist/fund manager and one of San Francisco's richer men. His car was a red Tesla Roadster Sport.

As the town car pulled up in front of the Johannsen house, Troy hesitated.

"You're coming, aren't you?" Caitlin asked him.

"You want to ride with me?" Shane called out the window of his Tesla. "We should talk."

Troy nodded. "Yeah. I guess we should."

A pro-legalization venture capitalist and an activist working on keeping drug users out of prison probably did have a few things to talk about, Michelle thought.

"You know, I'm really having a good time tonight," Caitlin said in the car. "Believe me, all the time I've been doing these events? That's rare."

Michelle forced a smile. "I'm glad to hear it."

As they followed Shane's Tesla through the San Francisco streets, losing the taillights now and again in the fog, Michelle tried to figure out how to tell Caitlin the truth, or at least to come up with a story that would make sense. One that Caitlin would believe.

"PEOPLE ARE RESPONSIBLE FOR their own choices."

Troy let out a sharp sigh, almost a huff. "That's a *thing*

with you masters of the universe, isn't it. You're in control, and if you're not, you're weak."

He leaned back in the booth, in that still, coiled way Michelle already recognized. "You know, for most people, getting lectures about choices when they don't have opportunities isn't all that useful."

He was clearly irritated, and Michelle couldn't blame him. Shane had been going on since they'd arrived about paths to success and personal freedom, a conversation that had presumably started in the car on the way over, and Michelle was already tired of it.

She wanted to get out of there. She needed to figure out what to do. She was going to have to call Gary, for one. Caitlin's reversal of Safer America's positions in this election was bound to get back to him, and if she didn't get in front of that, he'd take it out on her, and he'd take it out on Danny. She was sure of that.

The private bar of the speakeasy was down a flight of stairs, in a bricked basement that they claimed was used to smuggle booze during Prohibition. Who knew if that was really true? It was the kind of story Michelle could see making up to add a little burnish to your marketing. They'd gone with the theme down here, using old whiskey barrels for stools and installing a long, wooden bar scarred with cigarette burns.

"You're disadvantaged, you don't have a support system, you gotta make all the right choices, not slip up once," Troy continued. "There's no margin for error. Meanwhile, some people have the privilege to fuck up over and over again and still come out on top. You gonna talk to *them* about choices?"

"Life ain't fair." Shane raised his craft bourbon cocktail with its hand-chipped ice and sipped.

"That's your answer?"

Shane put down his drink and sat up straight, like he was suddenly energized. "Look at it this way. The ones who do make it through, who make all the right choices and succeed . . . they're going to be the best of the best. They're ones who push us all forward. What's that line by Hemingway, they are strong in the broken places."

"Oh lord," Caitlin said, rolling her eyes. "Let me tell you something. When some things get broken, they aren't stronger. They're just broken, healing up crooked and limping along as best as they can."

"Here's what I don't get," Troy said, jabbing his finger at Shane. "If you believe in some kind of survival of the fittest, you tell me how it is that most of the people making decisions in this country are the ones who've grown up being protected from their own mistakes. You tell me how that works."

Shane laughed. "Not very well. Tell you what." He leaned forward, elbows on the table, chin in hand. "If you have some opportunity-based programs in mind, let me know. Maybe we can help each other here."

"How's that?"

"I want both of these propositions to pass. I think that position is on the right side of history. It's also the position that's going to make me a lot of money. If you want to get the message out about how passing these propositions strengthens communities, I'll put some money into those efforts."

"Even though you don't care about the communities."

"Talk me into caring," Shane said with a grin.

Michelle stood. "Excuse me. I'll be right back."

The restrooms were upstairs. A good excuse to step outside the speakeasy and make a call.

It was chilly in the fog. A homeless man pissed against the wall just to the left of the bar's hidden entrance. The Tenderloin was a dicey neighborhood surrounded by gentrification, million-dollar lofts popping up here and there on its blocks like mushrooms after a rain.

Michelle buttoned her jacket and called Gary. She hoped he wouldn't answer.

"Hello?"

Shit.

"I don't have time to talk right now," she said. "But you might be hearing some things about the fundraiser tonight. Caitlin said she's on the fence about continuing to fund the Protect our Communities campaign."

"You mean No on 275 and 391?"

"Right."

"Tell me exactly what happened. This couldn't just have come out of the blue."

"I told you, I have to go. I'm with Caitlin. Let's talk tomorrow."

"Wait—"

"*No.* You don't want me to blow this, do you? I'm hanging up now."

"Okay, okay. Tomorrow. First thing."

"I'll call."

Then she disconnected.

WHEN SHE GOT BACK downstairs, Troy was standing at the bar, peering at the shelves of liquor. "Oh, good," he said. "Thought I'd get the next round. Wanted to see what kind of whiskey they had. What would you like?"

"Oh. Just a glass of wine."

"You have a preference?"

"The Napa cabernet. Thanks."

They stood in silence as the bartender, a twentysomething with a beard, tattoos, wearing a striped vest and suspenders, mixed what looked to be a complicated cocktail.

"You know," Troy said, "I get the feeling you maybe think I'm bad news for your boss."

Michelle's stomach lurched. This night wasn't going to get any easier. What should she say to him?

"I . . . I don't think that at all."

She risked a glance over at the table where Shane and Caitlin sat, Caitlin in full charm mode, leaning forward slightly, a bright smile on her lips.

"You just . . . you need to be careful," she said in a low voice. "Both of you. Some of the people involved with Safer America . . ."

Christ.

"They're not great people."

Troy rested his elbow on the bar and leaned back, looking at her with a puzzled, appraising expression. "What do you mean, exactly?"

The bartender turned in their direction. "Hi, folks. What can I get for you?"

Michelle shook her head. "That's all I can say."

And she probably shouldn't have said it.

SHANE OFFERED TO DROP Troy at his hotel—"It's on my way."

When the town car pulled up to the corner in front of the speakeasy, Caitlin and Troy hugged briefly. A friendly, collegial hug, Michelle thought. Maybe that was all there was to it.

"Talk tomorrow?" Caitlin asked him in a low voice.

"Definitely."

He glanced over at Michelle. Their eyes met briefly.

Just be careful.

CAITLIN STRETCHED IN HER seat in the back of the town car.

"What a night," she said.

Caitlin had been quiet on the ride back. Michelle was guessing that she had a lot to think about. She'd just more or less blown up Safer America's mission in California, and there was no way that wouldn't have larger consequences.

Just not necessarily the ones Caitlin was expecting.

Caitlin sighed. "I am gonna catch so much shit when we get back to Houston."

"You'll be fine," Michelle said automatically. "I mean, it's your organization. They have to go along with what you want, don't they?"

"Not necessarily. The board has the power to fire me, if they want to. But that could get pretty ugly too, if I want to make it ugly." Caitlin chuckled. "Who knows, maybe I do."

Michelle nodded. Things were building up to something very ugly, she was sure of it, but how could she talk Caitlin out of the confrontation? She had no leverage, no argument, other than a truth that sounded too crazy to believe.

❧ ❧ ❧

"LET'S JUST MEET FOR lunch tomorrow," Caitlin said, as they waited for the elevator in the hotel lobby. "I'm worn out. In a good way." She smiled. There was something thoughtful about the expression. "I can't tell you what a relief it is, to finally just . . . cast off this weight I've been carrying. Stop being this symbol all the time. Whatever happens when we get home . . : it's worth it."

It's not worth it if they kill you, Michelle almost blurted out.

You don't know if that's what they're planning, she told herself.

She smiled and nodded and said: "That's so great to hear."

But later, lying in bed, unable to sleep, she couldn't stop thinking about it.

If Caitlin really did intend to pull Safer America's resources out of the California campaign, or worse, put them on the other side of the propositions . . . Kicking her out of her own nonprofit might not be enough. Those kinds of battles often went public, and in Caitlin's current frame of mind, Michelle could see her relishing that fight.

Killing Caitlin made a sick kind of sense, the kind of sense Gary made.

And don't make it look like an accident, she thought. No. Make it a murder. Make it vicious. Senseless.

Caitlin O'Connor, tragic survivor, victimized a second time. A martyr.

A very useful symbol.

Think of the campaign ads and appeals for donations you could run with that.

It was too easy, putting herself in Gary's head.

Chapter Twenty-Six

THE ADVANTAGE TO CALLING Gary last night was that she'd done her job, technically. Now she could control the timing of when she called him again. She couldn't put him off for too long, she knew, but she could keep both her iPhones switched off until she was ready for the conversation. She needed to think about what to say, a way to word it that would be less damaging to Caitlin, if that was even possible.

Besides, she had things she needed to do first.

LOTUS HAD A TINY business center, for those who needed to print or fax and for the very few people who traveled without laptops or tablets or smartphones. The center was in an alcove, not even a separate room, to the side and behind the Buddha fountain.

6 A.M. The lobby was fairly quiet. A few guests sipped coffee and read newspapers in the couches and chairs adjacent to the bar.

"Just enter your name and room number on the screen," the desk clerk said, "and we'll charge it to your room."

"Actually, is there some way I can pay cash instead? My employer's covering my room, and this is my own business."

"Sure, not a problem. Type in 'Guest' and 'Guestroom1234' and tell me when you're done."

She'd given it a lot of thought. She couldn't trust that sending a flash drive to her old LA attorney would be enough. Maybe they'd find out what she was doing here, but that might not be an entirely bad thing either—it might distract them from looking into an obscure figure from her past. Or, it might make them think that she could have stashed this information in so many places that they'd never find them all.

Or, the whole thing was an exercise in futility.

But she had to take the chance, as bad as the odds were. Just going along with Gary and Sam and hoping that things would somehow work out gave her no chance at all.

Evergreen did email newsletters for subscribers, advertising seasonal menus, special events and deals, using a free web-based service. There weren't all that many subscribers, under two hundred last time she checked, but it was easy to add other addresses to the email list. She did that now, going to websites like the *New York Times* and the *Washington Post*, *Mother Jones*, *The Nation*, the *San Francisco Chronicle* and the *LA Times*, the *Wall Street Journal*, *Reason*, a few alternative online publications and local weeklies, finding a reporter's or editor's email address and adding it to the Evergreen mailing list.

Next, she opened a simple template and titled it: "A story you might be interested in."

Her heart was thudding hard now, sweat prickling her skin. If there was spyware on this computer . . . if they were monitoring it . . .

She drew in a deep breath and inserted the extra flash drive to which she'd copied Danny's logbook.

The PDF of the letter he'd written in the back opened immediately. This computer had Acrobat Pro installed. Good, she thought. You couldn't insert PDFs into one of these newsletters; she'd tried it before, and you had to use JPEGs or PNG files (whatever those were). She saved the file as a JPEG and uploaded it to the file manager section of the email service, where it appeared as a thumbnail above other thumbnails of images she'd used in newsletters past: Her shot of the redwoods, an artfully arranged plate of seasonal root vegetables, a staff photo celebrating Christmas last year.

She went back to the newsletter she'd started. If she'd had more time, she would have written something better, more persuasive, more informative. But she didn't have time.

She wrote:

> *My name is Michelle Mason. For the last two years I was known as Emily Carmichael, and I owned and operated the Evergreen Bistro in Arcata, CA. I lived with a man people knew as Jeff Gregerson. His real name is Daniel Finn.*
>
> *This is a crazy-sounding story, and if you'd tried to tell it to me a few years ago I never would have believed it. I wouldn't have even listened. But it's true, and the materials linked to this email can prove it. I've sent other people this infomation as well.*

She inserted the JPEG of Danny's note below that.

The email service offered file-hosting, where you could upload documents and then insert links to them in your email blasts. Using Acrobat, she combined the two hundred PDFs from Danny's logbook into nine files. She kept the links in her newsletter simple. "Captain Daniel Finn's Logbook, Part 1." "Part 2." "Part 3."

She'd send it to everyone on the email list. The more the

better. Maybe there were a few conspiracy theorists among Evergreen's clientele.

The last thing she did was schedule the email to go out in seven days.

When she cleared the browser and logged off, it was just after 8:30 A.M.

THE BANK OF AMERICA branch near Union Square opened at 9:00 A.M. Bank of America was where Emily had her checking account. With $10,000 of the cash she'd brought from Arcata, she purchased a cashier's check made out to Derek Girard. She wasn't sure how much of the original $10,000 retainer was left at this point, something she should have asked about but had been too distracted to even consider. He'd said the ten thousand would be more than enough to cover the costs if the case didn't go to trial, when he'd thought they'd bail Danny out and get the case dismissed or make some kind of deal. Now? With visits to jails six hours away from Houston? Who knew what the tab would be?

Next, she headed to a different bank, Chase, where Michelle had a bank account. On her way, she used one of her new burner cells to call Alan Bach.

"Michelle, good to hear from you."

She was a little surprised that he wasn't busy, that he took her call. If he hadn't been able to talk to her, she would've gone ahead to the bank and gotten another cashier's check and sent it to him anyway. She had no idea how much was appropriate for this situation, but where could you look up the going rate for receiving tinfoil-hat material that might get you killed?

"Hi, Alan. Thanks so much for taking my call. How's everything?"

"Great, fine." A pause. "I got your package."

"Oh, good. That's why I was calling, actually."

"Ah. Yeah. You know, I have to say, it's not every day I get that kind of . . . James Bond scenario in the mail."

She faked a chuckle. "I know, I know. That must have seemed . . . just completely melodramatic."

"Well, a little out of the ordinary."

"Yeah. It's . . . a complicated story. But I just wanted to make sure you got it, and I also wanted to let you know that I'm sending a retainer for any expenses you might have."

"For this?" He sounded in equal parts amused and puzzled. "Listen, why don't you save the money until you actually need me to do something? I know how difficult things have been for you."

"Well, I do have some money now. And . . . just in case . . . I'm going to send you something."

He laughed. "In case you need me to open this in a week and a half and do . . . something?"

"Hah, yeah, I know, it sounds a little . . . crazy, but . . . yes. Just in case."

"Okay, sure. If that's what you need, happy to do it for you." A pause. "And I meant what I said about it being good to hear your voice. The way you vanished a few years ago, as bad as things were . . . well, I'm glad that things seemed to have turned around for you."

Michelle laughed. "Yes. Things have definitely changed."

At the Chase Bank, she purchased a $5,000 cashier's check for Alan Bach.

Next, she went to the FedEx office on Kearny and sent the checks off to her two lawyers.

There was a Starbucks just around the block on Montgomery. She stood outside it and stared through the tinted windows. Not too long a line.

10:35 A.M. Plenty of time to do what she needed to do next.

She just was scared to death of doing it.

You have to, she told herself. It's either this, or go back to the hotel, pack your bag, take all the cash you have left out of the safe in the closet and run. Run, and don't look back. Leave Danny where he is and hope the $10,000 is enough for Derek and Marisol to work his case. Leave them to explain to the court why "Emily" had vanished without a word. Leave Caitlin to whatever fate Gary had in mind for her.

Or roll the dice and make the phone call.

"SAM. HI. IT'S MICHELLE."

She'd called him from the same burner she'd used to talk to him on Wednesday. She'd called Alan on one of her new phones. No way she wanted Alan associated with a number she'd used to call Sam.

"Do you have news?"

"I do," she said. "Danny's still at the Weaver Detention facility. It wasn't a mistake. They're putting pressure on him, and on me. I need you to do something about it."

"In other words, nothing's changed since our last conversation. I already told you how we should proceed."

She took in a deep breath. Stay calm, she told herself.

"I have something of Danny's," she said. "I think you should see it."

312   LISA BRACKMANN

"All right. I'll give you an address."

He already sounded wary. Good.

"I can email it. I think you'll want to see it right away."

A long moment of silence. Michelle waited.

"You'll need a pen," he finally said. "I'm going to give you an IP address."

SHE ORDERED A COFFEE of the day and bought a bottle of Eos water, which was supposed to be ethically sourced. Found a table in the corner and wiped off the crumbs and coffee ring and dribbles of milk with a napkin. Sat down and got out the iPad she'd bought at SFO. She'd never set up the internet on it; she'd wanted to keep it secure.

Now was the time.

After that was done, she went to Yahoo and created an email account. Hit the "Compose" link.

She wondered briefly what she should use for a subject line and settled on "Requested information." Then she slipped the flash drive into the USB port and attached one of the files she'd made from multiple pages of Danny's logbook, plus the note he'd written. She typed: "There's a lot more, but this will give you an idea. Call me when you've had a chance to review."

Her finger hovered above the SEND button on the touch screen.

You might as well do it, she told herself. You already hit the self-destruct button, and the clock's ticking.

She pushed SEND and waited.

SHE'D DRUNK HER CUP of coffee and was halfway through a refill when her burner cell rang.

"I don't know what the *fuck* you were thinking."

Her heart started pounding, and she felt a sudden damp chill on her skin. You can't panic, she told herself. Act like you're in control.

"Me? I'm not the one who wrote it," she said.

"What do you expect me to do with this?" He sounded angry.

Good. That meant she'd hit him where it hurt.

"I really don't care what you do with it. Danny wanted people to see this. What *I* want is for you to get him out of jail and to get Gary off of me. I want a life, like you promised me we were going to have. And just so we're clear about this, I've made sure that if you fuck with me, this information is going to get released, and I'm not bullshitting you about that, Sam. I mean it."

Michelle noticed, belatedly, a girl in her late teens or early twenties briefly look up from her tablet and glance in her direction. I probably shouldn't have said that in the Starbucks, Michelle thought, but the girl was wearing earbuds and nobody seemed to care.

Meanwhile, Sam was employing one of his strategic silences, but this time, Michelle wondered if it was because he really didn't know how to respond.

"I can't control Gary," he finally said.

"Maybe you can't control him, but you can negotiate with him, better than I can. You've got people behind you. You have influence."

Another silence.

"I assume if I do this, you won't release the information."

"Correct. I won't." She wanted to laugh. "That's how these things work, right?"

"What about Danny? You said he wanted people to see this."

"Danny's loyal. You know that. If we make this deal, he'll keep his end of it."

"All right. I'll see what I can do. Don't expect immediate results."

"How soon?"

"A few days. And it may not work."

"Then you can all live with the consequences," she said, and hung up.

SHE HAD ONE LAST thing to do before meeting Caitlin for lunch. She had to call Gary.

"Bout time you called," he said. "I hope you don't think you can just put me off like that, Michelle. You should've called me back last night."

"Sorry," she said, not even trying to sound apologetic. "We didn't get in till really late. And I told you the important part."

"Oh, really? So, just when were you gonna tell me about Troy Stone?"

Chapter Twenty-Seven

"I . . ." GODDAMMIT, SHE THOUGHT. No point in asking how he knew. She just had to somehow bullshit her way out of this.

"Well, today," she said. "Honestly, I didn't think it was that important until last night."

"You didn't think it was important." Michelle recognized that tone, the one that implied a threat. "They've been emailing each other since y'all met in Los Angeles."

"I didn't know that," Michelle said. "Because, funny, *I* don't read Caitlin's emails. Why didn't you tell *me*, if you thought it was important?"

Gary puffed out a sigh. "Well, to be honest with you, Caitlin did kind of an end-run. After the first couple of emails, she switched to texting and a non-Safer America email address, and not one of her usual ones either. I had some other stuff going on, and I just kind of dropped the ball. So, okay, that's on me, Michelle. But you know what, it's partly because I trusted you to keep me in the loop. I have a lot of respect for your abilities, I've told you that before."

"Look, Gary . . . you told me this was a babysitting job. You told me I was supposed to keep Caitlin healthy and focused. I've done that. Then you told me to let you know if she suddenly diverged from Safer America's agenda, and I did that too. Now I'm calling you back, like I said I would. What else do you want me to do?"

Gary laughed. "You really crack me up, you know that, Michelle?" He sounded genuinely amused. Jovial, in fact.

This was probably not a good thing.

"You're a smart woman. It's been so much fun, seeing your learning curve for this kind of work. But I gotta tell you, you almost outsmarted yourself here. Lucky for you, Troy Stone is going to save you a considerable amount of grief."

She felt that sick feeling in her stomach again.

"What do you mean?"

"Now it's my turn to be a little coy. You're just gonna have to wait till I set a few things up. I'll tell you what you need to know, when you need to know it."

Definitely not good.

JUST HOW WAS TROY Stone going to save her "a considerable amount of grief"?

"Hell, I wish I could just skip this CIAC convention," Caitlin said with a sigh. "It's such a bore. And so is Anaheim. What am I gonna say to them, anyway?"

Was it possible he was some kind of asset of the Boys?

No, that didn't make sense.

Focus, Michelle told herself.

"But you're not doing a speech or presentation, right?" she said. "It's a meet and greet?"

CIAC was the Correctional Industries Association . . . something. Michelle couldn't remember what the final "C" was for.

"Right," Caitlin said. "I guess I can just eat their food and drink their booze and call it a day."

They were having lunch at the hotel sushi restaurant.

Caitlin seemed to be addicted to the stuff. It was nice to see her eating, anyway.

Think like Gary, Michelle told herself. How would he see Troy Stone?

"You want some *toro* to finish?" Caitlin asked.

"Sure. That sounds great."

As someone he could set up, maybe. Like what he'd done to her in Mexico. Get Troy in trouble and use that as leverage against him.

"It's just . . . this convention, Michelle. It's huge and it's loud and it's full of people trying to sell you security cameras, cheap food service and handcuffs. The whole thing's kind of a bummer. And that's how I felt *before* I started really digging into the prison-industry numbers." Caitlin leaned forward, for a moment resting her face on her curled fingers. "I gotta tell you, last year when I was there, I was so stoned I can barely remember it. These meds I take, plus a few drinks, sometimes it's just all a blur. Thank god." She lifted her sake cup in a mock toast and drained it. "Maybe I should just ditch the meds and start smoking pot." She released that cackle of a laugh, the one that signaled she wasn't faking her amusement. "Wouldn't *that* make people's heads explode?"

You barely know Troy Stone, Michelle told herself. He's not your responsibility.

Neither was Caitlin.

"You know, the more research I do on this stuff, the more appalling I'm finding it all." Caitlin refilled Michelle's sake, and then her own. "And I swear, that's not just Troy talking through me."

I could tell you a few things, Michelle thought. About

Harris County Jail. About Weaver Detention Faciility, and Prostasis.

"You know what might be fun?" Caitlin said suddenly. "Filming it. Hire somebody with a video camera to follow me around."

Please, god, no. "You smoking pot?"

"Oh, no, I wasn't serious about that. I mean, me at the CAIC convention. I can talk a little bit about the prison industry. Shake some hands. See what happens."

"I . . . okay. And . . . I guess I'm not sure. Why do we want to do that?"

Caitlin shrugged. "Maybe we could use it somehow. Depending on where we go with this whole thing."

"You and Troy."

"And Shane, potentially. We'll see."

"Okay," Michelle said.

"I guess I need to decide pretty quick about what to do in California. It'll be bad enough when I tell the board I want to pull our resources out of Protect Our Communities. If I tell them I want to go in and campaign on the other side . . ." Caitlin chuckled, in a way that suggested she was faintly embarrassed. "Well, that's gonna be some fun times."

Michelle took a quick glance around the restaurant. A few Japanese businessmen, local hipster types with handcrafted leather messenger bags, well-heeled tourists, techies in hundred-dollar hoodies. No one who seemed to be watching them, though someone certainly could be.

She thought about her purse. Both of her iPhones were in it, and they were both switched on, Michelle's phone for work, and because she knew she could only be out of touch with Gary for so long before he'd retaliate, Emily's phone in case someone called about Danny. She didn't know if Gary could put spyware that switched on the mikes on her phones if he'd never physically gotten his hands on them. But she couldn't trust that they weren't being heard. There were plenty of other ways Gary could listen.

"Caitlin . . . are you sure you want to take this that far right now? Some of the donors . . . well, they're powerful people. And . . . I know the type. They can be pretty ruthless."

"Now, what are they gonna do?" Caitlin said with a snort. "Try and smear me? You know what, they can call me unstable, they can go ahead and try, but I'm not going to be doing this alone. I have people on my side too." She paused to refill Michelle's sake cup. "Besides, I don't give a shit what they think. They're free to take their money someplace else if they don't like it."

There had to be some way she could warn her, some story she could tell that Caitlin would believe.

Michelle drew in a deep breath. The air came with just the slightest hint of fish. It occurred to her that if Danny did get out, maybe he could back her up on this. The story would still sound crazy, but if there were two of them saying it . . .

And there was his logbook. Should she show it to Caitlin?

I have to time this right, she thought. I need to wait until Danny's out before I risk it. There were negotiations going on, she knew, and blowing up Gary's operation would only complicate them.

But what if Danny didn't get out? When was Gary going to pull the trigger on whatever he had planned for Troy Stone?

Where could she and Caitlin talk and not be overheard?

"Where did *you* go?"

"Sorry," Michelle said. "It's just . . . I was thinking of some things that happened a couple of years ago, when my husband died."

Caitlin leaned in closer. "Do you want to talk about it, hon? I get the feeling you had kind of a rough time."

Michelle manufactured a chuckle. "It's a long, complicated story. I'll tell you about it sometime. Just not right now."

It wasn't until the next morning, when they sat in their Business Class seats, plane waiting on the tarmac at SFO, and the flight attendant requested that all portable electronic devices be switched off for takeoff, that Michelle realized when and where might be the best opportunity for them to talk with some privacy.

No cell phone reception. No bugs. No van parked on a street outside with a high-powered mike aimed in their direction. Other passengers were a concern. But if she were careful . . .

She'd wait a day for Danny. But on the flight back to Houston on Sunday, she'd tell Caitlin the truth. Or some version of it.

In the meantime, she'd keep a close eye on Caitlin.

"You know," she said, "about filming you at the convention . . . I do a lot of still photography. I don't have that much experience with video, but in a pinch, if we can't find someone else on such short notice . . ."

"Oh, that sounds good," Caitlin said, between sips of her mimosa. "I mean, this is just an idea I had, it may or may not come to anything. No need to make a big production out of it."

Just the excuse Michelle needed to keep Caitlin in her sights.

Chapter Twenty-Eight

☙

"WELL, HERE WE ARE." Caitlin grinned at the camera. "Prepare yourself."

Michelle followed her onto the convention hall floor.

"Caitlin, can you hold up a minute? I want to get a few long-shots of all this."

The convention floor was huge, lit by fluorescent lights and ambient glow from displays in the booths that formed a maze across it. There was no natural light here, it was sealed off from the outside world like an indoor shopping mall or sports arena, its own disconnected environment, the constant chatter of the crowd forming an oceanic, discordant roar.

Michelle got her shot and half-jogged to catch up to Caitlin, who stood next to a booth for a company advertising itself as "The Next Generation in Correctional Healthcare."

"Ready?" Caitlin asked.

Michelle nodded. They'd stopped at a Best Buy a couple of miles from the convention center on their way from the airport and bought a Rode mike, some memory cards and an extra battery pack for her dSLR. A camcorder would have been better, but the camera would do, and at least Michelle already knew how to use it.

"So, the prison industry in the United States is big," Caitlin said. "State and federal governments spend around seventy-five billion dollars a year on corrections. We've got a total inmate population of two point three million people, which in terms of both the number of prisoners and as a percentage of the population, is the biggest in the world. We're five percent of the world's population, and we have twenty-five percent of the world's prison population. That's right—we're number one."

She paused. "You got all that?"

Michelle nodded.

"Let's walk a little, okay?"

"Sure."

Michelle followed alongside Caitlin as they moved down the row of booths. There were booths for food service. For secure payment systems. For vests that promised "ultimate stabbing protection." For tactical weapons, security cameras, prison architects, prison plumbing fixtures, drug-testing kits. Phone systems, correctional software, correctional pharmacies, prison ministries, sheriff's associations, insurance companies.

Caitlin halted again. "So I've been doing a lot of thinking about this. Wondering, is it really true that we just commit more crimes in America? And if so, why is that? Is this"—she made an open-palmed wave at the convention floor around her—"helping us fix that?"

They walked a little farther. Caitlin stopped in front of a booth for substance-abuse software. "Well, one thing I learned is that about half of the folks behind bars in state prisons are there for non-violent crimes. Ninety percent of federal prisoners are there for non-violent crimes. You know how many of those are there for drug offenses? About one quarter of the people held in US prisons and jails. You can add another seventeen percent who say they committed their crimes to get money for drugs. Around sixty-five percent of

prisoners have some kind of drug problem. Only eleven percent of them get treatment for it."

She really was good at this, Michelle thought. The way
she pulled up all those facts and figures without sounding
rehearsed or rushed, how she faced the camera with an easy
charm.

"Here's something else," Caitlin continued. "I was talking
to a representative from a correctional officer's union the
other night, and you know what he told me? More than half
of all male inmates have at least one significant mental health
problem. With women? Seventy-five percent."

She held the camera's gaze and said: "There are more seriously mentally ill people in the Los Angeles County Jail than
in any psychiatric hospital in the United States. Three times
more people with serious mental illness incarcerated than in
hospitals." She shook her head. "Now, that's a lot of numbers
and percentages I'm throwing out here. But to me, they all
started adding up to the same thing."

She paused. "Maybe we aren't doing this right."

By now they'd reached a huge display for Prostatis:
RESPONSIBILITY. EFFICIENCY. DIGNITY. was written across the
back of the booth, lit by dramatic spotlights.

Michelle's heart beat faster. Standing in front of display
was Randall Gates, shaking hands with another man in a
business suit.

"Keep filming," Caitlin said in a low voice. She pasted on
a smile and headed over to Gates.

"Caitlin!" Gates gave the other man's hand one last pump
and a good-bye pat on the shoulder. "So nice to see you
here."

"Hi, Randy," she said brightly.

By now, Gates had caught sight of Michelle and her camera. "What's this about?" he said, still smiling.

"I haven't exactly decided yet."

"Should we go have a little sit-down?" he said in a low voice.

"A sit-down? Is there something you'd like to discuss?"

"Maybe not with . . ." He turned to Michelle. "Could you . . . ?"

"No, she could not," Caitlin interrupted. "If there's something you want to say to me, why don't you just say it?"

"I . . ." He hesitated. Michelle zoomed in on his face. She watched his jaw tighten. His eyes flicked in her direction, then back to Caitlin. "I'm just a little confused about some of what I've heard coming out of the San Francisco event."

"I can imagine," Caitlin said. "And I'm still thinking it all through, to be honest with you. Why don't we table that sit-down till I get back to Houston and take it up at the next board meeting? We can call a special one if you'd like."

"I would. The sooner the better."

"Then we'll do that."

"Good." He hesitated, his eyes flicking at the camera again as though he couldn't help it, and then back to Caitlin. "I hope you know that I take my responsibilities as a member of the board very seriously."

"Of course I do, Randy," she said. "I know just how much Safer America means to you." She gave his arm a friendly squeeze. "We'll catch up later, okay?"

Caitlin turned back to Michelle. "I'm gonna walk down this aisle. Why don't you hang back and get a shot of me doing that?"

"Will do," Michelle said.

As Caitlin walked away, Michelle could sense Gates moving closer.

"Just what are you doing?"

Michelle gestured after Caitlin. "What she just asked me to do."

"Shut that off."

Something in his voice made her put the camera down. She looked at him. His face was tense, the lines around his mouth rigid.

"You're supposed to be looking after her," he said, staring hard at Michelle. "The fact that you're going along with this makes me wonder whose side you're really on."

Christ. Was he actively working with Gary? Did he know about her, about Danny?

Was this a threat?

She stared back. "I'm Caitlin's employee, Mr. Gates. It's my job to do what she asks me to do." She started to raise the camera, then stopped. "And just so you know . . . I *am* looking after her."

She wasn't in any position to threaten Randall Gates. But she hoped he knew that she meant every fucking word she'd just said.

BY THE TIME SHE got Caitlin in her sights again, Caitlin had gotten caught up in the traffic where two rows crossed. Michelle took a moment to zoom in on her. She wasn't sure if it would be a good shot or not, but Caitlin was smiling and making conversation with several in a crowd of young women in some kind of uniforms—police explorers? Junior correctional officers?

There was one woman not in a uniform standing just to

326 ☙ LISA BRACKMANN

Caitlin's side. Something about her felt familiar. Thirty-ish, a little heavy, baseball cap over brown hair pulled back in a ponytail. Michelle zoomed in on her.

A gold necklace with a Tinkerbell charm.

Carlene.

"Shit," Michelle said. She lowered the camera and ran.

Chapter Twenty-Nine

✣

"OH, THERE YOU ARE," Caitlin said. "Why were you running?"

Carlene ducked her head and swiveled on her heels.

"Where do you think you're going?" Michelle demanded. "What are you doing here?"

Carlene ignored her, pushing aside several junior correctional officers, or whatever they were, and hurried down the aisle.

Michelle caught up to her and grabbed her arm, yanked it hard. "I asked you a question."

"I don't have to answer you," Carlene spat out. "You better let go of me. Gary won't like it if you mess with me."

Michelle didn't let go. Not right away. "You tell Gary . . ."

What? What should she tell him?

Michelle released Carlene's arm, giving her a little push as she did. "Stay out of my way, Carlene. Leave Caitlin alone."

"Don't you think you can just order me around," Carlene muttered, her eyes glittering behind the lenses of her sturdy pewter glasses. "I'll kill you, you bitch. And you won't even see me coming."

With that, she turned and plunged into the crowd.

Christ, Michelle thought. She should have been more careful. Carlene might look harmless, but she was Gary's helper, after all. Who knew what she could really do?

She made her way back to Caitlin.

"What in the world was that all about?" Caitlin asked.

"I was filming you, and I saw her go for your purse," Michelle said. "I think she's some kind of pickpocket."

"At a correctional association convention?" Caitlin laughed. "That seems a little foolhardy. Should we call security?"

"I don't know. She's gone now. But if we see her again . . . yeah, we should call."

"Sounds good, hon." Caitlin took a step back and seemed to study Michelle. "You came running over like you were gonna tackle her," she said.

Michelle managed a smile. "I hate seeing people get ripped off."

"You know what, let's get out of here," Caitlin said abruptly. "I don't think there's any point in sticking around. All I'm going to do is piss people off."

"Where do you want to go?"

"I don't know." She suddenly looked exhausted, the recent liveliness that had animated her features drained away. "I need some time to think about how I'm going to handle all of this."

"Late lunch?" Michelle asked.

THIS PART OF ANAHEIM didn't feel anything like a real town or city. She didn't know what the rest of Anaheim was like. What there was here were broad streets, huge blocks of hotels, giant parking lots, a landscape that seemed both monumental and impermanent. There was nothing here with weight or history, nothing that seemed unique, no buildings constructed to human scale, just endless expanses of concrete, asphalt and stucco.

Their choices around the Anaheim Convention Center included something called the Anaheim GardenWalk, where they would find a Bubba Gump Shrimp, P. F. Chang's, and a Cheesecake Factory, among other things. There was also the Downtown Disney District, which had a La Brea Bakery and a House of Blues, along with a few more upscale options.

They chose a restaurant that offered "Disney Med"— "Modern spins on authentic Mediterranean cuisine." It also had an extensive wine list.

In the downstairs wood-floored and brick-walled bar, Caitlin picked at her tapas.

"I don't know, hon," she said. "I'm just wondering if I've bitten off more than I can chew here."

What should she say? Urge Caitlin to go back to supporting Safer America's status quo? Would that be enough to derail whatever it was Gary had planned?

"Maybe you shouldn't rush into anything," Michelle said.

"I think I have to, now. At least I have to move pretty quick. With this election coming up, I'm either on one side or the other. If I really can't support working against these propositions, then I have to say so, and I have to act on that."

Michelle leaned over and opened her purse. Felt around for the two iPhones and the signal-blocking bags.

"Well . . . you could always just take a couple of days," she said, as she tucked the phones into the bags. When she straightened up, she had a lipstick in her hand. "Maybe . . . get away someplace where you can really have time to think about things."

Someplace out of the country, preferably.

"Yeah." Caitlin sat up straighter. "You know what, maybe I'll go to the condo in San Diego for the rest of the weekend, fly home on Monday. Come up with some kind of a public statement. I'm not going to change my mind. I just need to figure out what I'm going to say and how I'm going to approach this." She took a healthy slug of her rioja. "And steel myself for this confrontation with the board. It's going to be ugly."

San Diego wasn't nearly far enough.

"You sure you wouldn't rather go to . . . I don't know, Maui?" She smiled and lifted her eyebrows, like it was a joke. One she hoped Caitlin might take seriously.

Caitlin snorted. "Wouldn't I, though? Maybe after I drop this little bomb." She pushed her plate aside. "Anyway, I can drive myself down. No need for you to come along if you need to get back to Houston."

"Oh, no, I don't have anything going on," Michelle said quickly. "I can drive us. And I can be close by in case . . . you need anything."

Caitlin smiled. One of her real ones.

"Thanks, Michelle. I really appreciate that. To tell you the truth, it'll be nice to have someone in my corner while I work through all of this."

"I'll email the office and tell them you won't be back till Tuesday. That way you won't get drawn into a conversation you're not ready to have. In the meantime . . ." Michelle smiled. "Maybe you should just turn off your phone."

"Maybe I will," Caitlin said, smiling back.

THEY DROVE BACK TO their hotel. It was close enough to rush hour that Caitlin wanted to wait a while to make the drive—"Since we have the rooms anyway. I'm beat, hon. I want to go get a massage and fall asleep on the table."

"Sounds good," Michelle said, though she didn't think it did. Even if she kept her phones off for the trip, even if Caitlin actually had powered hers down, there were so many other ways Gary could be tracking them, and the longer they stayed in one place, the more time Gary had to set up and change whatever plans he'd made to adapt to the new situation.

She went back up to her room. Her shoulders ached. Maybe she'd lie down. Maybe she'd go get a massage.

Christ, why am I doing this? she thought. It was stupid. She didn't know how she could protect Caitlin. She didn't have a plan. Except to try to sit Caitlin down and tell her an impossible story, show her Danny's logbook, and if Caitlin *did* believe her? *Then* what?

She took her phones out of the signal-blocking bags, plugged them both in and flopped down on the bed. She was so fucking tired, and there was just no end to it.

I should take the passport, the money and go, she thought. She wasn't sure to where. Maybe someplace in Asia or Africa. Somewhere off the grid.

Was there any such thing as off the grid any more? Timbuktu? Outer Mongolia?

She was dozing when her Emily phone rang. The default Marimba that she used for unknown callers.

SHE BOLTED OUT OF bed and grabbed the phone.

"Em? It's me."

"Danny?"

"Yeah."

"Are you . . . are you out?"

"Yeah." His voice caught. "I am."

"Oh thank god," she said in a rush. "Where are you?"

A shaky laugh. "Beautiful San Angelo, Texas."

"Are you . . . is this a good number?"

"Yeah."

"Let me call you back."

She disconnected and started to cry. "Not now," she muttered. She jotted down the number from her received calls, wiped her eyes, blew her nose and grabbed her last burner phone.

In the bathroom, she turned on the shower, full blast.

"Hey."

"We shouldn't talk too long," she said.

"Where are you?"

"California. Orange County."

"Do you know . . . why did I get out—?"

"I went home and got the book. I sent a copy to Sam. I didn't know what else to do."

A moment of silence on the other end.

"Em, why didn't you just go? I wanted you to take the money and the passport, and just . . ."

"Am I supposed to be a fucking mind reader?" she snapped. "And run . . . run where? What kind of life was I supposed to make for myself? If I have to live this way, I don't want to do it alone. Unless you're sick of me, and if that's the case, let's table it for now, and figure out what we're going to do to get out of this first."

A deep chuckle. "I told you I thought you could kick my ass."

The bathroom was steaming up from the running shower. She hated wasting water during a drought, and she was crying again.

"Aren't I allowed to care about you?" she asked.

"You're allowed. I'm just not the best investment you could've made."

"Better than my last one," she said.

"WE NEED TO POP smoke, get some distance between us and this shit storm. There's an expiration date on what my logbook's going to buy us."

"Why?" she asked. "I don't understand. Can't we hold it over them? Say we'll send it out if they don't leave us alone?"

He made a noise that was something between a laugh and a sigh. "There's stuff in that book that's pretty embarrassing. They're not going to want people talking about it. But it's all hard to prove, and if it does get out? They'll swamp it in a tide of shit. They'll smear me—and let's face it, that ain't too hard to do."

She sat down hard on the toilet. She realized that she'd thought of the logbook as a nearly magical object, something dangerous and powerful that could solve their problems if it didn't get them killed.

If it wasn't all that . . .

"Why did Sam get you out, then?"

"He looked at the options and figured getting me out was less risk and hassle than dealing with the flak from that logbook."

So she'd been right in her evaluation of Sam's character, at least.

"What do we do?" she asked.

"We just go far enough away that we're not worth the trouble for them to fuck with us. We don't make any more noise, they'll most likely leave us alone. But if someone like

334   LISA BRACKMANN

Gary decides he wants to take a shot while we're in range?
We're on our own."

"Okay." She thought about it. "Can you get to San Diego?"

"I have a buddy in Dallas with an SR20. Cute little bird,
comes with its own parachute, which given this guy's flying
chops is a good thing . . . Once he picks me up, we could get
to San Diego in about nine hours from here. We'd have to
stop once to refuel."

"When can he pick you up?"

"Don't know. Haven't asked him yet."

"Can you trust him?"

He chuckled. "I can pay him. If he fucks us over later, so
what? All we need is a little time. We go to Tijuana International and fly out with our new passports."

"I don't know if I can get to San Diego without being followed," she said. "I'm going to be with Caitlin."

"Caitlin?"

"The woman I've been working for."

"I'll call you when I have an ETA. You ditch her when
you can."

"I'll try," she said. "It's complicated."

"Do the best you can do. If you need me to, I'll come to
you. Just don't use the new passport unless you absolutely
have to. Those are the ones we use to get some distance
between us and them."

"And after that?"

"We become somebody else."

She laughed. "That part sounds good."

A hesitation on the other end of the line. She could hear
his exhalation of breath.

"Em . . . whatever Gary's doing, if you think it's about to

get hot, you need to bail, okay? Don't wait around and try to fix things."

"I won't," she said.

She'd do what she could do to warn Caitlin. She'd try to get her someplace safe. That was all she could do, and she knew it might not be enough.

Chapter Thirty

☙

THEY GOT ON THE road at 6:30 P.M. Still plenty of light. Michelle drove. She waited until they were passing through Irvine before she said anything.

She'd thought a lot about what to say. If she just dumped the whole insane story on Caitlin, if Caitlin decided she was crazy, then what? She'd lose any credibility she had, and there wouldn't be a thing she could do to help.

As they passed through the tan and cream stucco land-scape studded with trees, Michelle finally said: "So, you asked me about what happened a few years ago, around when my husband died."

"If you don't want to talk about it . . . really, hon, only if it's going to make you feel better."

Michelle let out a laugh. Nothing about this was going to make her feel better. "It's a hard thing to talk about," she said. "I thought maybe the best way to start was to show you something."

"All right." Caitlin sounded hesitant. God knows what she was thinking Michelle was about to show her.

"My purse is on the back seat. There's a book in it."

"A book?" A pause. "Sorry, but . . . there's no way I can look at a book right now. I get so carsick."

Michelle took a moment to glance at Caitlin. Not long, you had to be careful on these freeways. Caitlin was looking at her with what she thought was sympathy.

"I do want to know," Caitlin said. "I hope you don't think I'm putting you off."

"Oh. Well. We'll wait till we get to the condo, then."

"Let's stop at the Trader Joe's and get some snacks and wine," Caitlin said, resting her hand lightly on Michelle's shoulder for a moment. "We'll relax, and you can tell me all about it."

Great, Michelle thought. Just great. She didn't like the idea of delaying getting to the condo, someplace where people were likely to know Caitlin went, giving anyone tracking them more time to catch up. And that was assuming they'd bought any time by changing their travel plans.

"Would you rather just go out to dinner?" Having the conversation in a restaurant wasn't ideal, but maybe a public place was safer. "I mean, I don't want to invade your privacy at the condo."

"Oh, hon, it's not an invasion at all. I don't have a lot of memories there. It's just a vacation place I've hardly used. But it's quiet and private and I think that's about all I can handle right now. We can always order a pizza or something if you get hungry."

There's no reason to think something's going to happen tonight, Michelle told herself.

THE CONDO WAS NOT far from the University of Californa, San Diego campus, which was actually in La Jolla, north of the city proper. "Yeah," Caitlin said with a grin, "we couldn't really afford a second home in La Jolla, so I went for La Jolla adjacent. Close enough. It'd be nice to have a view of the ocean and a short walk to the beach, but at least I can get there pretty quick from here."

Michelle would have called it a townhouse, to be strictly accurate—a skinny, detached two-story building in a small complex overlooking a dark canyon. Eucalyptus trees clustered around the buildings and walkways. They were sometimes called "widow makers," Michelle recalled, due to their tendency to suddenly drop heavy branches.

Apt, she thought.

Caitlin fumbled around for the proper key and unlocked the front door, then deactivated the alarm system with a keychain fob. The security lights had come on when they stepped onto the walkway leading to the door—by now it was after 8:30 P.M., in spite of Michelle's best efforts to hurry them through Trader Joe's. The temperature was pleasant enough, in the high sixties, the air heavy and wet for San Diego, scented with eucalyptus. A quiet spot. Michelle couldn't hear much traffic. Mostly what she heard was the soft clatter of eucalyptus leaves and seed capsules stirred by the soft breeze.

Caitlin stepped inside and flicked on a light in the entry. "Lord, it's stuffy in here," she said.

"I'll open some windows," Michelle said. A good way for her to get an idea of the townhouse's layout.

Caitlin switched on a few lights. Michelle's first impression of the living room was sturdy, clean furniture, a rustic wood table with a light finish, off-white walls with some curves and arches, as if they'd gone for a slightly Spanish style for the interior. There were bright colors as well, pillows that looked like they were made from Mexican blankets on the couch, a few paintings, one done with swaths of purple hanging above a faux fireplace.

"You're welcome to stay the night in the spare room if

you'd like," Caitlin said. "But you'd probably be more comfortable over at the Hyatt."

"This is charming," Michelle said.

Caitlin made her little wave. "It's nothing fancy. We bought
it, oh, less than a year before . . . before Paul passed away.
I've mostly had it rented out since then. The last tenants
were some UCSD visiting professors. They moved out a few
months ago. I've been thinking about selling it."

"I like it," Michelle said truthfully. The townhouse wasn't
fancy, but it still felt more like a home than the River Oaks
house did.

Caitlin shrugged as she wheeled her suitcase down a small
hall that Michelle presumed led to a bedroom. "Maybe I'll
keep this and sell the place in Houston instead. If I'm gonna
blow everything else up, I might as well."

The townhouse had an open layout, with a dining area
and kitchen just beyond the living room. Michelle carried
the shopping bags with wine and snacks to the kitchen.
There was a deck there, with sliding glass doors, overlooking
the canyon. How accessible was it from outside? Michelle
wondered. Under any other circumstances, she'd prefer the
separate townhouse with a canyon view to, say, a condo with
shared walls and a couple of small windows facing the common grounds, but she didn't like the security implications
of this setup. Sure, there was an alarm, but look how easily
Gary had disabled hers.

The sliding doors had locks, at least, so that you could
open them partway, but not so wide that anyone larger than
a six-year old could squeeze through.

Here's hoping Gary doesn't employ any homicidal midg-
ets, Michelle thought.

"Well, I don't know about you, but I'm ready for a glass of wine."

Caitlin emerged from the bedroom, wearing some light sweats and a baggy T-shirt.

"Sure," Michelle said. "Where's the opener?"

"Oh, let me. Why don't you go sit down and relax? You want the red?"

"Whatever you'd like." Michelle wasn't planning on drinking.

She couldn't sit still, so she paced around the living room. How was she going to explain this to Caitlin? All the versions she tried in her head sounded equally absurd.

Just show her the logbook, she thought. Start with that. Take it from there.

The doorbell rang.

Michelle's heart started pounding hard.

"Would you mind seeing who that is?" Caitlin called from the kitchen.

"Sure."

Michelle padded as quietly as she could to the door. Peered through the peephole.

Troy Stone.

Why was he here? What had Gary planned?

What should she do?

"Who is it, hon?" Caitlin had come up behind her, holding two glasses of wine. She put them down on the coffee table.

"It's Troy," Michelle said in a low voice.

"Troy?" Caitlin frowned.

"Were you expecting him?"

"No. I mean, we talked about meeting, but we didn't make

any definite plans. I don't even remember giving him this address."

The doorbell rang again.

"Well, only one way to figure this out," Caitlin said.

"Don't—" Michelle began, as Caitlin stepped in front of her and unlocked the door.

"Hi, Troy! Come on in."

Chapter Thirty-One

⚜

"Hey, Caitlin. Michelle."

Troy Stone stood in the center of the living room. He seemed uncertain. Michelle was aware, suddenly, of how large a man he was, how much space he took up, how solid he appeared.

If he tried something . . . could she do anything to stop him?

"Would you like a glass of wine?" Caitlin asked him. "We were just sitting down for a drink."

"That'd be great," He sat down on the couch with that hint of stiffness Michelle had seen before, as though his back hurt. "Traffic wasn't bad, but I'm glad to be out of the car."

"Let me go pour another glass," Caitlin said.

"That's all right," Michelle said quickly. "I'll get it. Troy, the one on the coffee table's fresh. Why don't you take it?" She didn't want to turn her back on Caitlin, didn't want to leave her too close to Troy, but maybe she could find something in the kitchen she could use for a weapon, a knife.

"Yeah, I was already in the car so I just took the chance you'd be here," she heard Troy say. "Figured I'd hang out at the Hyatt bar if you weren't."

There was a paring knife in a butcher block on the counter, a good one, a Victorinox. Small enough to fit in her jacket pocket. She snatched it up and put it in her pocket, quickly poured a small glass of wine, to pretend that things were normal.

Maybe they were.

"Well, cheers," Caitlin said, lifting her glass.

"Cheers," Troy replied. Caitlin sat down on the chair across from him.

Michelle remained standing by the kitchen counter, so she could move quickly, if she had to.

"So, what's up?" Troy said at length.

Caitlin looked confused. "I was going to ask you the same thing."

"You texted *me*."

"I didn't."

Now it was Troy's turn to frown. "I have it right here. You said it was important, that we needed to talk tonight. I wouldn't have driven all the way down here from Venice otherwise."

Oh, shit, Michelle thought. She put down the wine. In a couple of strides she was across the room. "Let me see."

"What the hell, Michelle? You think I'm lying to you or something?"

"*No*." Or, probably not. "But it's important. Caitlin didn't send you a text."

He shrugged. Reached into his suit pocket and pulled out a smartphone. Unlocked the screen and pulled up a text screen.

There it was.

URGENT THAT WE TALK. SOMETHING BIG'S COME UP. CAN YOU COME TO SAN DIEGO TONIGHT? I KNOW IT'S A LOT TO ASK BUT IT'S EXTREMELY IMPORTANT.

I SHOULD BE THERE BY 9. CAN PUT YOU UP AT THE
HYATT AFTER.

Under that, Troy's reply:

WE CAN'T HANDLE ON THE PHONE?

And "Caitlin's":

AFRAID NOT. TOO COMPLICATED. COULD HAVE A HUGE
IMPACT ON OUR CAMPAIGN. BUT I THINK WE CAN MAKE
IT WORK FOR US. VERY EXCITING POSSIBILITIES!

Lucky for you, Troy Stone is going to save you a considerable amount of grief.

"We need to get out of here," Michelle said.

Caitlin laughed nervously. "You're scaring me a little, Michelle. What's going on?"

Troy stood up. "Yeah, Michelle. First you give me some cryptic warning, now this? I want an explanation."

"We don't have time—" Michelle began, and then the doorbell rang.

"Don't answer it!"

Troy beat her to the door. Looked through the keyhole. "What are you talking about? It's just a girl. There's nobody else."

He opened the door a crack, blocking it with his foot so no one could get past him. "Yeah?"

"I've lost my dog," Michelle heard. "Have you seen him?"

"What kind of dog?"

"A pug—"

"Close the door, Troy!" Michelle said, trying to keep her voice low.

Troy turned to her, with a look of pure exasperation. He suddenly swatted at his hip, exasperation turning to puzzlement. He took a few stumbling steps forward; then his eyes rolled back in his head, and he collapsed.

"Troy?" Caitlin started to move toward him as the door opened a crack, stopping for a moment as it hit Troy's foot. Whoever was behind the door pushed it again. The door opened wider.

Christ. She had no time. Michelle crouched behind the sofa, paring knife in hand, her back to the sliding glass doors.

"Who are you?" she heard Caitlin say. "What do you want? What did you—?"

Michelle heard the slightest puff of compressed air. A cry from Caitlin. The sound of stumbling footsteps, a body falling.

Then silence.

The front door closed.

Michelle risked a peek over the top of the couch. A short, slightly heavy woman was putting the chain on the front door. Michelle ducked down as she started to turn.

It had to be Carlene.

Was it possible she didn't know Michelle was here?

If she comes over here, grab a pillow, throw it at her, tackle her. She could take an unarmed Carlene, she was pretty sure. Just not whatever weapon Carlene had.

Michelle heard soft footsteps moving past her, toward the hall that led to the bedrooms. Saw a glow of light from the hall. She must be checking out the bedrooms, Michelle thought.

Now was her chance to get out. She rose up.

Troy and Caitlin lay on the floor, Troy by the door, Caitlin by the coffee table. Were they breathing?

Some kind of tranquilizer, maybe. But Carlene would have a gun, too.

Shit, she thought. I can't just leave them. If they're alive . . .

Besides, the woman was coming back.

From behind the couch, Michelle could hear her start to hum. Off-key, but it sounded like a Katy Perry song.

The humming continued as Michelle heard the sound of running water. She must have gone into the kitchen. Michelle risked another look.

She could see the woman's back. She was standing at the kitchen sink with the open bottle of wine, pouring the contents down the sink.

"Oh, oh, oh, California gurls . . ."

Michelle ducked back down.

She heard the sound of breaking glass. What was it? A wine glass?

"Oh, oh, oh . . ."

She heard a thud. A soft moan. Peeked over the couch. Saw Carlene standing over Caitlin, holding the wine bottle.

Fuck!

She crept around to the side of the couch. Got a glimpse of Carlene squatting by Caitlin, tugging down Caitlin's sweatpants, the empty wine bottle by her side.

Rage rose up from her gut, into her throat, and she made a sound halfway between a shriek and a bellow as she sprung to her feet.

Carlene's eyes went wide. "Stay out of this!" she cried, but as she saw Michelle close the gap between them, she reached for something beneath her shirt, tucked in her cleavage. Michelle glimpsed a pistol butt. She shoved Carlene to the ground, straddling her, grabbed her wrist with her free hand, slamming it against the carpet. Carlene didn't let go of the gun. She reached up and clutched a handful of Michelle's hair and yanked hard. Michelle fell to the side, landing on her own arm, still holding onto Carlene's other wrist, the hand that held the gun. Something, Carlene's knee maybe, struck her in the gut, and she nearly lost her grip, and then Carlene was punching the side of her head, grabbing her ear, twisting it.

With her free hand, Michelle reached out and stabbed the paring knife into Carlene's side, just under her arm. She caught a rib the first time. She reached out and stabbed again. Carlene screamed and kicked her in the shin. Michelle stabbed her again, this time in the fleshy part of her shoulder.

"Stop it!" Carlene shrieked. "Stop it!"

"You want me to stop it? *You want me to stop it?*" Michelle stabbed her again. "Let go of the fucking gun!"

Carlene let go. Michelle snatched it up and smacked her across the face with the butt end. Just because she felt like it.

"I'm bleeding!" Carlene sobbed.

"Well, that's what happens when you get stabbed, you stupid little bitch."

"I'll bleed out! I'll die!"

And the world will be a better place, Michelle thought. "Shut up," she said. "You're not bleeding that much." She stuck the pistol in the waistband of her pants, in the back. Even if it was a bad way to carry, Carlene couldn't reach it.

She wasn't sure what to do with the paring knife.

How the fuck was she going to clean up this mess? What should she do?

Caitlin was definitely breathing, at least, and over by the door, she saw Troy's arm move, his fingers clench.

"What did you give them?"

"It'll wear off in a few minutes," Carlene said, sniffling. She lay on the floor, clutching at her side. Blood oozed out between her fingers.

"Where is it? Where are the drugs?"

"In my purse." Her eyes flicked toward the door. A battered black cross-body bag leaned against the wall there. "Gary's gonna kill you."

"Gary can go fuck himself."

She stared at the scene for a moment, at Caitlin's unconscious form, her sweatpants pulled low on her hips, the wine bottle, the smashed wine glass. She shuddered. She had a pretty good idea what Carlene had planned to do.

Don't think about it now, she told herself.

"All right," she said to Carlene. "I'm going to give you a choice. I'll call an ambulance, and the police, and you can get a ride to the hospital in cuffs. Or you can get the fuck out of here and take your chances on making it to a hospital on your own and tell them whatever bullshit story you want. You decide. Now."

"I'll go," Carlene said. She slowly sat up. "Can I have a towel?"

"Oh for fuck's sake," Michelle muttered. She went into the kitchen and found a dishtowel. She left the paring knife on the counter by the sink. "Here." She threw it in Carlene's face.

"I can't stand up. You have to help me."

"God." Michelle grabbed Carlene's hand. It was slippery with blood. She pulled hard, until at last Carlene was on her feet.

Carlene took the dishtowel and held it against her side. With slow, shuffling steps, she headed toward the door.

"One more thing, Carlene," Michelle said. "You tell Gary I'm doing this as a favor to him. I figure it's one less mess he'll need to clean up later. You tell him that."

Carlene nodded. She opened the door. Michelle watched as the door closed behind her.

Shuddering, she quickly moved to the door and locked it. Peered out the peephole. Watched as Carlene shuffled down the path, into the night.

Maybe letting Carlene go was another rookie mistake.

How long would it take for Gary to arrange something worse?

But getting involved with the police . . . she didn't need that right now.

Not when she was trying to disappear.

Behind her, she heard a groan. Troy. His head turned to one side, then the other. His eyes opened. He rested his hand on his forehead. "Man . . . what? I don't know what . . ."

"Are you okay?" Michelle asked.

His eyes seemed to focus. "What happened?"

"You don't remember?"

His eyes squeezed shut for a moment. "That girl . . . lady . . . she'd lost her dog. She . . ."

He stared at Michelle's hand. Michelle followed his gaze. Her hand was covered in Carlene's blood. She'd forgotten for a moment.

"Things got a little ugly," she said.

"Sweet baby Jesus," Troy murmured. He tried to sit up, sunk back down, apparently still dizzy. "What the hell?"

Caitlin made a noise, a small grunt. Michelle crouched by her side. "It's okay," she said. Caitlin didn't respond. She was still out. Not surprising, given how much smaller she was than Troy. Michelle felt for a pulse at Caitlin's wrist. Slow and steady.

Troy rolled onto his side, then onto all fours, crawling the few feet from where he'd been lying to Michelle and Caitlin.

"Where is she?" he asked.

"Gone."

"What did she do to us?"

"Some kind of tranquilizer gun, I guess. I didn't really see. I ran out in to the kitchen and got a knife." She held up her hand. "Her blood, not mine."

"A tranquilizer gun? Are you shitting me?" Troy felt around the back of his thigh, flinched a little as he apparently found a tender spot. "This is insane." He stared at Caitlin. "Should we call an ambulance?"

Would an ambulance mean police?

"I guess. How are you feeling?"

"Better. Still a little woozy. Got kind of a headache." His eyes went a little wider. "Is that a gun?"

"Oh. Right." Michelle took the little pistol from where she'd tucked it against her pelvis and laid it on the coffee table. "Not mine. That was hers."

Now Caitlin began to stir. Her eyes fluttered open. For a moment she seemed to stare at nothing, her expression vaguely puzzled. Then it was as if something snapped into place, and her eyes grew wide with fear.

"It's okay," Michelle said quickly. "You're safe."

"Oh my god," Caitlin managed, her voice cracking. "Troy?"

He leaned over, rested his hand on hers. "I'm right here. I'm fine."

"We're going to call an ambulance," Michelle said. And while they were bundling up Caitlin and Troy, she'd slip away. She needed to bail, like Danny said. Not to try and fix this.

"No. No, I don't . . . I'm just a little dizzy, that's all." She took in a deep breath and winced, put her palm on her ribs. "I feel like I got kicked by a horse there." Caitlin slowly sat up. "What just happened?"

"I don't know," Michelle said. "She looked like the woman who tried to pick your purse at the conference. Remember? Maybe she's some kind of stalker."

At that moment, there was a huge bang, something solid crashing into the front door, then another as the door splintered and broke off its hinges. Bright lights, so light she couldn't see. And shouting: "On the floor! *On the floor! Now!*"

Men in black, wearing helmets, holding rifles.

"Hands behind your head! Behind your head, now! Motherfucker! *Get your motherfucking hands behind your head!*"

Michelle hit the floor and put her hands behind her head. Something, a knee, pinned her down. She could see the armed men swarming around Troy, one of them lifting a baton, slamming it down.

"No!" Caitlin was screaming. "*No!*"

Chapter Thirty-Two

⟐

"MY GOD, OFFICER." CAITLIN sat on the couch, shaking and furious. Troy sat next to her, resting his head in his hands. "You could've *killed* him. He's a *victim* here."

"We apologize, ma'am. But we had a report that . . ."

"I don't want to hear about your report. What the hell is wrong with you?"

Too bad, Michelle thought, because she actually would have liked to have heard about the report. She figured that Carlene had called it in, her last little "fuck you" to Michelle. But her guess was that this had been the plan all along.

Kill Caitlin. Make it ugly. Pin it on Troy.

Lucky for you, Troy Stone is going to save you a considerable amount of grief.

"Could've been worse," Troy said, finally lifting his head.

The police sergeant, or captain, or whatever he was, shifted back and forth from one foot to the other.

They'd cuffed Michelle and Troy and kept them on the floor until Caitlin had managed to convince the police that they weren't a threat. It took a while. The policemen with the big guns had left, replaced by several uniformed officers and a technician who took photos of the scene and Michelle's bruised face, the abraded patch on her scalp, her bloody hand, which he also swabbed, along with a few samples taken from underneath her nails—evidence of the fight she'd said she'd had with Carlene. Another officer bagged the paring knife and the gun and a sample of bloody carpet. The knife and the blood were probably the only things that made her story remotely credible, Michelle thought.

"The assailant's blood?" the lead officer asked.

"Of course it's her blood," Caitlin snapped. "None of us are bleeding, are we?"

He turned to Michelle. "So you fought her off? You stabbed her with the knife and took her gun?"

Michelle nodded.

The lead officer gave her a long look. "Well, I guess that was pretty lucky, wasn't it?"

"I guess so," she said. "Look, she wasn't exactly James Bond. Just some kind of crazy stalker."

"What about those text messages?" Troy asked suddenly. He patted his pants pocket. "Oh, man. My phone. It's gone. She must have stolen it."

"Text messages?" the officer asked.

Troy opened his mouth, then closed it.

"We'll be assigning this to a detective for a more extensive follow-up," the officer said. "Any other details, make a note if that helps. We'll get this whole thing sorted out."

Not likely, Michelle wanted to say, but of course, she didn't.

"THEY WANT US TO go up to the medical center and give blood samples and get more detailed exams. Have some other photos taken if need be." Caitlin shuddered. "I told them we'd take a cab over." She waved at the splintered front door. "After the board-up men come."

Michelle stood at the kitchen sink, scrubbing the blood off her hand. She'd already given all the evidence she planned on giving.

Don't wait around and try to fix things.

It was past time for her to make her move. To get away from Caitlin and Gary's surveillance, if she could.

Caitlin managed a shaky chuckle. "You think a glass of wine would get in the way of those tox screens they want to run?"

"I don't know," Michelle said. She turned off the water and dried her hands on a dishtowel. "After the drugs, maybe it's not a good mix."

"You're probably right about that. But you've been right about a lot of things, haven't you?"

Her voice had suddenly changed. She sounded steadier. More in control. And pissed as hell.

"Why don't you tell us the real story, Michelle? Because I know there *is* one."

Michelle considered the dishtowel in her hands. She folded it and hung it on the rack next to the sink. Got out three glasses from the cupboard and filled them with filtered water.

"Okay," she said. "But you're not going to like it."

She showed them Danny's logbook, the letter of explanation he'd written. Caitlin read it first, her brow wrinkling as she did. After she'd finished, she pushed the book over to Troy without comment, the expression on her face neutral, impossible to read.

Michelle waited, counting the minutes this was taking. There was a squad car parked in front of the house, and she didn't think Gary would try anything right now, not so soon after a major police incident. Not his style. He didn't have a platoon of men in black to storm in here and shoot up the place. She didn't think.

But she needed to make her move.

Pop smoke. Get the fuck out of here.

"What do you think?" Caitlin asked Troy.

He shrugged. "We've been saying for years the CIA's the ones behind all that crack cocaine in the eighties. People said we were paranoid."

"I know the person who wrote this," Michelle said. "And I know that it's true."

"Okay," Caitlin said. She still seemed oddly calm. "If this *is* true . . . I'm not sure I understand what it has to do with me."

"The people he's talking about . . ." Michelle began. "They've been using you and Safer America. They don't want you changing direction. They want the propositions here in California defeated. There's a lot of money tied up in keeping things the way they are."

"I . . ." Caitlin sat very still. She abruptly shook her head, like she could shake everything she'd heard out of it. Then she straightened up.

"And you? What's your part in all this?"

"They blackmailed me. Pulled strings to get me the job as your assistant. I was supposed to babysit you, they told me."

"You mean, spy on me. That's what you mean, isn't it? Spy on me and pretend to give a shit."

Her stillness had turned to rigidity, as if that was the only way she could hold herself together. She sounded furious.

Michelle couldn't really blame her. She nodded.

"And when you say 'pulled strings'—who's fucking me over in my own organization? Is it Porter?"

Michelle felt suddenly, utterly exhausted. Her head and ear and scalp throbbed. "Probably. I'm not sure. You can't trust any of them. That's all I know for certain."

"And now I'm supposed to trust *you*?"

Michelle shook her head. "I'm not asking you to trust me. Just . . . think about what happened tonight, and try to believe what I'm telling you."

Caitlin's head thumped back against the couch. "I don't know *what* to think."

"What do we do?" Troy clenched and unclenched his fists. "How are we supposed to protect ourselves against these people? We go to the police with this, they're just gonna laugh at us."

"I think you have two choices," Michelle said. She turned to Caitlin. Caitlin was overwhelmed, Michelle could tell—who wouldn't be? Michelle couldn't be sure that she'd absorbed it all or entirely believed it. But Caitlin needed to understand the situation she was in, and Michelle didn't have a lot of time to help her get it. "You forget about changing Safer America's direction, and go back to how things were before, do the election work they want you to do."

"I won't," Caitlin said. "I can't."

"Then you need to go public with your change of direction now. Don't wait to get back to Houston and talk to the board. Draft a press release, send it to the board, send it to everyone you can think of. Do it tonight. I don't think they'll try the same thing twice, not after it's too late for them to stop you from speaking out."

"I see." Caitlin nodded, like this was all some sort of normal business discussion. She sipped her glass of water. Swallowed hard. "That girl, she was here to kill me. Wasn't she?"

It was tempting to lie, to try and make it hurt less, but she needed to know the truth.

"Yes," Michelle said.

"To keep me from changing Safer America?"

"And to scare people, I think. Maybe influence the vote."

"And Troy?"

"I think they wanted to blame him for it."

The color drained from Caitlin's face. She suddenly looked as pale and insubstantial as when Michelle had first met her.

Troy's jaw worked. He stared down at his hands.

"I don't know what to do," he mumbled.

"You can walk away," Michelle said. "Pretend this never happened. Maybe they'll leave you alone."

Maybe they would. It wasn't like he had any proof of any of this. And his usefulness as a fall guy had probably expired.

Or maybe they'd kill him anyway.

Caitlin briefly rested her hand on his forearm. "You know what, Troy? If you don't want to partner up now, I understand. You don't need any more grief because of me."

"You're still going ahead?"

"Yeah. Yeah, I am." She laughed shakily. "Second time somebody's tried to kill me. Either third time's a charm, or the devil's used up his chances."

Troy was silent for a moment. Then he let out a chuff. "Good. Because I'm pissed off, and I want to do some damage to these assclowns. But the pretty white lady's the one they're gonna listen to. Not me."

They eyed each other.

"Well, I'm glad you think I'm pretty, anyway," Caitlin said.

"Come on, you know I do. It's just . . . *you*." He gestured at the broken door. "All this. It's a lot."

"Yeah." Caitlin sighed. "Yeah. It is."

Chapter Thirty-Three

THEY WAITED IN THE driveway for a taxi after the board-up men finished securing the door to Caitlin's condo. They'd left the porch light on, and now it lit a sheet of plywood. Michelle had Danny's ruck, Caitlin her small wheeled suitcase and Troy, a gym bag.

"I can drive the rental over," Michelle had said, but Caitlin rapidly shook her head.

"I don't think you should be driving," she said. "If you could see your face in a mirror right now . . ."

Funny, she'd thought she felt calm. She took a few deep breaths, drew in the scent of damp eucalyptus.

"I wish we weren't getting these damn exams," Caitlin said. "I'm of a mind to skip the whole thing and just check into the Hyatt."

"It's best we go along with it," Troy said.

Michelle wasn't planning on having an exam. She hadn't been drugged, and the cops had all the physical evidence from her they needed. What would be the point?

A few neighbors stood outside their townhouses in the dark, watching the scene. They'd had quite a show earlier, Michelle thought.

Caitlin smiled in their general direction. "If this whole thing gets out in the press, and I'm guessing it will, how do you think we should handle it?" she asked Troy.

"I think we stick with an attack by a nut job. Not comment

at all unless we have to. But we might as well get these tests done, just in case it comes up. We should have all the evidence we can on our side." He glanced sideways at Michelle. "In case."

"Maybe we could use it as a pivot, you know, say something about how it points to the need for more mental-health funding in communities."

Michelle could hear the enthusiasm in Caitlin's voice, the part of her that could make those speeches, that knew how to reach out and hook people, and enjoyed it.

Troy laughed a little and gave Caitlin's shoulder a tentative squeeze. "I like the way you think."

Michelle wondered what would happen to them. She hoped they'd make it. After all that Caitlin had been through, having her life upended a second time and still be willing to fight back . . . Whatever her partnership with Troy turned out to be, maybe they could find some strength and comfort in each other.

They'd need it.

I did what I could, she thought.

Caitlin suddenly turned to Michelle, as though she'd picked up on her attention.

"I guess I should thank you." She still sounded more angry than thankful. "I guess you could've just . . . let things take their course, and you didn't. Why is that?"

Why *wouldn't* Caitlin wonder? She had no reason to trust anything that Michelle had done, or might do.

Funny, how much it hurt being thought of that way.

"I didn't want to go along with these people," Michelle said. "I never did. I still know what's right, and what isn't."

Maybe she knew better now than she used to.

"I'll give you an email address," she said. "If something comes up . . . I don't know if I can help. But I'll try."

Caitlin seemed to study her. Michelle couldn't tell what sort of conclusions she might have reached.

"I guess there's nothing I can do to help *you*," Caitlin said.

"I doubt it."

Michelle fished around in her hobo for something to write on. Her hands closed on a business card at the bottom of her purse. She pulled it out. It was a card for Evergreen: the abstract redwood silhouette, the woodblock letters. She stared at it for a long moment, then carefully printed the email address she'd given to Maggie.

"Here," she said. "I hope . . . I hope you won't need it. But if there's anything . . ." She shrugged helplessly and held out the card.

Caitlin stared at her for a long moment. Then she took the card. She held it close to her chest and nodded.

"What are you going to do, Michelle?" she asked.

Michelle smiled tightly. "I'm going to disappear."

SHE TOOK A TAXI to Mission Valley and checked into the Motel 6. She debated about what name to use and decided on Emily. If the case against "Jeff" had been dropped, no one should be looking for her any more, should they? No one in law enforcement, anyway.

Gary would still be looking. If he didn't already know where she was.

But she didn't want to use the new passport. If she and Danny had any hope of really disappearing, she couldn't risk being Meredith Evelyn Jackson, not yet.

She paid cash for the room. No sense making it any easier for Gary to find her.

LYING IN BED, SHE thought about tomorrow, about what she was leaving behind her. The loose ends.

One of them was Evergreen.

Evergreen was hers. Her creation. Her responsibility.

Was there anything she could do to leave it the right way?

With the DEA out of the picture, maybe the restaurant could remain open, if Helen and the staff wanted to keep running it. She'd already cut her own salary in half when this whole thing started so she could bump up Helen and Joseph and Guillermo's pay. She could take herself off the books altogether, just draw a small percentage as a return on her investment, have Derek set that up so she'd still have money to send for her father's care and her nephew's college fund. All it would take was an email now and then, wouldn't it? That wouldn't be too much of a risk.

Be real, she told herself. It was tempting to think that something she'd created might go on without her, at least for a little while. But she had a long way to travel between here and some form of refuge, if there even was such a place.

Gary wouldn't give up so easily.

DANNY CALLED AT 6:15 A.M.

"I'm still a few hours out," he said. "Can you meet me at nine A.M. at the border crossing in San Ysidro? There's a trolley that takes you right to it."

"I'll be there."

"You okay? You sound a little rough."

She laughed. "I'm fine. It was a rough night."

"It's good to hear your voice, Em."

"It's good to hear you too. I'll see you soon."

A TAXI TOOK HER to Santa Fe Depot, the train and trolley station downtown. It looked to be a beautiful day, but most of them were here.

She drew in a deep breath, the air scented with brine from the harbor.

You can do this, she told herself.

She walked through the broad archway of the station entrance, flanked by Spanish-style towers that were topped with yellow and blue tiled domes.

The hall was an arched building with lines of copper chandeliers above, darkened wooden benches below. The station was close to one hundred years old; she'd read that when she was doing her research. The benches were mostly occupied; other people milled around the souvenir and snack counter, lingered by the arched exits onto the platform.

7:50 A.M. A busy morning.

The Amtrak counter was at the north end. Four people waited in line to buy tickets.

There's plenty of time, she told herself. The train didn't leave until 8:20.

Fifteen minutes later it was her turn.

"One to Los Angeles," she said. "Reserved coach is fine." She counted out fifty dollars.

"May I see some ID?"

This is it, she thought. It will either work, or it won't.

She slid Emily's license across the counter.

The clerk, a middle-aged black woman, held up the

license, glanced at Michelle. Typed at her terminal. A printer whirred and clattered.

"Here you go, Ms. Carmichael," the clerk said with a smile, the ticket in her outstretched hand. "Enjoy your trip."

"I will," she said. "Thanks. Have a nice day."

Passengers had started to line up out on the platform, the queue already stretching into the lobby. Michelle took her place at the end.

She glanced around, as normally as she could—just a tourist, taking in the sights—to see if she could spot any obvious tails. She couldn't, but then, Carlene had wanted to be spotted, back in Houston. There were so many people here. Any one of them might be following her. Or no one was. She couldn't know, one way or the other.

A few minutes later, she heard the warning bells that signaled an approaching train. Funny, because the train was already here, waiting across a set of tracks. The line started moving.

Now she was out on the platform and could see the gate that had lowered to protect passengers crossing the trolley tracks to reach their train. A trolley waited on the other side of the barrier, its doors open, passengers getting in and out.

Michelle stepped out of the line, walking quickly up the platform toward the trolley. She kept walking till she reached a gap between buildings at the end of the depot and turned right, passing trolley customers heading to the tracks. She turned right again, doubling back toward the front of the station. The back half of Santa Fe Depot had been turned into a contemporary art museum; she glimpsed vaguely sculptural shapes inside through the glassed-in archways, on the exterior wall, a black sign with scrolling red diode letters spelling BE ALL THAT YOU CAN BE.

Up ahead, at the back of the train station proper, two taxis waited at the curb.

The taxi stand was there, like her research said it would be. "Just don't expect to always find taxis waiting," a guy on TripAdvisor had said. If there hadn't been, she'd planned to walk to the closest big hotel.

Who knew if her feint to Los Angeles would work? But it was worth a try.

She approached the first cab. "Can you take me to San Ysidro, to the border?"

He nodded, and she climbed in.

SHE COULD SEE THE city changing as they headed south, from the harbor with the tall ships, the shiny highrises and condos of downtown, to a more industrial area: shipyards, a Navy base, car lots; then small, faded stucco houses, graffitied cinderblock walls, a weed-choked wetland, outlet stores. There was less money here.

Twenty-five minutes, and she was at the border.

The trolley station was a giant McDonald's: a cream and brick red stucco building that looked like it might have been a small warehouse once, or a garment factory, a long building with two low stories. There were three brick-red cement ellipses in descending order, like an upside-down series of steps, at the top of the building. McDONALD'S TROLLEY STATION was spelled out in square white plastic letters on the uppermost, largest step, next to a small pair of golden arches, just to clarify this was actually a McDonald's, maybe. The building also had signs for check-cashing and money-changing in English and Spanish, and something called "Saldos Gigantes: Ropa, Cosméticos, Miscelánea."

She'd gotten there early. It wasn't even 8:45. Maybe a cup of coffee, she thought. McDonald's coffee wasn't bad.

She went inside.

The McDonald's took up most of the back wall on the first floor. Above it was a Shoes for Less with a small neon sign that said ABIERTO. A few other small glassed-in stalls filled the remainder of the space. The middle was dedicated to seating for the McDonalds: Plastic-benched booths and tables divided by low orange walls topped with Plexiglas panels. The place was about three-quarters full, the languages she heard a mix of Spanish and English: tourists on their way to Tijuana, residents from both sides of the border. Michelle got her coffee and sat down at an empty table, facing the entrance, Danny's ruck on the bench by her side.

About ten minutes later, Gary walked in, wearing his Humboldt Crabs baseball hat.

There was no point in running. Where would she go?

She waited as he crossed the room, pulled out the chair across from her and sat.

"Pretty good try at evasion there, Michelle." He smiled, that phony grin she hated. "I'm sorry you and I never got a chance to work on that together." He gestured at her cup. "Coffee?"

She nodded.

"Why don't you go get me a cup? Black."

Of course he wouldn't get his own. Easier for him to watch her this way.

She returned with his cup of coffee. She thought about

throwing it in his face and trying to run. She wouldn't get away, but it would be satisfying, for a moment or two.

Instead she put the coffee in front of him and sat back down.

He sipped. Leaned back in his chair. "Do you know how much you piss me off, Michelle? I can't think of many people who piss me off more." He wagged a finger at her. "Believe it or not, I've got a pretty good track record with these kinds of ops. And this was gonna be so sweet."

Her stomach twisted, thinking of what he'd wanted to do.

"Thanks for the heads-up about Carlene," she said.

"Well, now, you turned off your phone. If you'd kept your phone on like you're supposed to, I would've been able to let you know what the plan was."

"Right," she said.

"Be fair. If I'd told you, would you've gone along with it?"

"Of course not," she snapped.

Gary sighed. "I told Carlene if you were in the frame, she'd better watch herself. She's a great little killer. But she's not the sharpest tool in the shed."

"She was going to kill me too?"

"Only if she had to. She was gonna trank you if you were around and being a problem. Having a second victim in that scenario . . . that would've been problematic."

"What about Troy?"

"He was going to kill himself. You know, in a fit of remorse. That's what the gun was for."

Gary took a sip of his coffee. "I always figured you for a practical woman, Michelle. Once it was done, you'd rather've lived, right?"

He leaned forward, with an expression that appeared

earnest, for Gary. "And I *did* want you to live. I've always liked you, Michelle. If Caitlin hadn't done her one-eighty, I would've been just fine with you babysitting her, like I said. I mean, it seems to me you've done her a world of good. What do the Jews call that? A mitzvah?"

It was always going to come down to this, she thought. Me, running out of options. Gary, pulling the strings.

"Just tell me," she said. "What are you going to do?"

Gary stretched out his legs, draped his arm awkwardly around the curved back of the metal chair. "Well, you know, it's not just me you've pissed off. There's some folks who are really upset with the way this whole thing's turned out. They're looking at losing a lot of money. Nobody likes that."

She thought she knew Gary pretty well. She knew his capacity for violence, and she knew that he could turn on a dime. But for all that he claimed to be angry right now, he didn't actually *seem* to be.

"I'm sure Safer America was a nice little racket for you. But what if Caitlin hadn't changed direction? Those propositions are still leading in the polls here. Say Safer America poured millions of dollars into this election, and they won anyway. Then what?"

"Yeah." Gary heaved a massive sigh. "Sometimes you can't hold back the tide. Just between you and me, I think that's what we're looking at here. With legal weed there's getting to be too much money on the other side of the equation. Oh well."

He straightened up. "But you know what, there's plenty of other ways to fill those prison beds. Can't pay your debts? Go to jail and work them off. Cheap labor! That's how we make America competitive again." A snort.

"God," Michelle muttered.

"And country," Gary said, lifting up his coffee cup. "Oh, hell, Michelle, would you just relax? Look, you and Danny can go off and do whatever you're gonna do. I'm not going to stop you."

Michelle sat there, stunned. Of all the things she'd thought Gary might say, this was not one of them.

Of course, he was probably lying.

"Why?"

It was the only thing she could think of to say.

He shrugged. "All of this, you know, I like to think of it as kind of a game. And let's face it, you won this time. I respect that."

He reached into the pocket of his chinos and pulled out a mini bottle of Herradura tequila. Cracked it open and poured half into Michelle's coffee and half into his own.

He raised his cup. After a moment of hesitation, she raised hers.

With Gary, it was generally better to play along.

They drank.

Finally he put his cup down. Rose. Tipped his Humboldt Crabs cap.

"See you around."

She watched him weave through the tables and out the door, into the bright light of day.

Chapter Thirty-Four

MICHELLE FINISHED HER COFFEE. Might as well, she thought, and as she lifted the cup to her lips, she noticed her hands were trembling. She realized now that ever since last night, after the attack and the police breaking down the door, she'd been detached from herself, not really inhabiting her own body, observing it along with everything else.

Detachment wasn't always a bad thing. It had gotten her through this, hadn't it?

She could feel herself coming back, like a limb that had fallen asleep. So far, it hurt.

9 A.M. Time to go outside, and see if Danny had made it. If he hadn't . . . ?

Cross the border? Go to the airport, get on a flight to somewhere as Meredith Evelyn Jackson?

She swallowed the dregs of her coffee and tequila and stood.

THE WEATHER HAD TURNED warmer. Still pleasant, but definitely shirtsleeve temperatures. She wished she had on shorts or a skirt instead of her jeans. It was nice to be someplace warm but not oppressive, where you wanted to get closer to the air.

She looked around. She didn't see Danny. Well, it was only just now 9 A.M.

If he was taking the trolley, this was where he would get off. A red train with a sign for Old Town waited to head back to San Diego proper, a tan, bunker-like, windowless building behind it. There was no place else the trains could go but north.

Palm trees. Fences. On the side of the street where the McDonald's was, a row of stucco, brick and cinderblock buildings, neon signs for money-changing and check cashing in English and Spanish, a 99-cent store and a *mercado*, behind them, a few small parking lots for people who wanted to leave their cars on this side of the border, brown rolling hills, dotted with scrub. On the other side of the tracks, a small shelter with an arched green roof and metal benches for trolley passengers, a drop-off and pick up area for taxis, a larger parking lot. Beyond that, the rush of a half-dozen lanes of cars driving into Mexico.

How did you even walk into Mexico? There wasn't an obvious gate or crossing. It was like being in a cul-de-sac. A dead-end.

Christ, what was she going to do?

Maybe I could get some restaurant work somewhere, she thought.

Another southbound trolley had arrived at the end of the line.

The doors opened. She waited as the cars emptied out.

Danny was one of the last passengers out of the third car.

He was scanning the opposite direction, so she couldn't see his face. But the shape of his body, the posture, the black duffel bag over one shoulder, the battered canvas messenger bag on the other, she was hit with a familiarity that felt like something falling into place.

He turned. She could see it on his face, that same recognition.

He came to her, going in and out of focus as he made his way through the tourists and the students and the house-keepers, all the people without cars who would be crossing into Tijuana this morning.

She slid the ruck off her shoulders. He dropped the duffel to his side. They held each other close, her head resting against his chest. His sweat had a sour, stale tang to it, but there was still his familiar scent. She'd missed it.

"I'm sorry," he said.

"I don't care right now. I don't care about any of it."

"You should. Pretty sure I'm the worst thing that ever happened to you."

If she looked at it rationally, maybe he was. But it didn't feel that way right now. "Not even close."

He exhaled a long sigh. "I guess we should get going."

He gave her a final squeeze and let go. Studied her face. He reached out and gently touched her cheek with his fingertips. "What the hell happened?"

"It's nothing. I'll tell you later."

The muscles in his jaw tightened; she could see the anger and frustration play out on his face, the helplessness.

"Later," she said. "It's actually a good story."

"Jesus. If you say so."

The two of them picked up their bags.

"You brought my ruck," Danny said, with a real smile.

She nodded. "And a few of your clothes and things."

"Man," he said, shaking his head. "You really are amazing."

He'd dropped weight in the month he'd been gone. His face was pale and haggard. His eyes looked lost.

"Which way?" she asked.

"I think it's over there." He gestured behind him, on the side of the tracks where the McDonald's was.

They crossed the tracks and found the footpath. It wound slightly uphill behind the buildings, a narrow channel between two high walls: on the eastern side, concrete panels that looked almost like blast walls, behind those a tall palisade fence topped by coils of razor wire. To the west, grids of open metal mesh. Security cameras were spaced in between the lights here and there.

Danny shuddered. "Looks like a fucking jail," he said.

Michelle reached out and took his hand.

It wasn't that crowded. There were knots of people walking ahead of them and behind them, most seeming not to be in any particular hurry.

We don't look any different than they do, Michelle told herself. We'll be fine.

She looked to the west, through the open mesh. She could see a large billboard, with an American eagle in front of a Mexican flag. 8 MILLION PEOPLE WILL SEE THIS SIGN YEARLY, it said. Call this number. Put up your ad.

Ahead of them the path broadened, ending in a huge concrete barrier with a giant metal sign attached that said, in block letters, MEXICO. The entrance was two full-height turnstiles, the kind you'd find exiting an amusement park. She had a sudden flash of memory from when she was a little girl, standing on the bottom arm as her dad gave the rotor a giant push, one last little ride before piling into the car and heading home.

"Here we go," Danny said. He grasped her hand tighter, and then he let go. She took a deep breath and pushed the arms and walked through.

On the other side was a single uniformed officer. He waved her through without a second glance.

She glanced over her shoulder.

"I'm right here," Danny said. He came up alongside her and took her hand again.

They walked a little ways, down a long concrete ramp, and the path narrowed to half the width of the US side. Now to their left was a long line of people, waiting to cross into the US. How long would it take? she wondered briefly. A crowded row of shops and stalls took up that side of the crossing. On their side was a wall separating them from all the lanes of cars heading north.

"Man, after a month of that shitty jail food, I could use a plate of tacos," Danny said.

Michelle laughed. "With guacamole. And margaritas."

They followed the people who had crossed ahead of them until the path turned into a street. Most of them walked up the stairs to a pedestrian bridge that spanned the auto crossing. Everything felt different: dustier, more crowded. Even the exhaust smelled different.

"What do we do now?" Michelle asked.

"I don't know," Danny said. "Who do you want us to be?"

END

Acknowledgments

My thanks go out to "the usual suspects"—Bronwen Hruska, Juliet Grames, Paul Oliver, Rachel Kowal, Rudy Martinez, Janine Agro, and the rest of the wonderful crew at Soho Press; also, the great folks at Curtis Brown—Holly Frederick, Kerry D'Agostino, Stuart Waterman, Sarah Gerton, and in particular my agent, Katherine Fausset, who has been a tremendous support for me. It is deeply appreciated.

Special thanks are due as well to some awesome people who helped me in the research of this novel: Jodie Evans, Nikki Corda, Brian Thomas, Judie and Jim Lutz, Sarah Cortez, Tom Abrahams, Jessica Willey, Teri Kanefield and the late Samantha Spangler – I wish I could tell her again how invaluable the information she gave me was.

Any mistakes in the book are the result of my own inadequacies, not theirs.

My gratitude as well to Pilar Perez, for giving me a wonderful "getaway" refuge when I needed it.

As is often said, writing is a solitary occupation. I'm fortunate to have a great support system of fellow authors. My thanks go out to the Fiction Co-op, the Writing Wombats, the Purgatorians and especially to beta readers Dana Fredsti, Bryn Greenwood, Kris Herndon, Kat Sheridan and Catherine McKenzie.